octopus pie

volume 2

by Meredith Gran

IMAGE COMICS, INC.
Robert Kirkman – Chief Operating Officer
Erik Larsen – Chief Financial Officer
Todd McFarlane – President
Marc Silvestri – Chief Executive Officer
Jim Valentino – Vice-President

Eric Stephenson – Publisher
Corey Murphy – Director of Sales
Jeff Boison – Director of Publishing Planning & Book Trade Sales
Jeremy Sullivan – Director of Digital Sales
Kat Salazar – Director of PR & Marketing
Emily Miller – Director of Operations
Branwyn Bigglestone – Senior Accounts Manager
Sarah Mello – Accounts Manager
Drew Gill – Art Director
Jonathan Chan – Production Manager
Meredith Wallace – Print Manager
Briah Skelly – Publicity Assistant
Randy Okamura – Digital Production Designer
David Brothers – Branding Manager
Ally Power – Content Manager
Addison Duke – Production Artist
Vincent Kukua – Production Artist
Sasha Head – Production Artist
Tricia Ramos – Production Artist
Jeff Stang – Direct Market Sales Representative
Emilio Bautista – Digital Sales Associate
Chloe Ramos-Peterson – Administrative Assistant
IMAGECOMICS.COM

For the readers who've been around since the late 2000s and helped me raise funds to get these pages into print. I see you and I'm happy you're here.

Thanks to Kate Beaton for her steadfast wisdom and support, and to the amazing ladies at Pizza Island for welcoming me back to New York when I accidentally left. Thanks to my friends at TopatoCo for letting me make books while living in small spaces.

Thanks always to Mike Holmes for telling me my work has value, even when I'm skeptical.

Now that some fleeting years have passed, I'd like to ask the court of public opinion, filtered generously through an early-20s brain, how harshly our heroes should be judged for their crimes. Is kissing your friend's boyfriend unforgivable? (Even if they JUST started dating, like, ten seconds ago?) Is retroactively admitting to cheating - after you've already broken up and gotten back together - no longer punishable by firing squad? If the Hanna in your life finds out what you did, is THAT retribution enough?

In this volume, there is a shift from poetic justice. In the past the characters had (mostly) done right by one another, always reverting to peace and understanding, closing every verse with a rhyme. Increasingly they're given opportunities to withhold their intent, their disappointments, and friendship-breaking truths. They have the security of a tight social group, but continue to exist in shameful minds. It's the small, lonely truths that cause them to hurt one another and themselves.

I was ashamed, for one thing, that I drew none of this book in New York. It was a hole in the assured narrative of my young life, a breach I'd neglect to mention if I had the chance. I'd left the city to pursue a relationship and supposedly figure life out. I lived in cheap, spacious buildings surrounded by living plants. The crowds and the noise and the piss-filled trains faded away, to be replaced by silent questions.

Was this the space I needed to be truly, unstoppably, mind-bogglingly, generation-voicingly, *very* creative? Or was I being dishonest by writing about a life I no longer lived? Does analogue really produce a warmer sound? Could I convey the unpleasant nature of piss without smelling it every day?

The pull for authenticity and geographical escape was so strong in those years. It overshadowed life itself. It stretched out over these stories, blurring the borders of Brooklyn and New England and the Pacific Northwest. It slept on my couch and ate my baked goods. At some point the physical settings were merely an examining table for the aforementioned shame. It became easier to write it down, tear it open and see just how avoidant and irrelevant these questions were. The "better place" sought in Volume 2 is not in the arms of a cool stranger, or neatly outlined in a series of Yelp reviews. For Eve and her friends it's simply a matter of looking within, and trying not to be repulsed.

When I first collected these stories, a theme of nostalgia seemed appropriate. Now I think disillusionment describes it better. Maybe the two go hand in hand. The characters are starting to feel the pressure of time and searching for a fonder point, either in the past or the completely vague future. Living for the moment just doesn't seem possible. Too many memories to recover, too many opportunities threatening to be missed.

In hindsight, that threat *was* the moment. By the time this book was finished, I was ready to go back to New York. Is that shit poetic or what?

-Meredith Gran,
February 2016

Contents

octopus pie

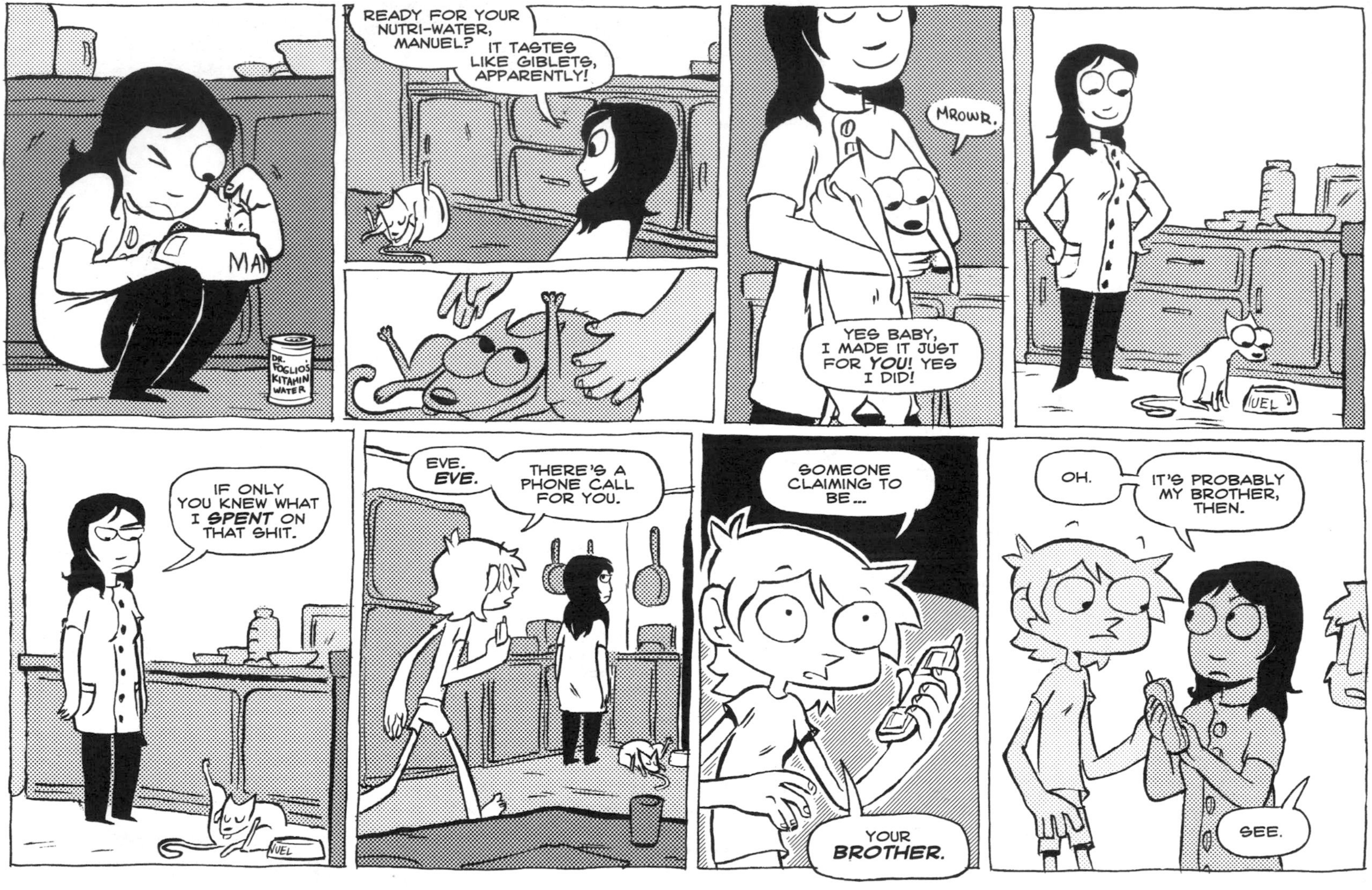
MA
DR. FOGLIO'S KITAMIN WATER
READY FOR YOUR NUTRI-WATER, MANUEL?
IT TASTES LIKE GIBLETS, APPARENTLY!
MROWR.
YES BABY, I MADE IT JUST FOR YOU! YES I DID!
UEL
IF ONLY YOU KNEW WHAT I SPENT ON THAT SHIT.
NUEL
EVE. EVE.
THERE'S A PHONE CALL FOR YOU.
SOMEONE CLAIMING TO BE...
YOUR BROTHER.
OH.
IT'S PROBABLY MY BROTHER, THEN.
SEE.

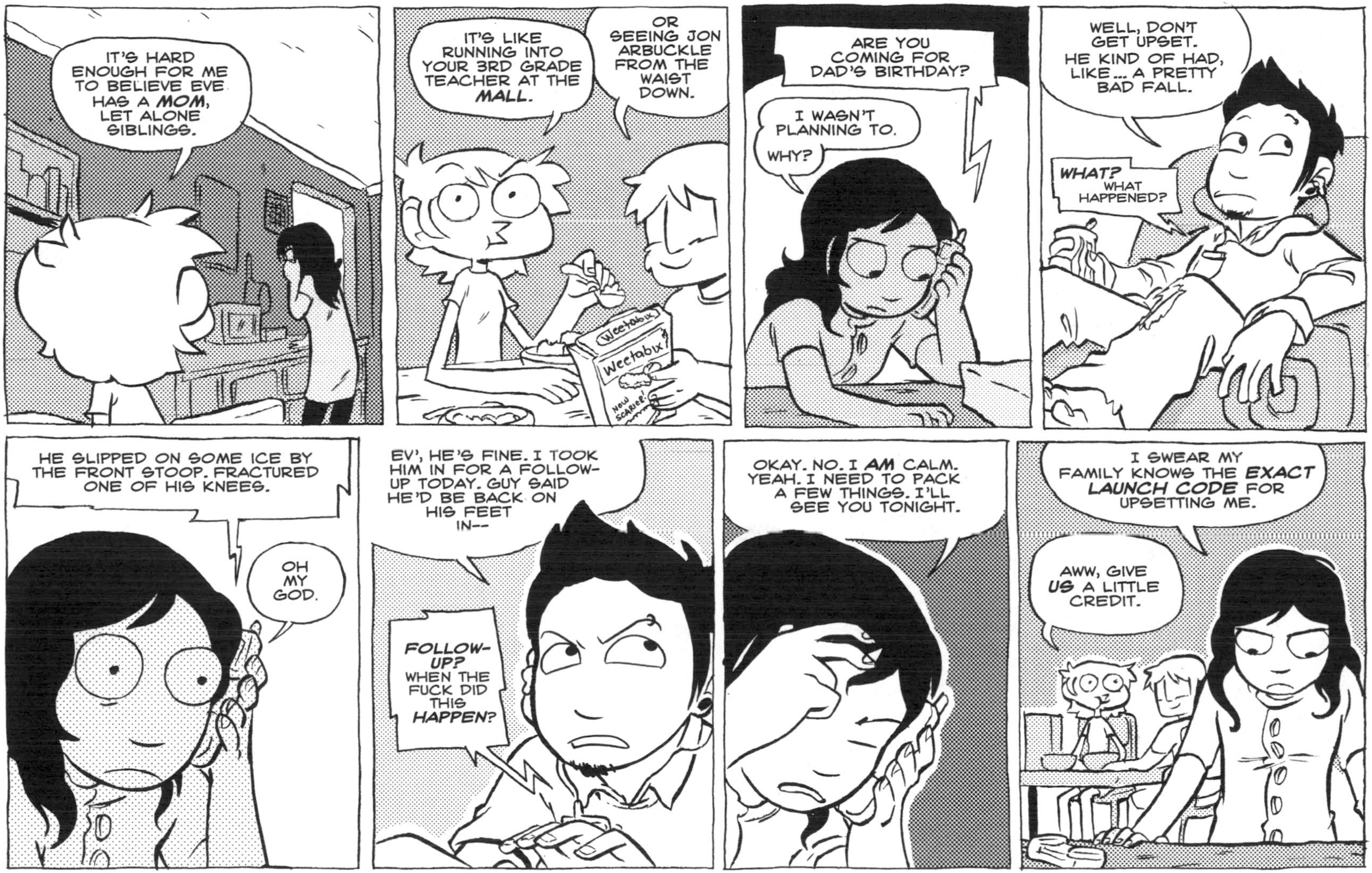
IT'S HARD ENOUGH FOR ME TO BELIEVE EVE HAS A **MOM**, LET ALONE SIBLINGS.
IT'S LIKE RUNNING INTO YOUR 3RD GRADE TEACHER AT THE **MALL**.
OR SEEING JON ARBUCKLE FROM THE WAIST DOWN.
Weetabix
NOW SCARIER!
ARE YOU COMING FOR DAD'S BIRTHDAY?
I WASN'T PLANNING TO.
WHY?
WELL, DON'T GET UPSET. HE KIND OF HAD, LIKE... A PRETTY BAD FALL.
WHAT? WHAT HAPPENED?
HE SLIPPED ON SOME ICE BY THE FRONT STOOP. FRACTURED ONE OF HIS KNEES.
OH MY GOD.
EV', HE'S FINE. I TOOK HIM IN FOR A FOLLOW-UP TODAY. GUY SAID HE'D BE BACK ON HIS FEET IN--
FOLLOW-UP? WHEN THE FUCK DID THIS **HAPPEN**?
OKAY. NO. I **AM** CALM. YEAH. I NEED TO PACK A FEW THINGS. I'LL SEE YOU TONIGHT.
I SWEAR MY FAMILY KNOWS THE **EXACT LAUNCH CODE** FOR UPSETTING ME.
AWW, GIVE **US** A LITTLE CREDIT.

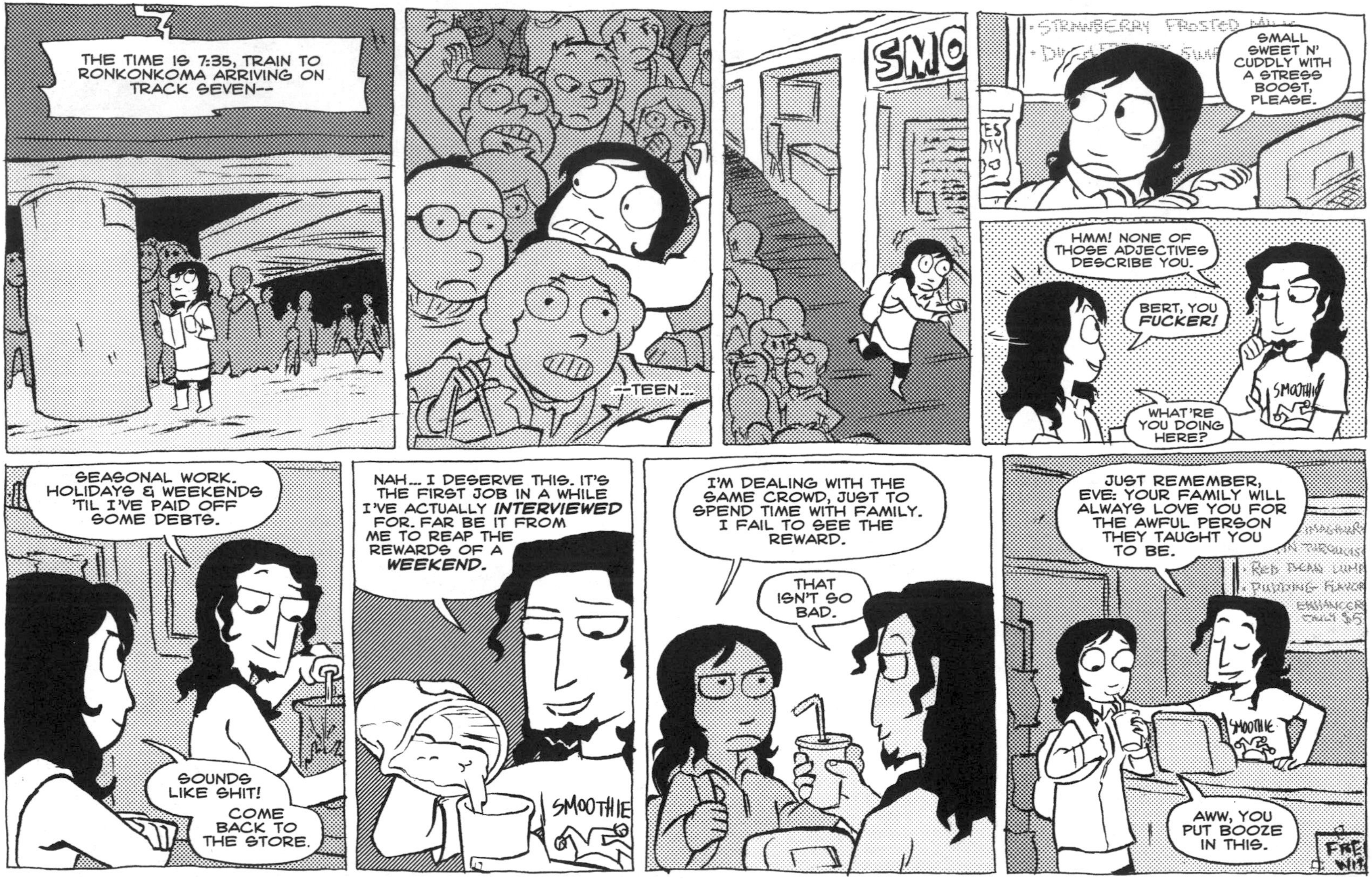
THE TIME IS 7:35, TRAIN TO RONKONKOMA ARRIVING ON TRACK SEVEN--
--TEEN...
SMALL SWEET N' CUDDLY WITH A STRESS BOOST, PLEASE.
HMM! NONE OF THOSE ADJECTIVES DESCRIBE YOU.
BERT, YOU FUCKER!
WHAT'RE YOU DOING HERE?
SEASONAL WORK. HOLIDAYS & WEEKENDS 'TIL I'VE PAID OFF SOME DEBTS.
SOUNDS LIKE SHIT!
COME BACK TO THE STORE.
NAH... I DESERVE THIS. IT'S THE FIRST JOB IN A WHILE I'VE ACTUALLY INTERVIEWED FOR. FAR BE IT FROM ME TO REAP THE REWARDS OF A WEEKEND.
I'M DEALING WITH THE SAME CROWD, JUST TO SPEND TIME WITH FAMILY. I FAIL TO SEE THE REWARD.
THAT ISN'T SO BAD.
JUST REMEMBER, EVE: YOUR FAMILY WILL ALWAYS LOVE YOU FOR THE AWFUL PERSON THEY TAUGHT YOU TO BE.
AWW, YOU PUT BOOZE IN THIS.

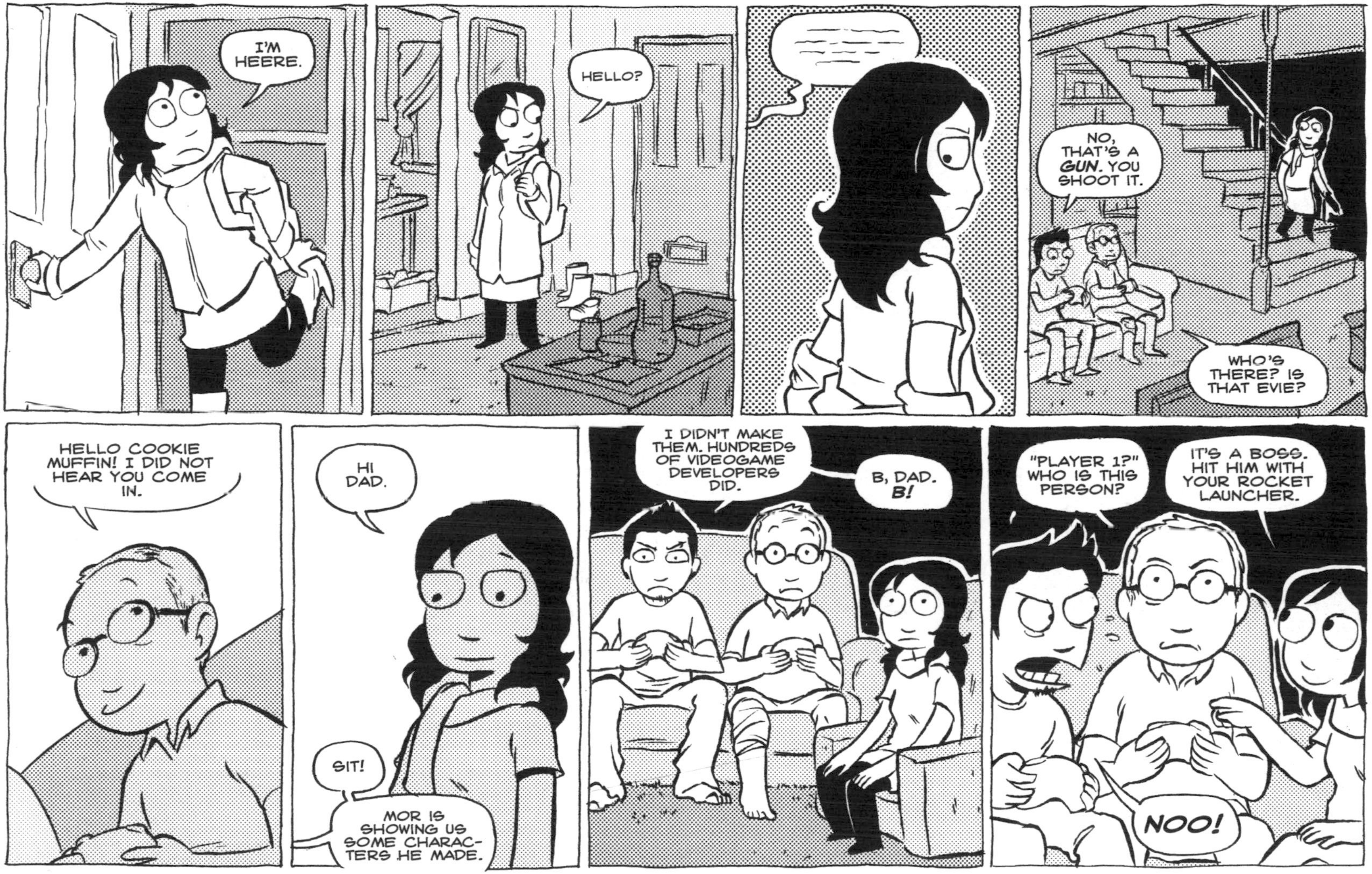
I'M HEERE.
HELLO?
NO, THAT'S A *GUN*. YOU SHOOT IT.
WHO'S THERE? IS THAT EVIE?
HELLO COOKIE MUFFIN! I DID NOT HEAR YOU COME IN.
HI DAD.
SIT!
MOR IS SHOWING US SOME CHARACTERS HE MADE.
I DIDN'T MAKE THEM. HUNDREDS OF VIDEOGAME DEVELOPERS DID.
B, DAD. *B!*
"PLAYER 1?" WHO IS THIS PERSON?
IT'S A BOSS. HIT HIM WITH YOUR ROCKET LAUNCHER.
NOO!

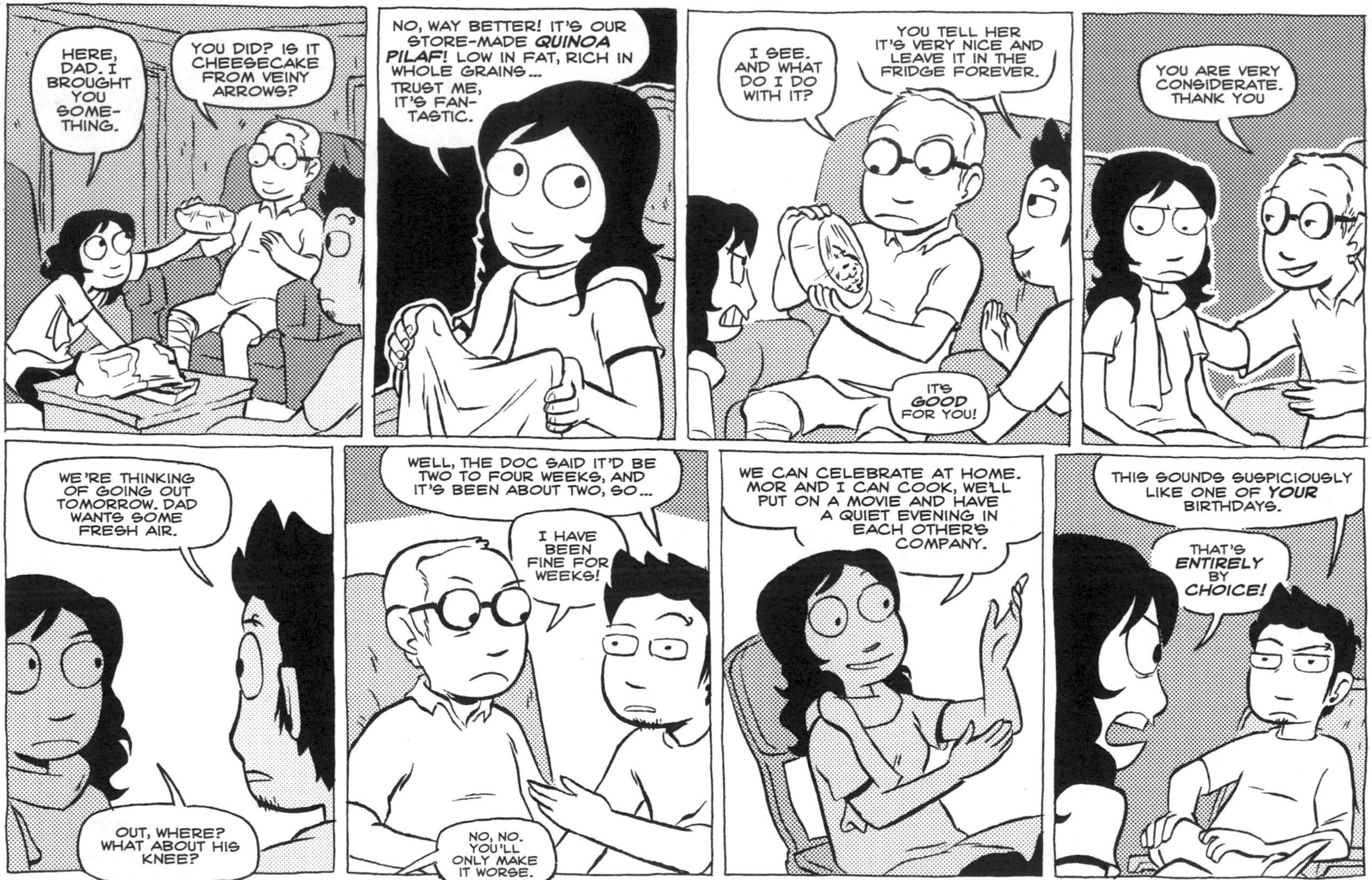
HERE, DAD. I BROUGHT YOU SOME-THING.
YOU DID? IS IT CHEESECAKE FROM VEINY ARROWS?
NO, WAY BETTER! IT'S OUR STORE-MADE *QUINOA PILAF!* LOW IN FAT, RICH IN WHOLE GRAINS... TRUST ME, IT'S FAN-TASTIC.
I SEE. AND WHAT DO I DO WITH IT?
YOU TELL HER IT'S VERY NICE AND LEAVE IT IN THE FRIDGE FOREVER.
IT'S *GOOD* FOR YOU!
YOU ARE VERY CONSIDERATE. THANK YOU
WE'RE THINKING OF GOING OUT TOMORROW. DAD WANTS SOME FRESH AIR.
OUT, WHERE? WHAT ABOUT HIS KNEE?
WELL, THE DOC SAID IT'D BE TWO TO FOUR WEEKS, AND IT'S BEEN ABOUT TWO, SO...
I HAVE BEEN FINE FOR WEEKS!
NO, NO. YOU'LL ONLY MAKE IT WORSE.
WE CAN CELEBRATE AT HOME. MOR AND I CAN COOK, WE'LL PUT ON A MOVIE AND HAVE A QUIET EVENING IN EACH OTHER'S COMPANY.
THIS SOUNDS SUSPICIOUSLY LIKE ONE OF *YOUR* BIRTHDAYS.
THAT'S *ENTIRELY* BY *CHOICE!*

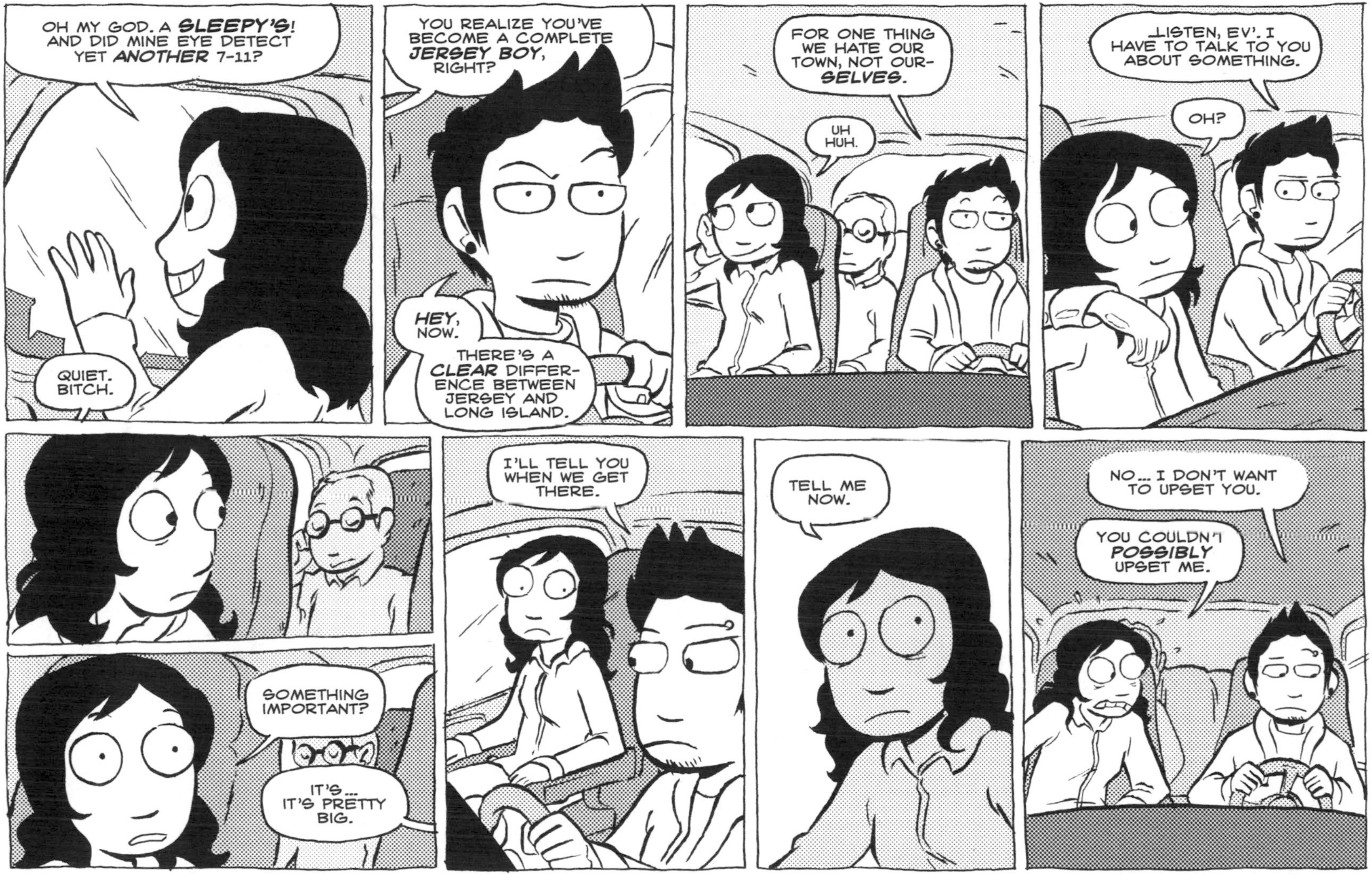
OH MY GOD. A **SLEEPY'S**! AND DID MINE EYE DETECT YET **ANOTHER** 7-11?
QUIET. BITCH.
YOU REALIZE YOU'VE BECOME A COMPLETE **JERSEY BOY**, RIGHT?
HEY, NOW.
THERE'S A **CLEAR** DIFFERENCE BETWEEN JERSEY AND LONG ISLAND.
FOR ONE THING WE HATE OUR TOWN, NOT OUR-**SELVES**.
UH HUH.
LISTEN, EV'. I HAVE TO TALK TO YOU ABOUT SOMETHING.
OH?
SOMETHING IMPORTANT?
IT'S... IT'S PRETTY BIG.
I'LL TELL YOU WHEN WE GET THERE.
TELL ME NOW.
NO... I DON'T WANT TO UPSET YOU.
YOU COULDN'T **POSSIBLY** UPSET ME.

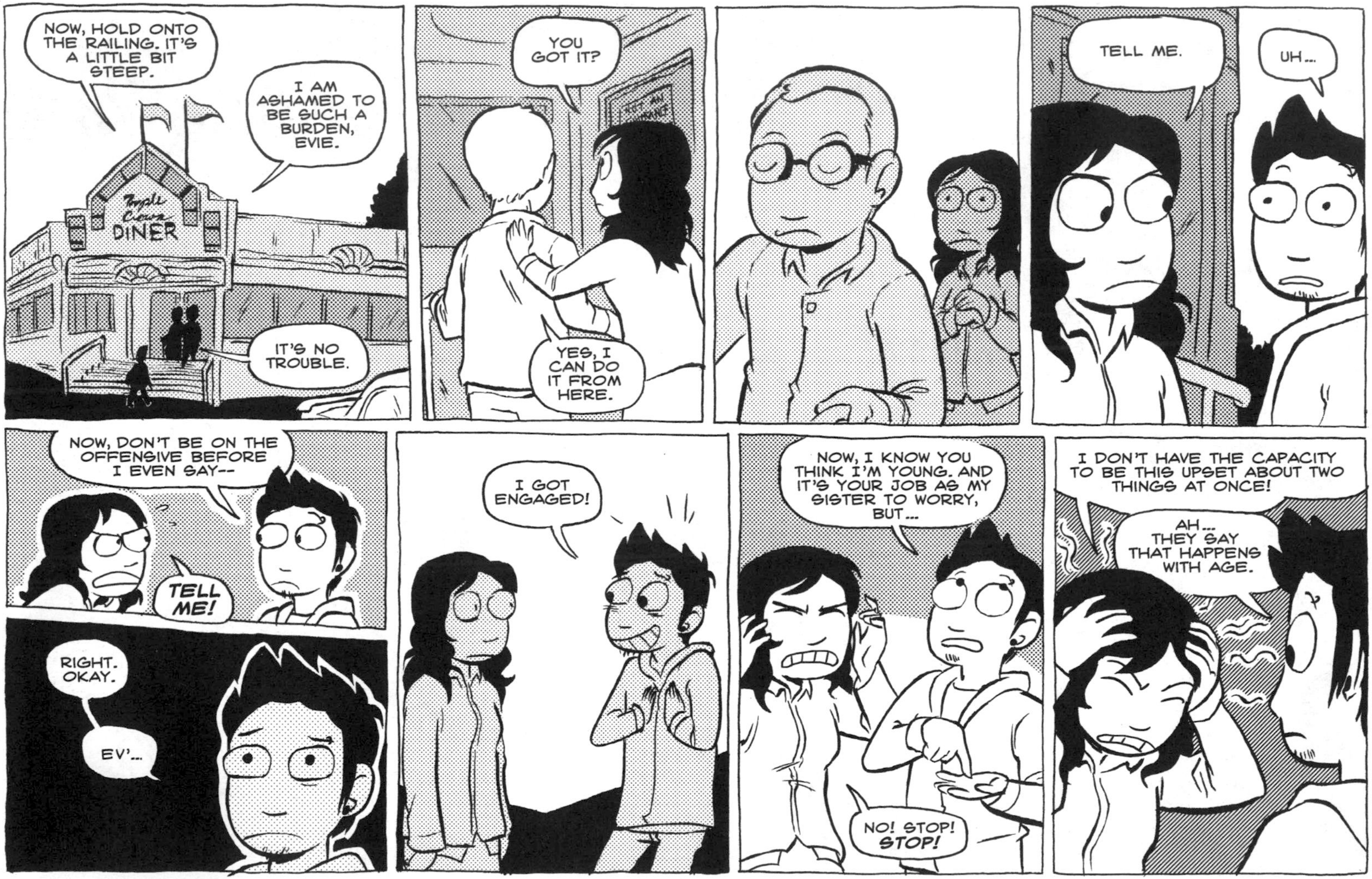
NOW, HOLD ONTO THE RAILING. IT'S A LITTLE BIT STEEP.
I AM ASHAMED TO BE SUCH A BURDEN, EVIE.
DINER
IT'S NO TROUBLE.
YOU GOT IT?
YES, I CAN DO IT FROM HERE.
TELL ME.
UH...
NOW, DON'T BE ON THE OFFENSIVE BEFORE I EVEN SAY--
TELL ME!
RIGHT. OKAY.
EV'...
I GOT ENGAGED!
NOW, I KNOW YOU THINK I'M YOUNG. AND IT'S YOUR JOB AS MY SISTER TO WORRY, BUT...
NO! STOP! STOP!
I DON'T HAVE THE CAPACITY TO BE THIS UPSET ABOUT TWO THINGS AT ONCE!
AH... THEY SAY THAT HAPPENS WITH AGE.

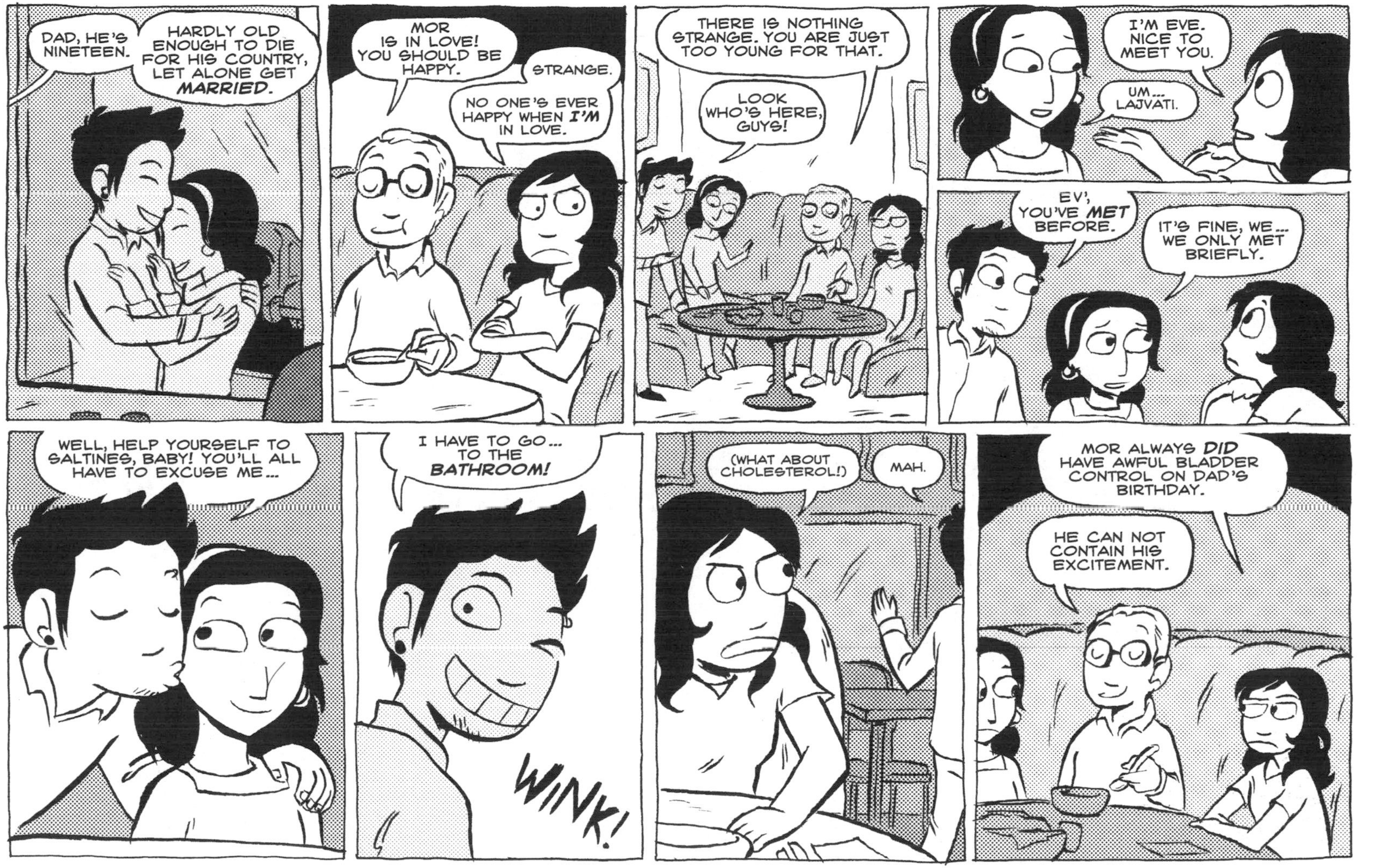
DAD, HE'S NINETEEN.
HARDLY OLD ENOUGH TO DIE FOR HIS COUNTRY, LET ALONE GET MARRIED.
MOR IS IN LOVE! YOU SHOULD BE HAPPY.
STRANGE.
NO ONE'S EVER HAPPY WHEN I'M IN LOVE.
THERE IS NOTHING STRANGE. YOU ARE JUST TOO YOUNG FOR THAT.
LOOK WHO'S HERE, GUYS!
I'M EVE. NICE TO MEET YOU.
UM... LAJVATI.
EV', YOU'VE MET BEFORE.
IT'S FINE, WE... WE ONLY MET BRIEFLY.
WELL, HELP YOURSELF TO SALTINES, BABY! YOU'LL ALL HAVE TO EXCUSE ME...
I HAVE TO GO... TO THE BATHROOM!
WINK!
(WHAT ABOUT CHOLESTEROL!)
MAH.
MOR ALWAYS DID HAVE AWFUL BLADDER CONTROL ON DAD'S BIRTHDAY.
HE CAN NOT CONTAIN HIS EXCITEMENT.

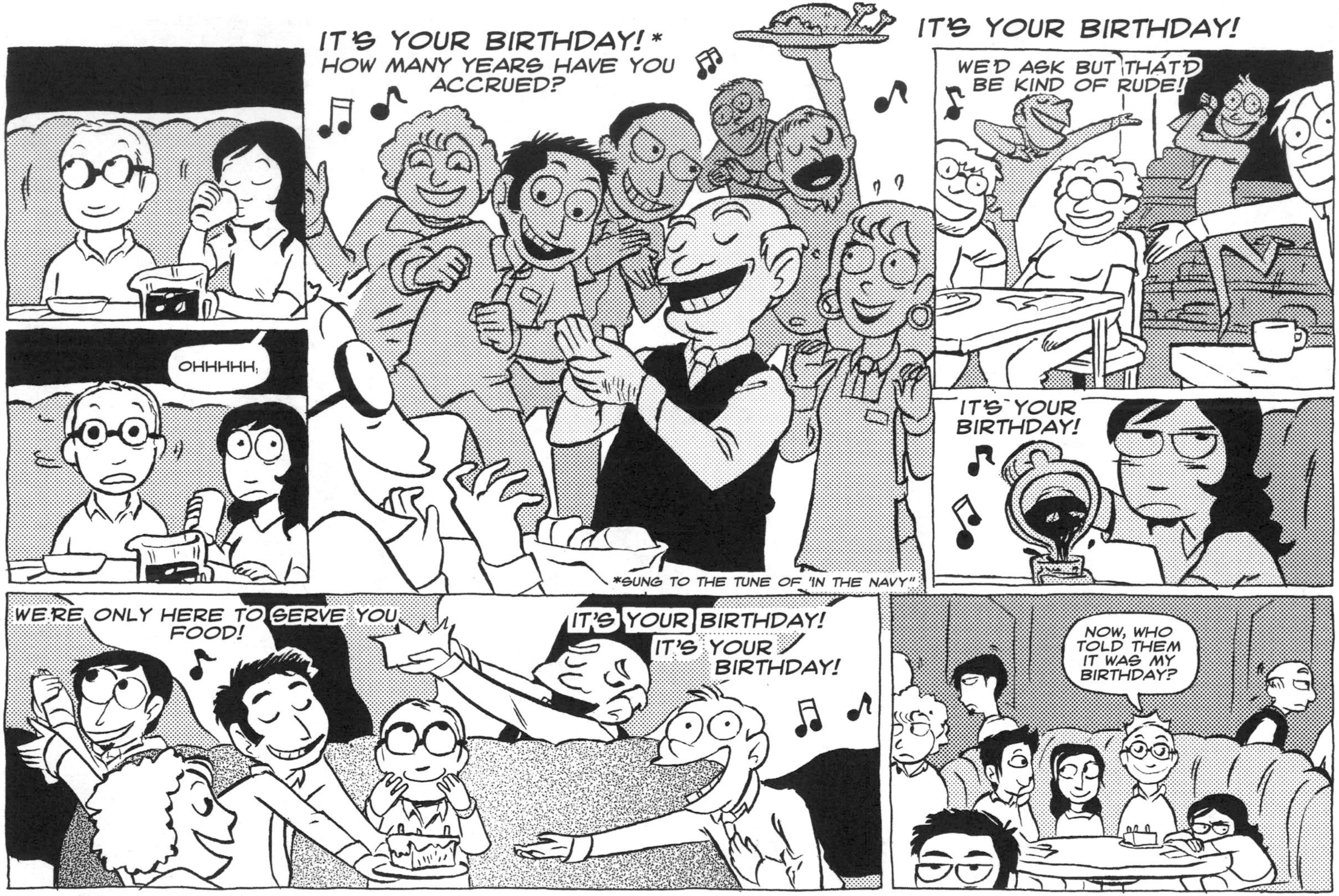
OHHHHH,
IT'S YOUR BIRTHDAY! *
HOW MANY YEARS HAVE YOU ACCRUED?
IT'S YOUR BIRTHDAY!
WE'D ASK BUT THAT'D BE KIND OF RUDE!
IT'S YOUR BIRTHDAY!
*SUNG TO THE TUNE OF "IN THE NAVY"
WE'RE ONLY HERE TO SERVE YOU FOOD!
IT'S YOUR BIRTHDAY!
IT'S YOUR BIRTHDAY!
NOW, WHO TOLD THEM IT WAS MY BIRTHDAY?

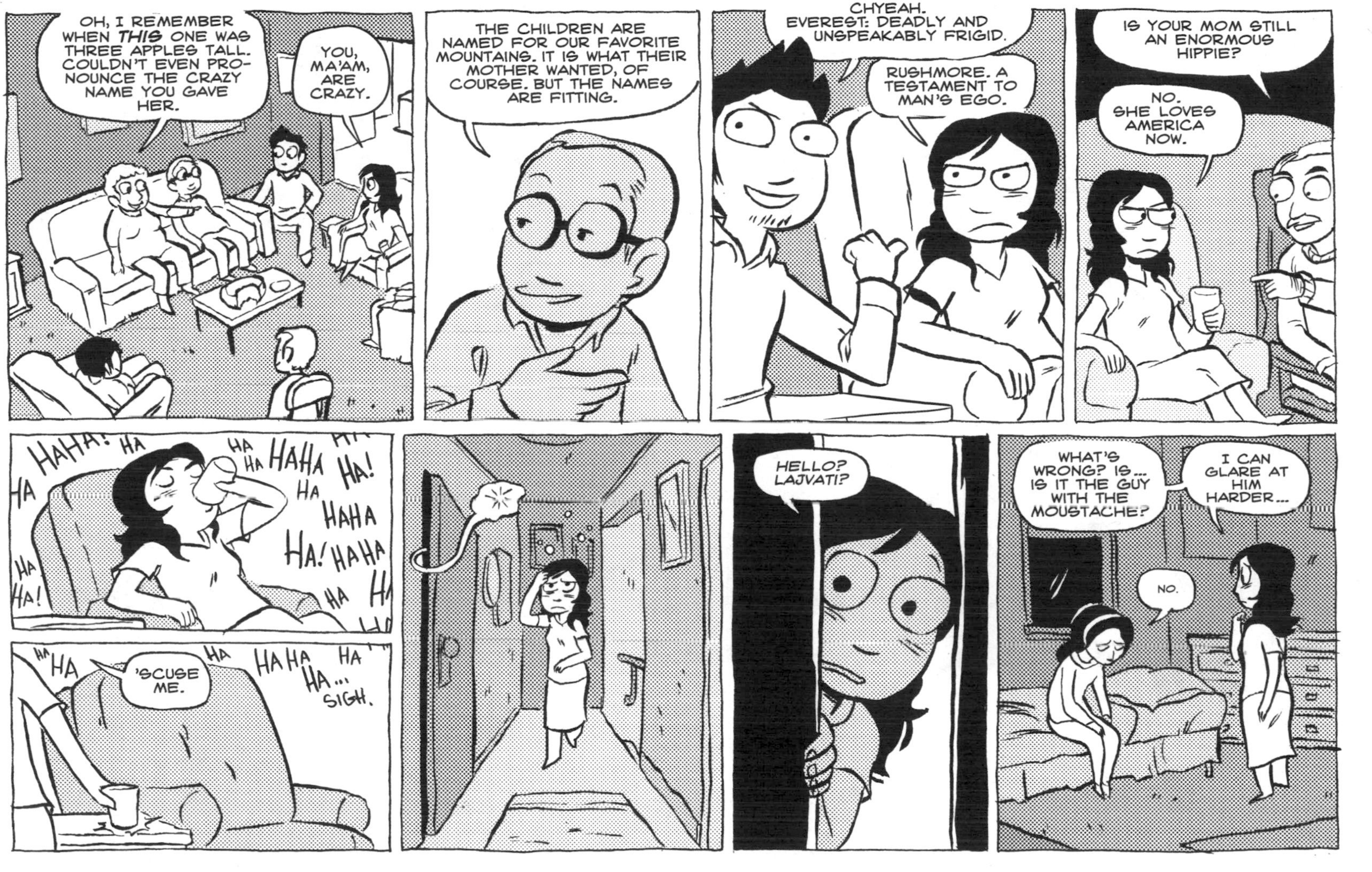
OH, I REMEMBER WHEN THIS ONE WAS THREE APPLES TALL. COULDN'T EVEN PRONOUNCE THE CRAZY NAME YOU GAVE HER.
YOU, MA'AM, ARE CRAZY.
THE CHILDREN ARE NAMED FOR OUR FAVORITE MOUNTAINS. IT IS WHAT THEIR MOTHER WANTED, OF COURSE. BUT THE NAMES ARE FITTING.
CHYEAH. EVEREST: DEADLY AND UNSPEAKABLY FRIGID.
RUSHMORE. A TESTAMENT TO MAN'S EGO.
IS YOUR MOM STILL AN ENORMOUS HIPPIE?
NO. SHE LOVES AMERICA NOW.
HAHA! HA HA HA HAHA HA! HA HAHA HA! HAHA HA HA HA!
HA HA 'SCUSE ME. HA HAHA HA HA... SIGH.
HELLO? LAJVATI?
WHAT'S WRONG? IS... IS IT THE GUY WITH THE MOUSTACHE?
I CAN GLARE AT HIM HARDER...
NO.

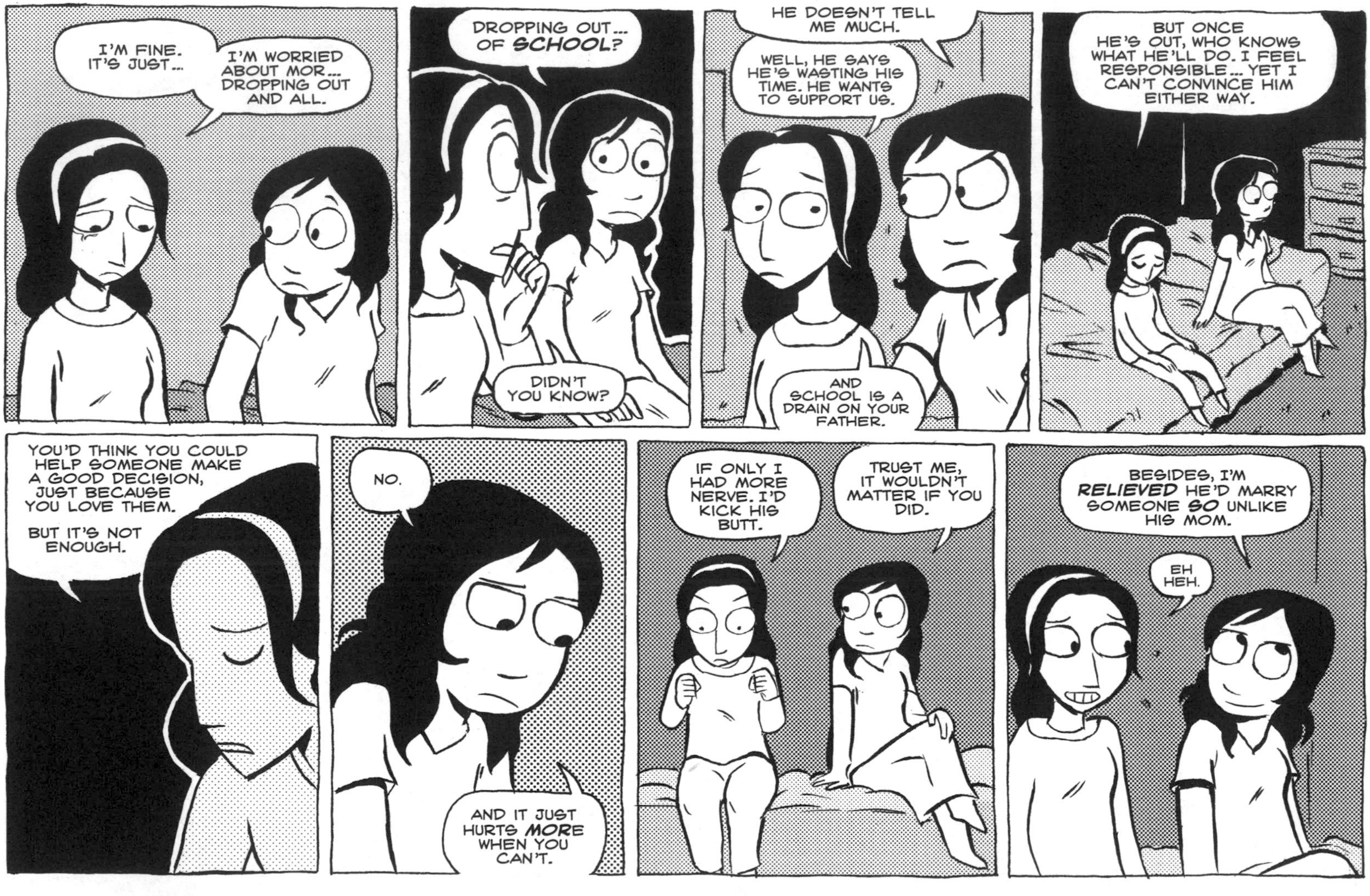
I'M FINE. IT'S JUST...
I'M WORRIED ABOUT MOR... DROPPING OUT AND ALL.
DROPPING OUT... OF SCHOOL?
DIDN'T YOU KNOW?
HE DOESN'T TELL ME MUCH.
WELL, HE SAYS HE'S WASTING HIS TIME. HE WANTS TO SUPPORT US.
AND SCHOOL IS A DRAIN ON YOUR FATHER.
BUT ONCE HE'S OUT, WHO KNOWS WHAT HE'LL DO. I FEEL RESPONSIBLE... YET I CAN'T CONVINCE HIM EITHER WAY.
YOU'D THINK YOU COULD HELP SOMEONE MAKE A GOOD DECISION, JUST BECAUSE YOU LOVE THEM.
BUT IT'S NOT ENOUGH.
NO.
AND IT JUST HURTS MORE WHEN YOU CAN'T.
IF ONLY I HAD MORE NERVE. I'D KICK HIS BUTT.
TRUST ME, IT WOULDN'T MATTER IF YOU DID.
BESIDES, I'M RELIEVED HE'D MARRY SOMEONE SO UNLIKE HIS MOM.
EH HEH.

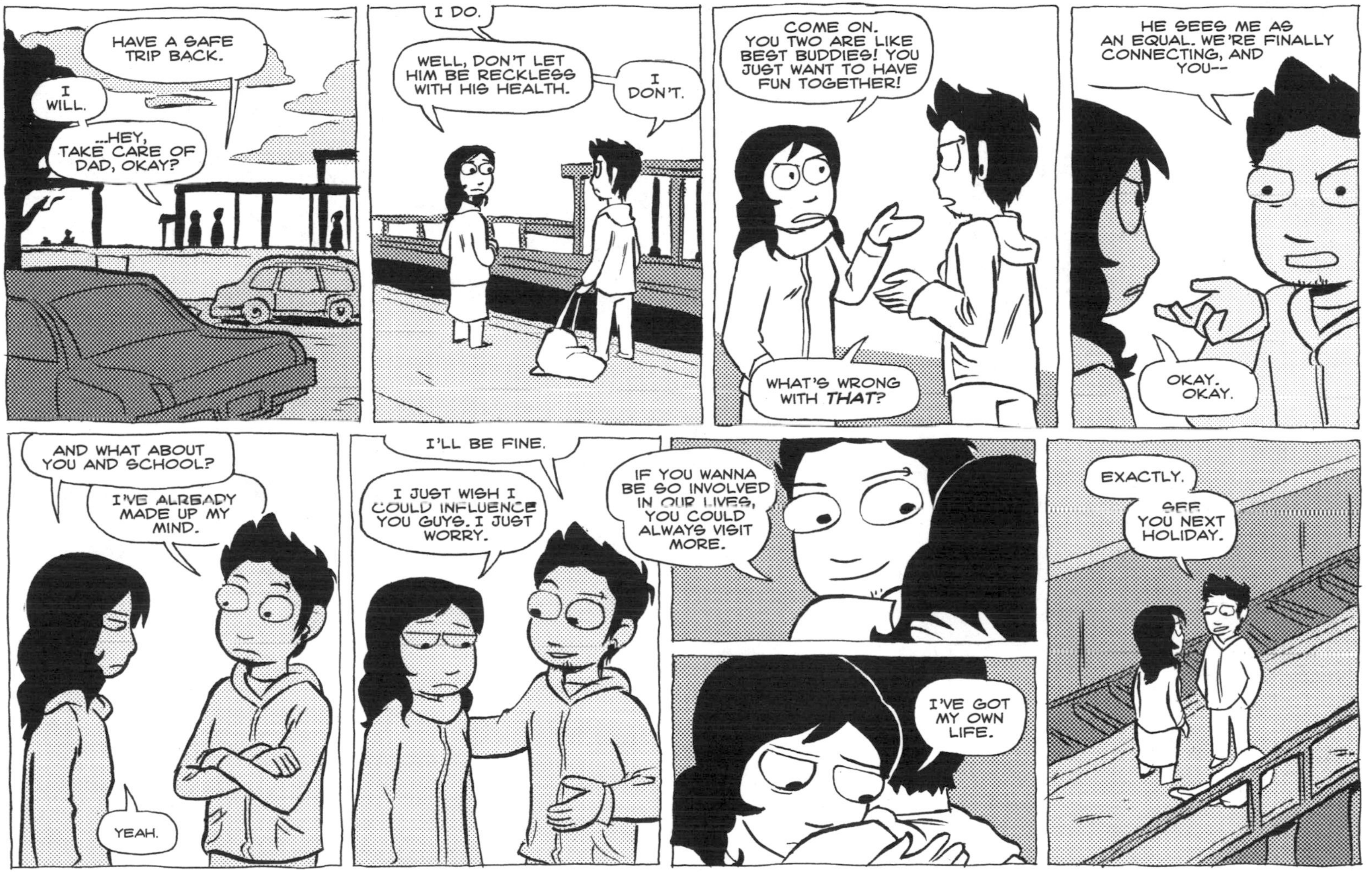
HAVE A SAFE TRIP BACK.
I WILL.
...HEY, TAKE CARE OF DAD, OKAY?
I DO.
WELL, DON'T LET HIM BE RECKLESS WITH HIS HEALTH.
I DON'T.
COME ON. YOU TWO ARE LIKE BEST BUDDIES! YOU JUST WANT TO HAVE FUN TOGETHER!
WHAT'S WRONG WITH *THAT*?
HE SEES ME AS AN EQUAL. WE'RE FINALLY CONNECTING, AND YOU--
OKAY. OKAY.
AND WHAT ABOUT YOU AND SCHOOL?
I'VE ALREADY MADE UP MY MIND.
YEAH.
I'LL BE FINE.
I JUST WISH I COULD INFLUENCE YOU GUYS. I JUST WORRY.
IF YOU WANNA BE SO INVOLVED IN OUR LIVES, YOU COULD ALWAYS VISIT MORE.
I'VE GOT MY OWN LIFE.
EXACTLY.
SEE YOU NEXT HOLIDAY.

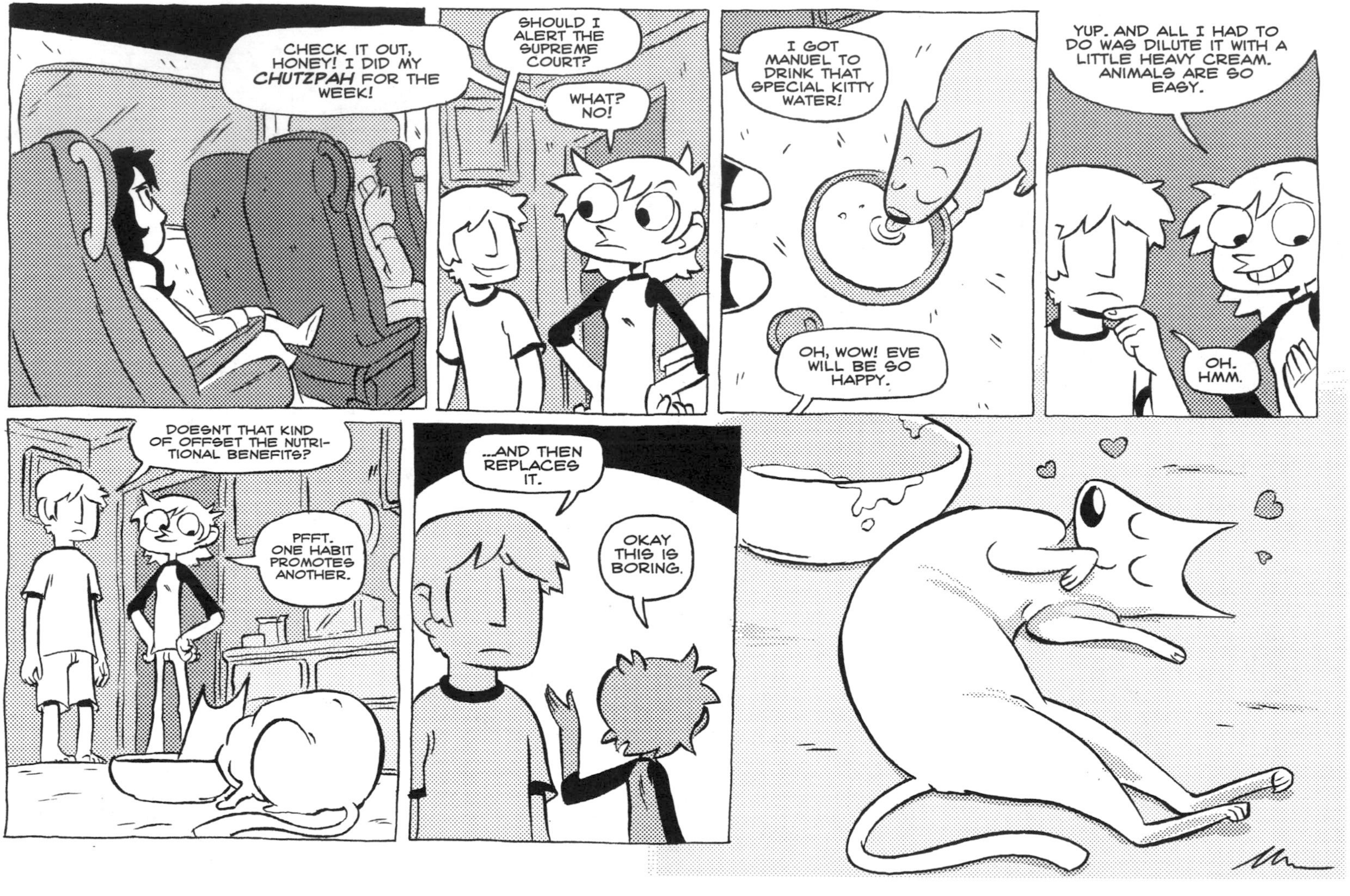
CHECK IT OUT, HONEY! I DID MY *CHUTZPAH* FOR THE WEEK!
SHOULD I ALERT THE SUPREME COURT?
WHAT? NO!
I GOT MANUEL TO DRINK THAT SPECIAL KITTY WATER!
OH, WOW! EVE WILL BE SO HAPPY.
YUP. AND ALL I HAD TO DO WAS DILUTE IT WITH A LITTLE HEAVY CREAM. ANIMALS ARE SO EASY.
OH. HMM.
DOESN'T THAT KIND OF OFFSET THE NUTRITIONAL BENEFITS?
PFFT. ONE HABIT PROMOTES ANOTHER.
...AND THEN REPLACES IT.
OKAY THIS IS BORING.

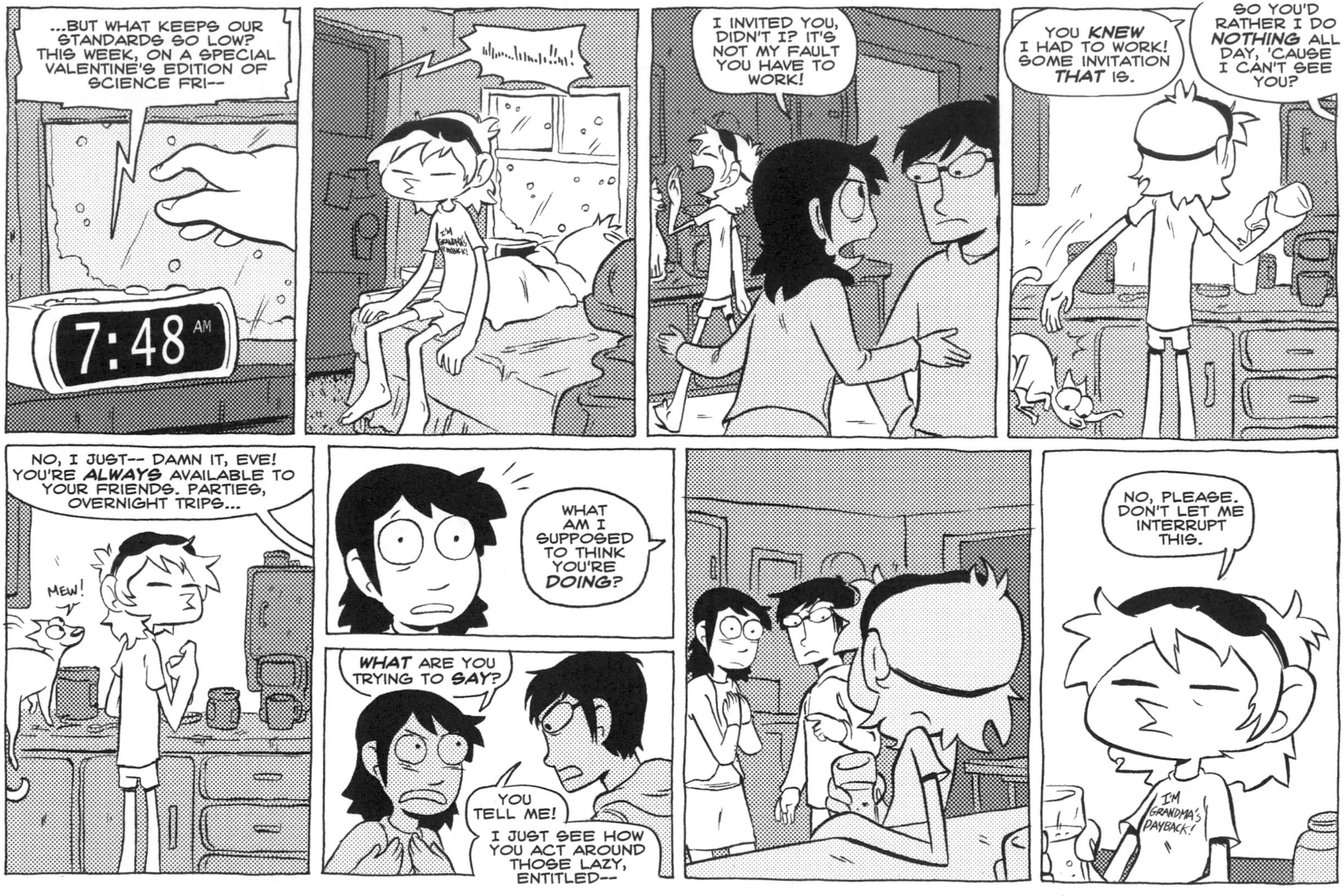
...BUT WHAT KEEPS OUR STANDARDS SO LOW? THIS WEEK, ON A SPECIAL VALENTINE'S EDITION OF SCIENCE FRI--
7:48 AM
I'M GRANDMA'S PAYBACK!
I INVITED YOU, DIDN'T I? IT'S NOT MY FAULT YOU HAVE TO WORK!
YOU **KNEW** I HAD TO WORK! SOME INVITATION **THAT** IS.
SO YOU'D RATHER I DO **NOTHING** ALL DAY, 'CAUSE I CAN'T SEE YOU?
NO, I JUST-- DAMN IT, EVE! YOU'RE **ALWAYS** AVAILABLE TO YOUR FRIENDS. PARTIES, OVERNIGHT TRIPS...
MEW!
WHAT AM I SUPPOSED TO THINK YOU'RE **DOING**?
WHAT ARE YOU TRYING TO **SAY**?
YOU TELL ME!
I JUST SEE HOW YOU ACT AROUND THOSE LAZY, ENTITLED--
NO, PLEASE. DON'T LET ME INTERRUPT THIS.
I'M GRANDMA'S PAYBACK!

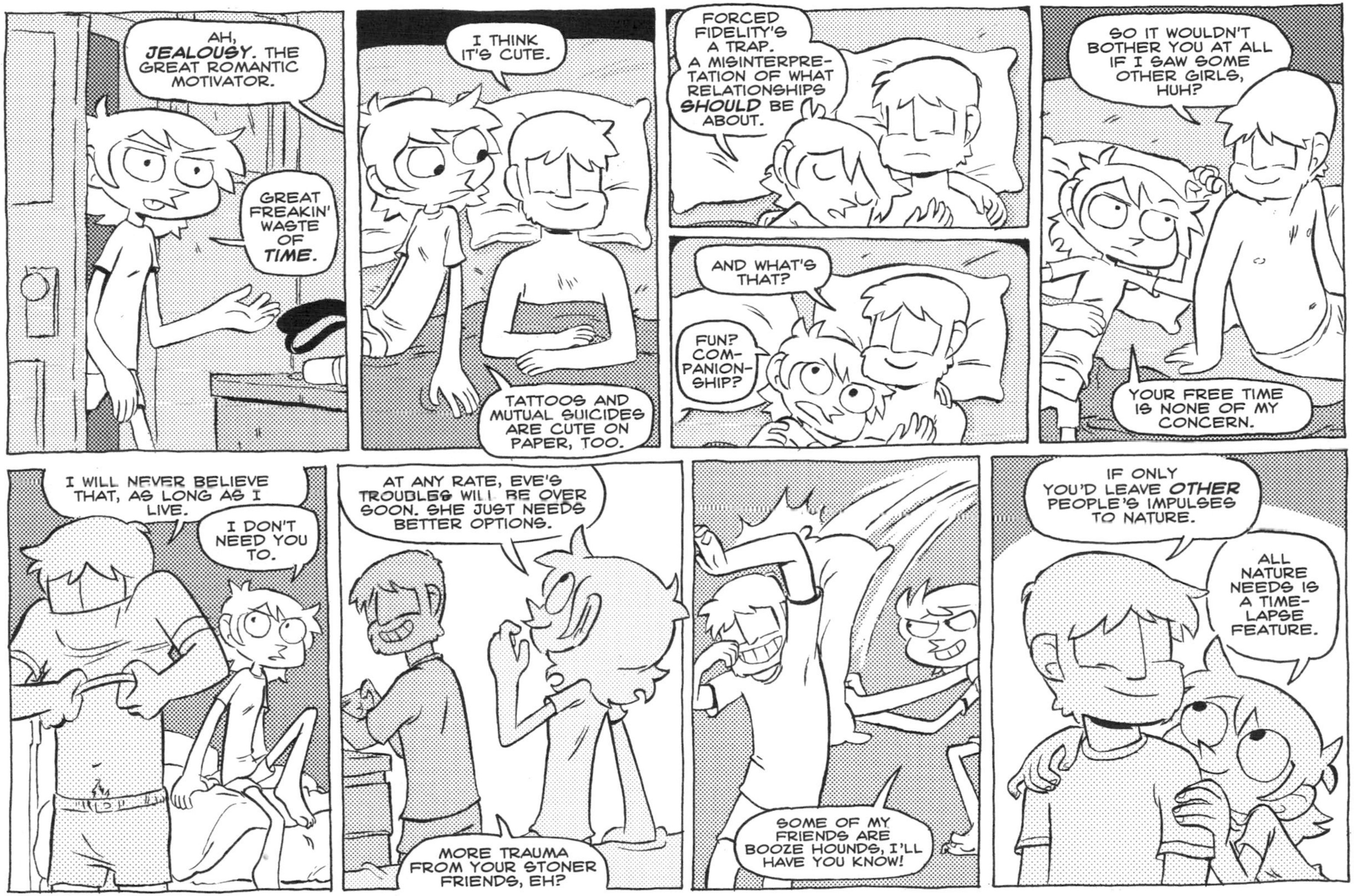
AH, JEALOUSY. THE GREAT ROMANTIC MOTIVATOR.
GREAT FREAKIN' WASTE OF TIME.
I THINK IT'S CUTE.
TATTOOS AND MUTUAL SUICIDES ARE CUTE ON PAPER, TOO.
FORCED FIDELITY'S A TRAP. A MISINTERPRETATION OF WHAT RELATIONSHIPS SHOULD BE ABOUT.
AND WHAT'S THAT?
FUN? COMPANIONSHIP?
SO IT WOULDN'T BOTHER YOU AT ALL IF I SAW SOME OTHER GIRLS, HUH?
YOUR FREE TIME IS NONE OF MY CONCERN.
I WILL NEVER BELIEVE THAT, AS LONG AS I LIVE.
I DON'T NEED YOU TO.
AT ANY RATE, EVE'S TROUBLES WILL BE OVER SOON. SHE JUST NEEDS BETTER OPTIONS.
MORE TRAUMA FROM YOUR STONER FRIENDS, EH?
SOME OF MY FRIENDS ARE BOOZE HOUNDS, I'LL HAVE YOU KNOW!
IF ONLY YOU'D LEAVE OTHER PEOPLE'S IMPULSES TO NATURE.
ALL NATURE NEEDS IS A TIME-LAPSE FEATURE.

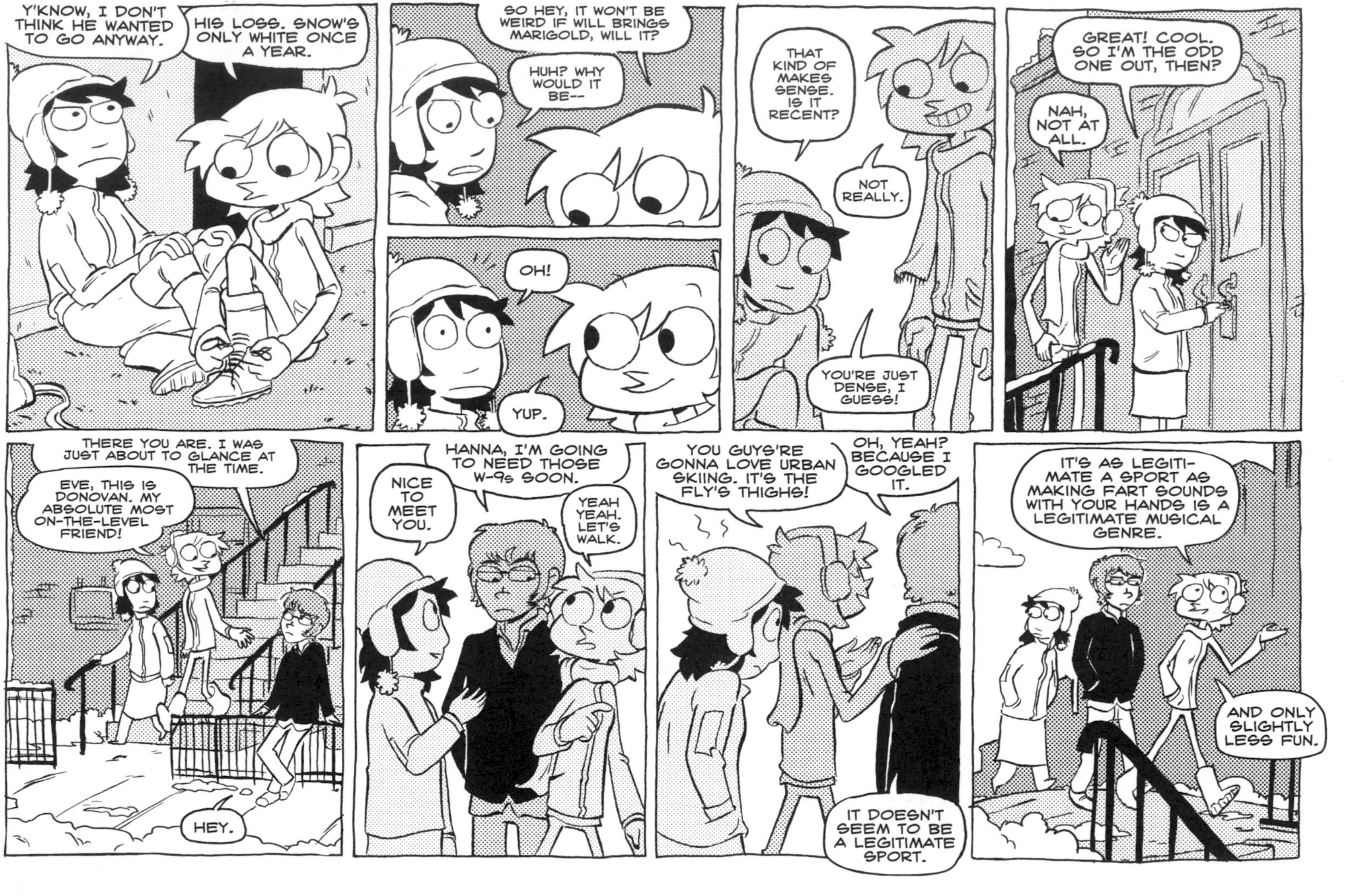

Y'KNOW, I DON'T THINK HE WANTED TO GO ANYWAY.
HIS LOSS. SNOW'S ONLY WHITE ONCE A YEAR.
SO HEY, IT WON'T BE WEIRD IF WILL BRINGS MARIGOLD, WILL IT?
HUH? WHY WOULD IT BE--
OH!
YUP.
THAT KIND OF MAKES SENSE. IS IT RECENT?
NOT REALLY.
YOU'RE JUST DENSE, I GUESS!
GREAT! COOL. SO I'M THE ODD ONE OUT, THEN?
NAH, NOT AT ALL.
THERE YOU ARE. I WAS JUST ABOUT TO GLANCE AT THE TIME.
EVE, THIS IS DONOVAN. MY ABSOLUTE MOST ON-THE-LEVEL FRIEND!
HEY.
NICE TO MEET YOU.
HANNA, I'M GOING TO NEED THOSE W-9s SOON.
YEAH YEAH. LET'S WALK.
YOU GUYS'RE GONNA LOVE URBAN SKIING. IT'S THE FLY'S THIGHS!
OH, YEAH? BECAUSE I GOOGLED IT.
IT DOESN'T SEEM TO BE A LEGITIMATE SPORT.
IT'S AS LEGITI-MATE A SPORT AS MAKING FART SOUNDS WITH YOUR HANDS IS A LEGITIMATE MUSICAL GENRE.
AND ONLY SLIGHTLY LESS FUN.

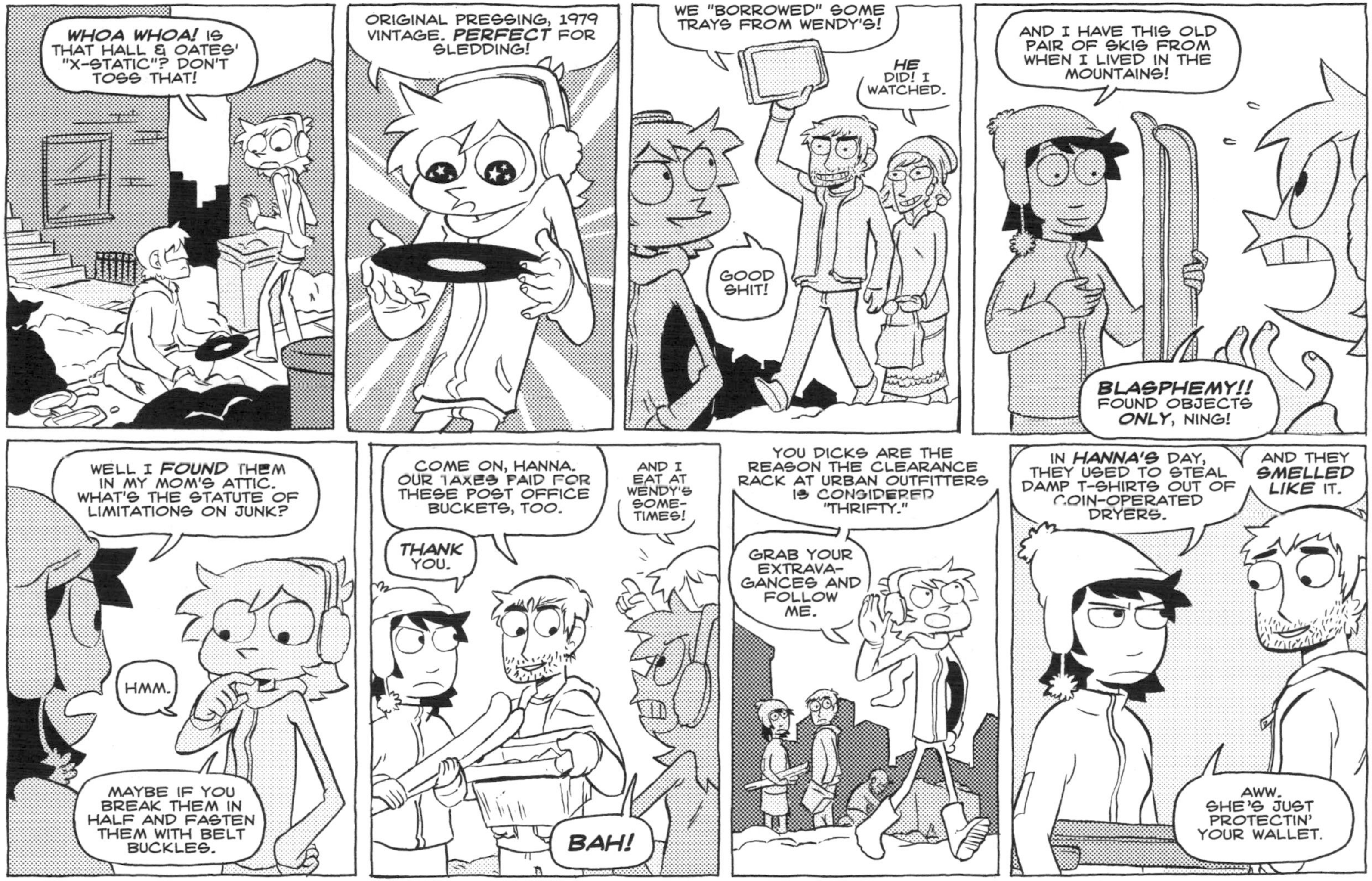
WHOA WHOA! IS THAT HALL & OATES' "X-STATIC"? DON'T TOSS THAT!
ORIGINAL PRESSING, 1979 VINTAGE. PERFECT FOR SLEDDING!
WE "BORROWED" SOME TRAYS FROM WENDY'S!
HE DID! I WATCHED.
GOOD SHIT!
AND I HAVE THIS OLD PAIR OF SKIS FROM WHEN I LIVED IN THE MOUNTAINS!
BLASPHEMY!! FOUND OBJECTS ONLY, NING!
WELL I FOUND THEM IN MY MOM'S ATTIC. WHAT'S THE STATUTE OF LIMITATIONS ON JUNK?
HMM.
MAYBE IF YOU BREAK THEM IN HALF AND FASTEN THEM WITH BELT BUCKLES.
COME ON, HANNA. OUR TAXES PAID FOR THESE POST OFFICE BUCKETS, TOO.
AND I EAT AT WENDY'S SOME-TIMES!
THANK YOU.
BAH!
YOU DICKS ARE THE REASON THE CLEARANCE RACK AT URBAN OUTFITTERS IS CONSIDERED "THRIFTY."
GRAB YOUR EXTRAVA-GANCES AND FOLLOW ME.
IN HANNA'S DAY, THEY USED TO STEAL DAMP T-SHIRTS OUT OF COIN-OPERATED DRYERS.
AND THEY SMELLED LIKE IT.
AWW. SHE'S JUST PROTECTIN' YOUR WALLET.

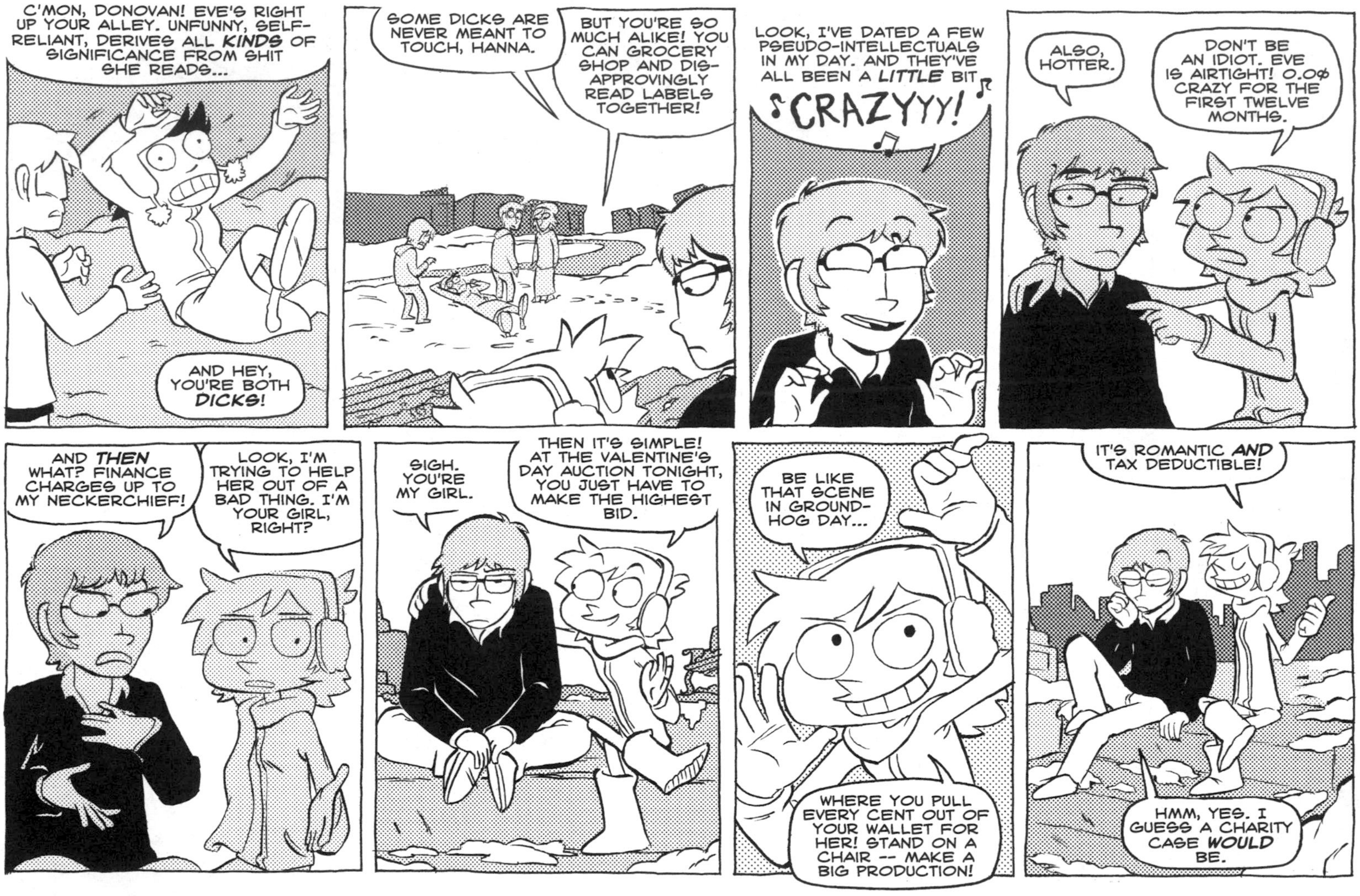
C'MON, DONOVAN! EVE'S RIGHT UP YOUR ALLEY. UNFUNNY, SELF-RELIANT, DERIVES ALL KINDS OF SIGNIFICANCE FROM SHIT SHE READS...
AND HEY, YOU'RE BOTH DICKS!
SOME DICKS ARE NEVER MEANT TO TOUCH, HANNA.
BUT YOU'RE SO MUCH ALIKE! YOU CAN GROCERY SHOP AND DIS-APPROVINGLY READ LABELS TOGETHER!
LOOK, I'VE DATED A FEW PSEUDO-INTELLECTUALS IN MY DAY. AND THEY'VE ALL BEEN A LITTLE BIT
CRAZYYYY!
ALSO, HOTTER.
DON'T BE AN IDIOT. EVE IS AIRTIGHT! 0.0% CRAZY FOR THE FIRST TWELVE MONTHS.
AND THEN WHAT? FINANCE CHARGES UP TO MY NECKERCHIEF!
LOOK, I'M TRYING TO HELP HER OUT OF A BAD THING. I'M YOUR GIRL, RIGHT?
SIGH. YOU'RE MY GIRL.
THEN IT'S SIMPLE! AT THE VALENTINE'S DAY AUCTION TONIGHT, YOU JUST HAVE TO MAKE THE HIGHEST BID.
BE LIKE THAT SCENE IN GROUND-HOG DAY...
WHERE YOU PULL EVERY CENT OUT OF YOUR WALLET FOR HER! STAND ON A CHAIR -- MAKE A BIG PRODUCTION!
IT'S ROMANTIC AND TAX DEDUCTIBLE!
HMM, YES. I GUESS A CHARITY CASE WOULD BE.

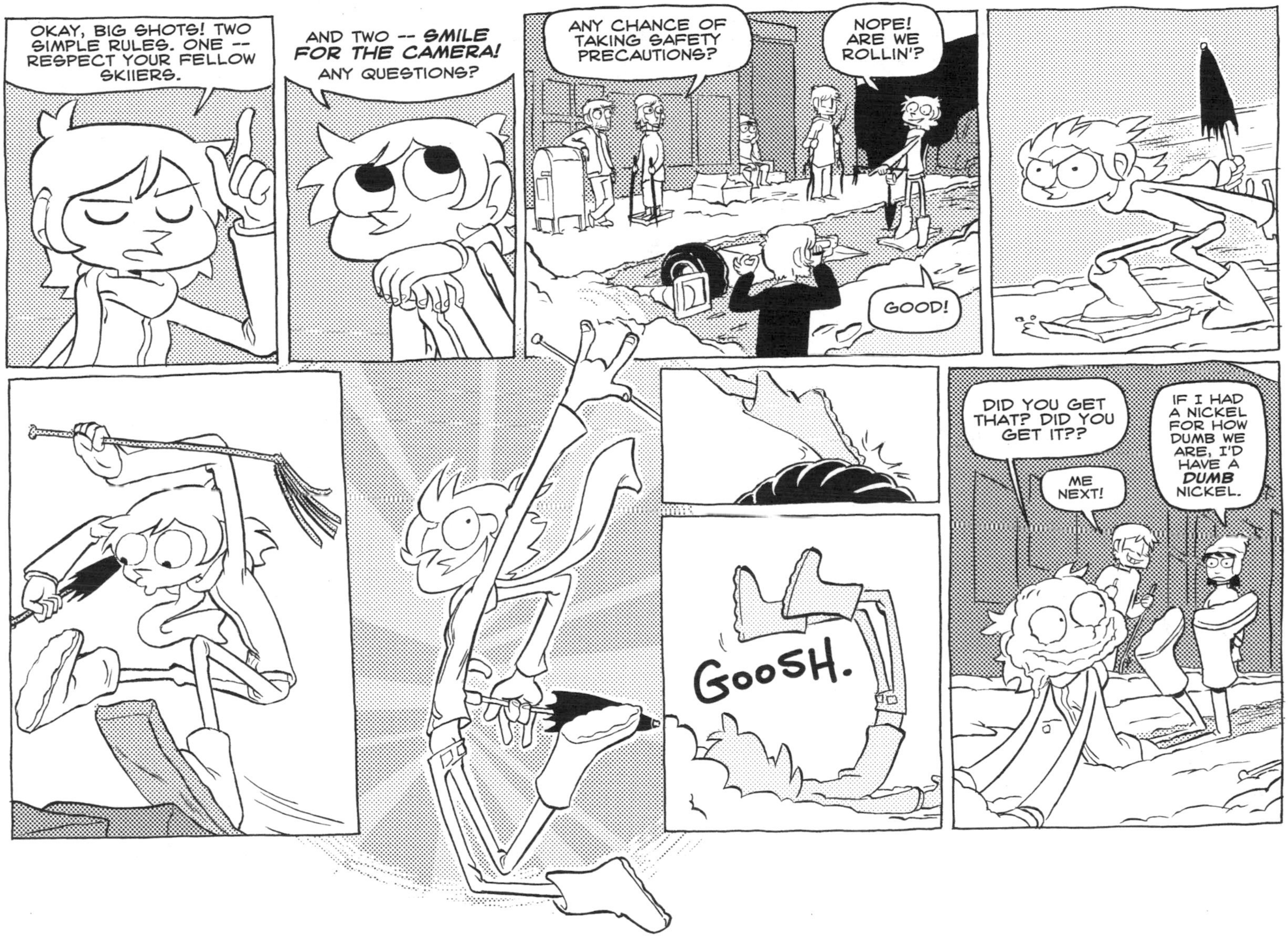
OKAY, BIG SHOTS! TWO SIMPLE RULES. ONE -- RESPECT YOUR FELLOW SKIIERS.
AND TWO -- SMILE FOR THE CAMERA! ANY QUESTIONS?
ANY CHANCE OF TAKING SAFETY PRECAUTIONS?
NOPE! ARE WE ROLLIN'?
GOOD!
GOOSH.
DID YOU GET THAT? DID YOU GET IT??
ME NEXT!
IF I HAD A NICKEL FOR HOW DUMB WE ARE, I'D HAVE A DUMB NICKEL.

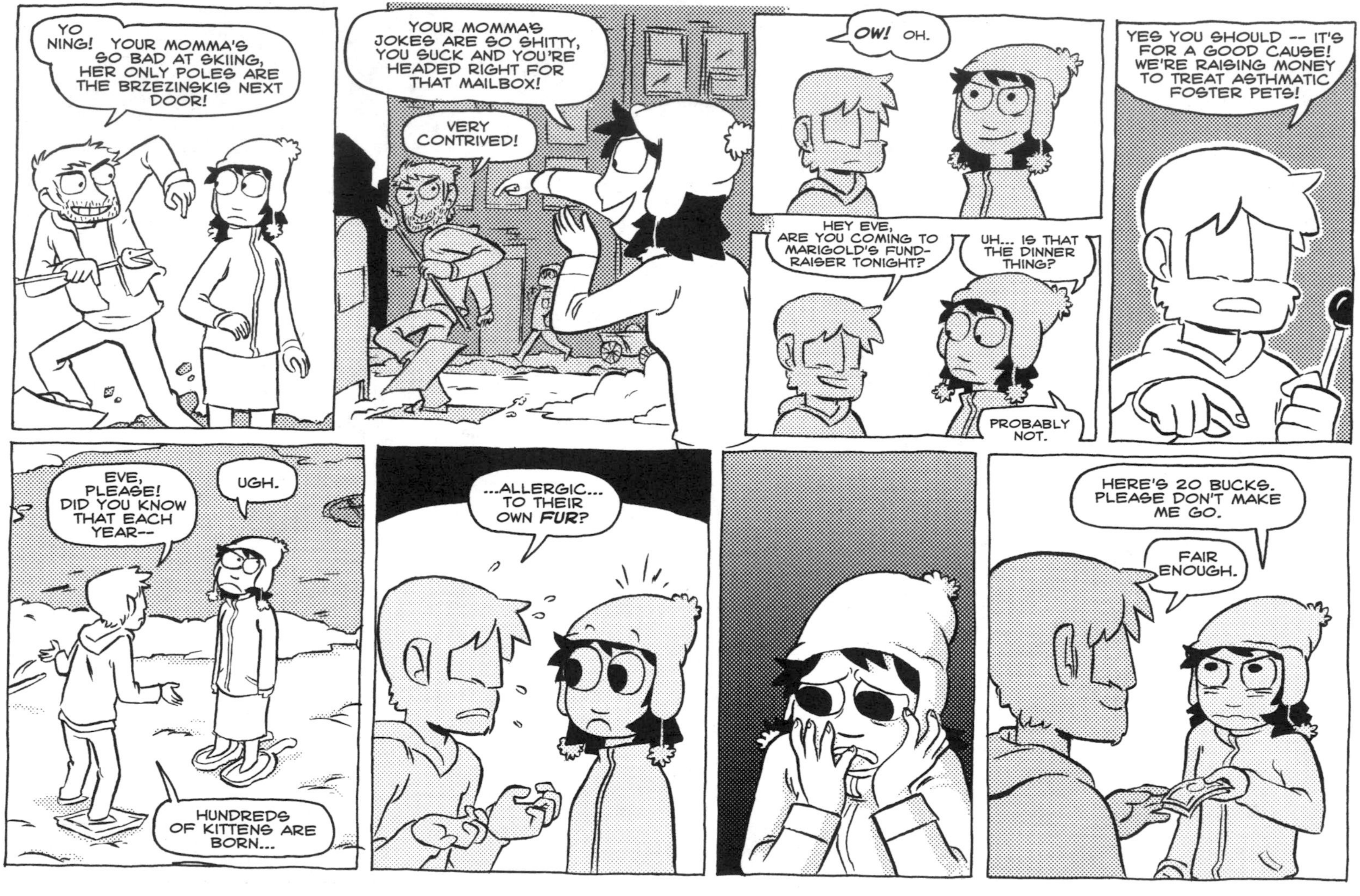
YO NING! YOUR MOMMA'S SO BAD AT SKIING, HER ONLY POLES ARE THE BRZEZINSKIS NEXT DOOR!
YOUR MOMMA'S JOKES ARE SO SHITTY, YOU SUCK AND YOU'RE HEADED RIGHT FOR THAT MAILBOX!
VERY CONTRIVED!
OW! OH.
YES YOU SHOULD -- IT'S FOR A GOOD CAUSE! WE'RE RAISING MONEY TO TREAT ASTHMATIC FOSTER PETS!
HEY EVE, ARE YOU COMING TO MARIGOLD'S FUND-RAISER TONIGHT?
UH... IS THAT THE DINNER THING?
PROBABLY NOT.
EVE, PLEASE! DID YOU KNOW THAT EACH YEAR--
UGH.
HUNDREDS OF KITTENS ARE BORN...
...ALLERGIC... TO THEIR OWN FUR?
HERE'S 20 BUCKS. PLEASE DON'T MAKE ME GO.
FAIR ENOUGH.

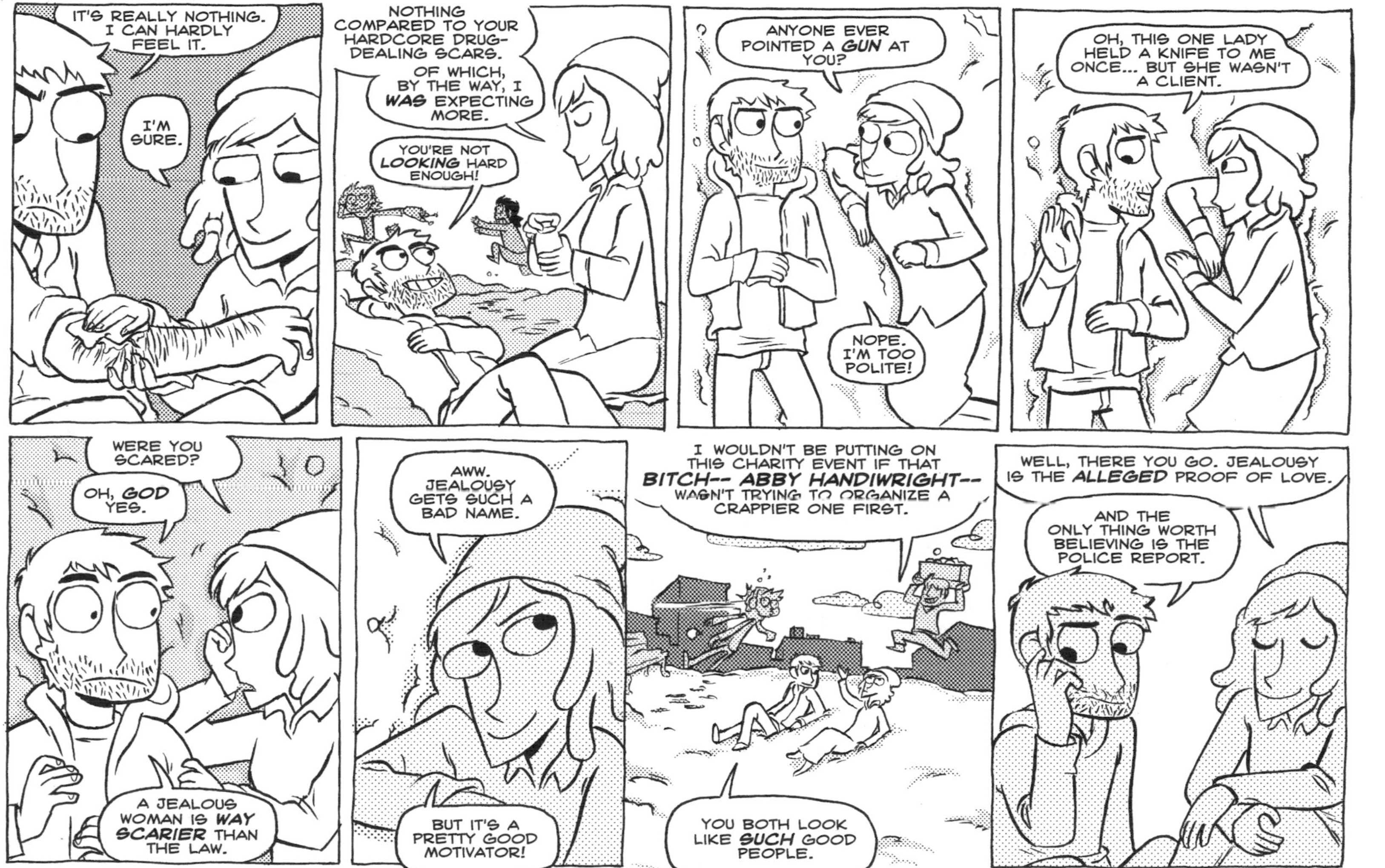
IT'S REALLY NOTHING. I CAN HARDLY FEEL IT.
I'M SURE.
NOTHING COMPARED TO YOUR HARDCORE DRUG-DEALING SCARS.
OF WHICH, BY THE WAY, I WAS EXPECTING MORE.
YOU'RE NOT LOOKING HARD ENOUGH!
ANYONE EVER POINTED A GUN AT YOU?
NOPE. I'M TOO POLITE!
OH, THIS ONE LADY HELD A KNIFE TO ME ONCE... BUT SHE WASN'T A CLIENT.
WERE YOU SCARED?
OH, GOD YES.
A JEALOUS WOMAN IS WAY SCARIER THAN THE LAW.
AWW. JEALOUSY GETS SUCH A BAD NAME.
BUT IT'S A PRETTY GOOD MOTIVATOR!
I WOULDN'T BE PUTTING ON THIS CHARITY EVENT IF THAT BITCH-- ABBY HANDIWRIGHT-- WASN'T TRYING TO ORGANIZE A CRAPPIER ONE FIRST.
YOU BOTH LOOK LIKE SUCH GOOD PEOPLE.
WELL, THERE YOU GO. JEALOUSY IS THE ALLEGED PROOF OF LOVE.
AND THE ONLY THING WORTH BELIEVING IS THE POLICE REPORT.

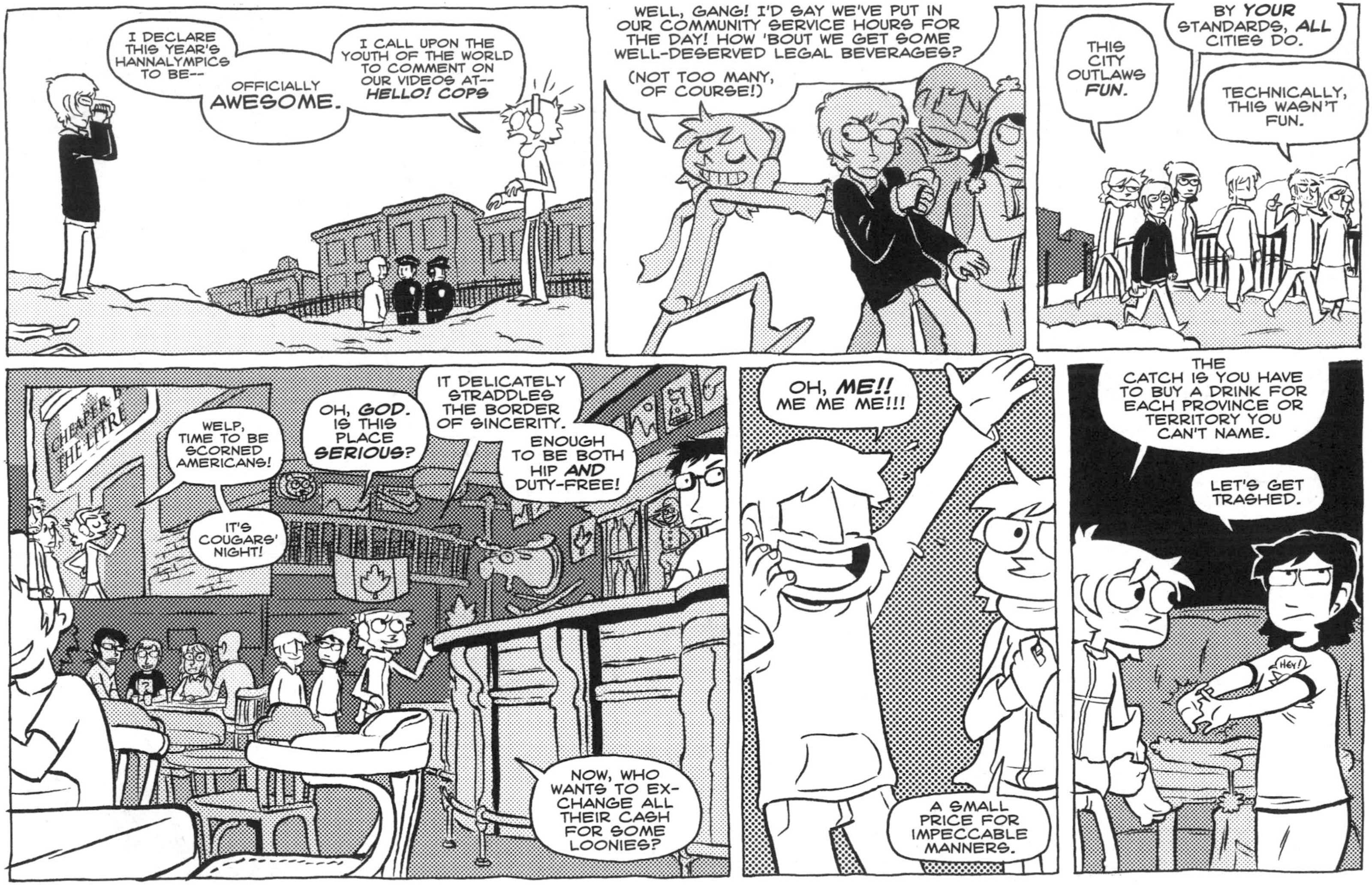
I DECLARE THIS YEAR'S HANNALYMPICS TO BE--
OFFICIALLY AWESOME.
I CALL UPON THE YOUTH OF THE WORLD TO COMMENT ON OUR VIDEOS AT-- HELLO! COPS
WELL, GANG! I'D SAY WE'VE PUT IN OUR COMMUNITY SERVICE HOURS FOR THE DAY! HOW 'BOUT WE GET SOME WELL-DESERVED LEGAL BEVERAGES?
(NOT TOO MANY, OF COURSE!)
THIS CITY OUTLAWS FUN.
BY YOUR STANDARDS, ALL CITIES DO.
TECHNICALLY, THIS WASN'T FUN.
CHEAPER BY THE LITRE
WELP, TIME TO BE SCORNED AMERICANS!
IT'S COUGARS' NIGHT!
OH, GOD. IS THIS PLACE SERIOUS?
IT DELICATELY STRADDLES THE BORDER OF SINCERITY.
ENOUGH TO BE BOTH HIP AND DUTY-FREE!
NOW, WHO WANTS TO EXCHANGE ALL THEIR CASH FOR SOME LOONIES?
OH, ME!! ME ME ME!!!
A SMALL PRICE FOR IMPECCABLE MANNERS.
THE CATCH IS YOU HAVE TO BUY A DRINK FOR EACH PROVINCE OR TERRITORY YOU CAN'T NAME.
LET'S GET TRASHED.
HEY!

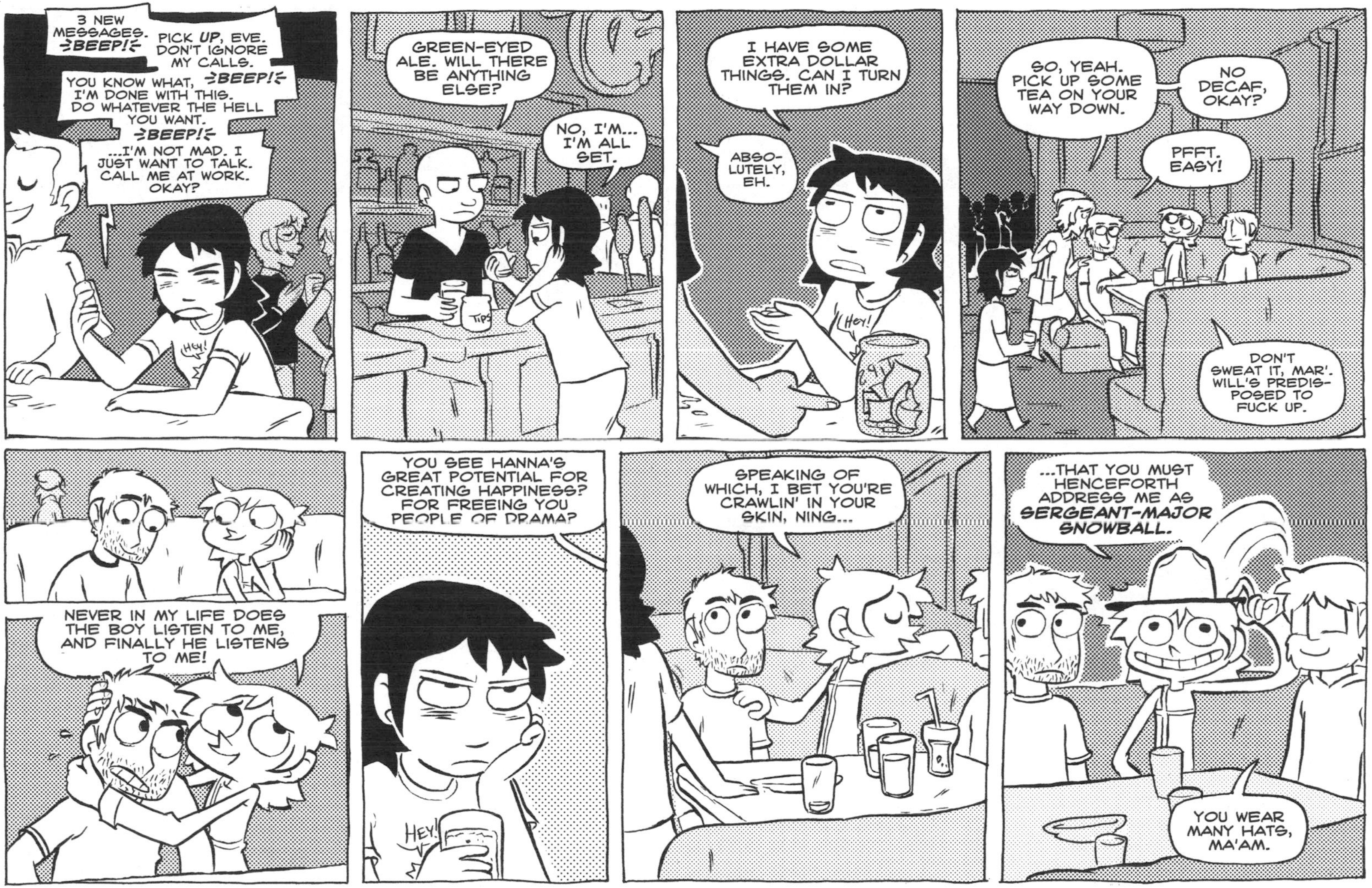
3 NEW MESSAGES. ⪢BEEP!⪡
PICK UP, EVE. DON'T IGNORE MY CALLS.
YOU KNOW WHAT, ⪢BEEP!⪡ I'M DONE WITH THIS. DO WHATEVER THE HELL YOU WANT.
⪢BEEP!⪡
...I'M NOT MAD. I JUST WANT TO TALK. CALL ME AT WORK. OKAY?
GREEN-EYED ALE. WILL THERE BE ANYTHING ELSE?
NO, I'M... I'M ALL SET.
TIPS
I HAVE SOME EXTRA DOLLAR THINGS. CAN I TURN THEM IN?
ABSO-LUTELY, EH.
SO, YEAH. PICK UP SOME TEA ON YOUR WAY DOWN.
NO DECAF, OKAY?
PFFT. EASY!
DON'T SWEAT IT, MAR'. WILL'S PREDIS-POSED TO FUCK UP.
NEVER IN MY LIFE DOES THE BOY LISTEN TO ME, AND FINALLY HE LISTENS TO ME!
YOU SEE HANNA'S GREAT POTENTIAL FOR CREATING HAPPINESS? FOR FREEING YOU PEOPLE OF DRAMA?
SPEAKING OF WHICH, I BET YOU'RE CRAWLIN' IN YOUR SKIN, NING...
...THAT YOU MUST HENCEFORTH ADDRESS ME AS **SERGEANT-MAJOR SNOWBALL.**
YOU WEAR MANY HATS, MA'AM.

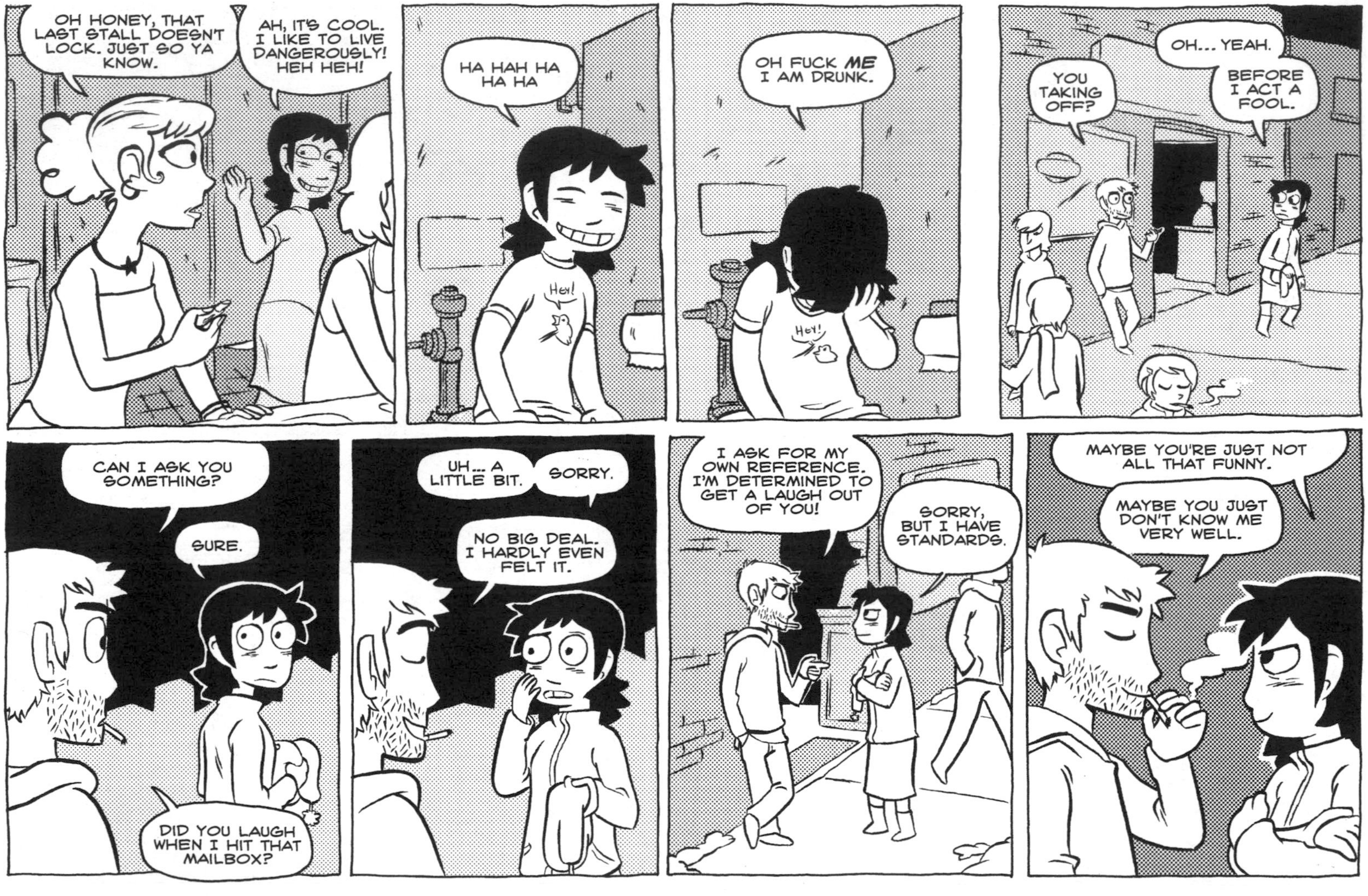
OH HONEY, THAT LAST STALL DOESN'T LOCK. JUST SO YA KNOW.
AH, IT'S COOL. I LIKE TO LIVE DANGEROUSLY! HEH HEH!
HA HAH HA HA HA
Hey!
OH FUCK ME I AM DRUNK.
Hey!
YOU TAKING OFF?
OH... YEAH.
BEFORE I ACT A FOOL.
CAN I ASK YOU SOMETHING?
SURE.
DID YOU LAUGH WHEN I HIT THAT MAILBOX?
UH... A LITTLE BIT.
SORRY.
NO BIG DEAL. I HARDLY EVEN FELT IT.
I ASK FOR MY OWN REFERENCE. I'M DETERMINED TO GET A LAUGH OUT OF YOU!
SORRY, BUT I HAVE STANDARDS.
MAYBE YOU'RE JUST NOT ALL THAT FUNNY.
MAYBE YOU JUST DON'T KNOW ME VERY WELL.

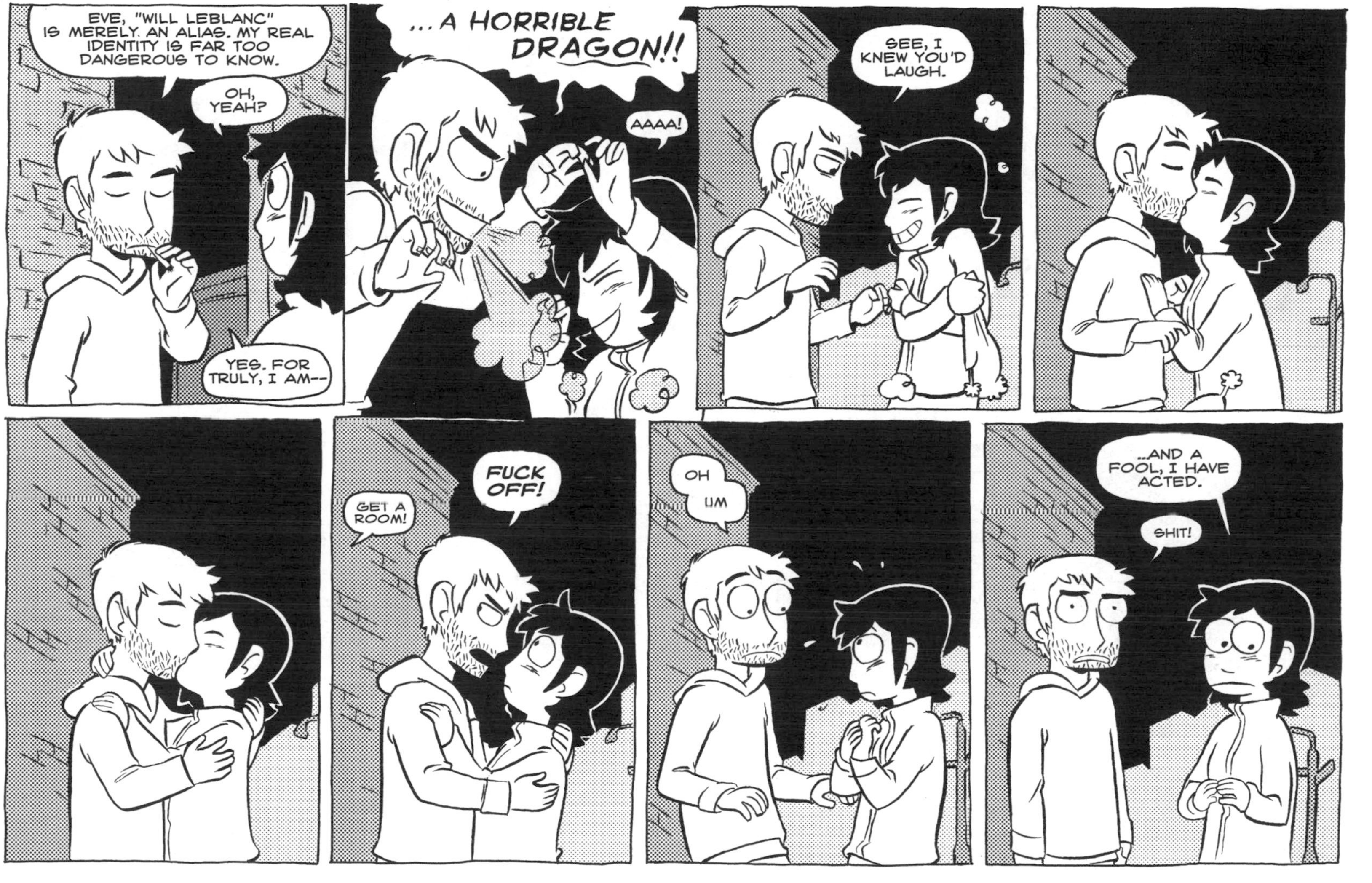
EVE, "WILL LEBLANC" IS MERELY AN ALIAS. MY REAL IDENTITY IS FAR TOO DANGEROUS TO KNOW.
OH, YEAH?
YES. FOR TRULY, I AM--
...A HORRIBLE DRAGON!!
AAAA!
SEE, I KNEW YOU'D LAUGH.
GET A ROOM!
FUCK OFF!
OH
UM
...AND A FOOL, I HAVE ACTED.
SHIT!

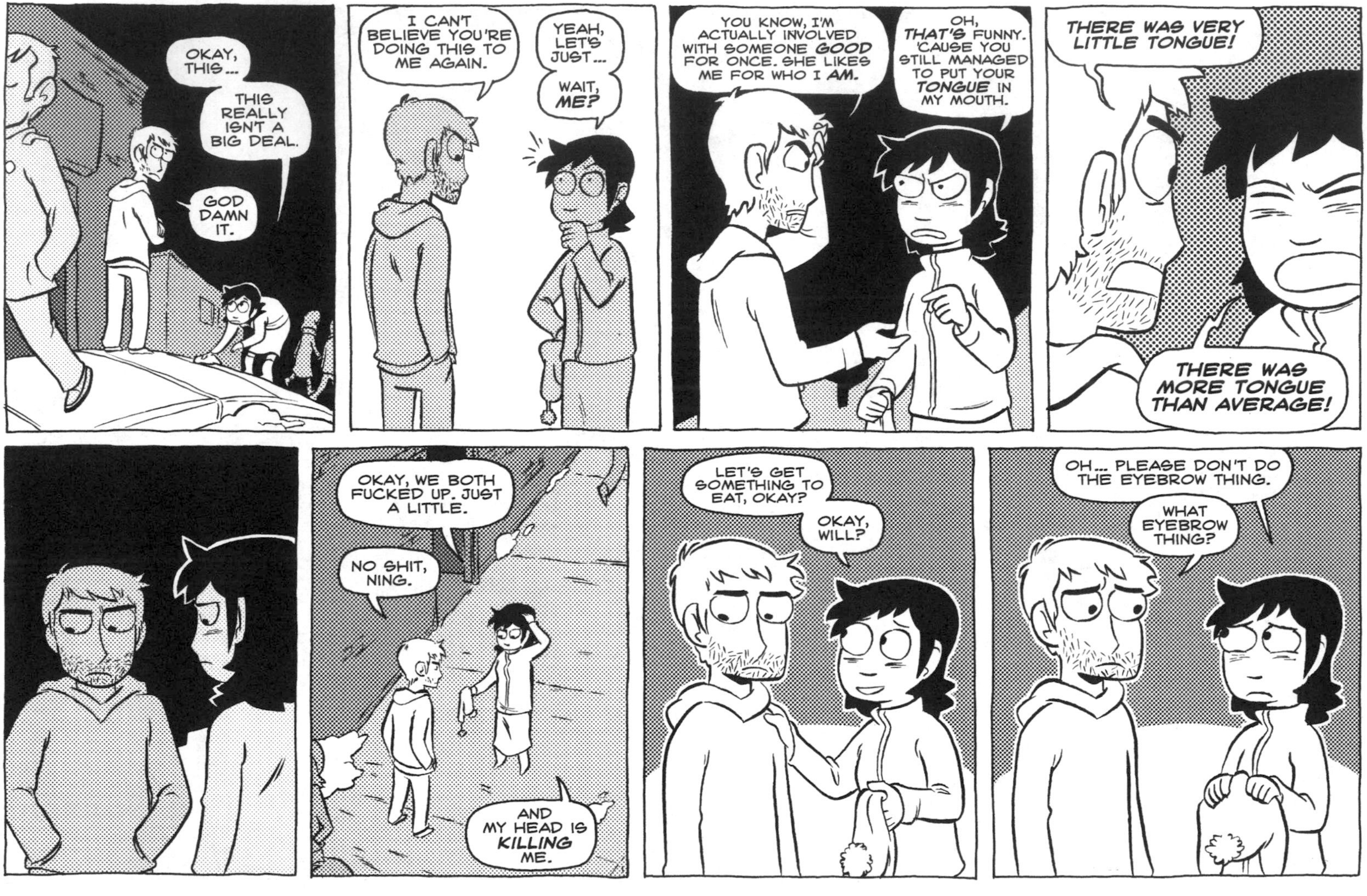
OKAY, THIS...
THIS REALLY ISN'T A BIG DEAL.
GOD DAMN IT.
I CAN'T BELIEVE YOU'RE DOING THIS TO ME AGAIN.
YEAH, LET'S JUST...
WAIT, ME?
YOU KNOW, I'M ACTUALLY INVOLVED WITH SOMEONE GOOD FOR ONCE. SHE LIKES ME FOR WHO I AM.
OH, THAT'S FUNNY. 'CAUSE YOU STILL MANAGED TO PUT YOUR TONGUE IN MY MOUTH.
THERE WAS VERY LITTLE TONGUE!
THERE WAS MORE TONGUE THAN AVERAGE!
OKAY, WE BOTH FUCKED UP. JUST A LITTLE.
NO SHIT, NING.
AND MY HEAD IS KILLING ME.
LET'S GET SOMETHING TO EAT, OKAY?
OKAY, WILL?
OH... PLEASE DON'T DO THE EYEBROW THING.
WHAT EYEBROW THING?

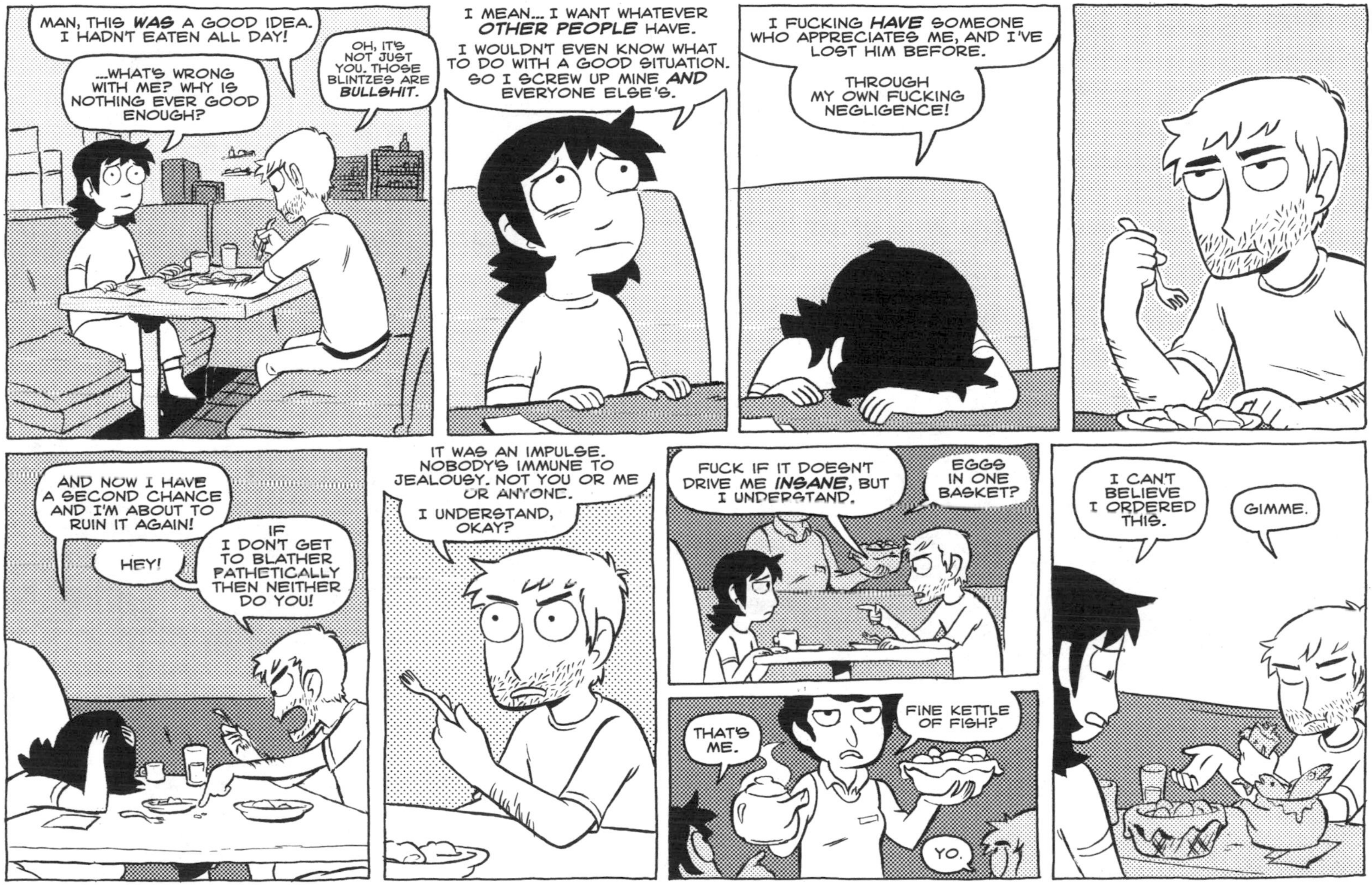

MAN, THIS WAS A GOOD IDEA. I HADN'T EATEN ALL DAY!
...WHAT'S WRONG WITH ME? WHY IS NOTHING EVER GOOD ENOUGH?
OH, IT'S NOT JUST YOU. THOSE BLINTZES ARE BULLSHIT.
I MEAN... I WANT WHATEVER OTHER PEOPLE HAVE.
I WOULDN'T EVEN KNOW WHAT TO DO WITH A GOOD SITUATION. SO I SCREW UP MINE AND EVERYONE ELSE'S.
I FUCKING HAVE SOMEONE WHO APPRECIATES ME, AND I'VE LOST HIM BEFORE.
THROUGH MY OWN FUCKING NEGLIGENCE!
AND NOW I HAVE A SECOND CHANCE AND I'M ABOUT TO RUIN IT AGAIN!
HEY!
IF I DON'T GET TO BLATHER PATHETICALLY THEN NEITHER DO YOU!
IT WAS AN IMPULSE. NOBODY'S IMMUNE TO JEALOUSY. NOT YOU OR ME OR ANYONE.
I UNDERSTAND, OKAY?
FUCK IF IT DOESN'T DRIVE ME INSANE, BUT I UNDERSTAND.
EGGS IN ONE BASKET?
THAT'S ME.
FINE KETTLE OF FISH?
YO.
I CAN'T BELIEVE I ORDERED THIS.
GIMME.

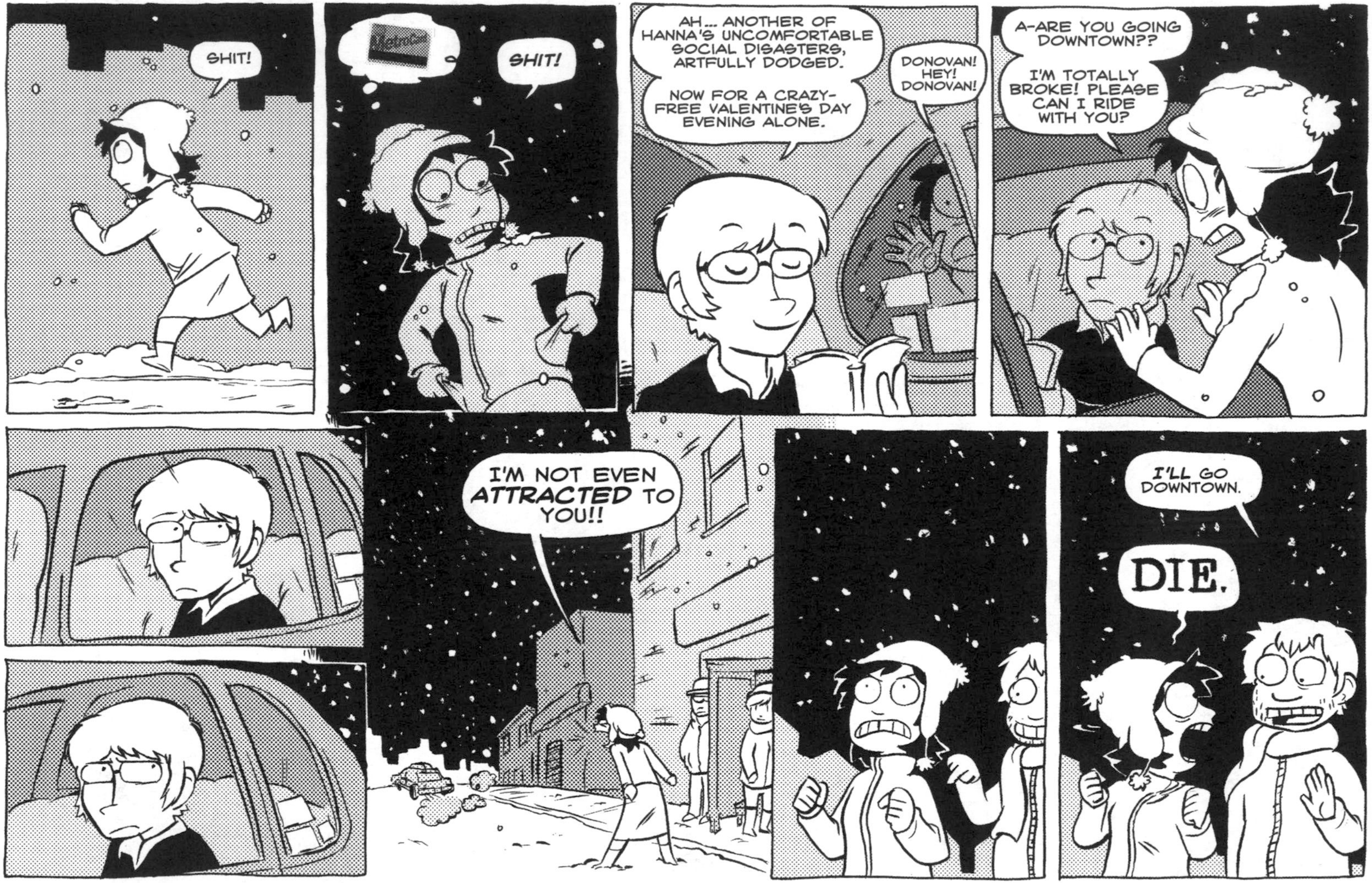
SHIT!
SHIT!
AH... ANOTHER OF HANNA'S UNCOMFORTABLE SOCIAL DISASTERS, ARTFULLY DODGED.
NOW FOR A CRAZY-FREE VALENTINE'S DAY EVENING ALONE.
DONOVAN! HEY! DONOVAN!
A-ARE YOU GOING DOWNTOWN??
I'M TOTALLY BROKE! PLEASE CAN I RIDE WITH YOU?
I'M NOT EVEN ATTRACTED TO YOU!!
I'LL GO DOWNTOWN.
DIE.

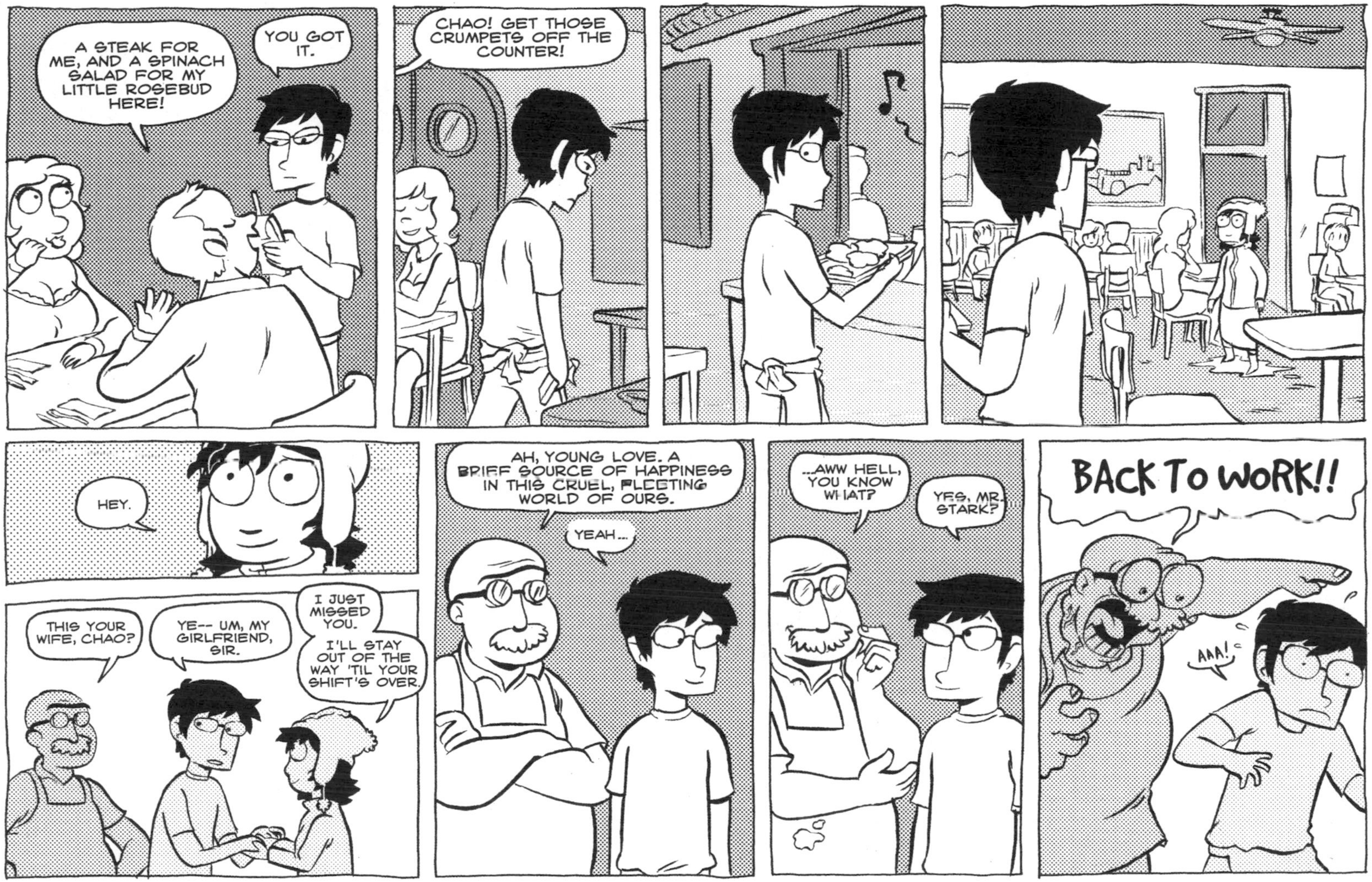
A STEAK FOR ME, AND A SPINACH SALAD FOR MY LITTLE ROSEBUD HERE!
YOU GOT IT.
CHAO! GET THOSE CRUMPETS OFF THE COUNTER!
HEY.
THIS YOUR WIFE, CHAO?
YE-- UM, MY GIRLFRIEND, SIR.
I JUST MISSED YOU.
I'LL STAY OUT OF THE WAY 'TIL YOUR SHIFT'S OVER.
AH, YOUNG LOVE. A BRIEF SOURCE OF HAPPINESS IN THIS CRUEL, FLEETING WORLD OF OURS.
YEAH...
...AWW HELL, YOU KNOW WHAT?
YES, MR. STARK?
BACK TO WORK!!
AAA!

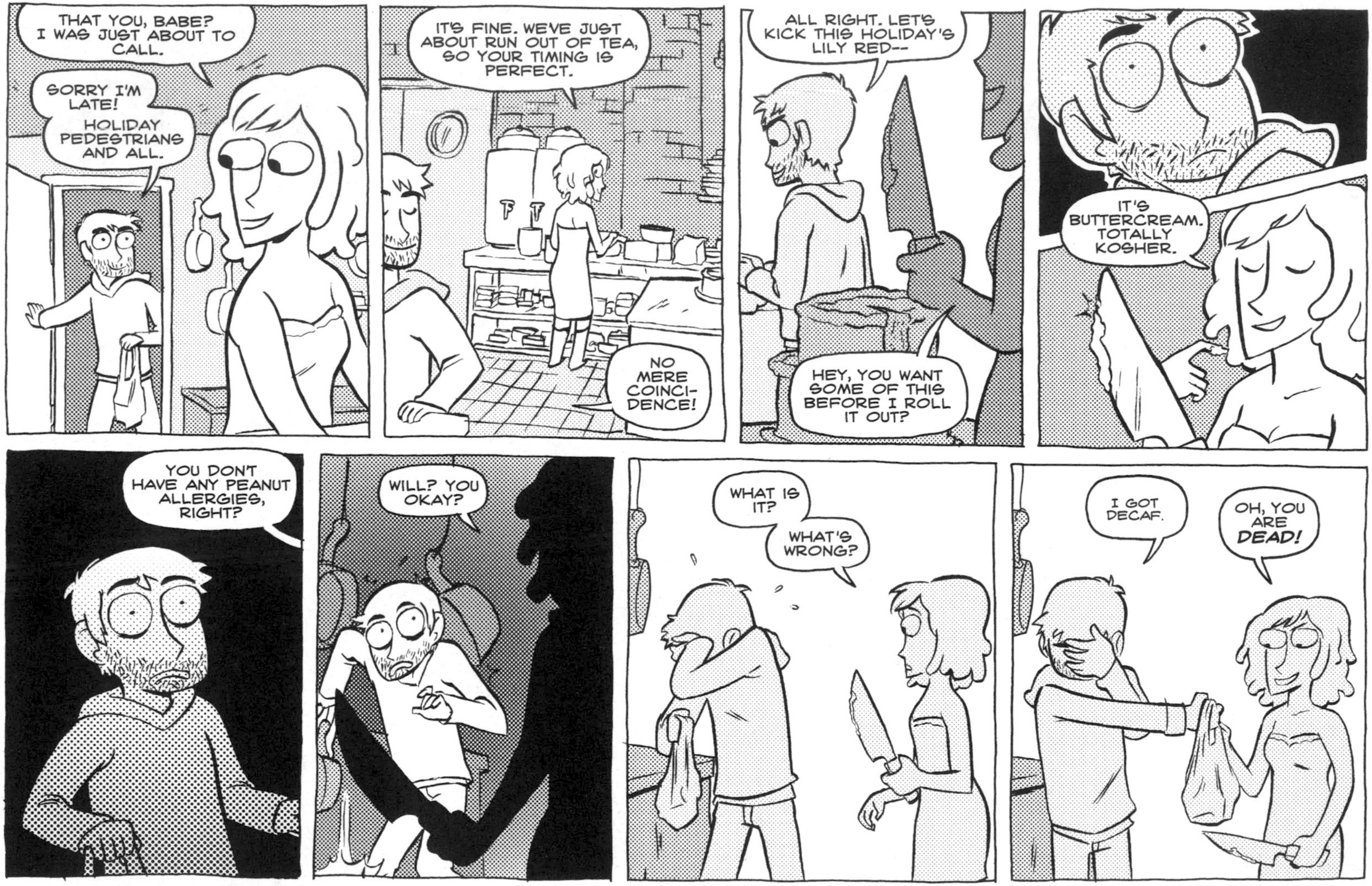
THAT YOU, BABE? I WAS JUST ABOUT TO CALL.
SORRY I'M LATE!
HOLIDAY PEDESTRIANS AND ALL.
IT'S FINE. WE'VE JUST ABOUT RUN OUT OF TEA, SO YOUR TIMING IS PERFECT.
NO MERE COINCI-DENCE!
ALL RIGHT. LET'S KICK THIS HOLIDAY'S LILY RED--
HEY, YOU WANT SOME OF THIS BEFORE I ROLL IT OUT?
IT'S BUTTERCREAM. TOTALLY KOSHER.
YOU DON'T HAVE ANY PEANUT ALLERGIES, RIGHT?
WILL? YOU OKAY?
WHAT IS IT?
WHAT'S WRONG?
I GOT DECAF.
OH, YOU ARE *DEAD!*

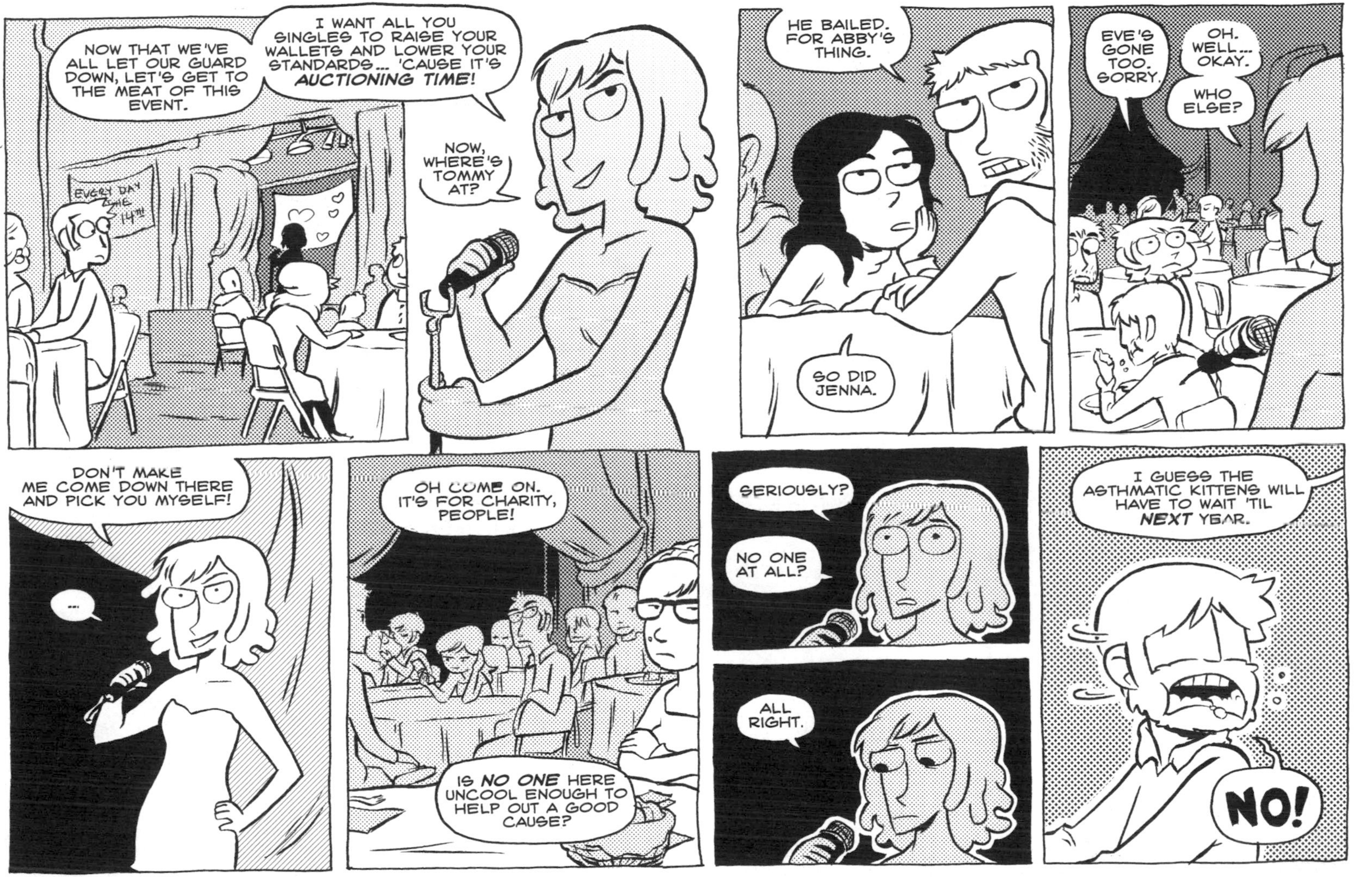
NOW THAT WE'VE ALL LET OUR GUARD DOWN, LET'S GET TO THE MEAT OF THIS EVENT.
EVERY DAY THE 14TH
I WANT ALL YOU SINGLES TO RAISE YOUR WALLETS AND LOWER YOUR STANDARDS... 'CAUSE IT'S AUCTIONING TIME!
NOW, WHERE'S TOMMY AT?
HE BAILED. FOR ABBY'S THING.
SO DID JENNA.
EVE'S GONE TOO. SORRY.
OH. WELL... OKAY.
WHO ELSE?
DON'T MAKE ME COME DOWN THERE AND PICK YOU MYSELF!
...
OH COME ON. IT'S FOR CHARITY, PEOPLE!
IS NO ONE HERE UNCOOL ENOUGH TO HELP OUT A GOOD CAUSE?
SERIOUSLY?
NO ONE AT ALL?
ALL RIGHT.
I GUESS THE ASTHMATIC KITTENS WILL HAVE TO WAIT 'TIL NEXT YEAR.
NO!

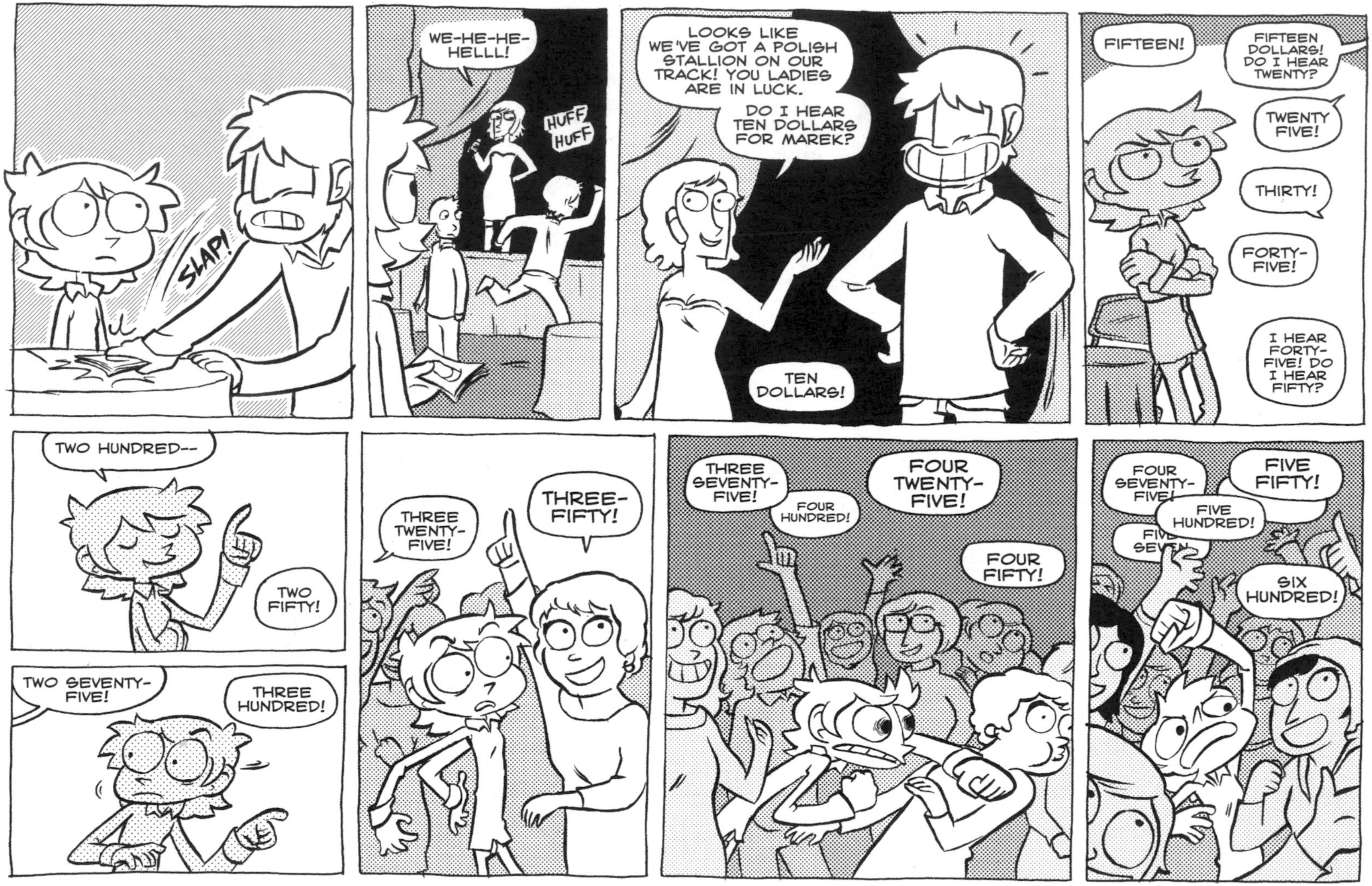
SLAP!
WE-HE-HE-HELLL!
HUFF HUFF
LOOKS LIKE WE'VE GOT A POLISH STALLION ON OUR TRACK! YOU LADIES ARE IN LUCK.
DO I HEAR TEN DOLLARS FOR MAREK?
TEN DOLLARS!
FIFTEEN!
FIFTEEN DOLLARS! DO I HEAR TWENTY?
TWENTY FIVE!
THIRTY!
FORTY-FIVE!
I HEAR FORTY-FIVE! DO I HEAR FIFTY?
TWO HUNDRED--
TWO FIFTY!
TWO SEVENTY-FIVE!
THREE HUNDRED!
THREE TWENTY-FIVE!
THREE-FIFTY!
THREE SEVENTY-FIVE!
FOUR HUNDRED!
FOUR TWENTY-FIVE!
FOUR FIFTY!
FOUR SEVENTY-FIVE!
FIVE HUNDRED!
FIVE FIFTY!
SIX HUNDRED!

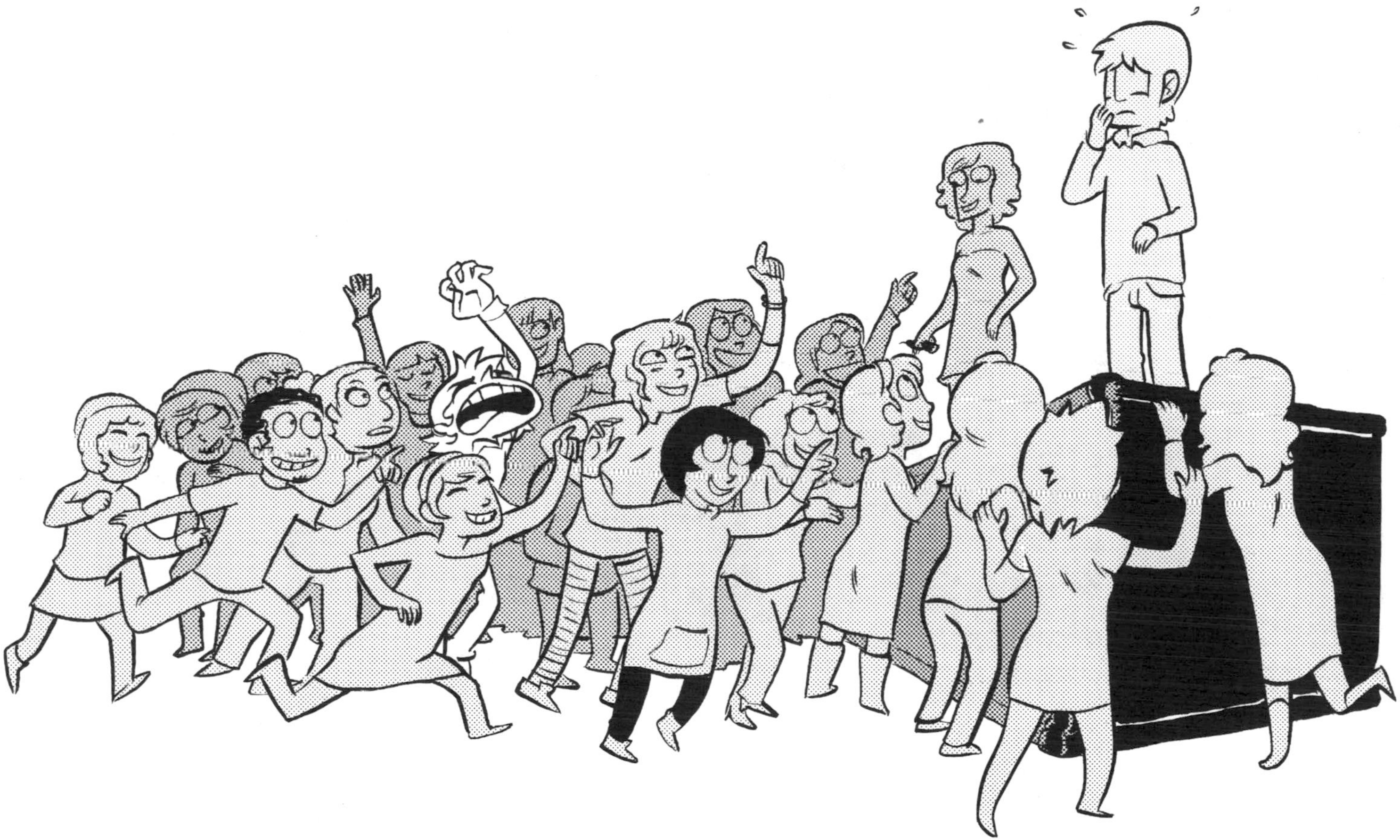

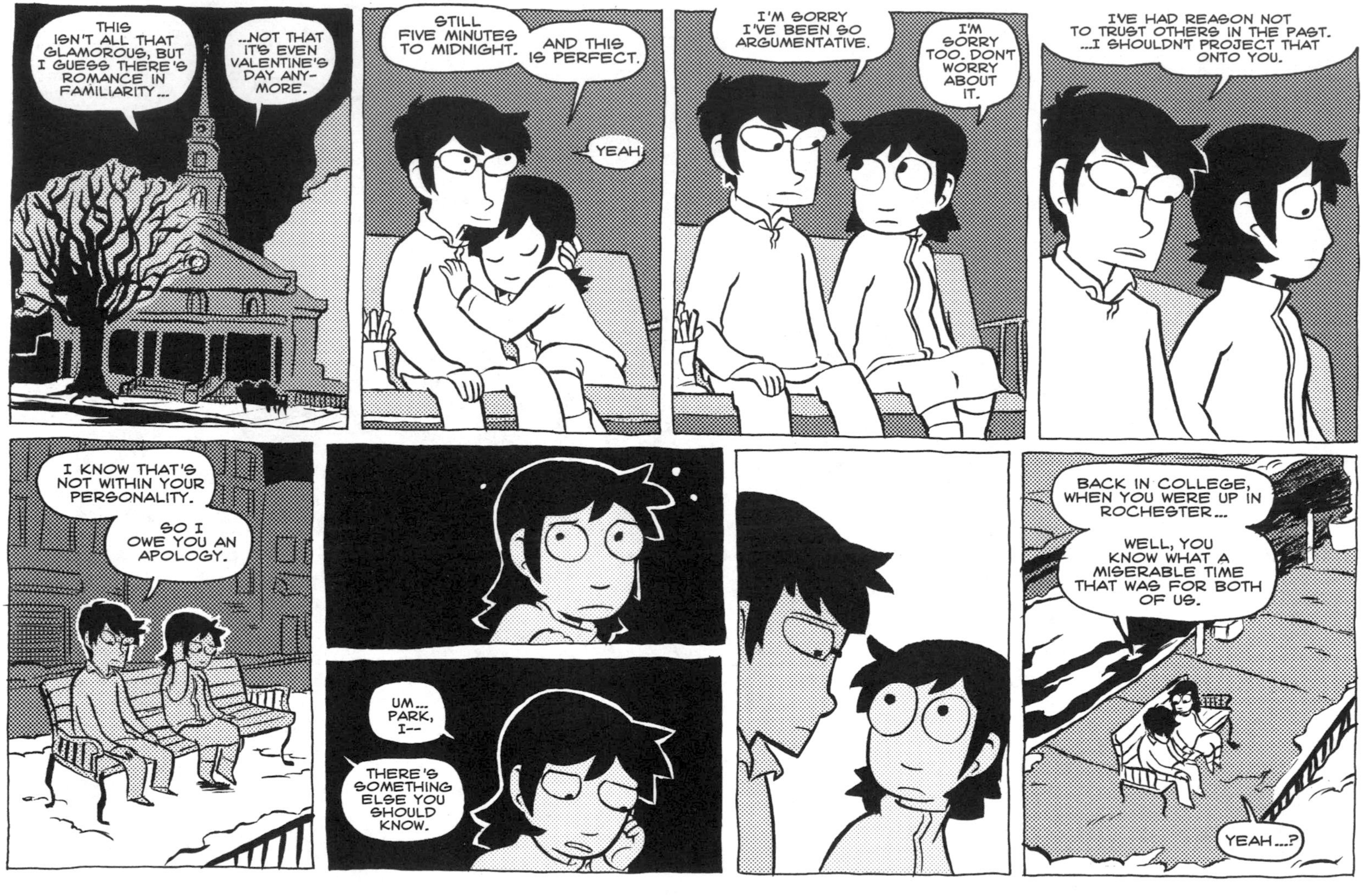
THIS ISN'T ALL THAT GLAMOROUS, BUT I GUESS THERE'S ROMANCE IN FAMILIARITY...
...NOT THAT IT'S EVEN VALENTINE'S DAY ANY-MORE.
STILL FIVE MINUTES TO MIDNIGHT.
AND THIS IS PERFECT.
YEAH.
I'M SORRY I'VE BEEN SO ARGUMENTATIVE.
I'M SORRY TOO. DON'T WORRY ABOUT IT.
I'VE HAD REASON NOT TO TRUST OTHERS IN THE PAST. ...I SHOULDN'T PROJECT THAT ONTO YOU.
I KNOW THAT'S NOT WITHIN YOUR PERSONALITY.
SO I OWE YOU AN APOLOGY.
UM... PARK, I--
THERE'S SOMETHING ELSE YOU SHOULD KNOW.
BACK IN COLLEGE, WHEN YOU WERE UP IN ROCHESTER...
WELL, YOU KNOW WHAT A MISERABLE TIME THAT WAS FOR BOTH OF US.
YEAH...?

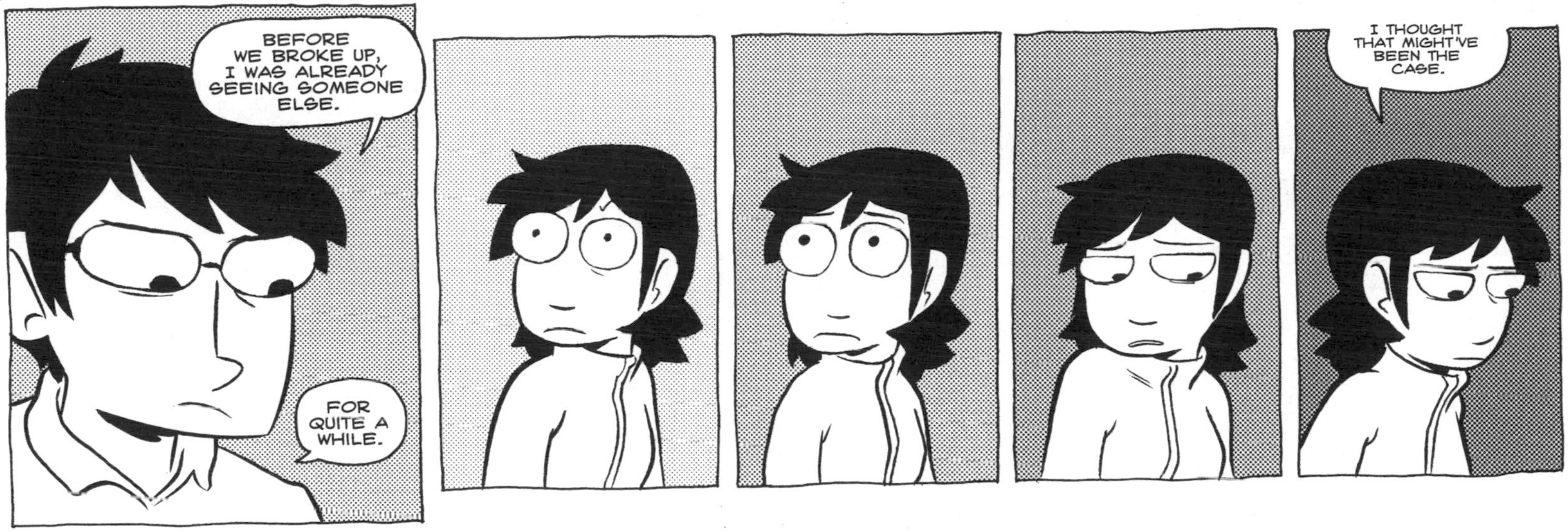
BEFORE WE BROKE UP, I WAS ALREADY SEEING SOMEONE ELSE.
FOR QUITE A WHILE.
I THOUGHT THAT MIGHT'VE BEEN THE CASE.

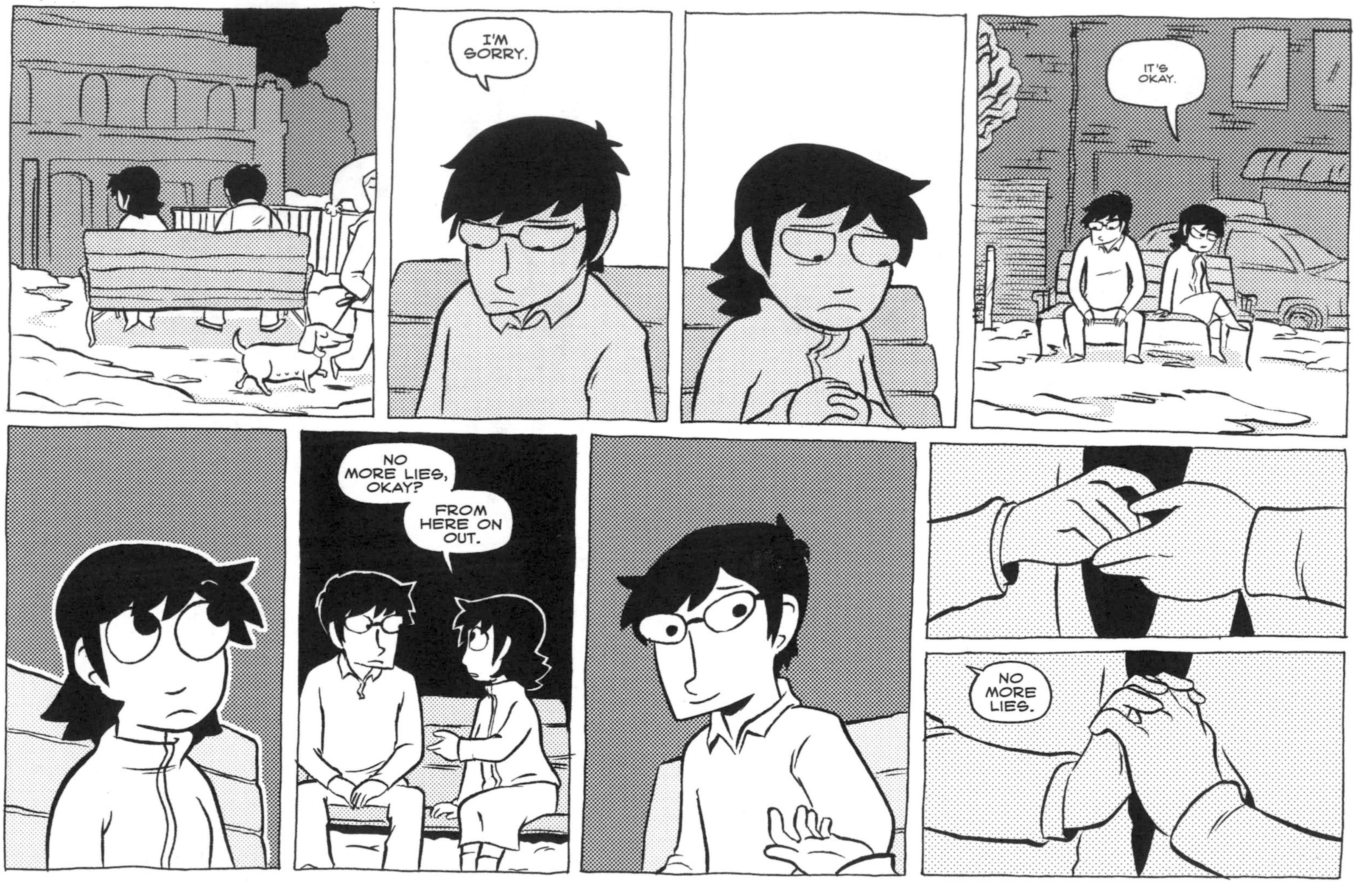
I'M SORRY.
IT'S OKAY.
NO MORE LIES, OKAY?
FROM HERE ON OUT.
NO MORE LIES.

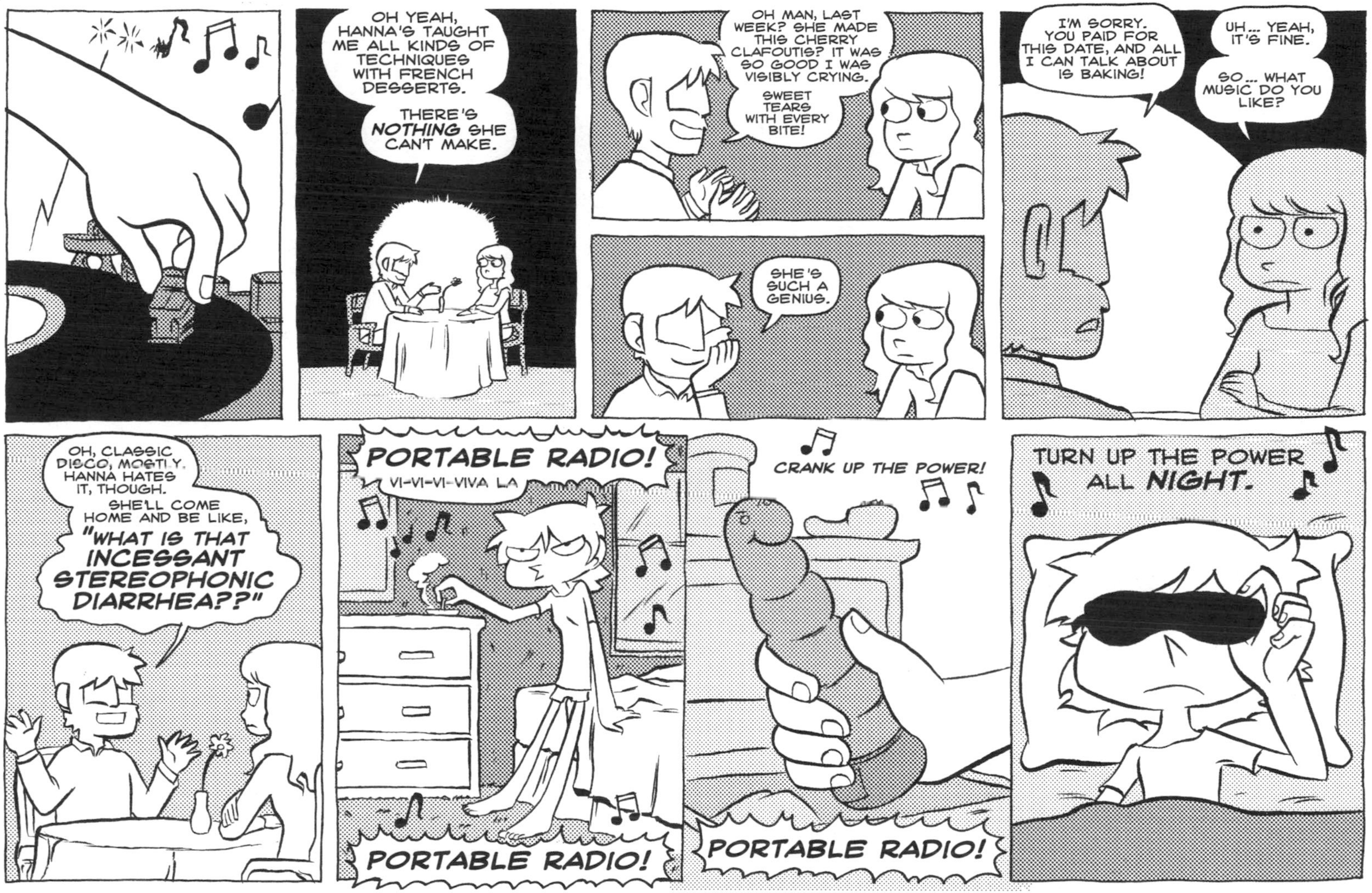
OH YEAH, HANNA'S TAUGHT ME ALL KINDS OF TECHNIQUES WITH FRENCH DESSERTS.
THERE'S NOTHING SHE CAN'T MAKE.
OH MAN, LAST WEEK? SHE MADE THIS CHERRY CLAFOUTIS? IT WAS SO GOOD I WAS VISIBLY CRYING.
SWEET TEARS WITH EVERY BITE!
SHE'S SUCH A GENIUS.
I'M SORRY. YOU PAID FOR THIS DATE, AND ALL I CAN TALK ABOUT IS BAKING!
UH... YEAH, IT'S FINE.
SO... WHAT MUSIC DO YOU LIKE?
OH, CLASSIC DISCO, MOSTLY. HANNA HATES IT, THOUGH.
SHE'LL COME HOME AND BE LIKE, "WHAT IS THAT INCESSANT STEREOPHONIC DIARRHEA??"
PORTABLE RADIO!
VI-VI-VI-VIVA LA
PORTABLE RADIO!
CRANK UP THE POWER!
PORTABLE RADIO!
TURN UP THE POWER ALL NIGHT.

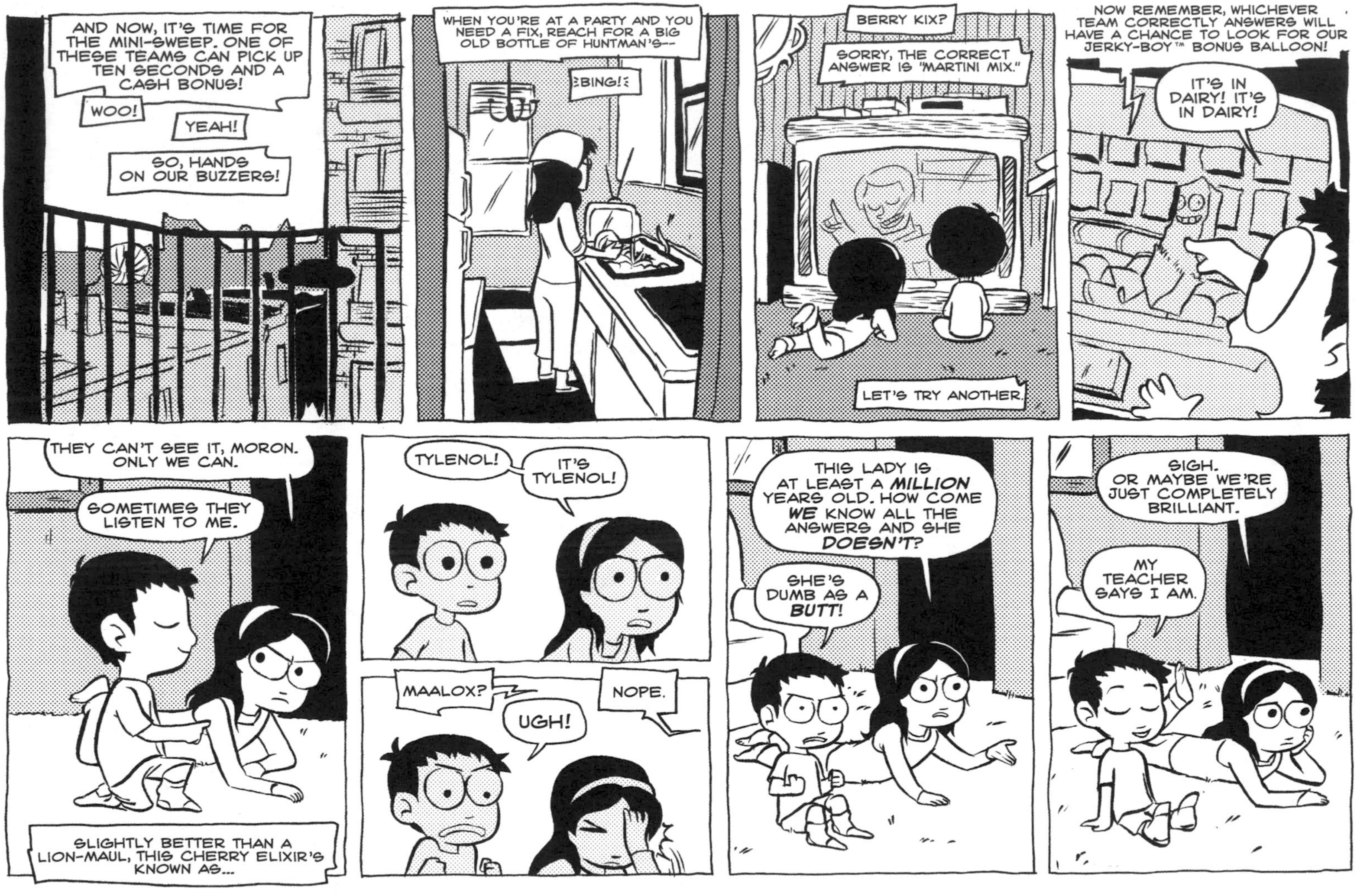
AND NOW, IT'S TIME FOR THE MINI-SWEEP. ONE OF THESE TEAMS CAN PICK UP TEN SECONDS AND A CASH BONUS!
WOO!
YEAH!
SO, HANDS ON OUR BUZZERS!
WHEN YOU'RE AT A PARTY AND YOU NEED A FIX, REACH FOR A BIG OLD BOTTLE OF HUNTMAN'S--
BING!
BERRY KIX?
SORRY, THE CORRECT ANSWER IS "MARTINI MIX."
LET'S TRY ANOTHER.
NOW REMEMBER, WHICHEVER TEAM CORRECTLY ANSWERS WILL HAVE A CHANCE TO LOOK FOR OUR JERKY-BOY™ BONUS BALLOON!
IT'S IN DAIRY! IT'S IN DAIRY!
THEY CAN'T SEE IT, MORON. ONLY WE CAN.
SOMETIMES THEY LISTEN TO ME.
SLIGHTLY BETTER THAN A LION-MAUL, THIS CHERRY ELIXIR'S KNOWN AS...
TYLENOL!
IT'S TYLENOL!
MAALOX?
NOPE.
UGH!
THIS LADY IS AT LEAST A MILLION YEARS OLD. HOW COME WE KNOW ALL THE ANSWERS AND SHE DOESN'T?
SHE'S DUMB AS A BUTT!
SIGH. OR MAYBE WE'RE JUST COMPLETELY BRILLIANT.
MY TEACHER SAYS I AM.

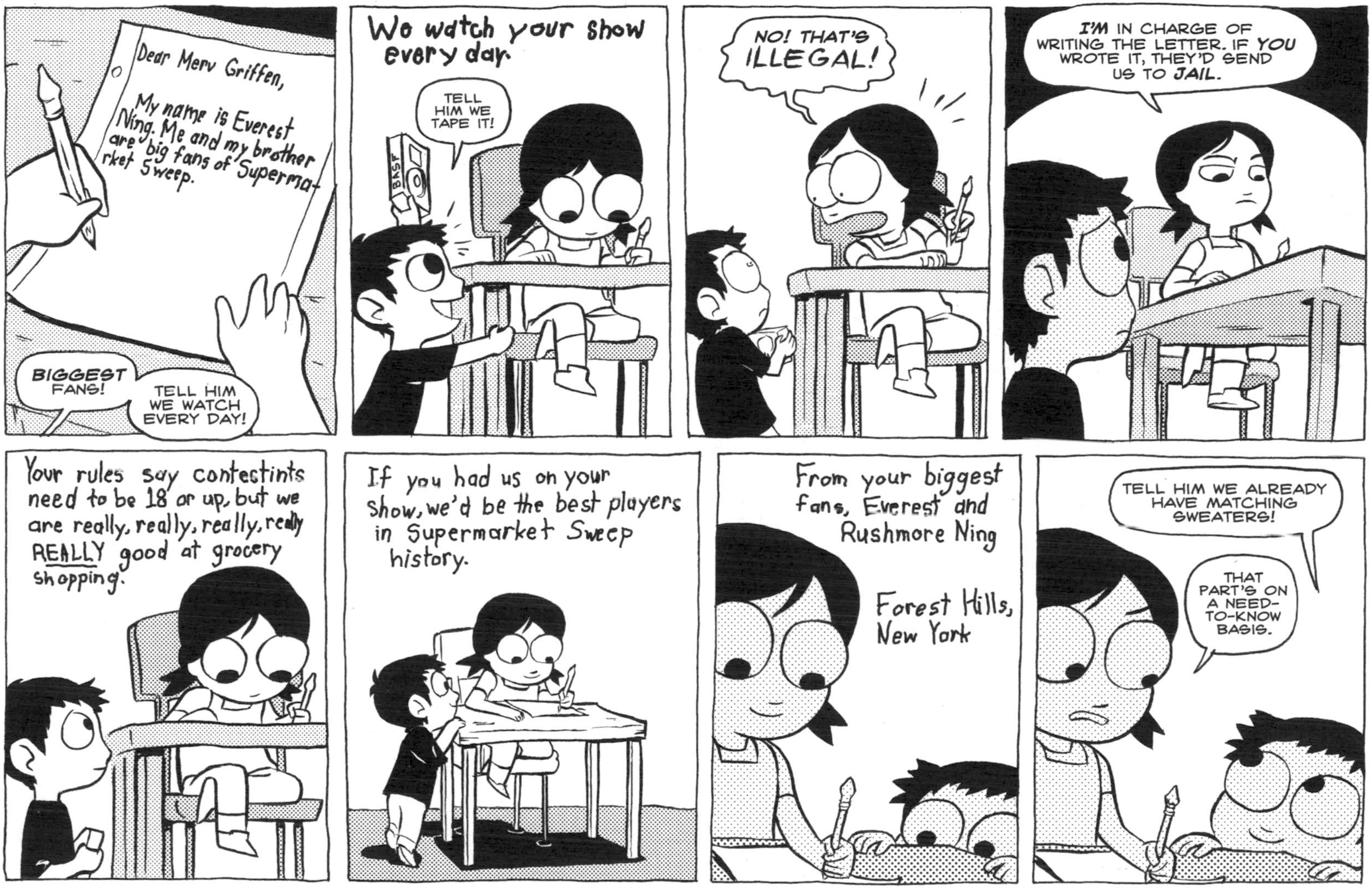
Dear Merv Griffen,
My name is Everest Ning. Me and my brother are big fans of Supermarket Sweep.
BIGGEST FANS!
TELL HIM WE WATCH EVERY DAY!
We watch your show every day.
TELL HIM WE TAPE IT!
BASF
NO! THAT'S ILLEGAL!
I'M IN CHARGE OF WRITING THE LETTER. IF YOU WROTE IT, THEY'D SEND US TO JAIL.
Your rules say contestints need to be 18 or up, but we are really, really, really, really REALLY good at grocery shopping.
If you had us on your show, we'd be the best players in Supermarket Sweep history.
From your biggest fans, Everest and Rushmore Ning
Forest Hills, New York
TELL HIM WE ALREADY HAVE MATCHING SWEATERS!
THAT PART'S ON A NEED-TO-KNOW BASIS.

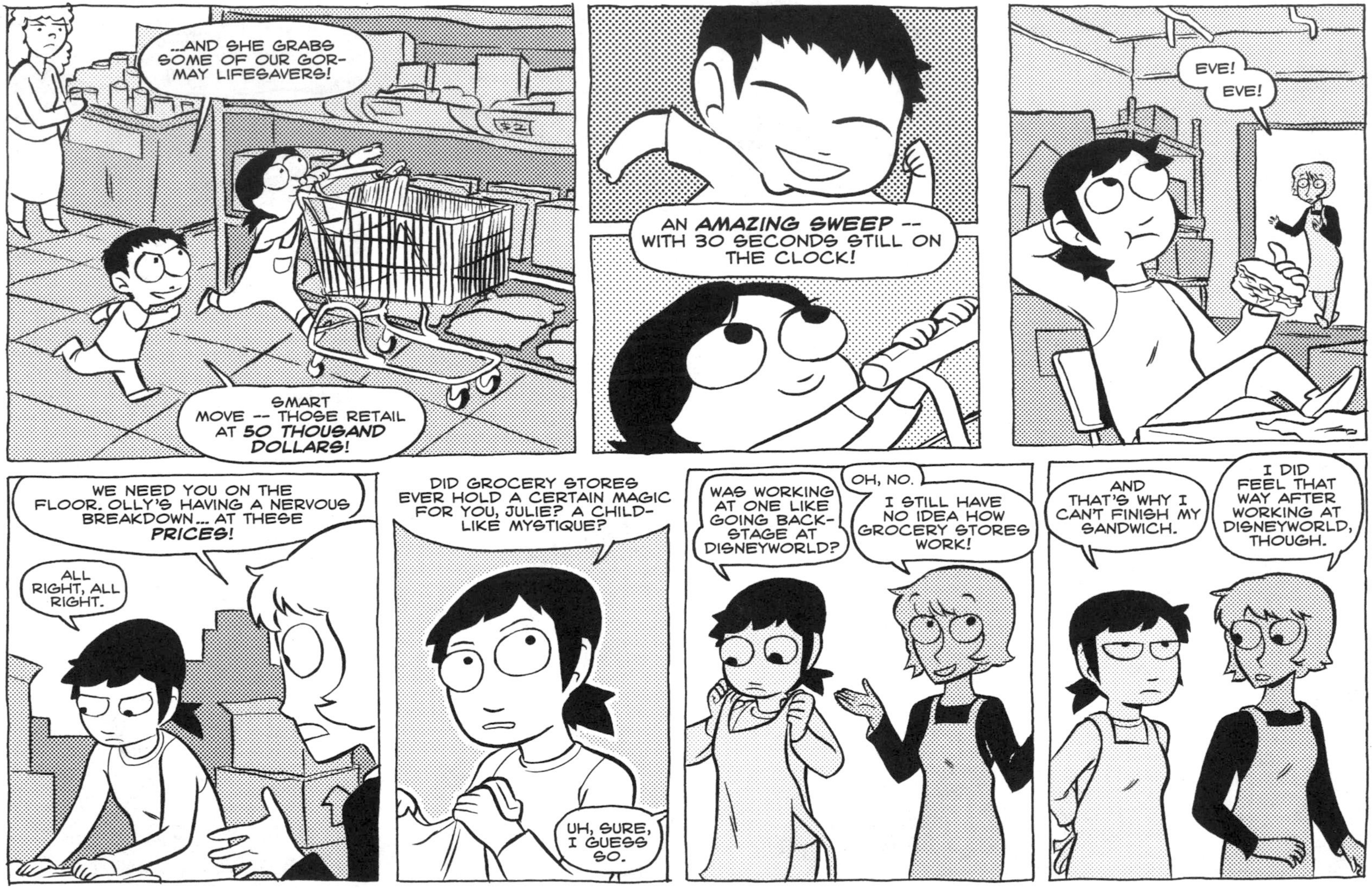

...AND SHE GRABS SOME OF OUR GOR-MAY LIFESAVERS!
$2
SMART MOVE -- THOSE RETAIL AT **50 THOUSAND DOLLARS!**
AN ***AMAZING SWEEP*** -- WITH 30 SECONDS STILL ON THE CLOCK!
EVE!
EVE!
WE NEED YOU ON THE FLOOR. OLLY'S HAVING A NERVOUS BREAKDOWN... AT THESE ***PRICES!***
ALL RIGHT, ALL RIGHT.
DID GROCERY STORES EVER HOLD A CERTAIN MAGIC FOR YOU, JULIE? A CHILD-LIKE MYSTIQUE?
UH, SURE, I GUESS SO.
WAS WORKING AT ONE LIKE GOING BACK-STAGE AT DISNEYWORLD?
OH, NO.
I STILL HAVE NO IDEA HOW GROCERY STORES WORK!
AND THAT'S WHY I CAN'T FINISH MY SANDWICH.
I DID FEEL THAT WAY AFTER WORKING AT DISNEYWORLD, THOUGH.

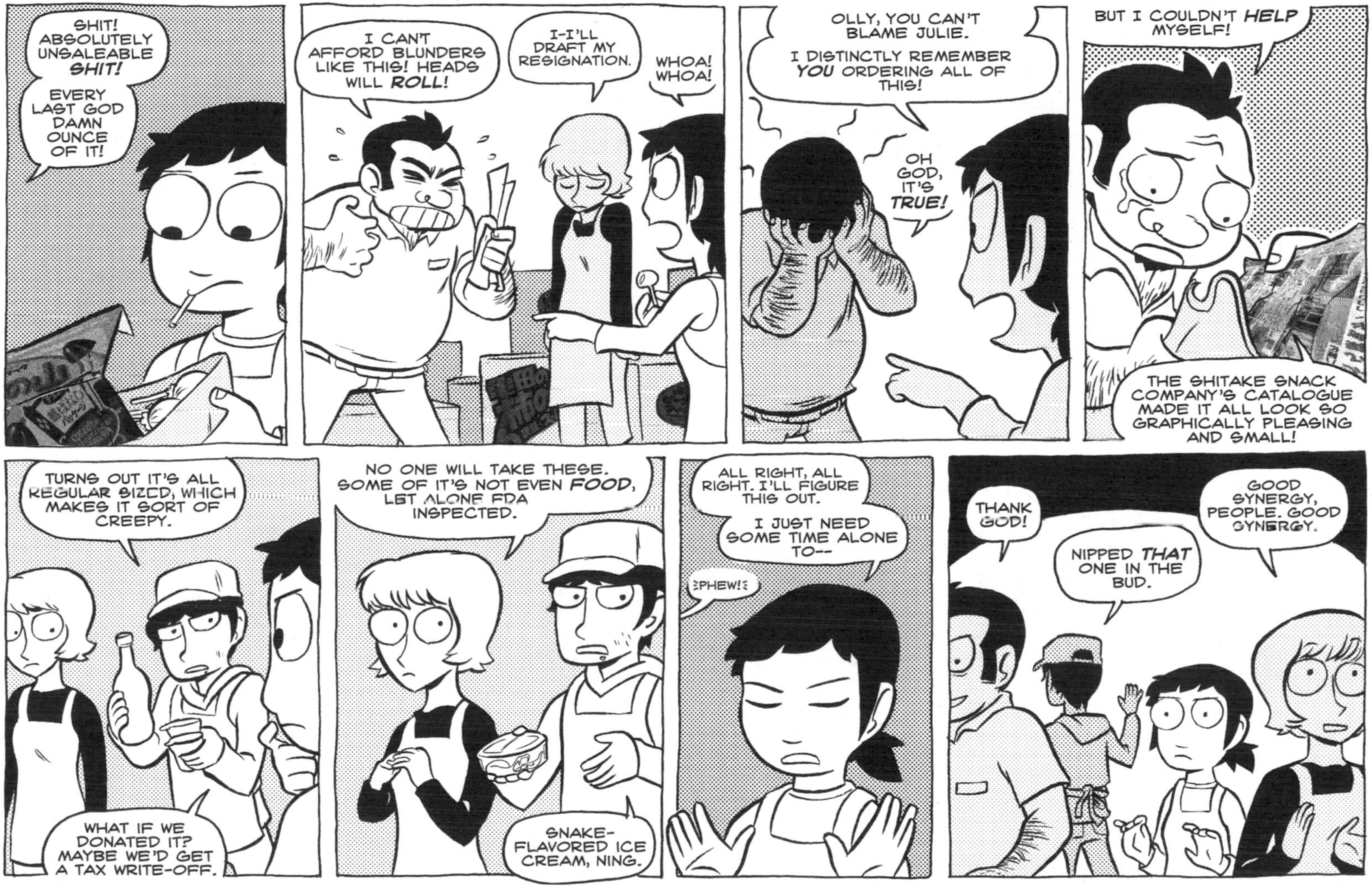
SHIT! ABSOLUTELY UNSALEABLE SHIT!
EVERY LAST GOD DAMN OUNCE OF IT!
I CAN'T AFFORD BLUNDERS LIKE THIS! HEADS WILL ROLL!
I-I'LL DRAFT MY RESIGNATION.
WHOA! WHOA!
OLLY, YOU CAN'T BLAME JULIE.
I DISTINCTLY REMEMBER YOU ORDERING ALL OF THIS!
OH GOD, IT'S TRUE!
BUT I COULDN'T HELP MYSELF!
THE SHITAKE SNACK COMPANY'S CATALOGUE MADE IT ALL LOOK SO GRAPHICALLY PLEASING AND SMALL!
TURNS OUT IT'S ALL REGULAR SIZED, WHICH MAKES IT SORT OF CREEPY.
WHAT IF WE DONATED IT? MAYBE WE'D GET A TAX WRITE-OFF.
NO ONE WILL TAKE THESE. SOME OF IT'S NOT EVEN FOOD, LET ALONE FDA INSPECTED.
SNAKE-FLAVORED ICE CREAM, NING.
ALL RIGHT, ALL RIGHT. I'LL FIGURE THIS OUT.
I JUST NEED SOME TIME ALONE TO--
PHEW!
THANK GOD!
NIPPED THAT ONE IN THE BUD.
GOOD SYNERGY, PEOPLE. GOOD SYNERGY.

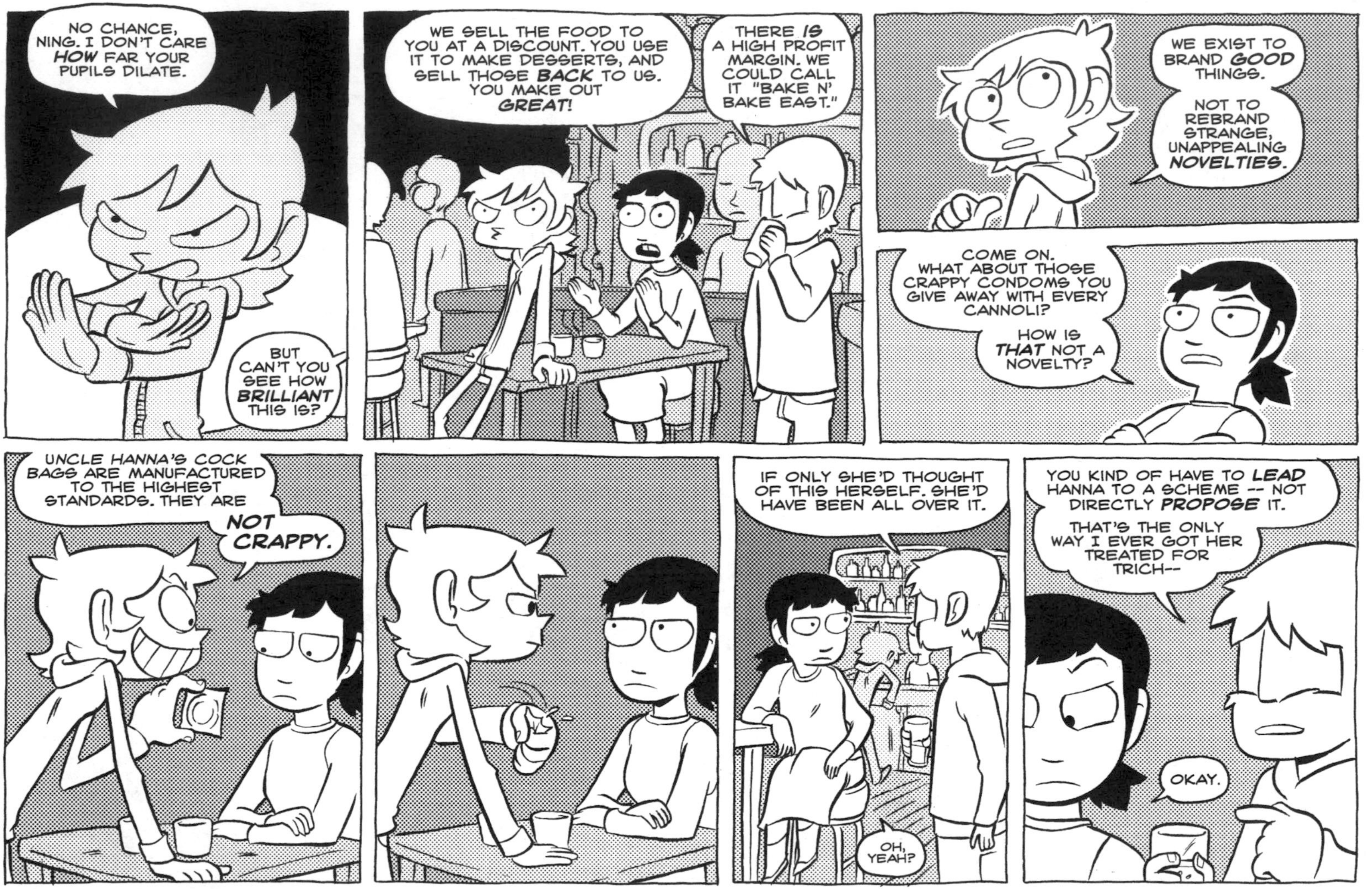
NO CHANCE, NING. I DON'T CARE HOW FAR YOUR PUPILS DILATE.
BUT CAN'T YOU SEE HOW BRILLIANT THIS IS?
WE SELL THE FOOD TO YOU AT A DISCOUNT. YOU USE IT TO MAKE DESSERTS, AND SELL THOSE BACK TO US. YOU MAKE OUT GREAT!
THERE IS A HIGH PROFIT MARGIN. WE COULD CALL IT "BAKE N' BAKE EAST."
WE EXIST TO BRAND GOOD THINGS.
NOT TO REBRAND STRANGE, UNAPPEALING NOVELTIES.
COME ON. WHAT ABOUT THOSE CRAPPY CONDOMS YOU GIVE AWAY WITH EVERY CANNOLI?
HOW IS THAT NOT A NOVELTY?
UNCLE HANNA'S COCK BAGS ARE MANUFACTURED TO THE HIGHEST STANDARDS. THEY ARE
NOT CRAPPY.
IF ONLY SHE'D THOUGHT OF THIS HERSELF. SHE'D HAVE BEEN ALL OVER IT.
OH, YEAH?
YOU KIND OF HAVE TO LEAD HANNA TO A SCHEME -- NOT DIRECTLY PROPOSE IT.
THAT'S THE ONLY WAY I EVER GOT HER TREATED FOR TRICH--
OKAY.

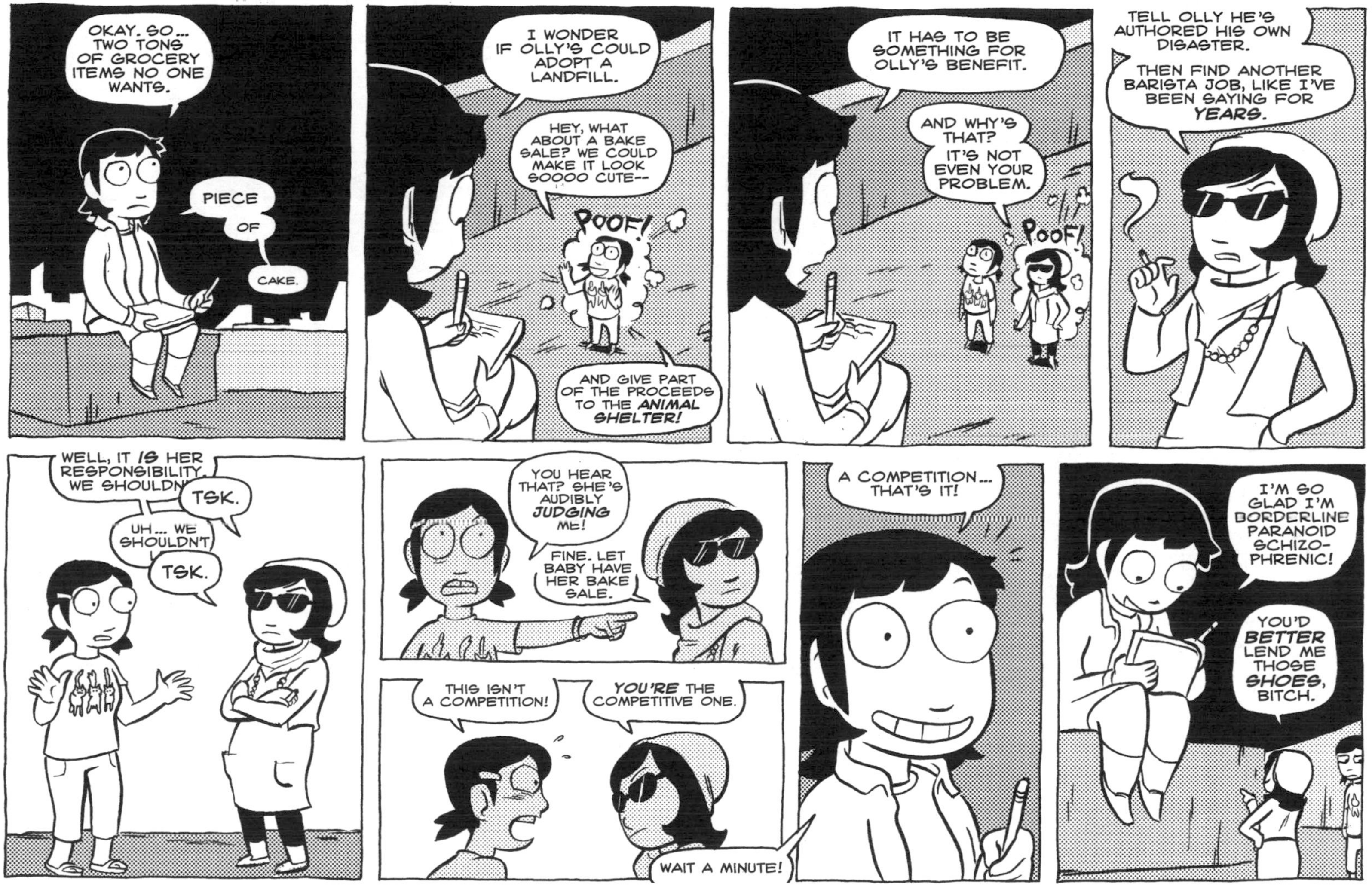
OKAY. SO... TWO TONS OF GROCERY ITEMS NO ONE WANTS.
PIECE
OF
CAKE.
I WONDER IF OLLY'S COULD ADOPT A LANDFILL.
HEY, WHAT ABOUT A BAKE SALE? WE COULD MAKE IT LOOK SOOOO CUTE--
POOF!
AND GIVE PART OF THE PROCEEDS TO THE ANIMAL SHELTER!
IT HAS TO BE SOMETHING FOR OLLY'S BENEFIT.
AND WHY'S THAT?
IT'S NOT EVEN YOUR PROBLEM.
POOF!
TELL OLLY HE'S AUTHORED HIS OWN DISASTER.
THEN FIND ANOTHER BARISTA JOB, LIKE I'VE BEEN SAYING FOR YEARS.
WELL, IT IS HER RESPONSIBILITY. WE SHOULDN'T
TSK.
UH... WE SHOULDN'T
TSK.
YOU HEAR THAT? SHE'S AUDIBLY JUDGING ME!
FINE. LET BABY HAVE HER BAKE SALE.
THIS ISN'T A COMPETITION!
YOU'RE THE COMPETITIVE ONE.
WAIT A MINUTE!
A COMPETITION... THAT'S IT!
I'M SO GLAD I'M BORDERLINE PARANOID SCHIZO-PHRENIC!
YOU'D BETTER LEND ME THOSE SHOES, BITCH.

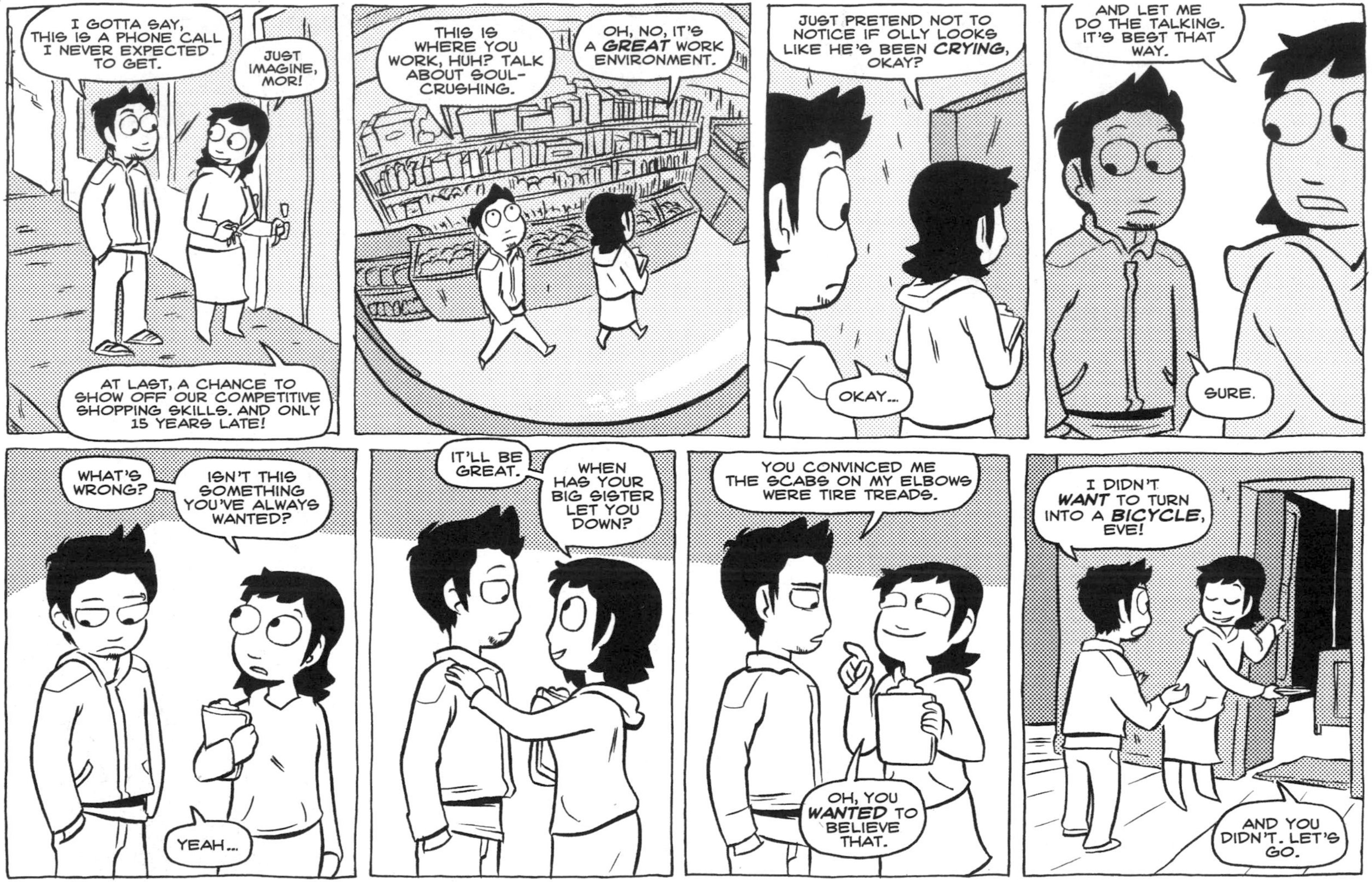
I GOTTA SAY, THIS IS A PHONE CALL I NEVER EXPECTED TO GET.
JUST IMAGINE, MOR!
AT LAST, A CHANCE TO SHOW OFF OUR COMPETITIVE SHOPPING SKILLS. AND ONLY 15 YEARS LATE!
THIS IS WHERE YOU WORK, HUH? TALK ABOUT SOUL-CRUSHING.
OH, NO, IT'S A GREAT WORK ENVIRONMENT.
JUST PRETEND NOT TO NOTICE IF OLLY LOOKS LIKE HE'S BEEN CRYING, OKAY?
OKAY...
AND LET ME DO THE TALKING. IT'S BEST THAT WAY.
SURE.
WHAT'S WRONG?
ISN'T THIS SOMETHING YOU'VE ALWAYS WANTED?
YEAH...
IT'LL BE GREAT.
WHEN HAS YOUR BIG SISTER LET YOU DOWN?
YOU CONVINCED ME THE SCABS ON MY ELBOWS WERE TIRE TREADS.
OH, YOU WANTED TO BELIEVE THAT.
I DIDN'T WANT TO TURN INTO A BICYCLE, EVE!
AND YOU DIDN'T. LET'S GO.

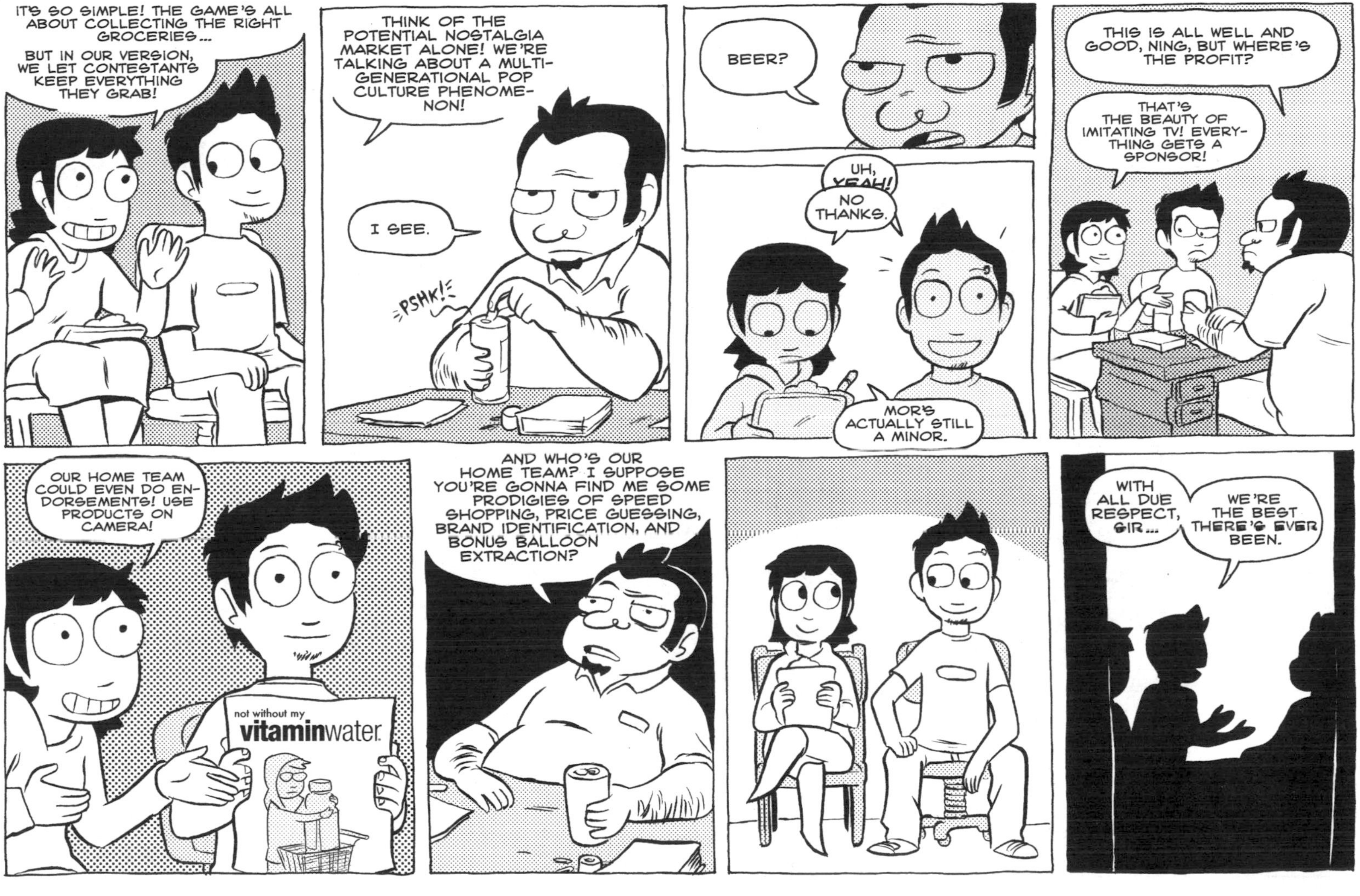
IT'S SO SIMPLE! THE GAME'S ALL ABOUT COLLECTING THE RIGHT GROCERIES...
BUT IN OUR VERSION, WE LET CONTESTANTS KEEP EVERYTHING THEY GRAB!
THINK OF THE POTENTIAL NOSTALGIA MARKET ALONE! WE'RE TALKING ABOUT A MULTI-GENERATIONAL POP CULTURE PHENOMENON!
I SEE.
PSHK!
BEER?
UH, YEAH!
NO THANKS.
MOR'S ACTUALLY STILL A MINOR.
THIS IS ALL WELL AND GOOD, NING, BUT WHERE'S THE PROFIT?
THAT'S THE BEAUTY OF IMITATING TV! EVERYTHING GETS A SPONSOR!
OUR HOME TEAM COULD EVEN DO ENDORSEMENTS! USE PRODUCTS ON CAMERA!
not without my vitaminwater.
AND WHO'S OUR HOME TEAM? I SUPPOSE YOU'RE GONNA FIND ME SOME PRODIGIES OF SPEED SHOPPING, PRICE GUESSING, BRAND IDENTIFICATION, AND BONUS BALLOON EXTRACTION?
WITH ALL DUE RESPECT, SIR...
WE'RE THE BEST THERE'S EVER BEEN.

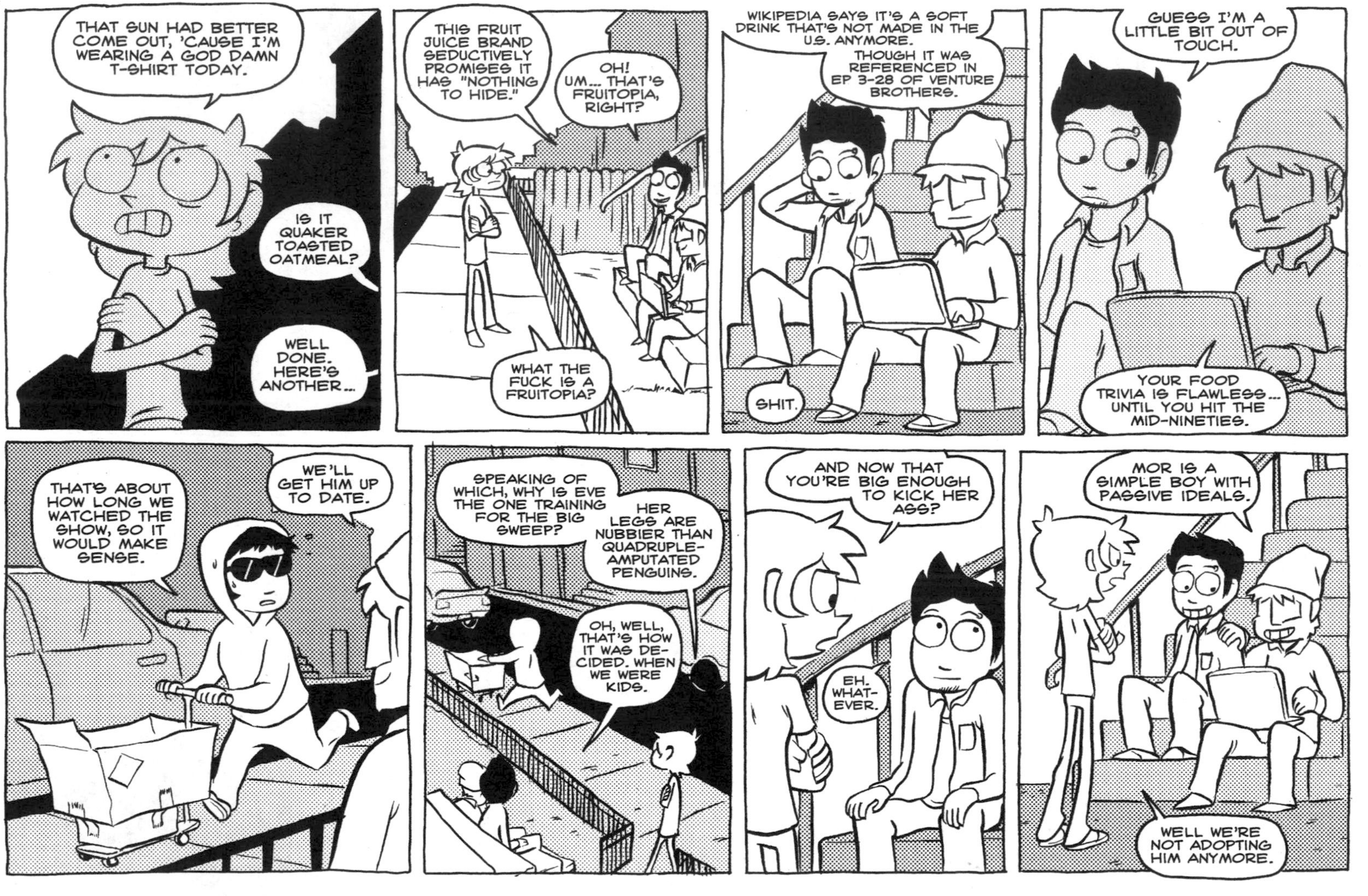

THAT SUN HAD BETTER COME OUT, 'CAUSE I'M WEARING A GOD DAMN T-SHIRT TODAY.
IS IT QUAKER TOASTED OATMEAL?
WELL DONE. HERE'S ANOTHER...
THIS FRUIT JUICE BRAND SEDUCTIVELY PROMISES IT HAS "NOTHING TO HIDE."
OH! UM... THAT'S FRUITOPIA, RIGHT?
WHAT THE FUCK IS A FRUITOPIA?
WIKIPEDIA SAYS IT'S A SOFT DRINK THAT'S NOT MADE IN THE U.S. ANYMORE.
THOUGH IT WAS REFERENCED IN EP 3-28 OF VENTURE BROTHERS.
SHIT.
GUESS I'M A LITTLE BIT OUT OF TOUCH.
YOUR FOOD TRIVIA IS FLAWLESS... UNTIL YOU HIT THE MID-NINETIES.
THAT'S ABOUT HOW LONG WE WATCHED THE SHOW, SO IT WOULD MAKE SENSE.
WE'LL GET HIM UP TO DATE.
SPEAKING OF WHICH, WHY IS EVE THE ONE TRAINING FOR THE BIG SWEEP?
HER LEGS ARE NUBBIER THAN QUADRUPLE-AMPUTATED PENGUINS.
OH, WELL, THAT'S HOW IT WAS DE-CIDED. WHEN WE WERE KIDS.
AND NOW THAT YOU'RE BIG ENOUGH TO KICK HER ASS?
EH. WHAT-EVER.
MOR IS A SIMPLE BOY WITH PASSIVE IDEALS.
WELL WE'RE NOT ADOPTING HIM ANYMORE.

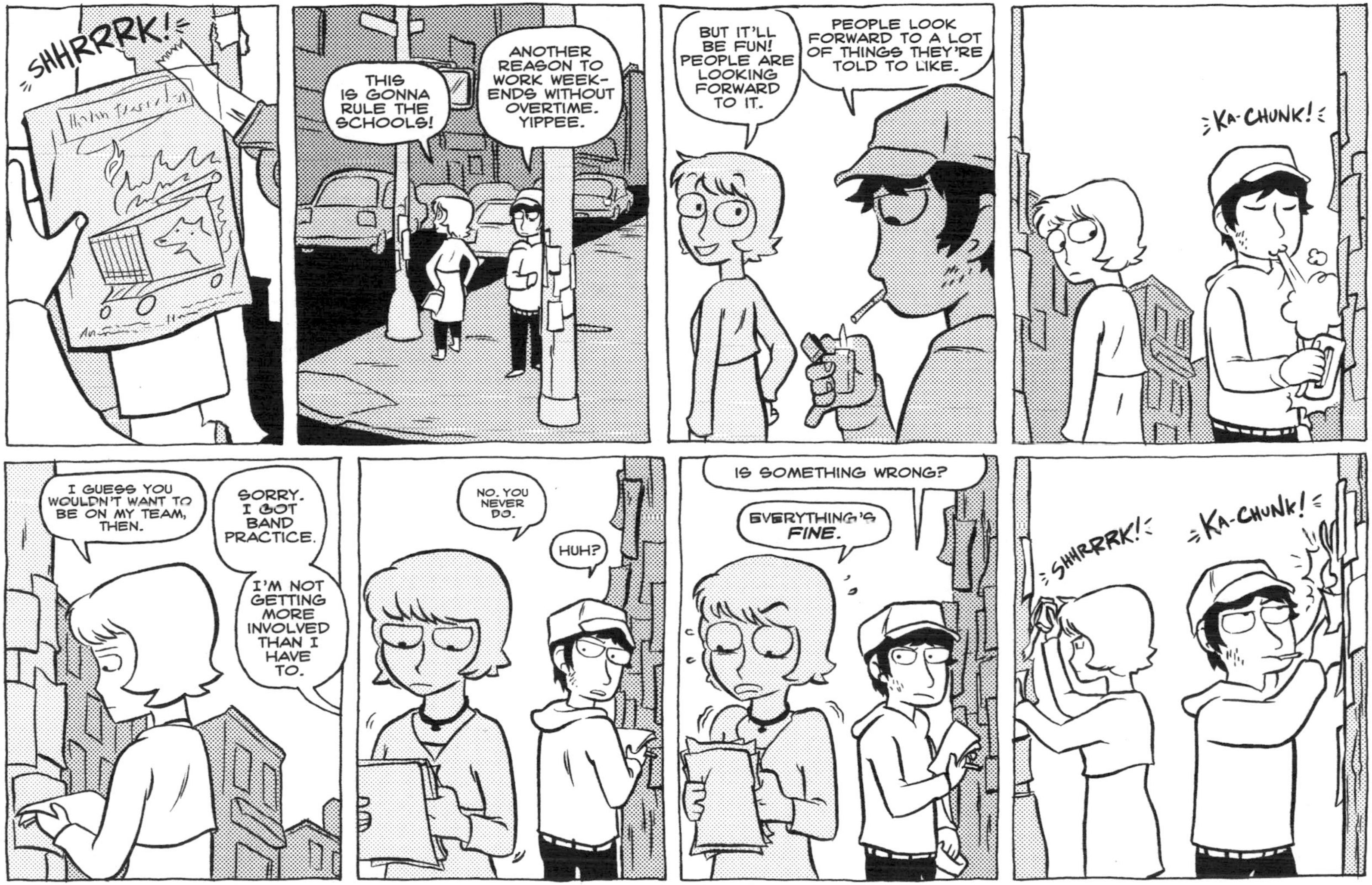
SHHRRRK!
THIS IS GONNA RULE THE SCHOOLS!
ANOTHER REASON TO WORK WEEK-ENDS WITHOUT OVERTIME. YIPPEE.
BUT IT'LL BE FUN! PEOPLE ARE LOOKING FORWARD TO IT.
PEOPLE LOOK FORWARD TO A LOT OF THINGS THEY'RE TOLD TO LIKE.
KA-CHUNK!
I GUESS YOU WOULDN'T WANT TO BE ON MY TEAM, THEN.
SORRY. I GOT BAND PRACTICE.
I'M NOT GETTING MORE INVOLVED THAN I HAVE TO.
NO. YOU NEVER DO.
HUH?
IS SOMETHING WRONG?
EVERYTHING'S FINE.
SHHRRRK!
KA-CHUNK!

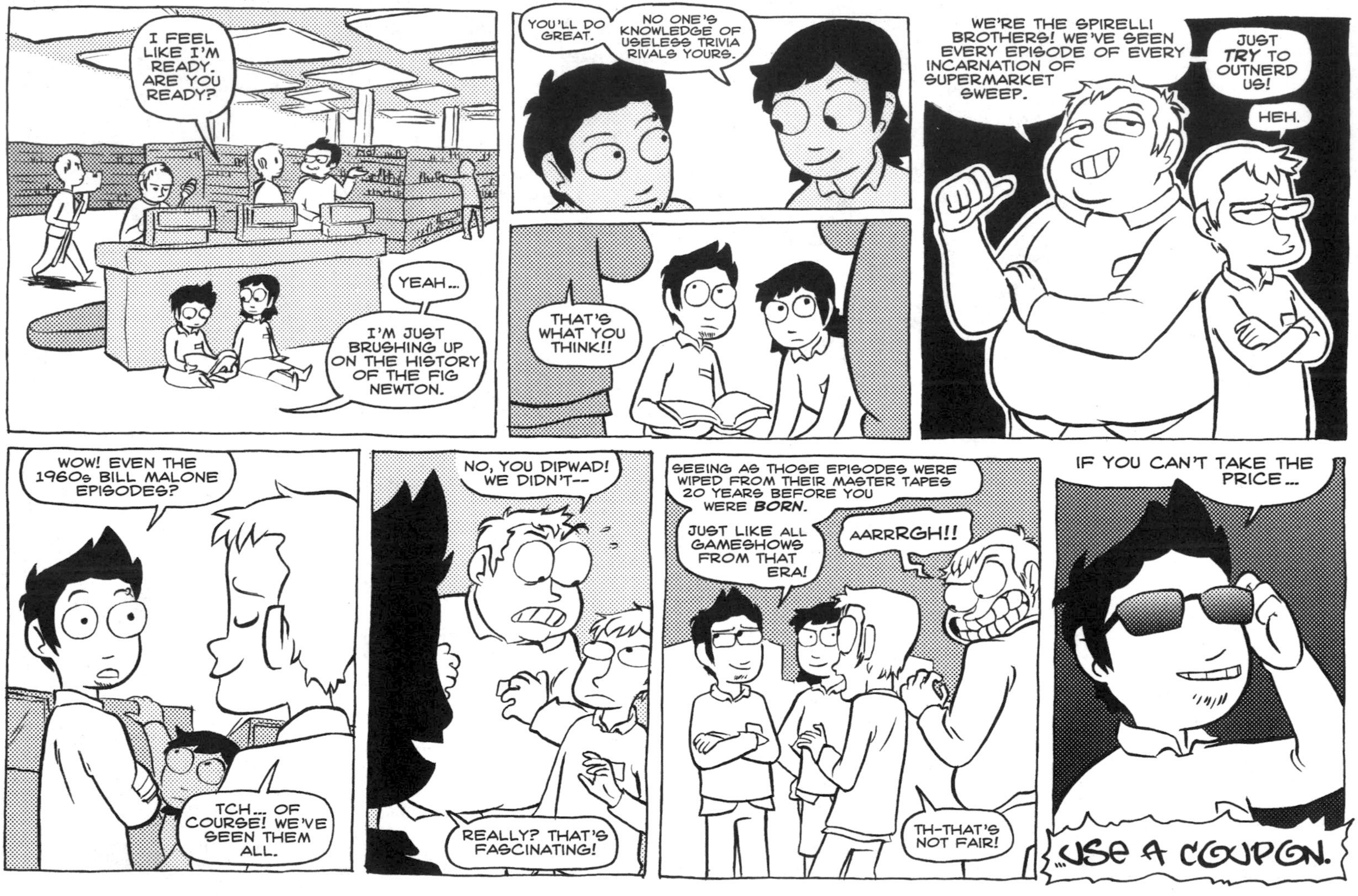

I FEEL LIKE I'M READY. ARE YOU READY?
YEAH...
I'M JUST BRUSHING UP ON THE HISTORY OF THE FIG NEWTON.
YOU'LL DO GREAT.
NO ONE'S KNOWLEDGE OF USELESS TRIVIA RIVALS YOURS.
THAT'S WHAT YOU THINK!!
WE'RE THE SPIRELLI BROTHERS! WE'VE SEEN EVERY EPISODE OF EVERY INCARNATION OF SUPERMARKET SWEEP.
JUST *TRY* TO OUTNERD US!
HEH.
WOW! EVEN THE 1960s BILL MALONE EPISODES?
TCH... OF COURSE! WE'VE SEEN THEM ALL.
NO, YOU DIPWAD! WE DIDN'T--
REALLY? THAT'S FASCINATING!
SEEING AS THOSE EPISODES WERE WIPED FROM THEIR MASTER TAPES 20 YEARS BEFORE YOU WERE **BORN**.
JUST LIKE ALL GAMESHOWS FROM THAT ERA!
AARRRGH!!
TH-THAT'S NOT FAIR!
IF YOU CAN'T TAKE THE PRICE...
...USE A COUPON.

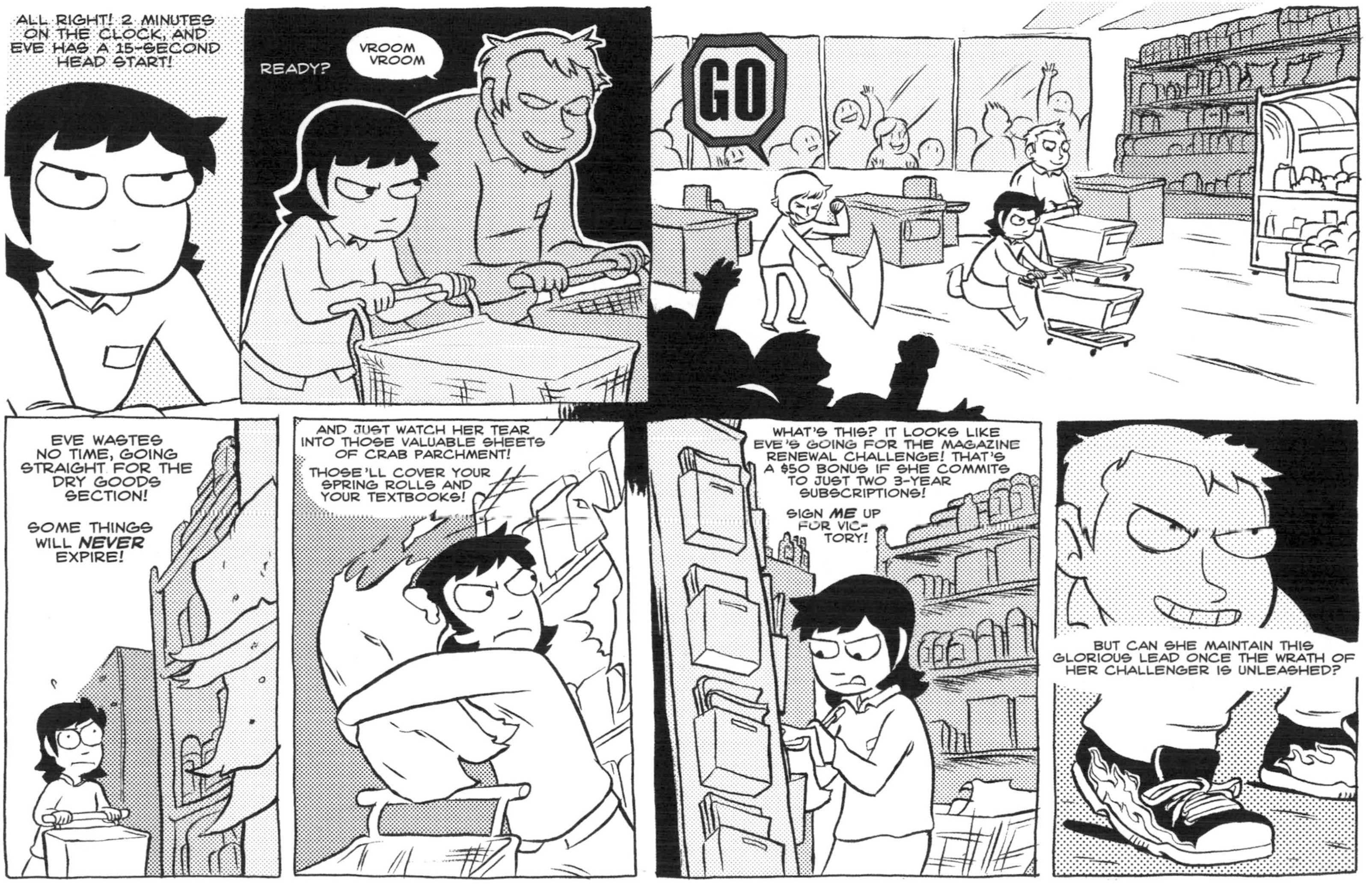
ALL RIGHT! 2 MINUTES ON THE CLOCK, AND EVE HAS A 15-SECOND HEAD START!
READY?
VROOM VROOM
GO
EVE WASTES NO TIME, GOING STRAIGHT FOR THE DRY GOODS SECTION!
SOME THINGS WILL NEVER EXPIRE!
AND JUST WATCH HER TEAR INTO THOSE VALUABLE SHEETS OF CRAB PARCHMENT!
THOSE'LL COVER YOUR SPRING ROLLS AND YOUR TEXTBOOKS!
WHAT'S THIS? IT LOOKS LIKE EVE'S GOING FOR THE MAGAZINE RENEWAL CHALLENGE! THAT'S A $50 BONUS IF SHE COMMITS TO JUST TWO 3-YEAR SUBSCRIPTIONS!
SIGN ME UP FOR VIC-TORY!
BUT CAN SHE MAINTAIN THIS GLORIOUS LEAD ONCE THE WRATH OF HER CHALLENGER IS UNLEASHED?

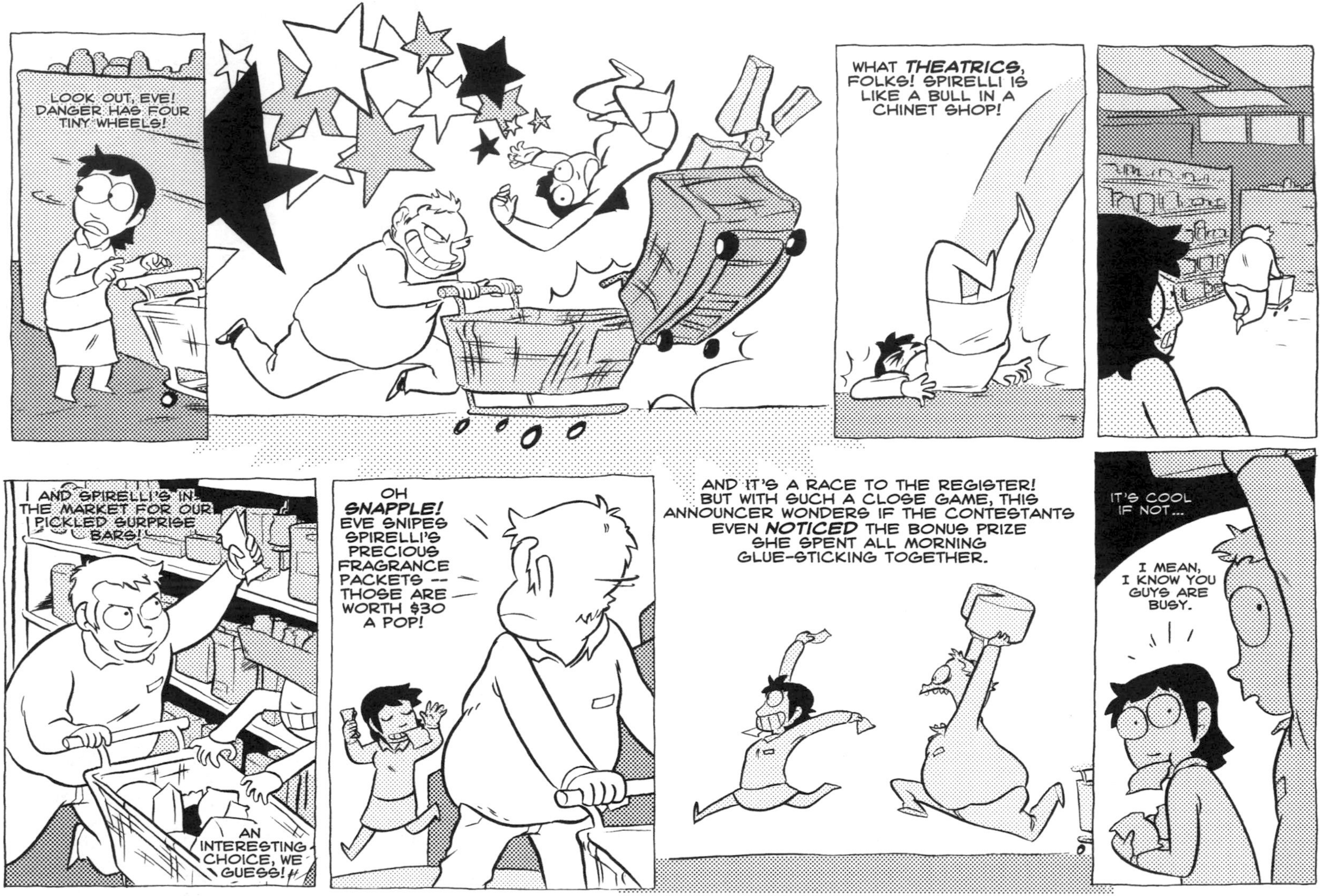
LOOK OUT, EVE! DANGER HAS FOUR TINY WHEELS!
WHAT *THEATRICS*, FOLKS! SPIRELLI IS LIKE A BULL IN A CHINET SHOP!
AND SPIRELLI'S IN THE MARKET FOR OUR PICKLED SURPRISE BARS!
AN INTERESTING CHOICE, WE GUESS!
OH *SNAPPLE!* EVE SNIPES SPIRELLI'S PRECIOUS FRAGRANCE PACKETS -- THOSE ARE WORTH $30 A POP!
AND IT'S A RACE TO THE REGISTER! BUT WITH SUCH A CLOSE GAME, THIS ANNOUNCER WONDERS IF THE CONTESTANTS EVEN *NOTICED* THE BONUS PRIZE SHE SPENT ALL MORNING GLUE-STICKING TOGETHER.
IT'S COOL IF NOT...
I MEAN, I KNOW YOU GUYS ARE BUSY.

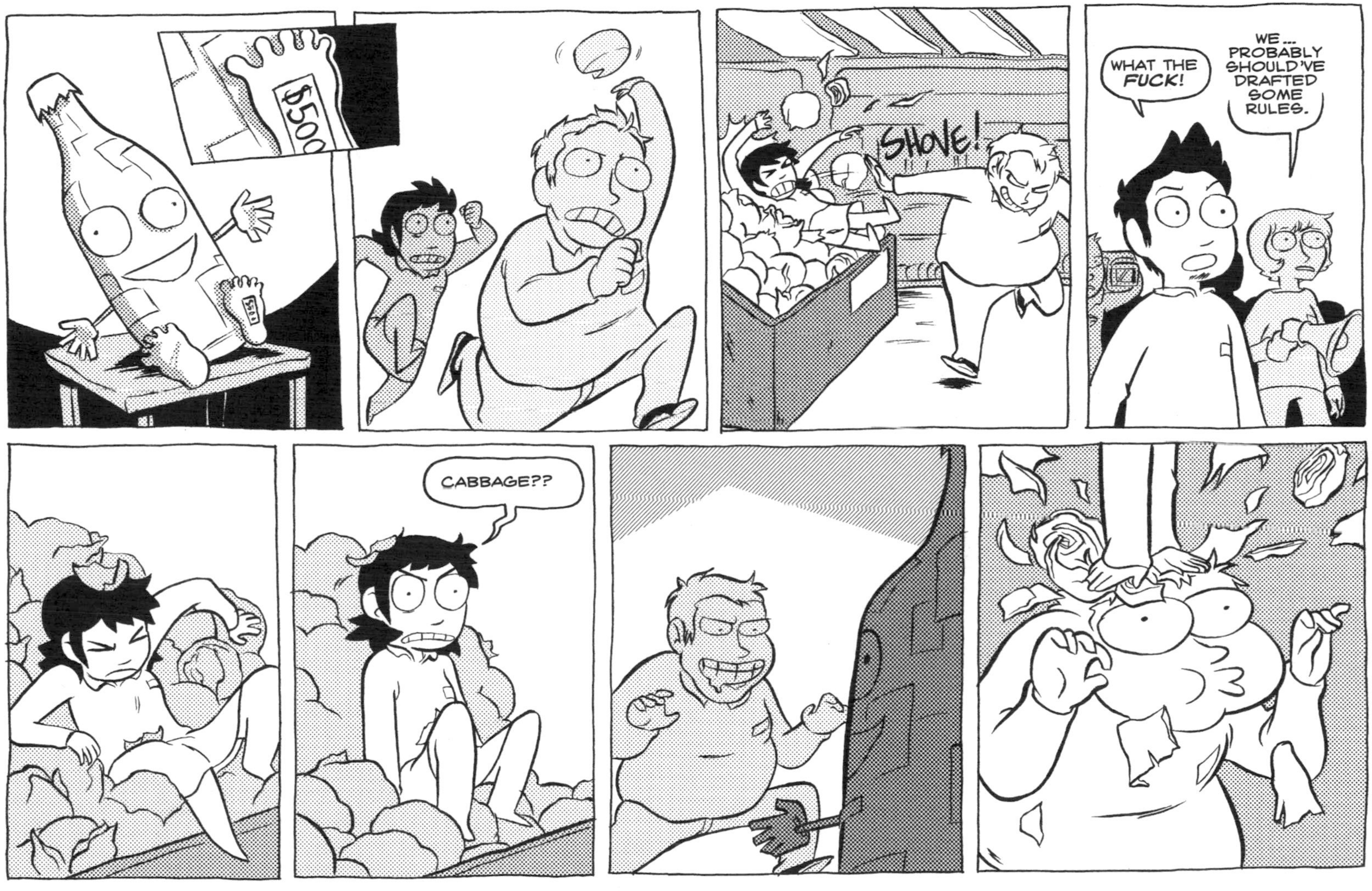
$500
SHOVE!
WHAT THE FUCK!
WE... PROBABLY SHOULD'VE DRAFTED SOME RULES.
CABBAGE??

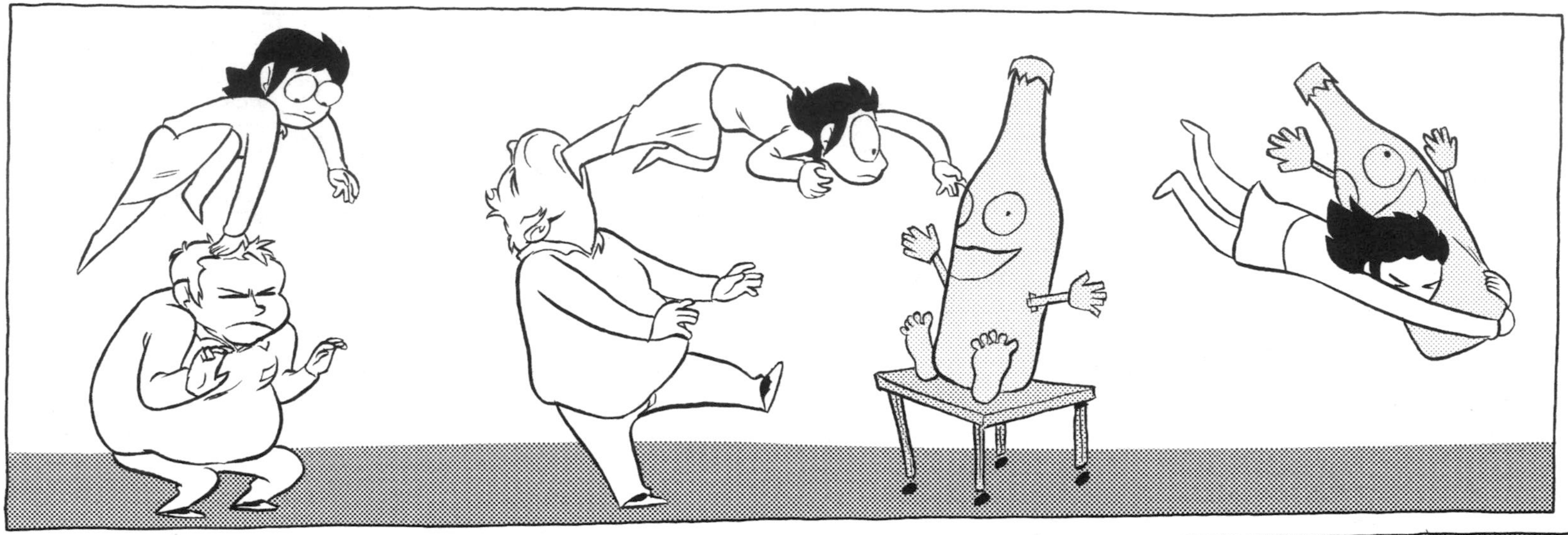

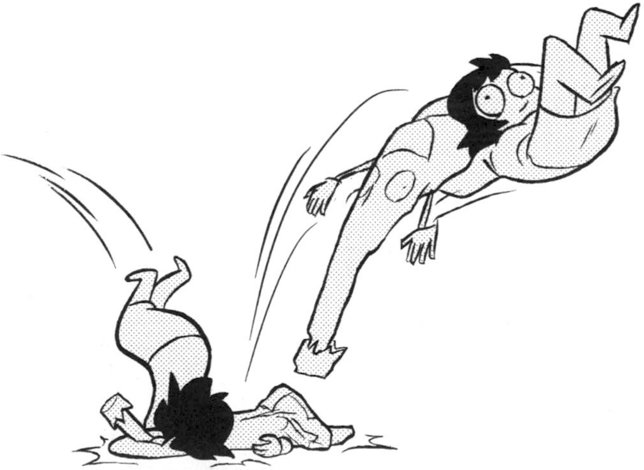

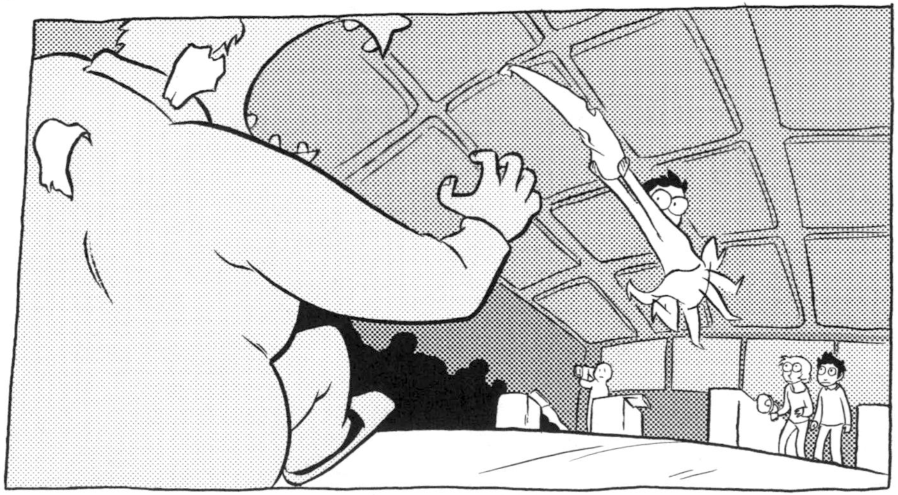

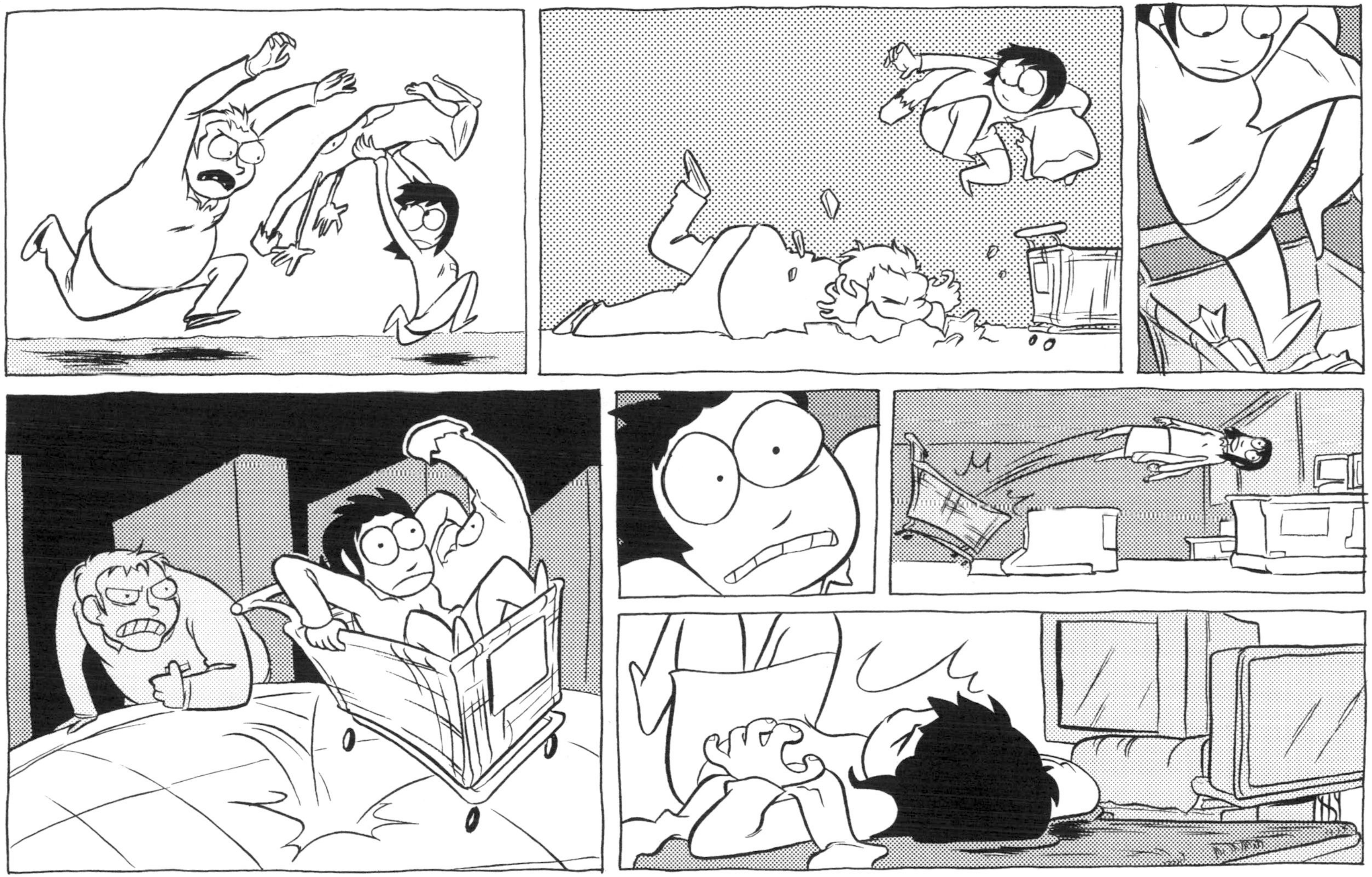

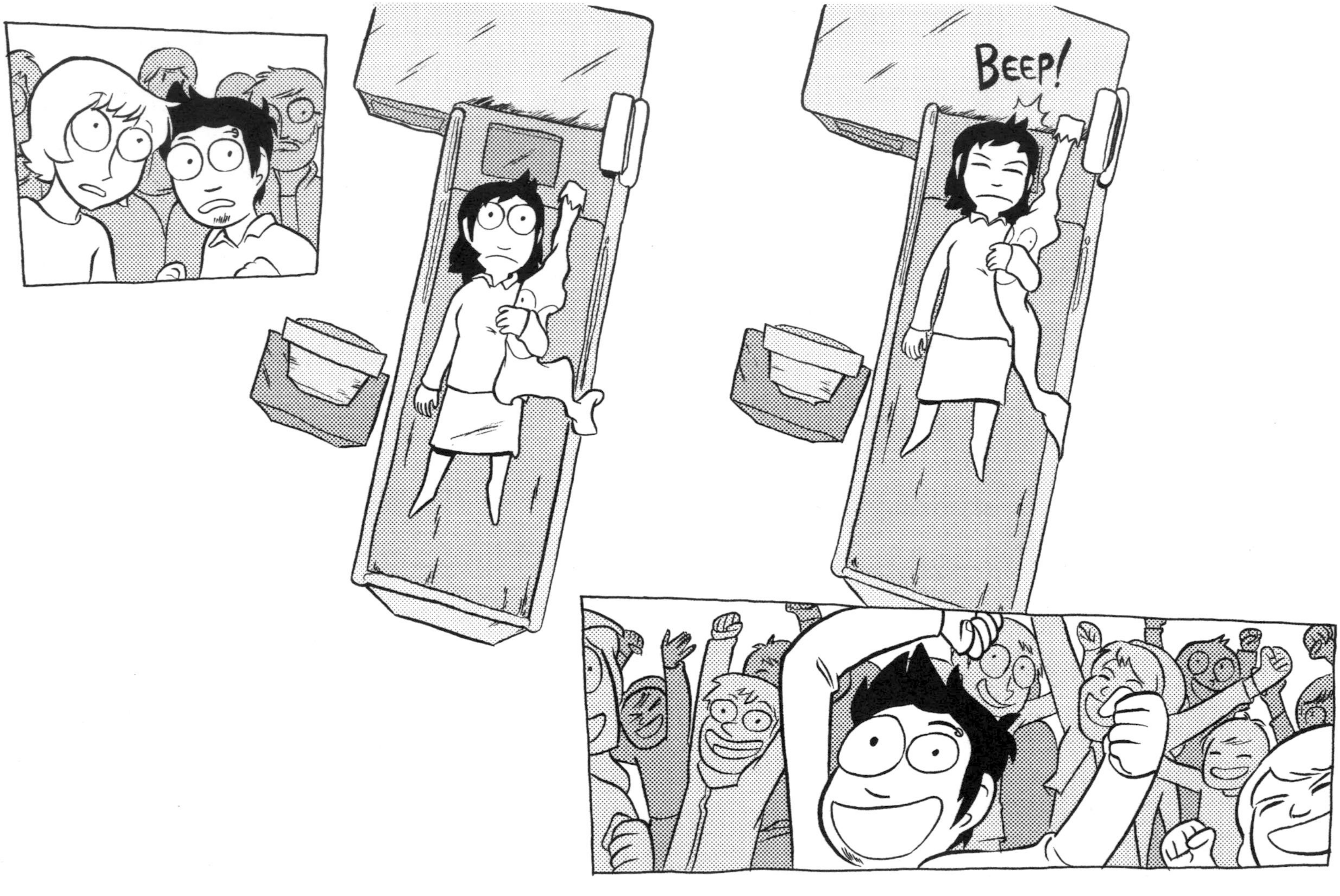
BEEP!

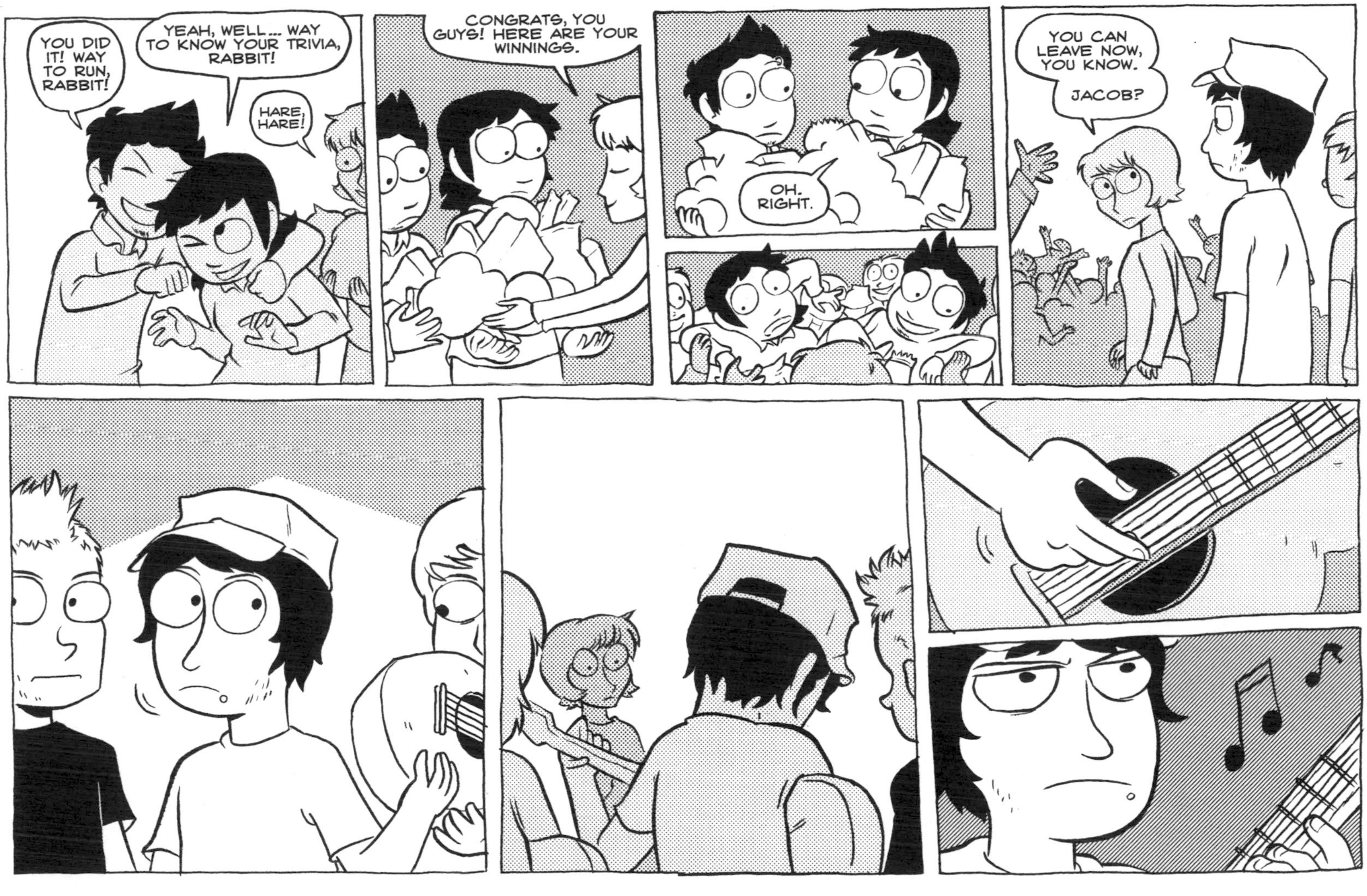

YOU DID IT! WAY TO RUN, RABBIT!
YEAH, WELL... WAY TO KNOW YOUR TRIVIA, RABBIT!
HARE, HARE!
CONGRATS, YOU GUYS! HERE ARE YOUR WINNINGS.
OH. RIGHT.
YOU CAN LEAVE NOW, YOU KNOW.
JACOB?

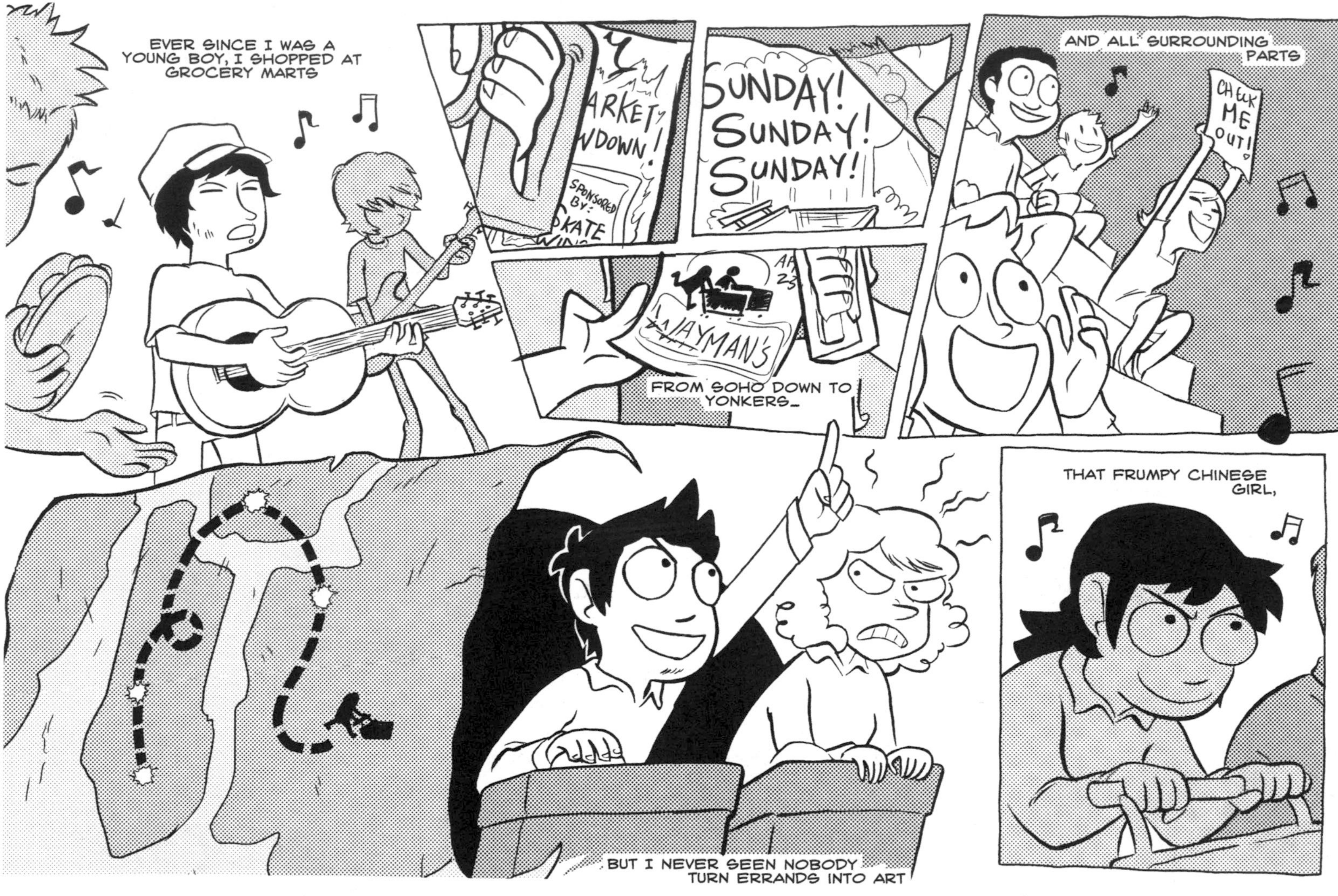
EVER SINCE I WAS A YOUNG BOY, I SHOPPED AT GROCERY MARTS
ARKET
WDOWN!
SPONSORED BY:
SKATE
SUNDAY! SUNDAY! SUNDAY!
AND ALL SURROUNDING PARTS
CHECK ME OUT!
WAYMAN'S
FROM SOHO DOWN TO YONKERS_
BUT I NEVER SEEN NOBODY TURN ERRANDS INTO ART
THAT FRUMPY CHINESE GIRL,

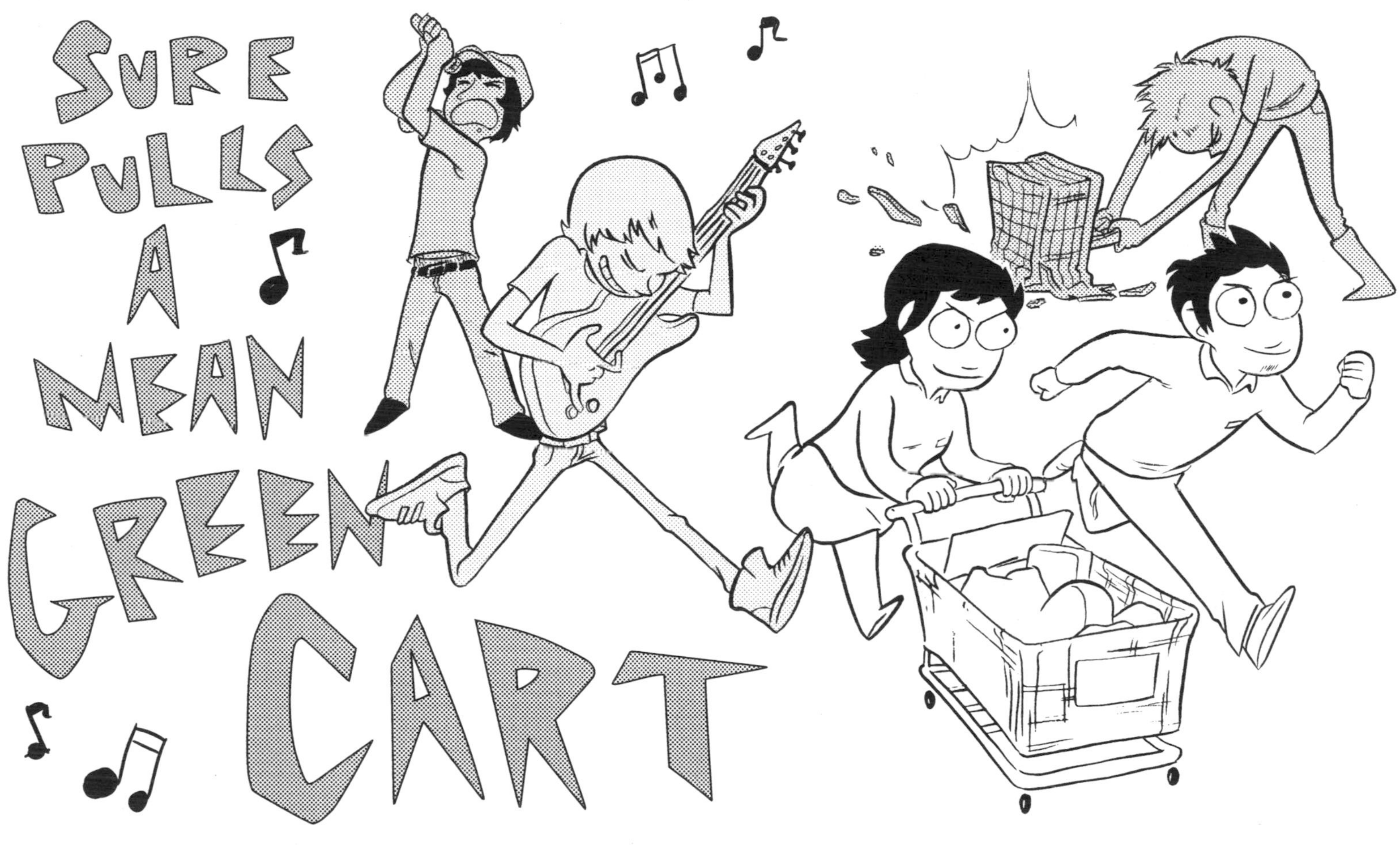
SURE PULLS A MEAN GREEN CART

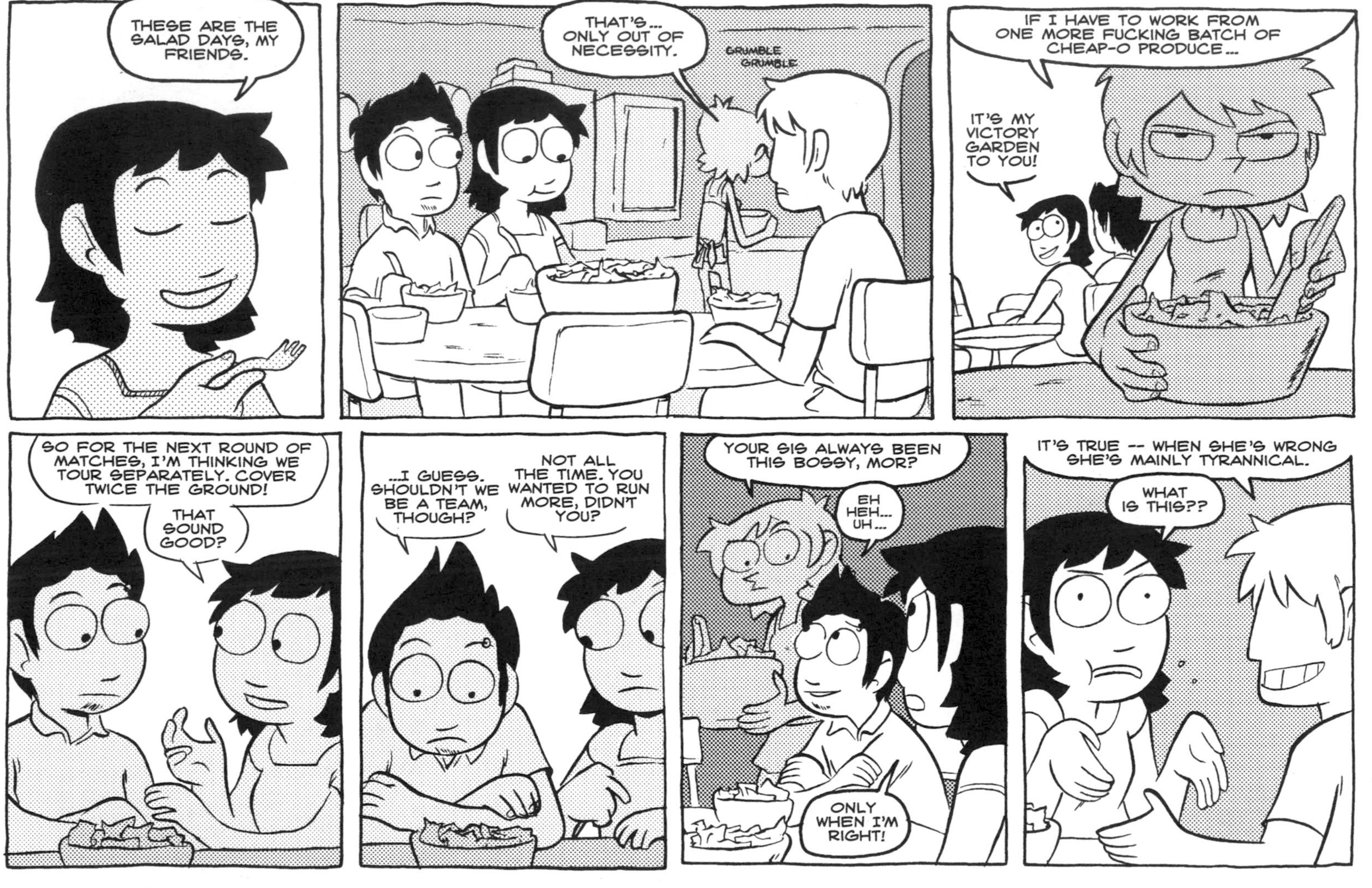
THESE ARE THE SALAD DAYS, MY FRIENDS.
THAT'S... ONLY OUT OF NECESSITY.
GRUMBLE GRUMBLE
IF I HAVE TO WORK FROM ONE MORE FUCKING BATCH OF CHEAP-O PRODUCE...
IT'S MY VICTORY GARDEN TO YOU!
SO FOR THE NEXT ROUND OF MATCHES, I'M THINKING WE TOUR SEPARATELY. COVER TWICE THE GROUND!
THAT SOUND GOOD?
...I GUESS. SHOULDN'T WE BE A TEAM, THOUGH?
NOT ALL THE TIME. YOU WANTED TO RUN MORE, DIDN'T YOU?
YOUR SIS ALWAYS BEEN THIS BOSSY, MOR?
EH HEH... UH...
ONLY WHEN I'M RIGHT!
IT'S TRUE -- WHEN SHE'S WRONG SHE'S MAINLY TYRANNICAL.
WHAT IS THIS??

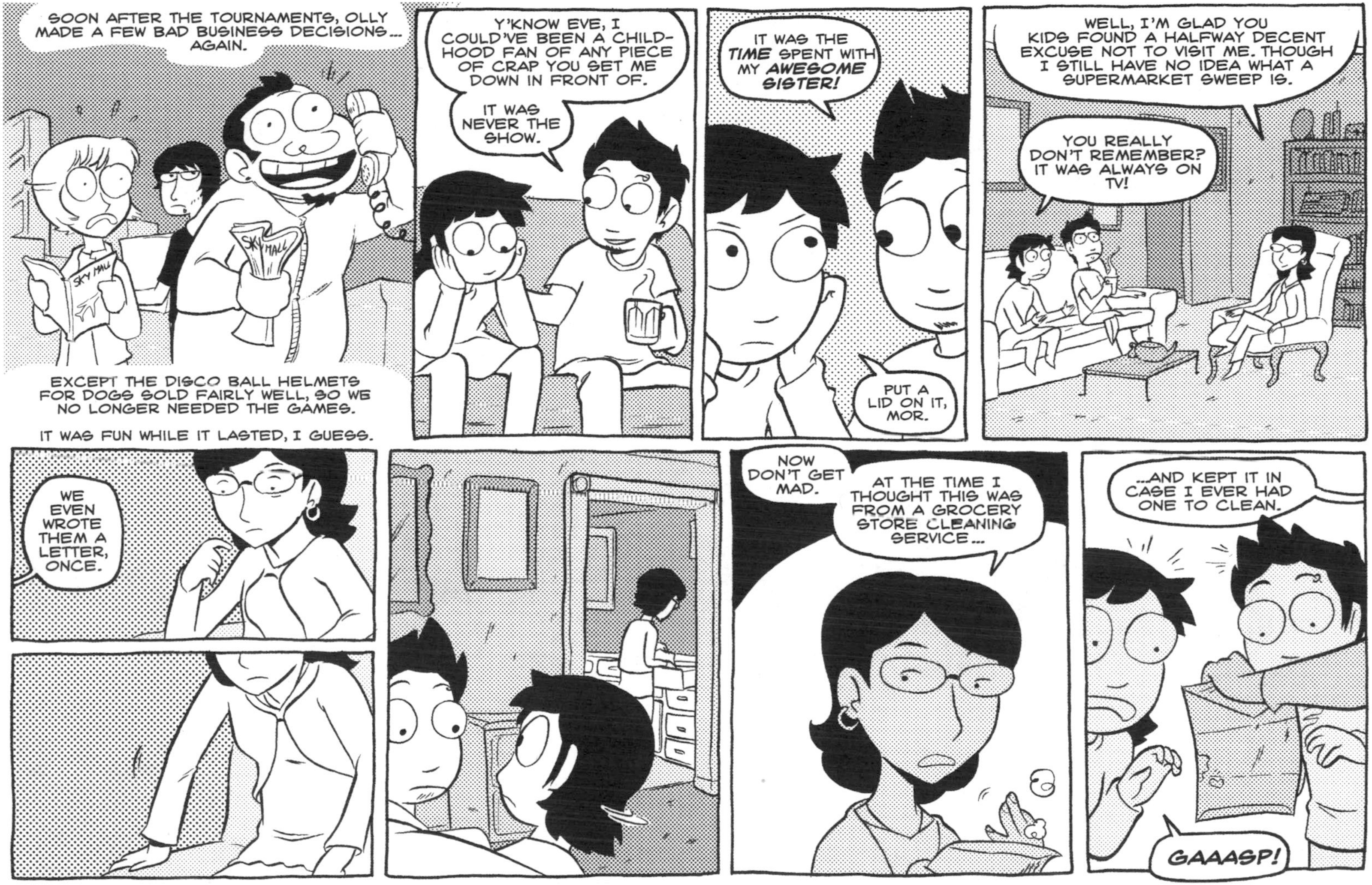
SOON AFTER THE TOURNAMENTS, OLLY MADE A FEW BAD BUSINESS DECISIONS... AGAIN.
SKY MALL
SKY MALL
EXCEPT THE DISCO BALL HELMETS FOR DOGS SOLD FAIRLY WELL, SO WE NO LONGER NEEDED THE GAMES.
IT WAS FUN WHILE IT LASTED, I GUESS.
Y'KNOW EVE, I COULD'VE BEEN A CHILDHOOD FAN OF ANY PIECE OF CRAP YOU SET ME DOWN IN FRONT OF.
IT WAS NEVER THE SHOW.
IT WAS THE *TIME* SPENT WITH MY ***AWESOME SISTER!***
PUT A LID ON IT, MOR.
WELL, I'M GLAD YOU KIDS FOUND A HALFWAY DECENT EXCUSE NOT TO VISIT ME. THOUGH I STILL HAVE NO IDEA WHAT A SUPERMARKET SWEEP IS.
YOU REALLY DON'T REMEMBER? IT WAS ALWAYS ON TV!
WE EVEN WROTE THEM A LETTER, ONCE.
NOW DON'T GET MAD.
AT THE TIME I THOUGHT THIS WAS FROM A GROCERY STORE CLEANING SERVICE...
...AND KEPT IT IN CASE I EVER HAD ONE TO CLEAN.
GAAASP!

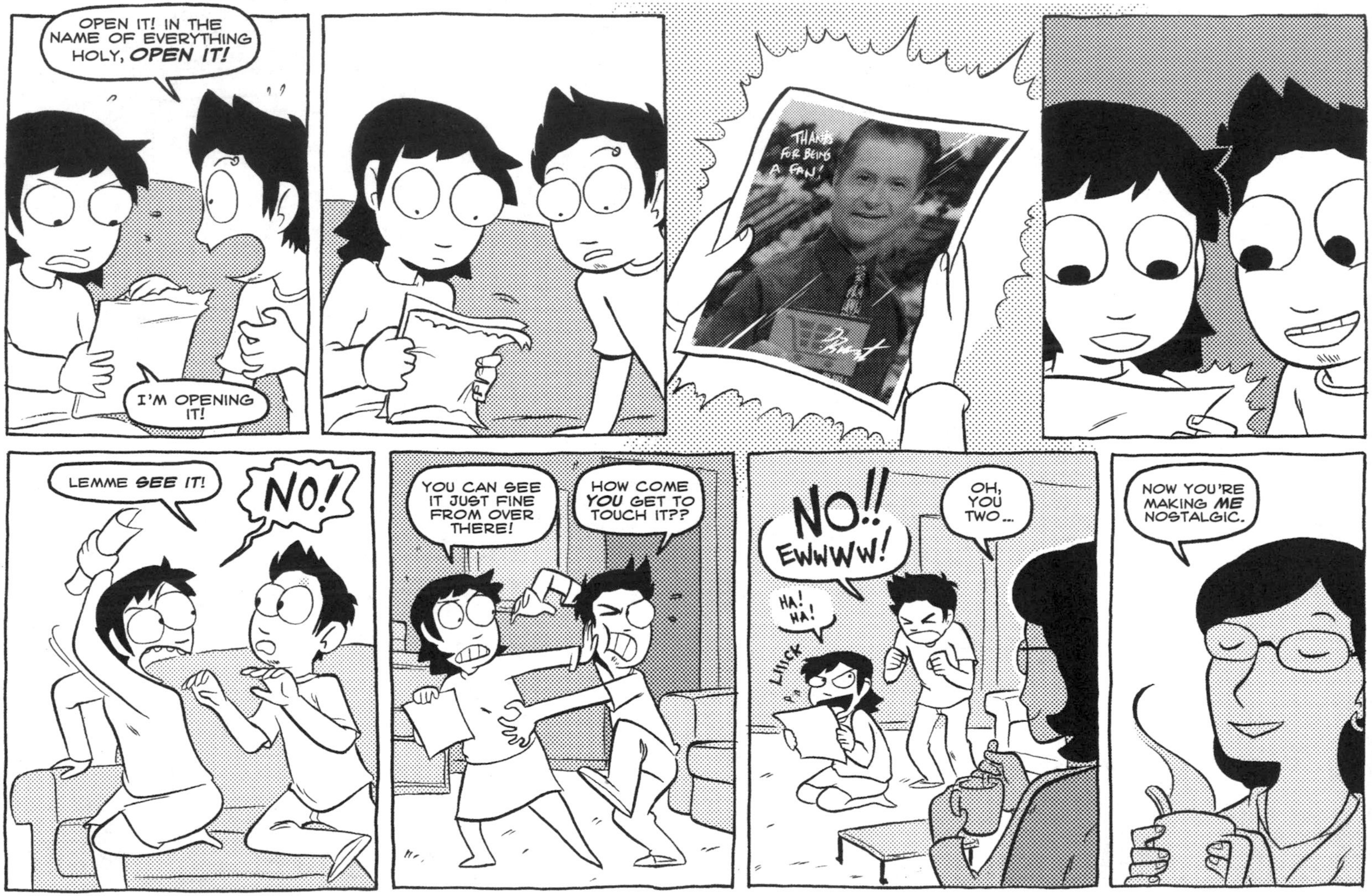
OPEN IT! IN THE NAME OF EVERYTHING HOLY, OPEN IT!
I'M OPENING IT!
THANKS FOR BEING A FAN!
LEMME SEE IT!
NO!
YOU CAN SEE IT JUST FINE FROM OVER THERE!
HOW COME YOU GET TO TOUCH IT??
NO!! EWWWW!
HA! HA!
OH, YOU TWO...
NOW YOU'RE MAKING ME NOSTALGIC.

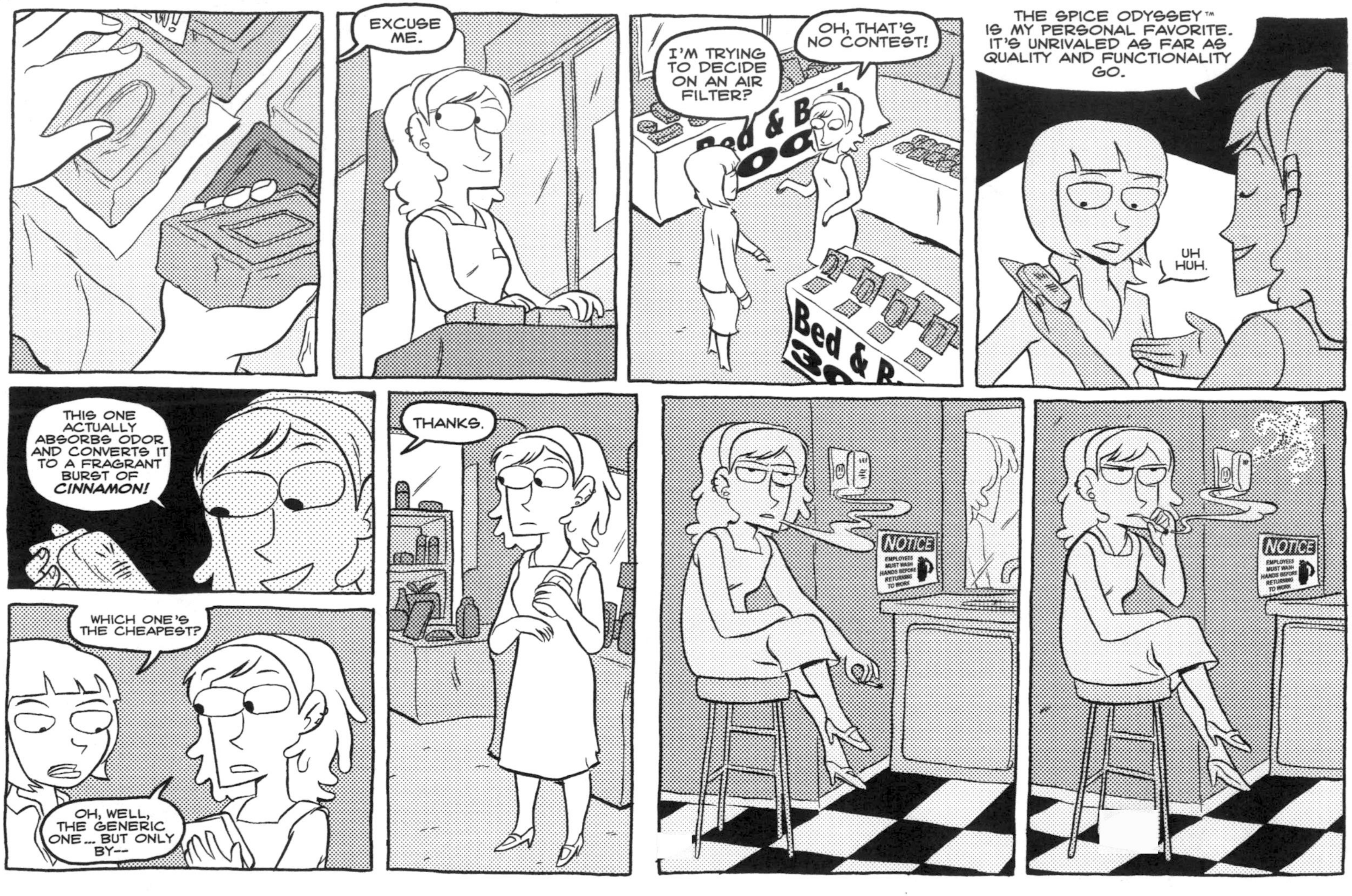
EXCUSE ME.
I'M TRYING TO DECIDE ON AN AIR FILTER?
OH, THAT'S NO CONTEST!
THE SPICE ODYSSEY™ IS MY PERSONAL FAVORITE. IT'S UNRIVALED AS FAR AS QUALITY AND FUNCTIONALITY GO.
UH HUH.
THIS ONE ACTUALLY ABSORBS ODOR AND CONVERTS IT TO A FRAGRANT BURST OF CINNAMON!
WHICH ONE'S THE CHEAPEST?
OH, WELL, THE GENERIC ONE... BUT ONLY BY--
THANKS.
NOTICE
EMPLOYEES MUST WASH HANDS BEFORE RETURNING TO WORK
NOTICE
EMPLOYEES MUST WASH HANDS BEFORE RETURNING TO WORK

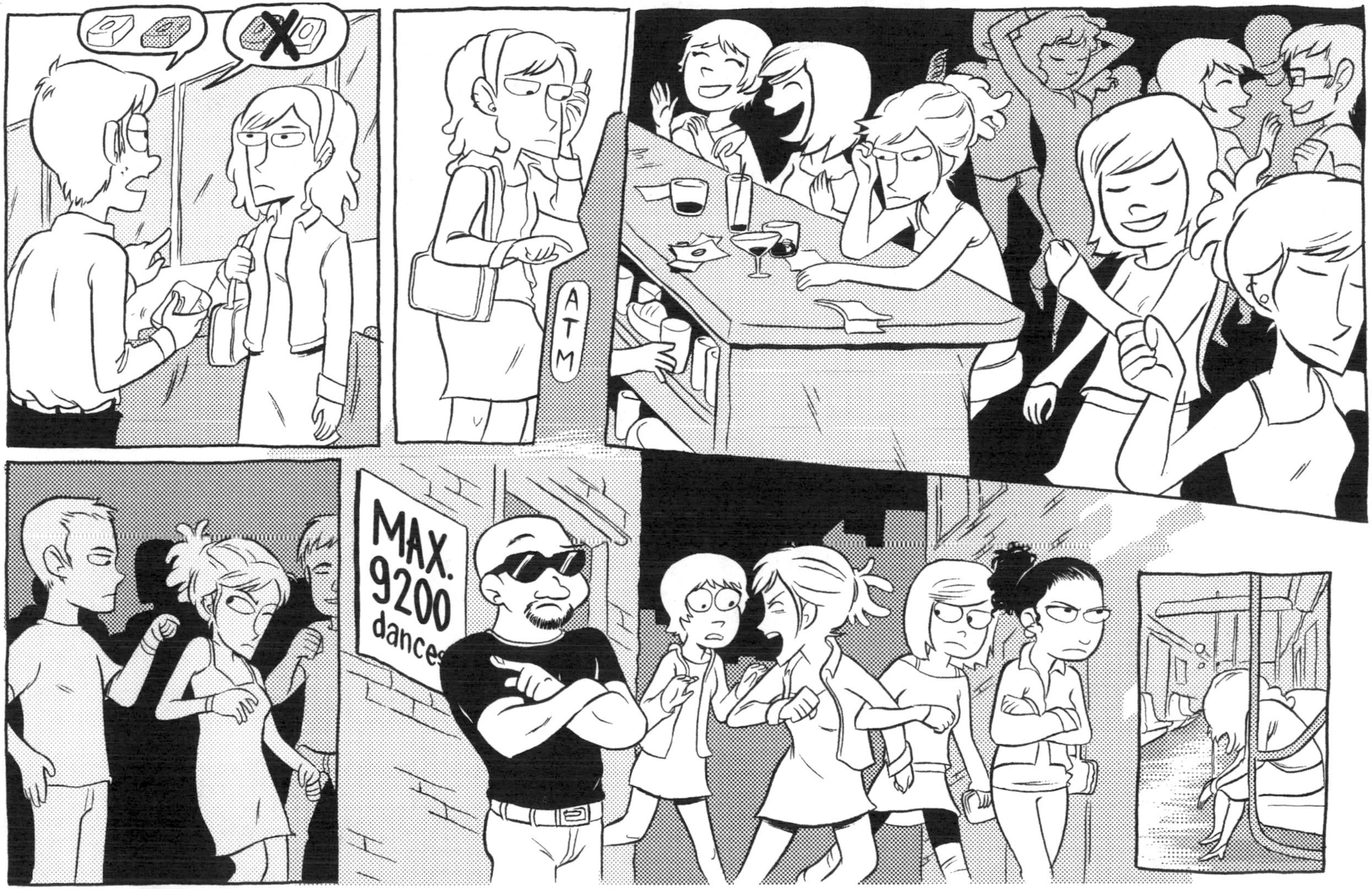
ATM
MAX.
9200
dances

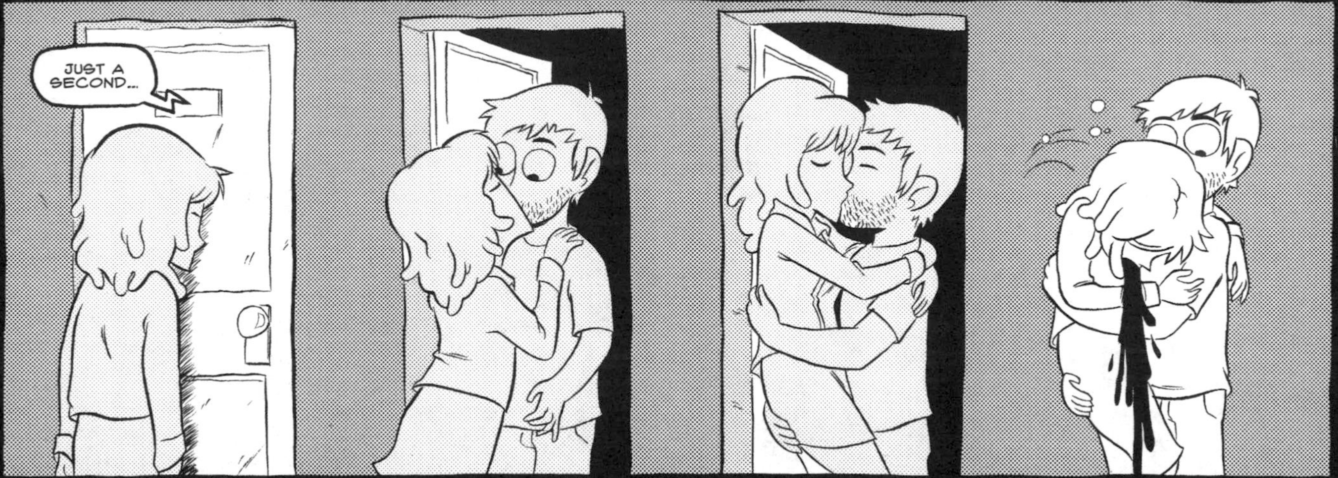
JUST A SECOND...

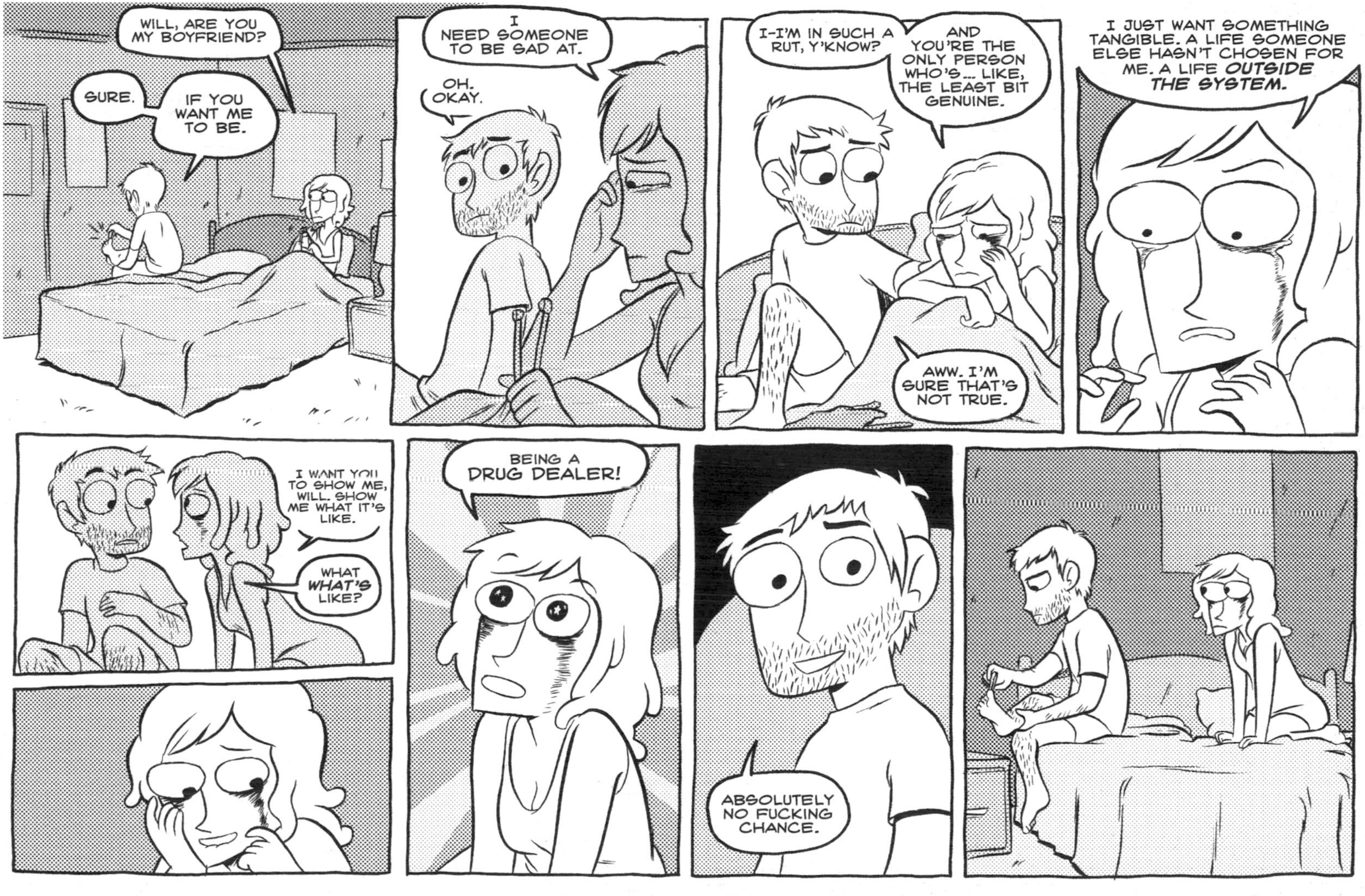

WILL, ARE YOU MY BOYFRIEND?
SURE.
IF YOU WANT ME TO BE.
I NEED SOMEONE TO BE SAD AT.
OH. OKAY.
I-I'M IN SUCH A RUT, Y'KNOW?
AND YOU'RE THE ONLY PERSON WHO'S... LIKE, THE LEAST BIT GENUINE.
AWW. I'M SURE THAT'S NOT TRUE.
I JUST WANT SOMETHING TANGIBLE. A LIFE SOMEONE ELSE HASN'T CHOSEN FOR ME. A LIFE *OUTSIDE THE SYSTEM.*
I WANT YOU TO SHOW ME, WILL. SHOW ME WHAT IT'S LIKE.
WHAT *WHAT'S* LIKE?
BEING A DRUG DEALER!
ABSOLUTELY NO FUCKING CHANCE.

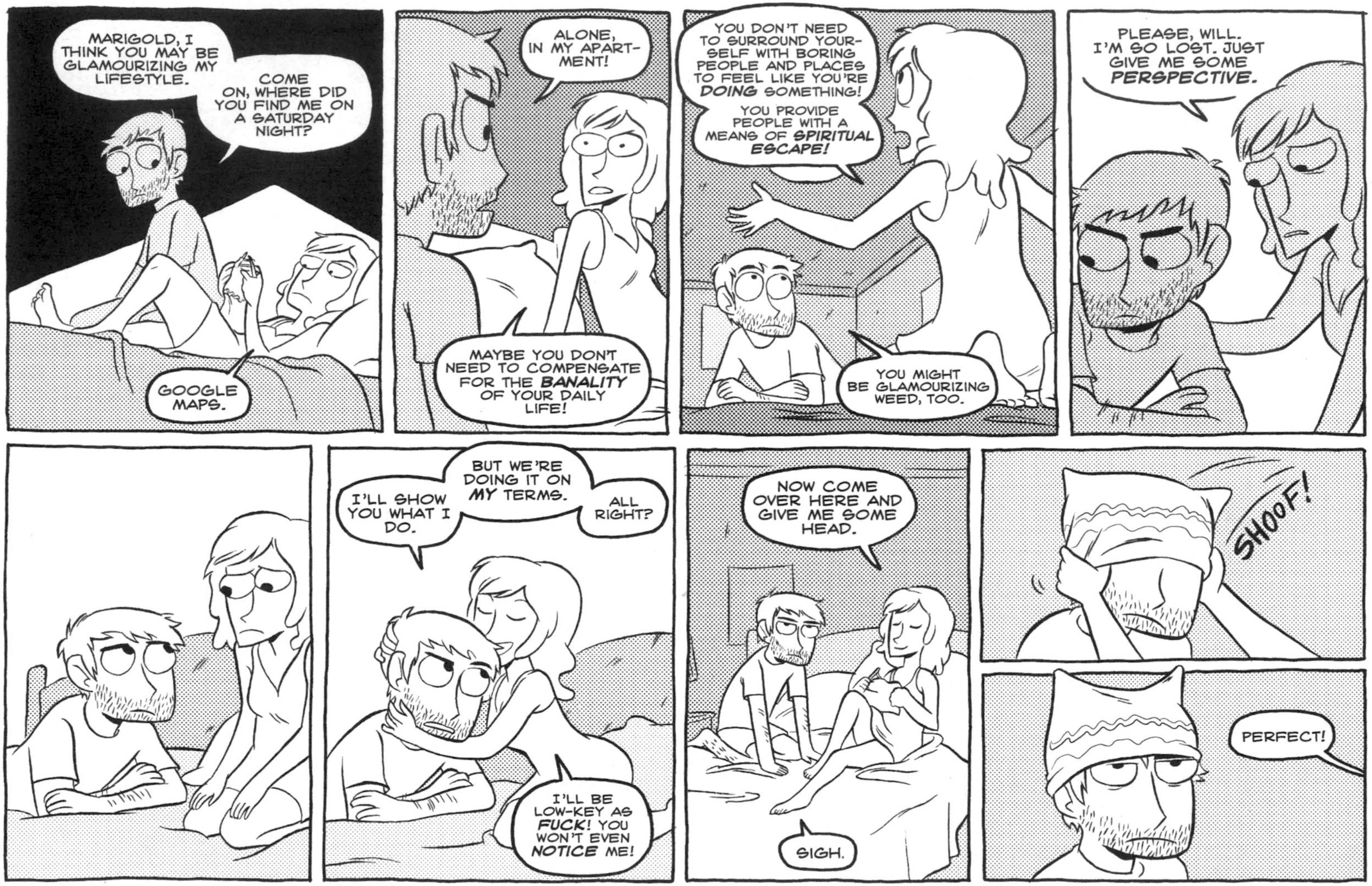
MARIGOLD, I THINK YOU MAY BE GLAMOURIZING MY LIFESTYLE.
COME ON, WHERE DID YOU FIND ME ON A SATURDAY NIGHT?
GOOGLE MAPS.
ALONE, IN MY APARTMENT!
MAYBE YOU DON'T NEED TO COMPENSATE FOR THE BANALITY OF YOUR DAILY LIFE!
YOU DON'T NEED TO SURROUND YOURSELF WITH BORING PEOPLE AND PLACES TO FEEL LIKE YOU'RE DOING SOMETHING!
YOU PROVIDE PEOPLE WITH A MEANS OF SPIRITUAL ESCAPE!
YOU MIGHT BE GLAMOURIZING WEED, TOO.
PLEASE, WILL. I'M SO LOST. JUST GIVE ME SOME PERSPECTIVE.
I'LL SHOW YOU WHAT I DO.
BUT WE'RE DOING IT ON MY TERMS.
ALL RIGHT?
I'LL BE LOW-KEY AS FUCK! YOU WON'T EVEN NOTICE ME!
NOW COME OVER HERE AND GIVE ME SOME HEAD.
SIGH.
SHOOF!
PERFECT!

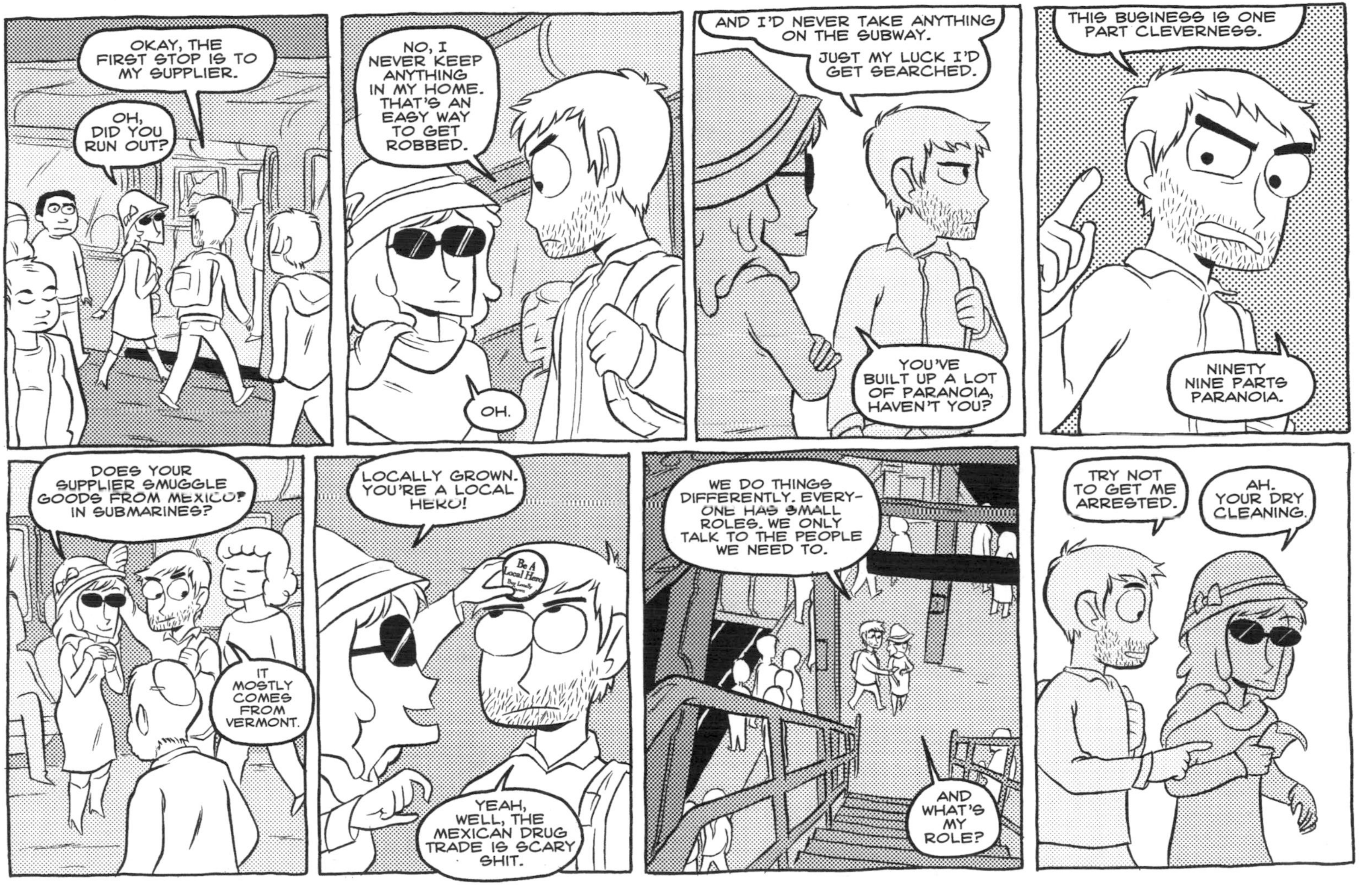
OKAY, THE FIRST STOP IS TO MY SUPPLIER.
OH, DID YOU RUN OUT?
NO, I NEVER KEEP ANYTHING IN MY HOME. THAT'S AN EASY WAY TO GET ROBBED.
OH.
AND I'D NEVER TAKE ANYTHING ON THE SUBWAY.
JUST MY LUCK I'D GET SEARCHED.
YOU'VE BUILT UP A LOT OF PARANOIA, HAVEN'T YOU?
THIS BUSINESS IS ONE PART CLEVERNESS.
NINETY NINE PARTS PARANOIA.
DOES YOUR SUPPLIER SMUGGLE GOODS FROM MEXICO IN SUBMARINES?
IT MOSTLY COMES FROM VERMONT.
LOCALLY GROWN. YOU'RE A LOCAL HERO!
Be A Local Hero
YEAH, WELL, THE MEXICAN DRUG TRADE IS SCARY SHIT.
WE DO THINGS DIFFERENTLY. EVERYONE HAS SMALL ROLES. WE ONLY TALK TO THE PEOPLE WE NEED TO.
AND WHAT'S MY ROLE?
TRY NOT TO GET ME ARRESTED.
AH. YOUR DRY CLEANING.

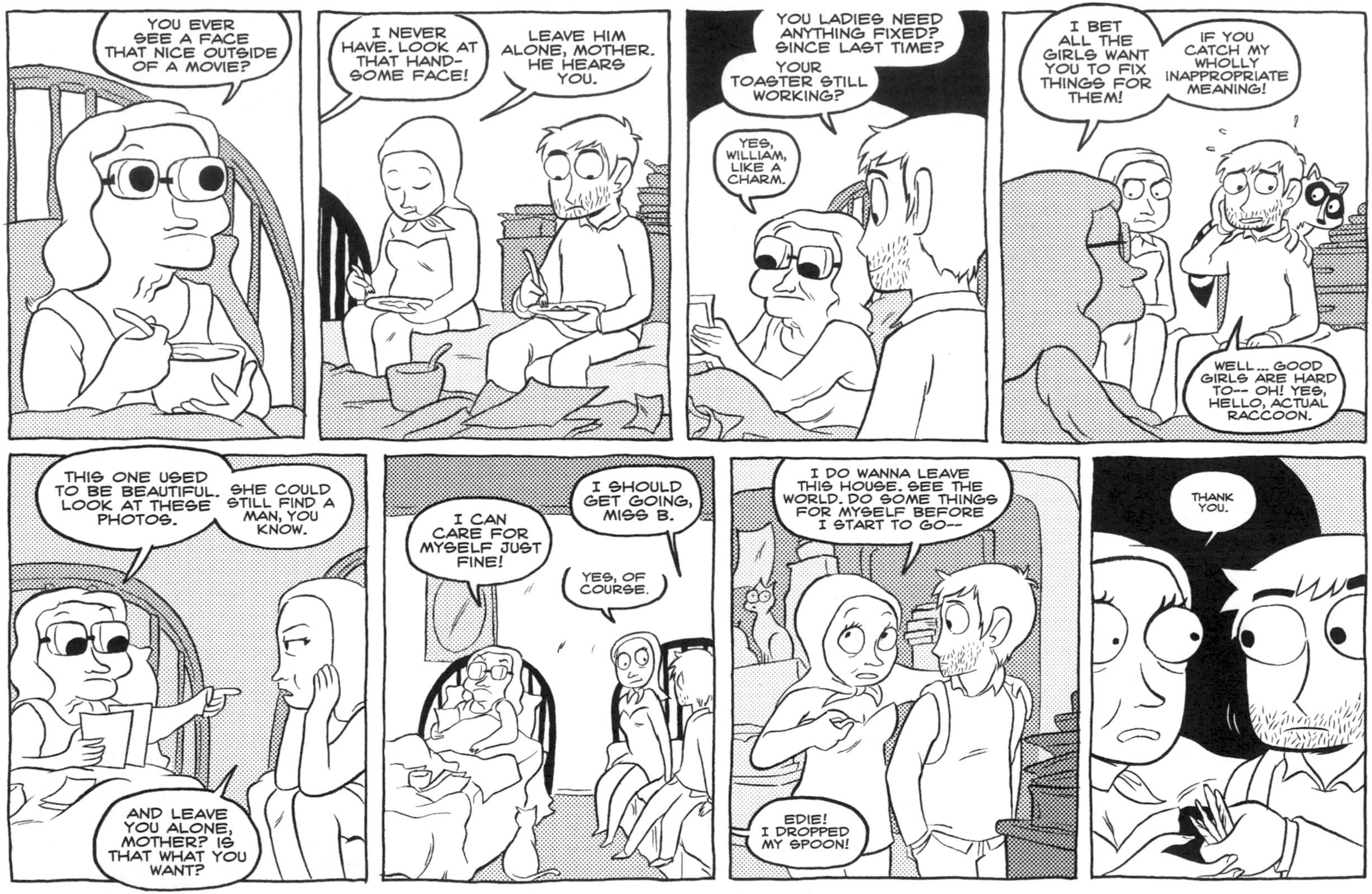
YOU EVER SEE A FACE THAT NICE OUTSIDE OF A MOVIE?
I NEVER HAVE. LOOK AT THAT HAND-SOME FACE!
LEAVE HIM ALONE, MOTHER. HE HEARS YOU.
YOU LADIES NEED ANYTHING FIXED? SINCE LAST TIME?
YOUR TOASTER STILL WORKING?
YES, WILLIAM, LIKE A CHARM.
I BET ALL THE GIRLS WANT YOU TO FIX THINGS FOR THEM!
IF YOU CATCH MY WHOLLY INAPPROPRIATE MEANING!
WELL... GOOD GIRLS ARE HARD TO-- OH! YES, HELLO, ACTUAL RACCOON.
THIS ONE USED TO BE BEAUTIFUL. LOOK AT THESE PHOTOS.
SHE COULD STILL FIND A MAN, YOU KNOW.
AND LEAVE YOU ALONE, MOTHER? IS THAT WHAT YOU WANT?
I CAN CARE FOR MYSELF JUST FINE!
I SHOULD GET GOING, MISS B.
YES, OF COURSE.
I DO WANNA LEAVE THIS HOUSE. SEE THE WORLD. DO SOME THINGS FOR MYSELF BEFORE I START TO GO--
EDIE! I DROPPED MY SPOON!
THANK YOU.

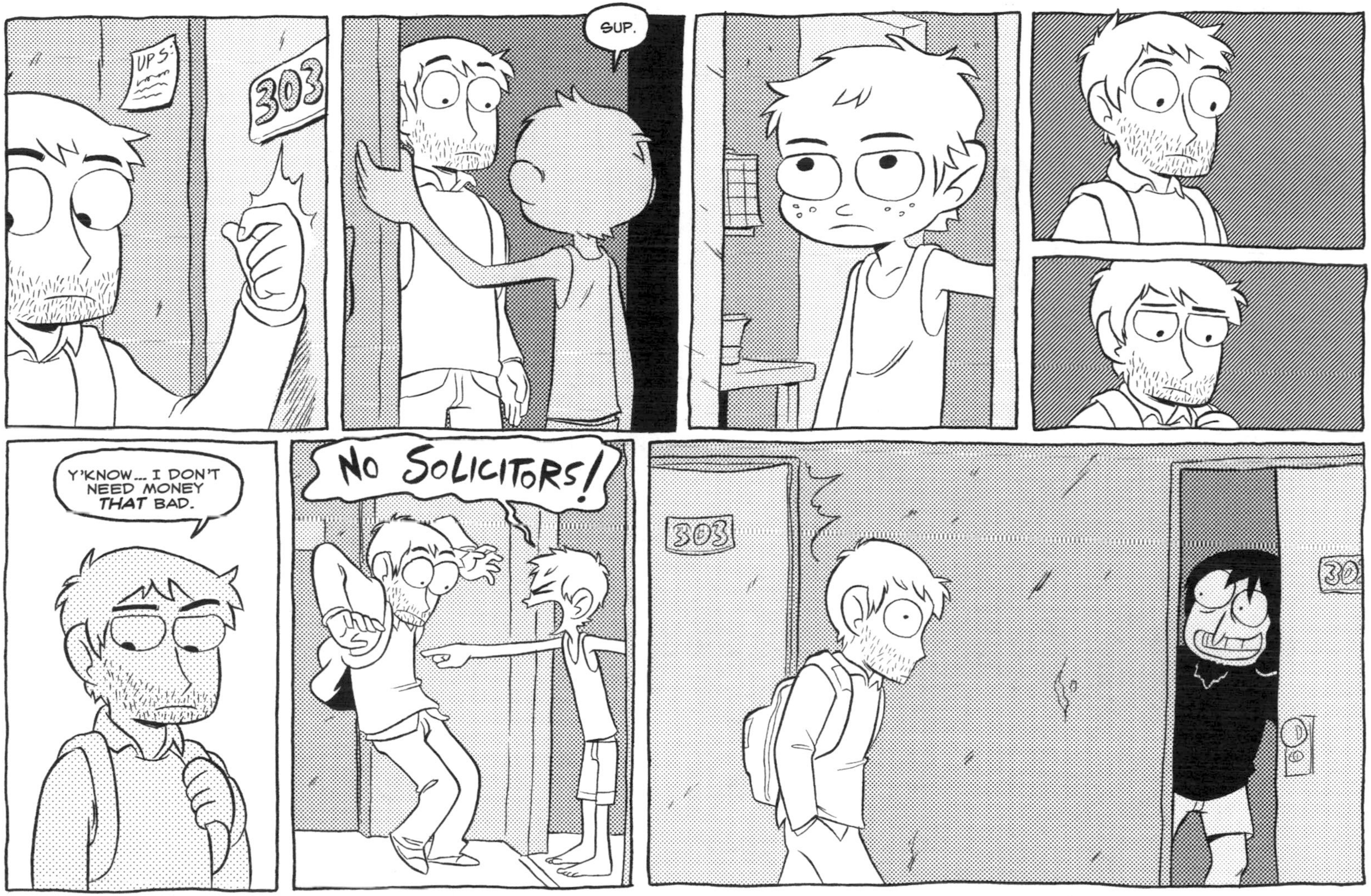
UPS:
303
SUP.
Y'KNOW... I DON'T NEED MONEY *THAT* BAD.
NO SOLICITORS!
303

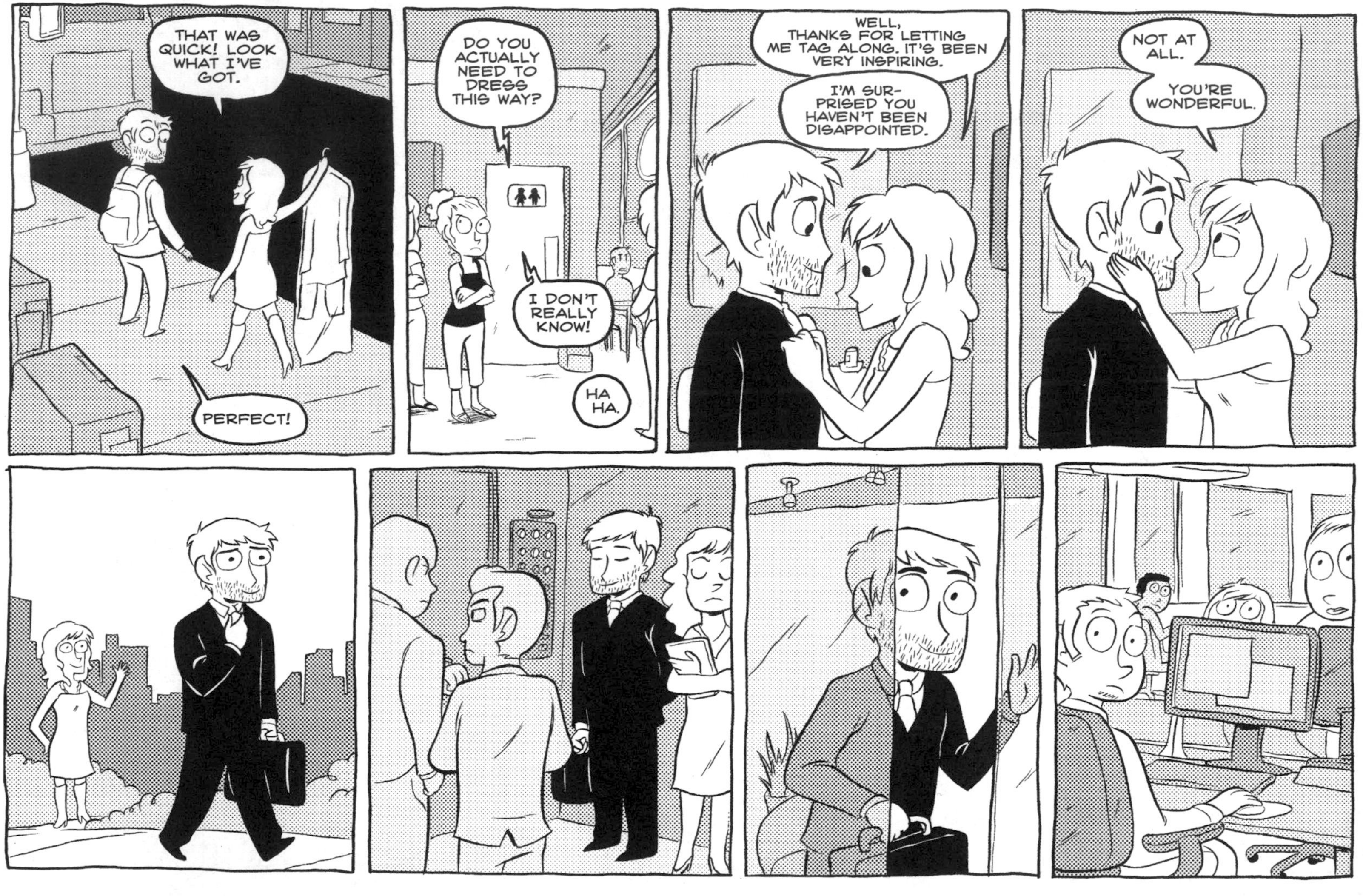
THAT WAS QUICK! LOOK WHAT I'VE GOT.
PERFECT!
DO YOU ACTUALLY NEED TO DRESS THIS WAY?
I DON'T REALLY KNOW!
HA HA.
WELL, THANKS FOR LETTING ME TAG ALONG. IT'S BEEN VERY INSPIRING.
I'M SUR-PRISED YOU HAVEN'T BEEN DISAPPOINTED.
NOT AT ALL.
YOU'RE WONDERFUL.

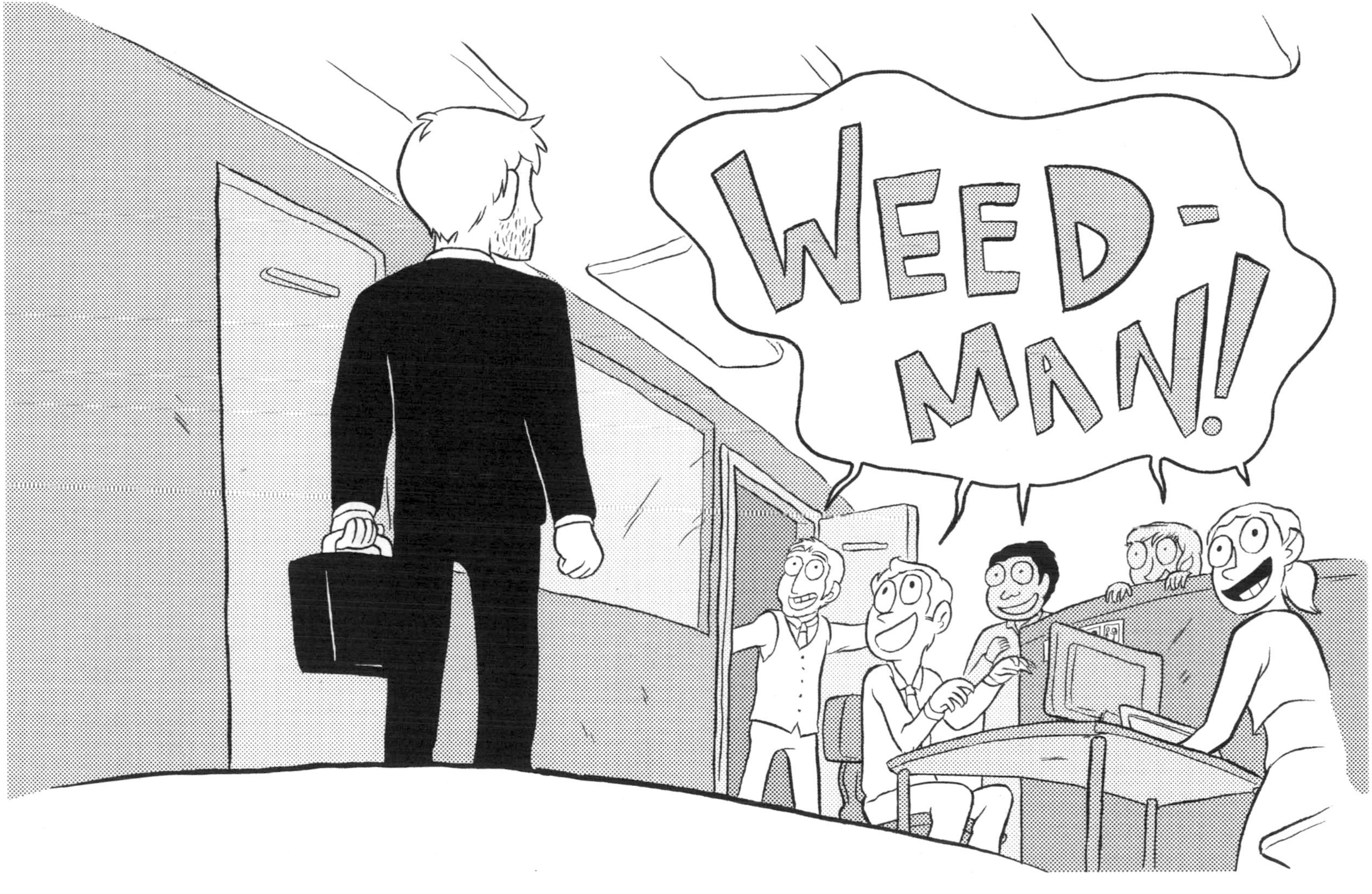
WEED-MAN!

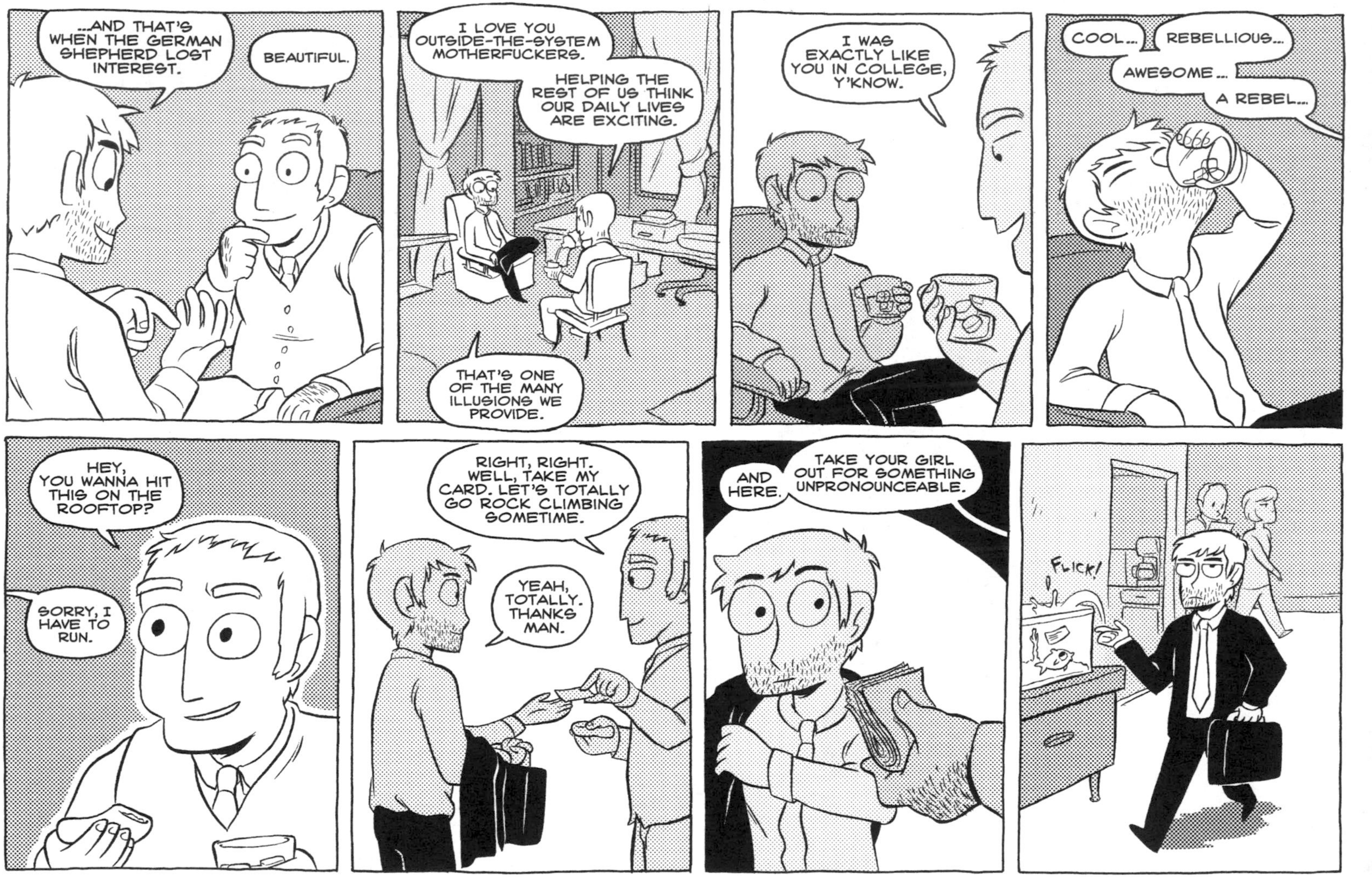
...AND THAT'S WHEN THE GERMAN SHEPHERD LOST INTEREST.
BEAUTIFUL.
I LOVE YOU OUTSIDE-THE-SYSTEM MOTHERFUCKERS.
HELPING THE REST OF US THINK OUR DAILY LIVES ARE EXCITING.
THAT'S ONE OF THE MANY ILLUSIONS WE PROVIDE.
I WAS EXACTLY LIKE YOU IN COLLEGE, Y'KNOW.
COOL...
REBELLIOUS...
AWESOME...
A REBEL...
HEY, YOU WANNA HIT THIS ON THE ROOFTOP?
SORRY, I HAVE TO RUN.
RIGHT, RIGHT. WELL, TAKE MY CARD. LET'S TOTALLY GO ROCK CLIMBING SOMETIME.
YEAH, TOTALLY. THANKS MAN.
AND HERE.
TAKE YOUR GIRL OUT FOR SOMETHING UNPRONOUNCEABLE.
FLICK!

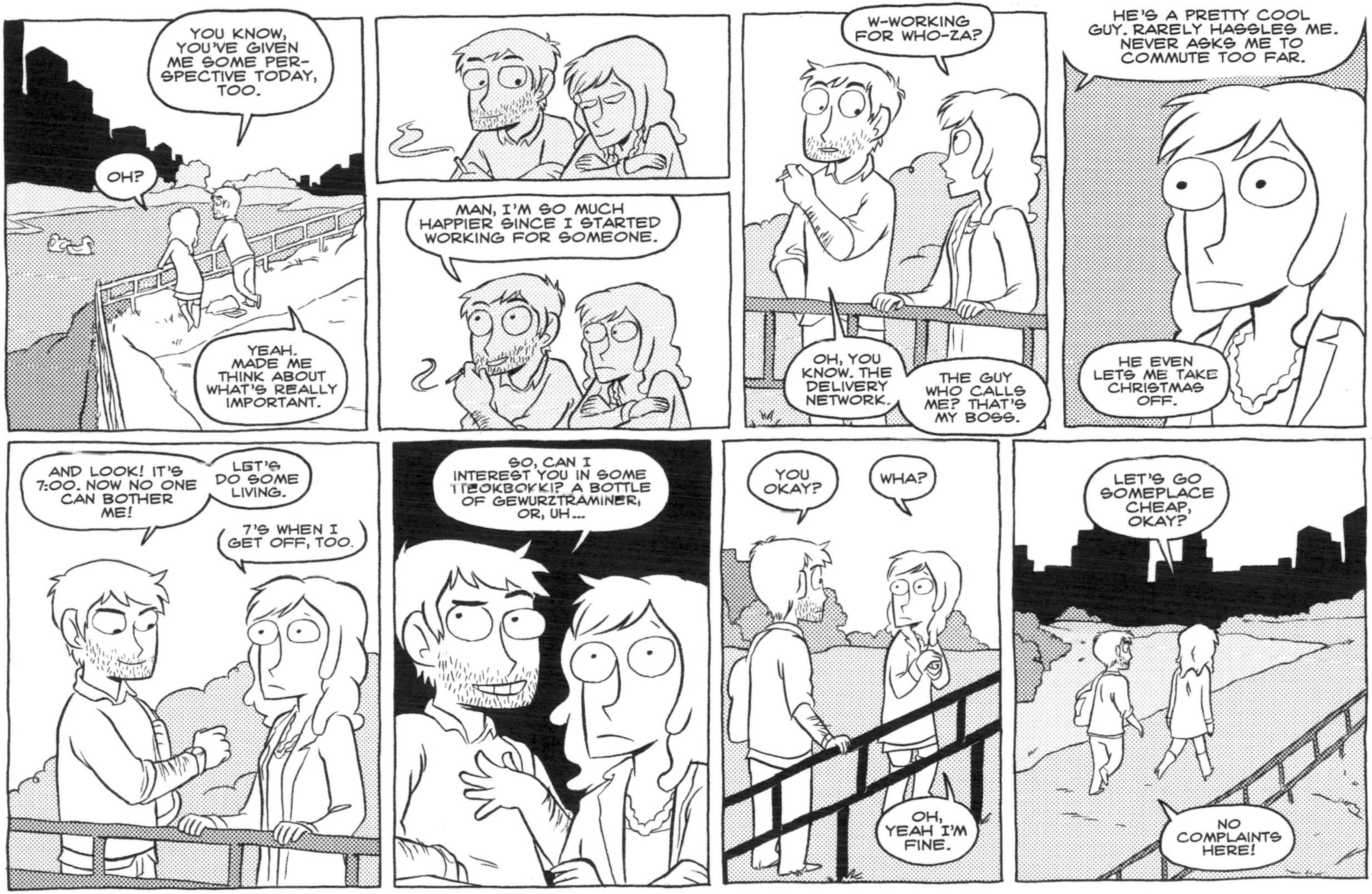
YOU KNOW, YOU'VE GIVEN ME SOME PER-SPECTIVE TODAY, TOO.
OH?
YEAH. MADE ME THINK ABOUT WHAT'S REALLY IMPORTANT.
MAN, I'M SO MUCH HAPPIER SINCE I STARTED WORKING FOR SOMEONE.
W-WORKING FOR WHO-ZA?
OH, YOU KNOW. THE DELIVERY NETWORK.
THE GUY WHO CALLS ME? THAT'S MY BOSS.
HE'S A PRETTY COOL GUY. RARELY HASSLES ME. NEVER ASKS ME TO COMMUTE TOO FAR.
HE EVEN LETS ME TAKE CHRISTMAS OFF.
AND LOOK! IT'S 7:00. NOW NO ONE CAN BOTHER ME!
LET'S DO SOME LIVING.
7'S WHEN I GET OFF, TOO.
SO, CAN I INTEREST YOU IN SOME TTEOKBOKKI? A BOTTLE OF GEWURZTRAMINER, OR, UH...
YOU OKAY?
WHA?
OH, YEAH I'M FINE.
LET'S GO SOMEPLACE CHEAP, OKAY?
NO COMPLAINTS HERE!

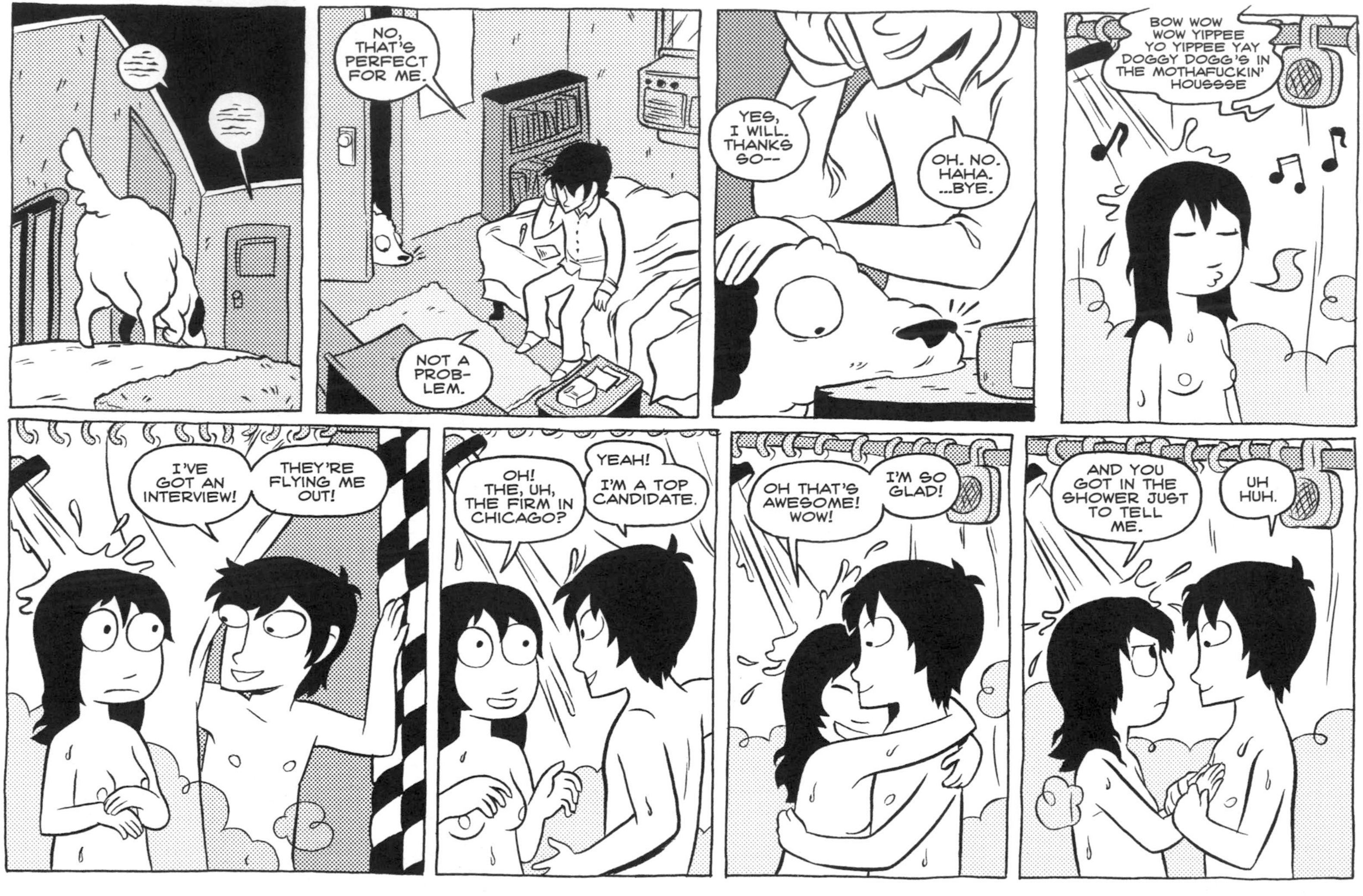
NO, THAT'S PERFECT FOR ME.
NOT A PROB-LEM.
YES, I WILL. THANKS SO--
OH. NO. HAHA. ...BYE.
BOW WOW WOW YIPPEE YO YIPPEE YAY DOGGY DOGG'S IN THE MOTHAFUCKIN' HOUSSSE
I'VE GOT AN INTERVIEW!
THEY'RE FLYING ME OUT!
OH! THE, UH, THE FIRM IN CHICAGO?
YEAH!
I'M A TOP CANDIDATE.
OH THAT'S AWESOME! WOW!
I'M SO GLAD!
AND YOU GOT IN THE SHOWER JUST TO TELL ME.
UH HUH.

93

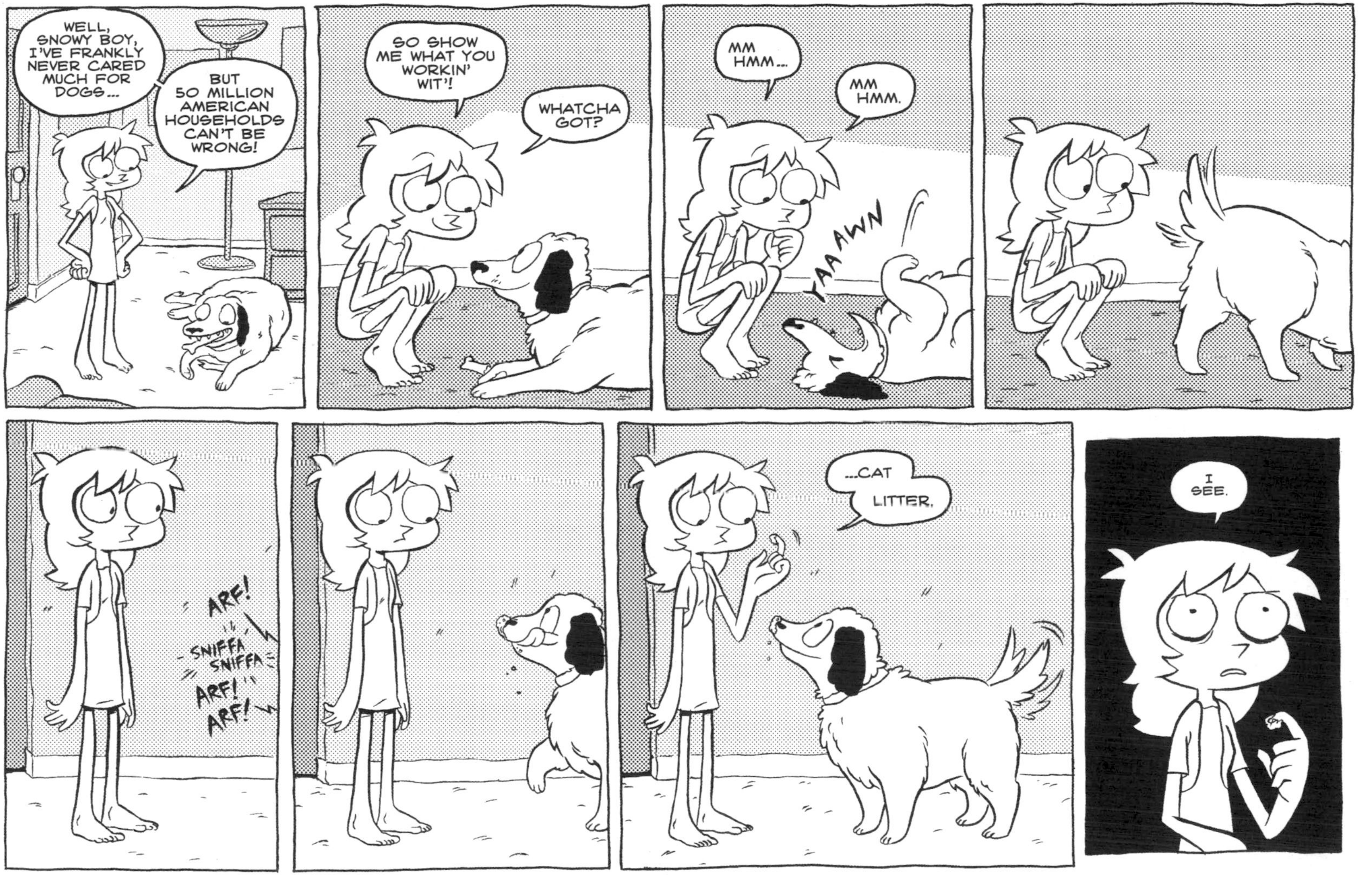
WELL, SNOWY BOY, I'VE FRANKLY NEVER CARED MUCH FOR DOGS...
BUT 50 MILLION AMERICAN HOUSEHOLDS CAN'T BE WRONG!
SO SHOW ME WHAT YOU WORKIN' WIT'!
WHATCHA GOT?
MM HMM...
MM HMM.
YAAAWN
ARF!
SNIFFA SNIFFA
ARF!
ARF!
...CAT LITTER.
I SEE.

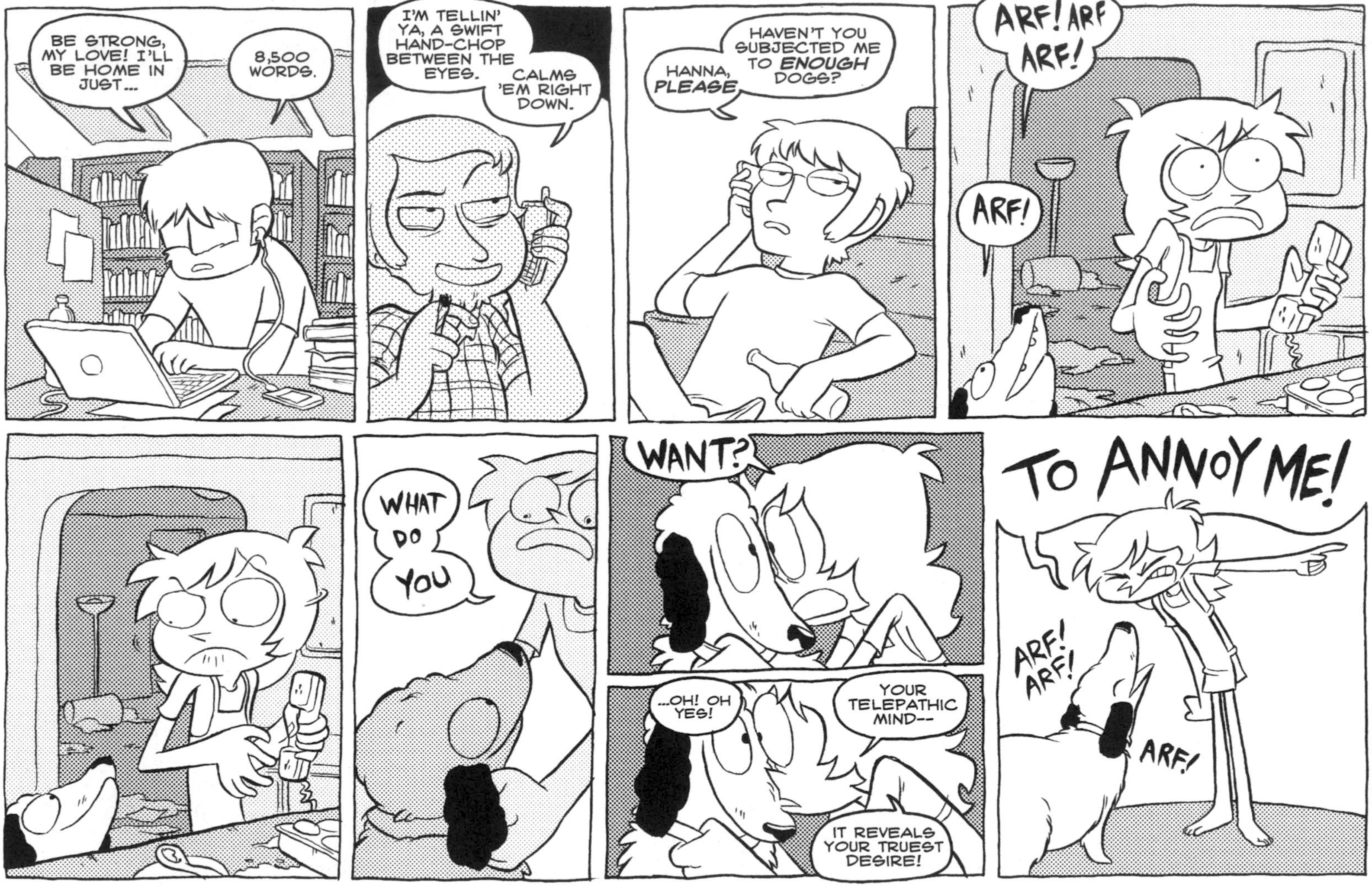
BE STRONG, MY LOVE! I'LL BE HOME IN JUST...
8,500 WORDS.
I'M TELLIN' YA, A SWIFT HAND-CHOP BETWEEN THE EYES.
CALMS 'EM RIGHT DOWN.
HANNA, PLEASE
HAVEN'T YOU SUBJECTED ME TO ENOUGH DOGS?
ARF! ARF ARF!
ARF!
WHAT DO YOU
WANT?
...OH! OH YES!
YOUR TELEPATHIC MIND--
IT REVEALS YOUR TRUEST DESIRE!
TO ANNOY ME!
ARF! ARF!
ARF!

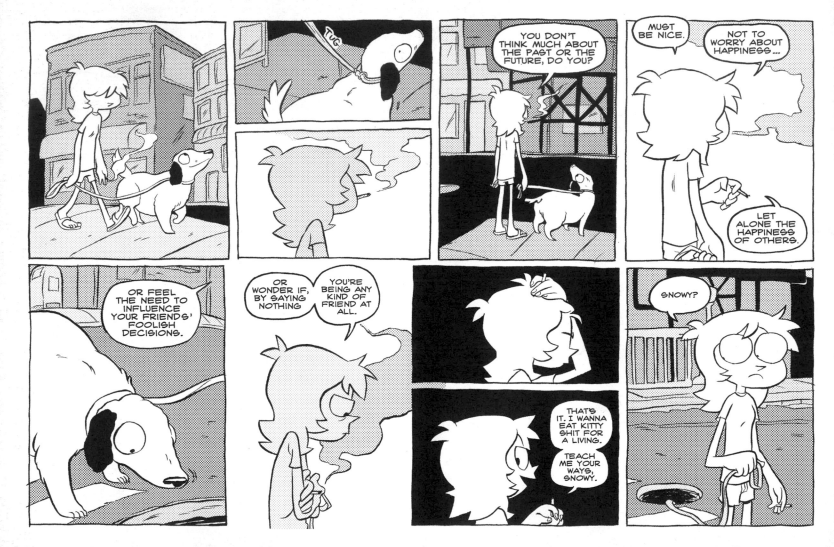

100

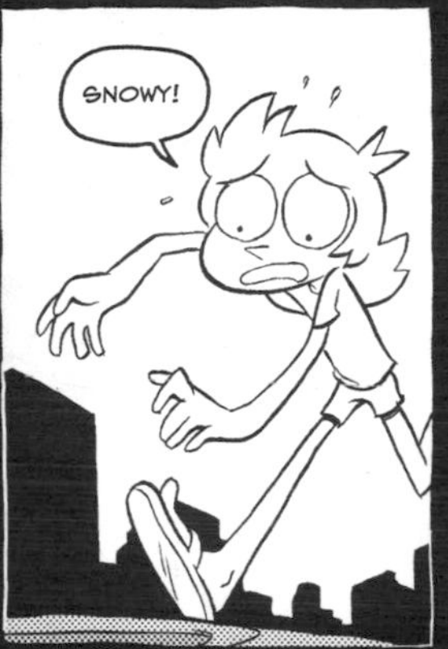
SNOWY!

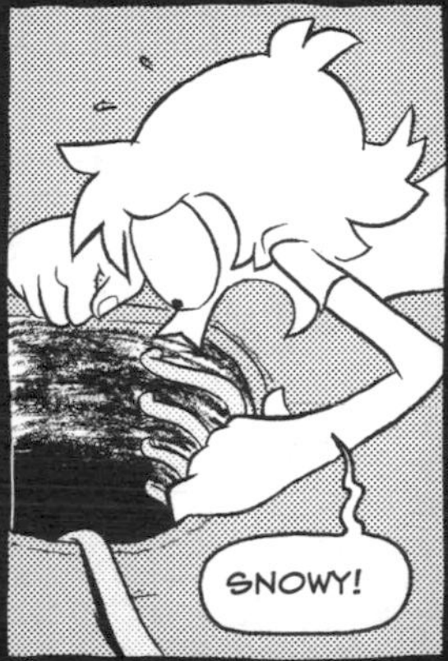
SNOWY!

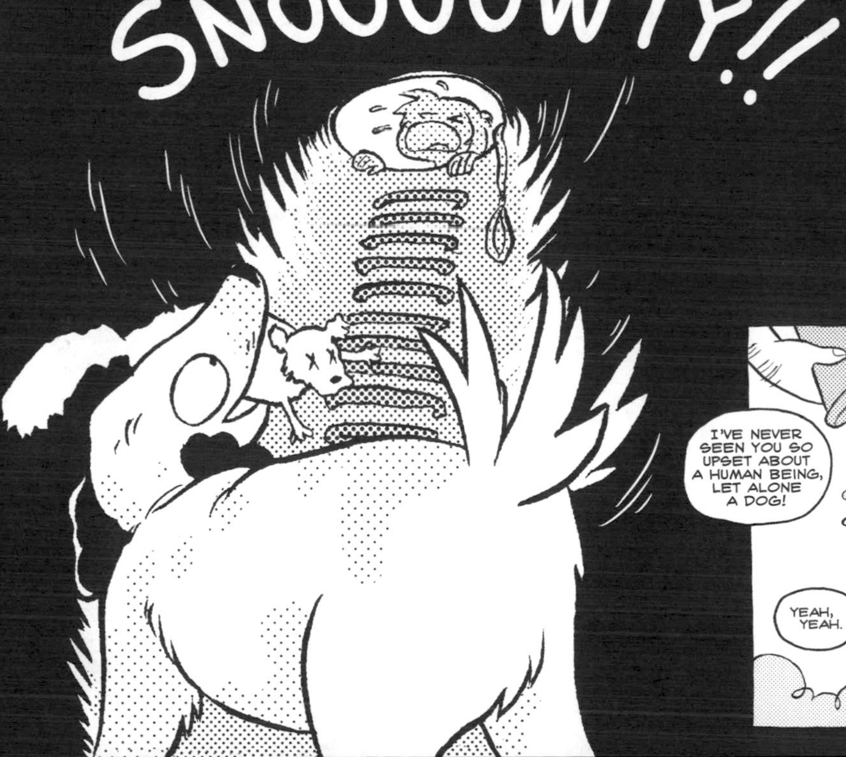
SNOOOOWYY!!

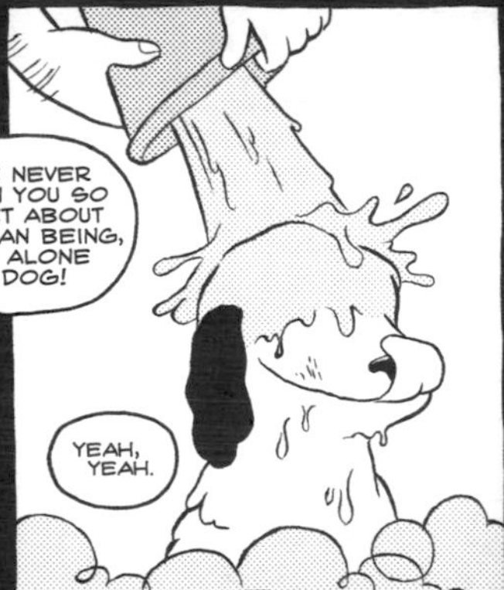
I'VE NEVER SEEN YOU SO UPSET ABOUT A HUMAN BEING, LET ALONE A DOG!
YEAH, YEAH.

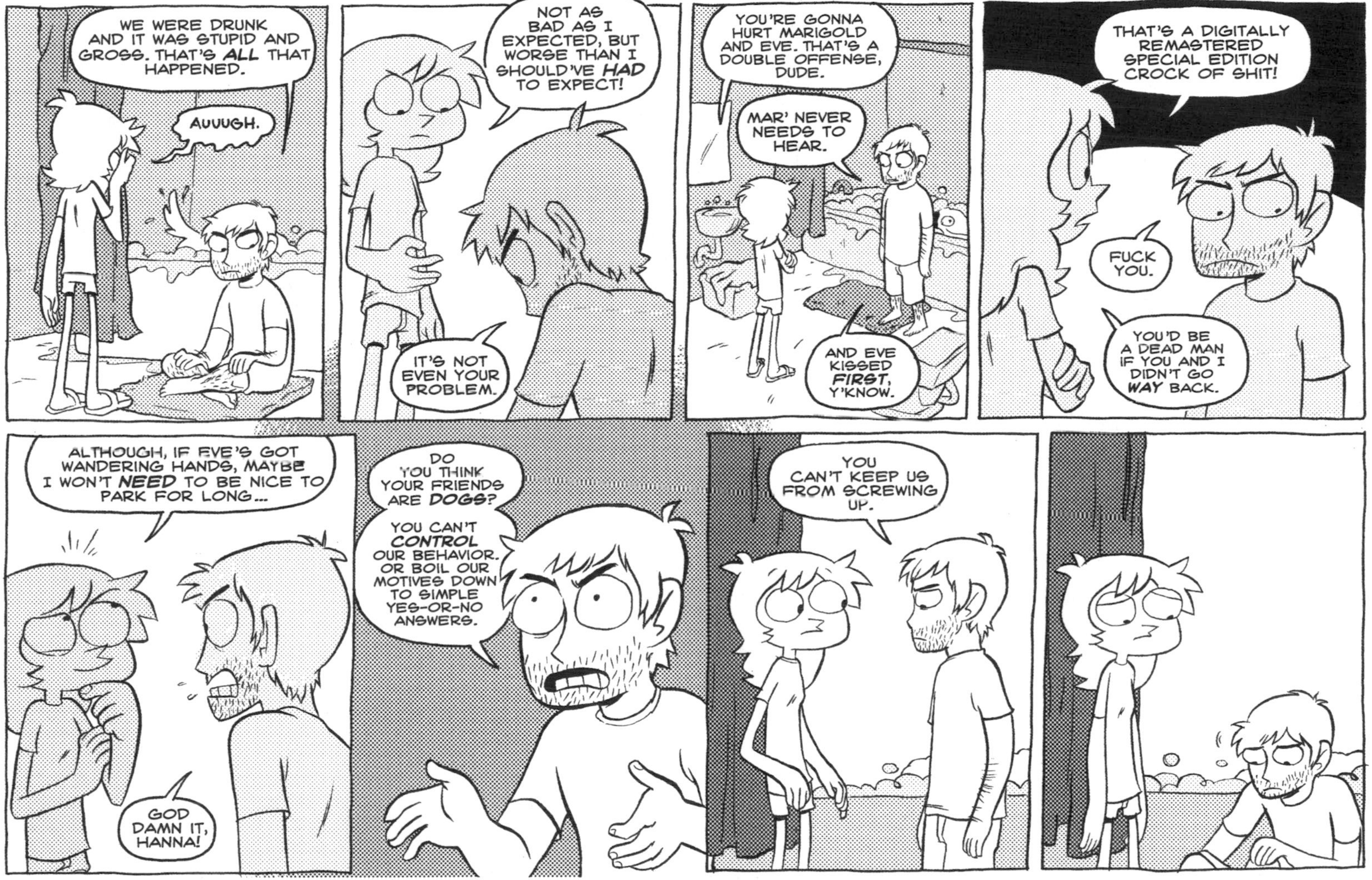
WE WERE DRUNK AND IT WAS STUPID AND GROSS. THAT'S **ALL** THAT HAPPENED.
AUUUGH.
NOT AS BAD AS I EXPECTED, BUT WORSE THAN I SHOULD'VE **HAD** TO EXPECT!
IT'S NOT EVEN YOUR PROBLEM.
YOU'RE GONNA HURT MARIGOLD AND EVE. THAT'S A DOUBLE OFFENSE, DUDE.
MAR' NEVER NEEDS TO HEAR.
AND EVE KISSED **FIRST**, Y'KNOW.
THAT'S A DIGITALLY REMASTERED SPECIAL EDITION CROCK OF SHIT!
FUCK YOU.
YOU'D BE A DEAD MAN IF YOU AND I DIDN'T GO **WAY** BACK.
ALTHOUGH, IF EVE'S GOT WANDERING HANDS, MAYBE I WON'T **NEED** TO BE NICE TO PARK FOR LONG...
GOD DAMN IT, HANNA!
DO YOU THINK YOUR FRIENDS ARE **DOGS**?
YOU CAN'T **CONTROL** OUR BEHAVIOR. OR BOIL OUR MOTIVES DOWN TO SIMPLE YES-OR-NO ANSWERS.
YOU CAN'T KEEP US FROM SCREWING UP.

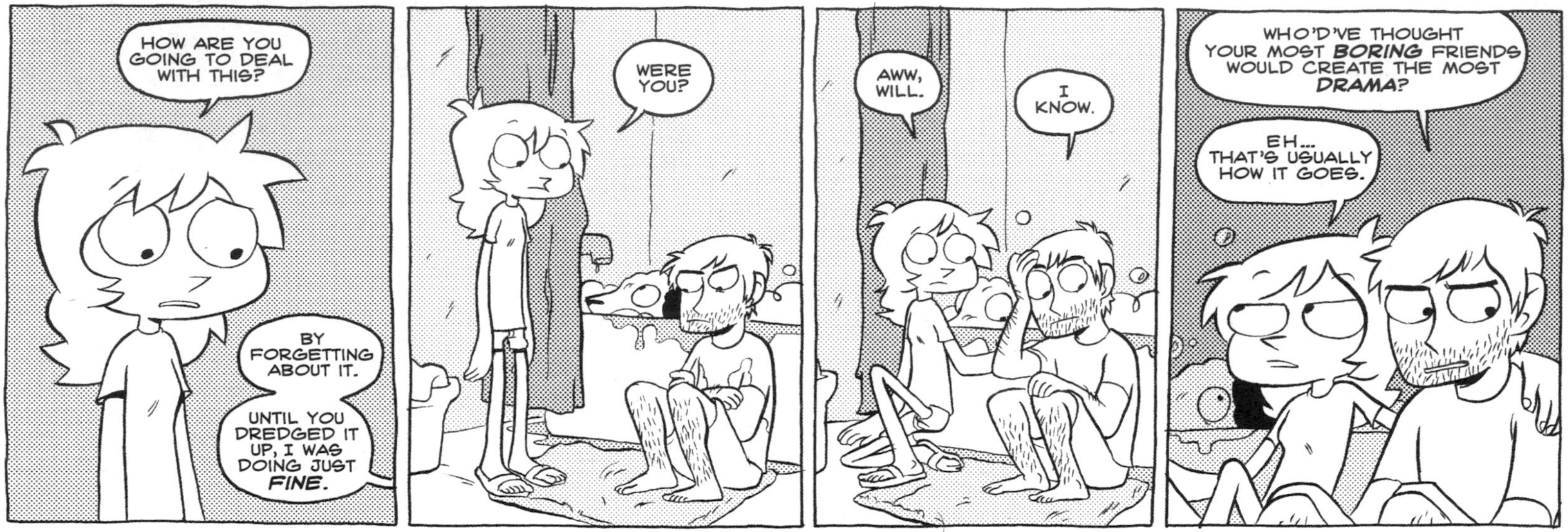
HOW ARE YOU GOING TO DEAL WITH THIS?
BY FORGETTING ABOUT IT.
UNTIL YOU DREDGED IT UP, I WAS DOING JUST **FINE**.
WERE YOU?
AWW, WILL.
I KNOW.
WHO'D'VE THOUGHT YOUR MOST **BORING** FRIENDS WOULD CREATE THE MOST **DRAMA**?
EH... THAT'S USUALLY HOW IT GOES.

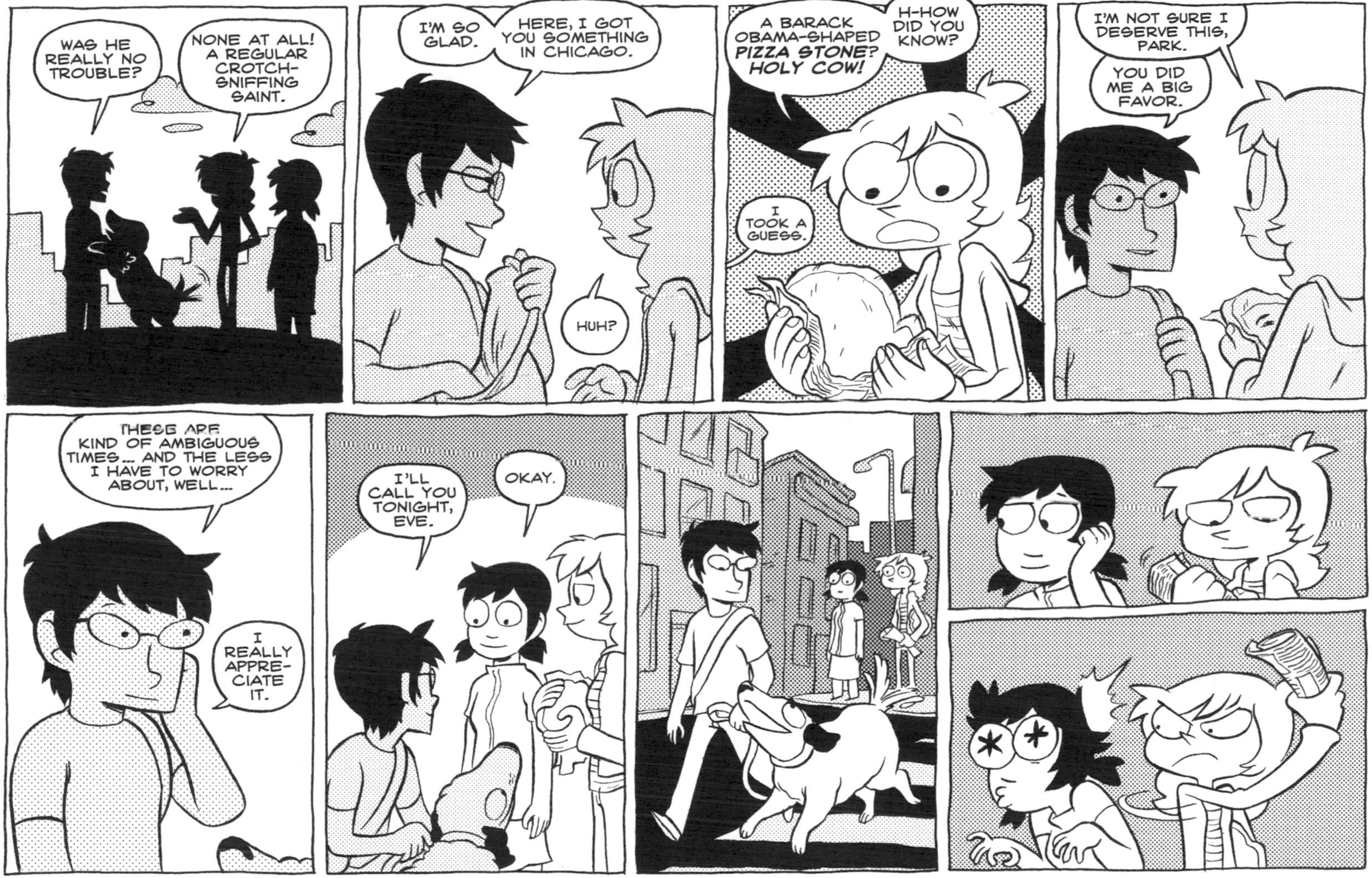

WAS HE REALLY NO TROUBLE?
NONE AT ALL! A REGULAR CROTCH-SNIFFING SAINT.
I'M SO GLAD.
HERE, I GOT YOU SOMETHING IN CHICAGO.
HUH?
A BARACK OBAMA-SHAPED PIZZA STONE? HOLY COW!
H-HOW DID YOU KNOW?
I TOOK A GUESS.
I'M NOT SURE I DESERVE THIS, PARK.
YOU DID ME A BIG FAVOR.
THESE ARE KIND OF AMBIGUOUS TIMES... AND THE LESS I HAVE TO WORRY ABOUT, WELL...
I REALLY APPRECIATE IT.
I'LL CALL YOU TONIGHT, EVE.
OKAY.

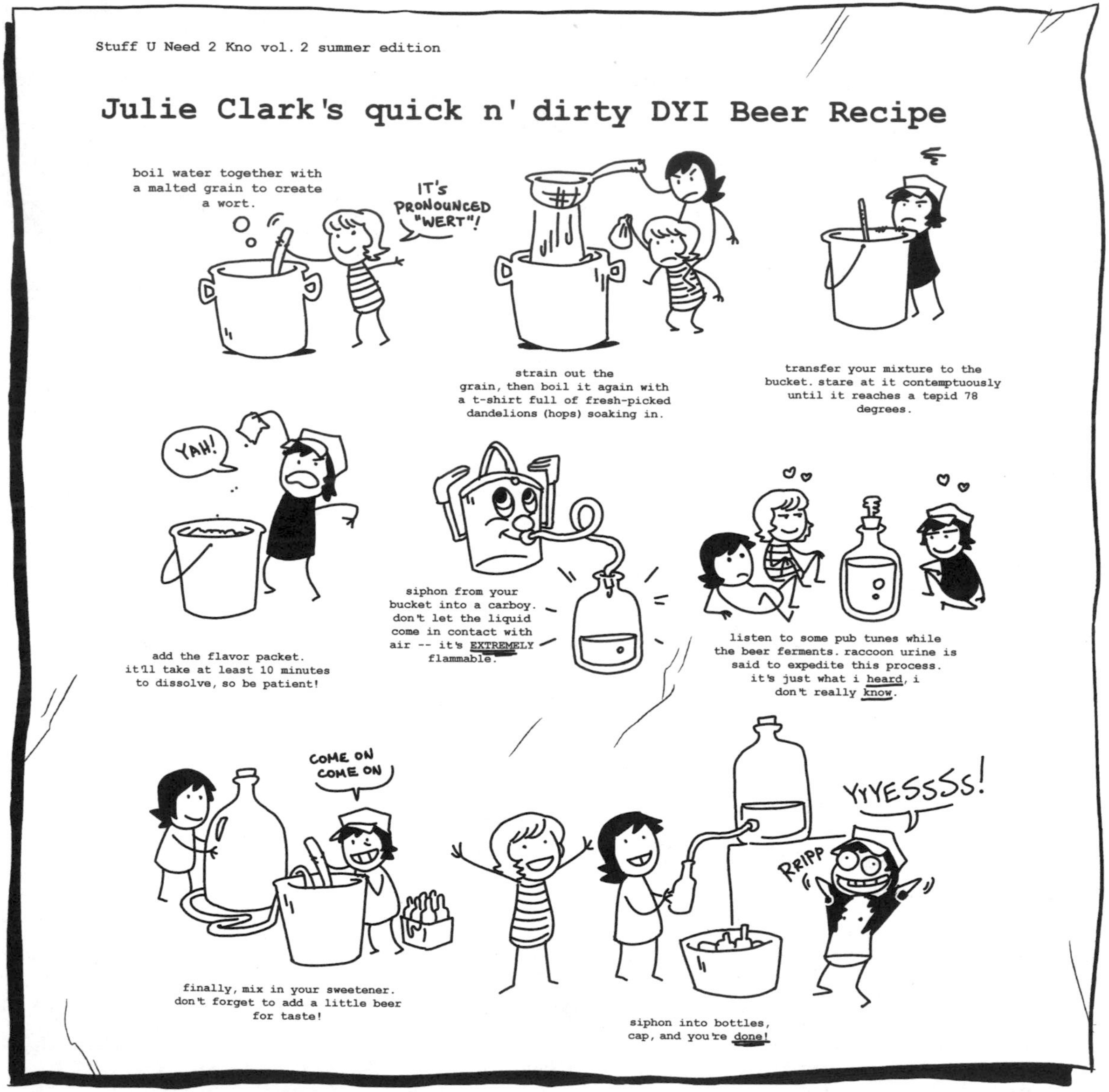
Stuff U Need 2 Kno vol. 2 summer edition
Julie Clark's quick n' dirty DYI Beer Recipe
boil water together with a malted grain to create a wort.
IT'S PRONOUNCED "WERT"!
strain out the grain, then boil it again with a t-shirt full of fresh-picked dandelions (hops) soaking in.
transfer your mixture to the bucket. stare at it contemptuously until it reaches a tepid 78 degrees.
YAH!
add the flavor packet. it'll take at least 10 minutes to dissolve, so be patient!
siphon from your bucket into a carboy. don't let the liquid come in contact with air -- it's EXTREMELY flammable.
listen to some pub tunes while the beer ferments. raccoon urine is said to expedite this process. it's just what i heard, i don't really know.
COME ON COME ON
finally, mix in your sweetener. don't forget to add a little beer for taste!
YYYESSSSS!
RRIPP
siphon into bottles, cap, and you're done!

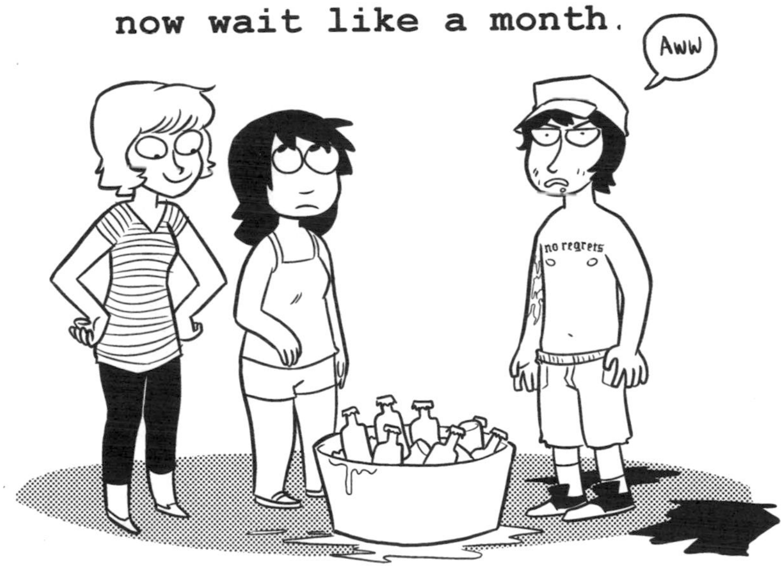
now wait like a month.
AWW
no regrets

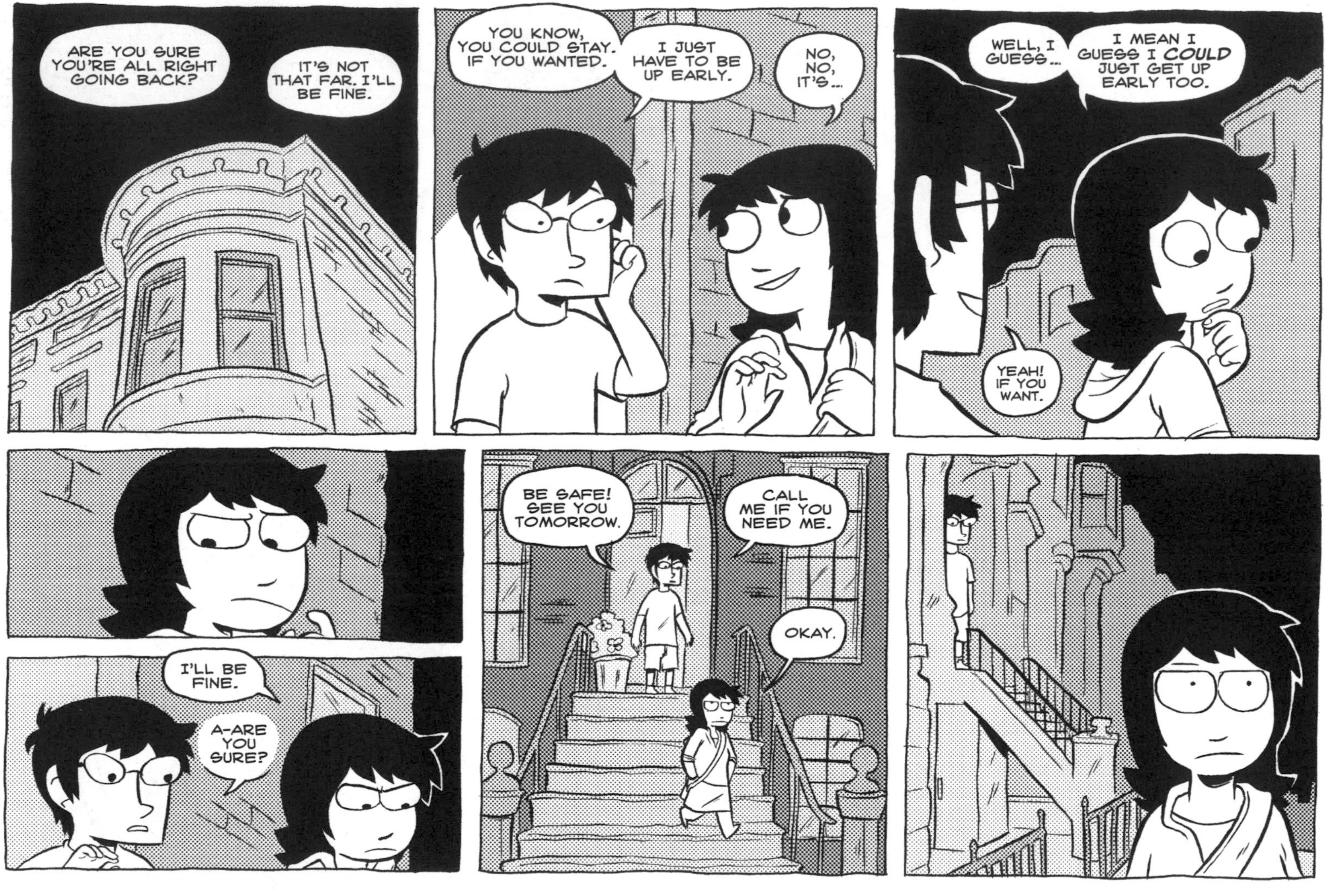
ARE YOU SURE YOU'RE ALL RIGHT GOING BACK?
IT'S NOT THAT FAR. I'LL BE FINE.
YOU KNOW, YOU COULD STAY. IF YOU WANTED.
I JUST HAVE TO BE UP EARLY.
NO, NO, IT'S...
WELL, I GUESS...
I MEAN I GUESS I *COULD* JUST GET UP EARLY TOO.
YEAH! IF YOU WANT.
I'LL BE FINE.
A-ARE YOU SURE?
BE SAFE! SEE YOU TOMORROW.
CALL ME IF YOU NEED ME.
OKAY.

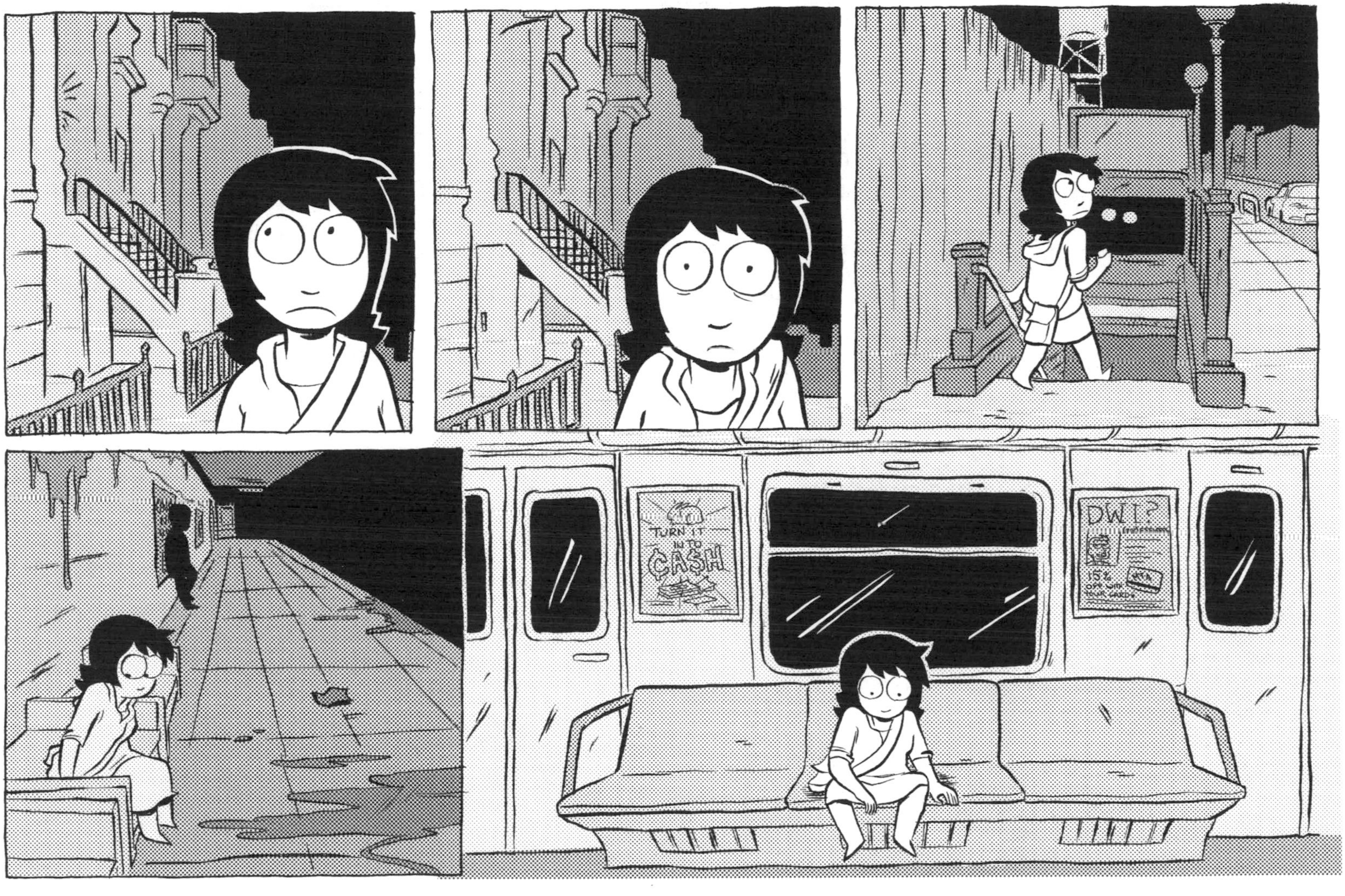
TURN IT INTO CASH
DWI?
15%
OFF WITH YOUR CARD

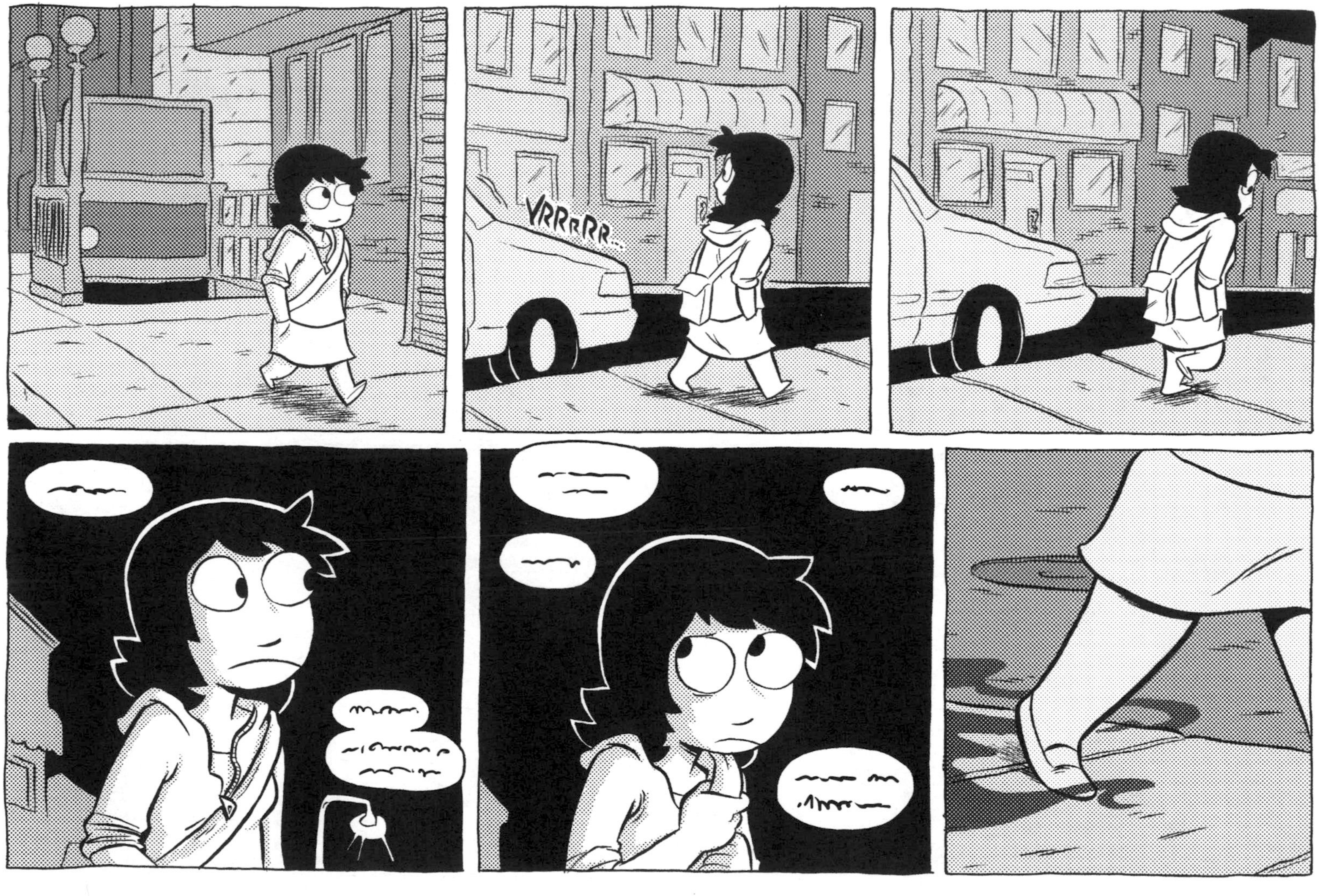
VRRrRRR...

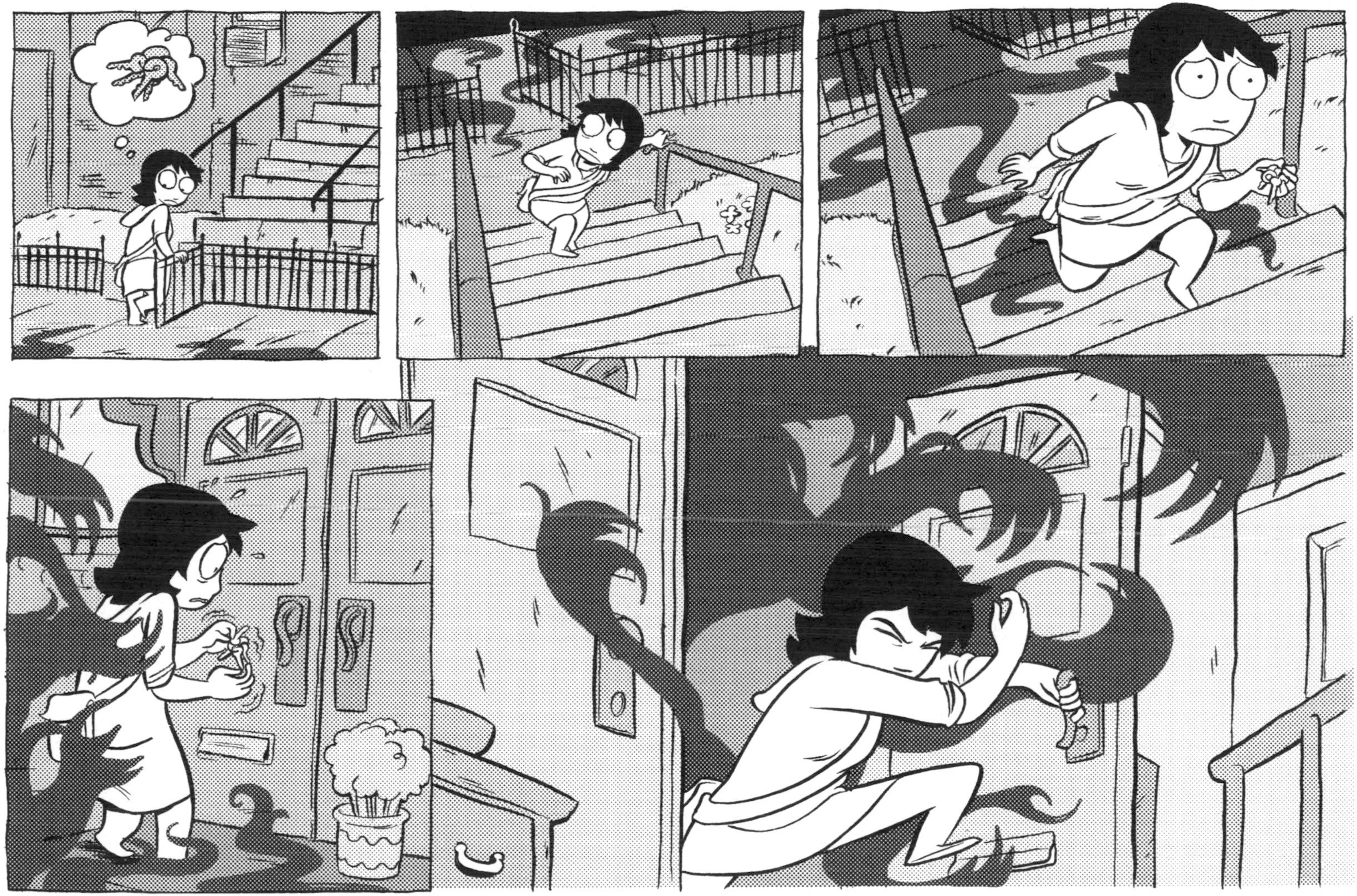

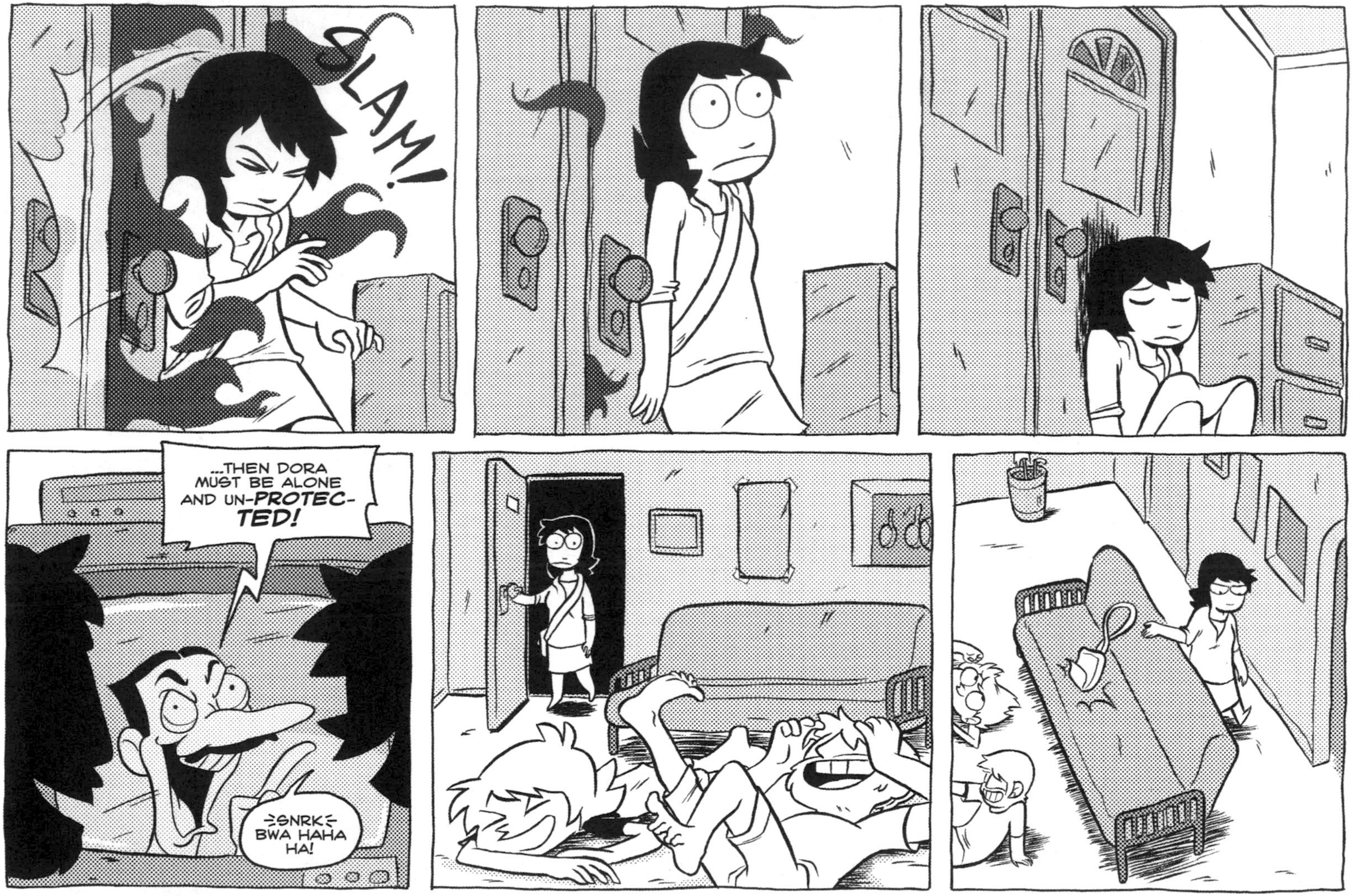
SLAM!
...THEN DORA MUST BE ALONE AND UN-PROTEC-TED!
=SNRK= BWA HAHA HA!

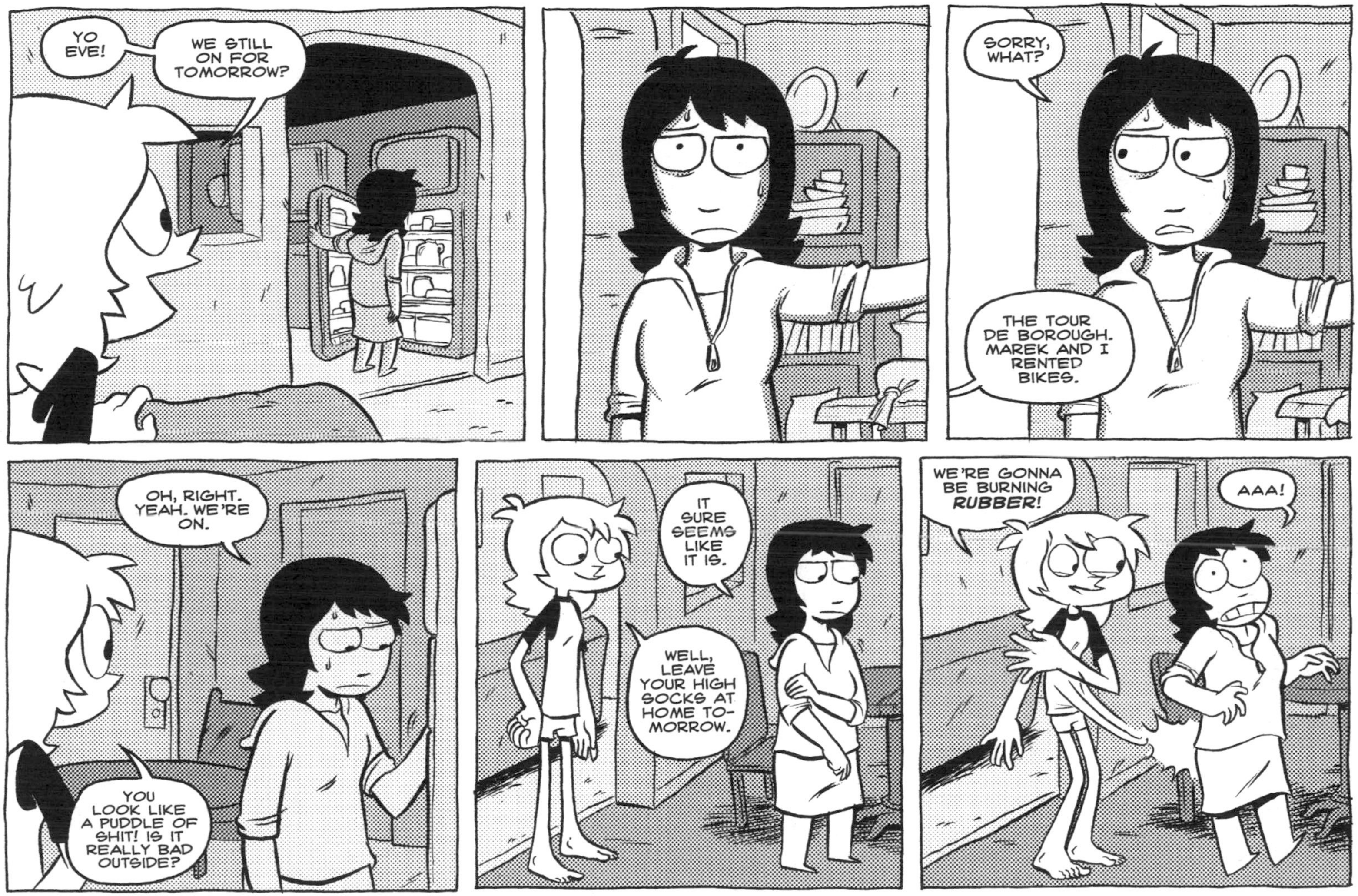
YO EVE!
WE STILL ON FOR TOMORROW?
SORRY, WHAT?
THE TOUR DE BOROUGH. MAREK AND I RENTED BIKES.
OH, RIGHT. YEAH. WE'RE ON.
YOU LOOK LIKE A PUDDLE OF SHIT! IS IT REALLY BAD OUTSIDE?
IT SURE SEEMS LIKE IT IS.
WELL, LEAVE YOUR HIGH SOCKS AT HOME TOMORROW.
WE'RE GONNA BE BURNING ***RUBBER***!
AAA!

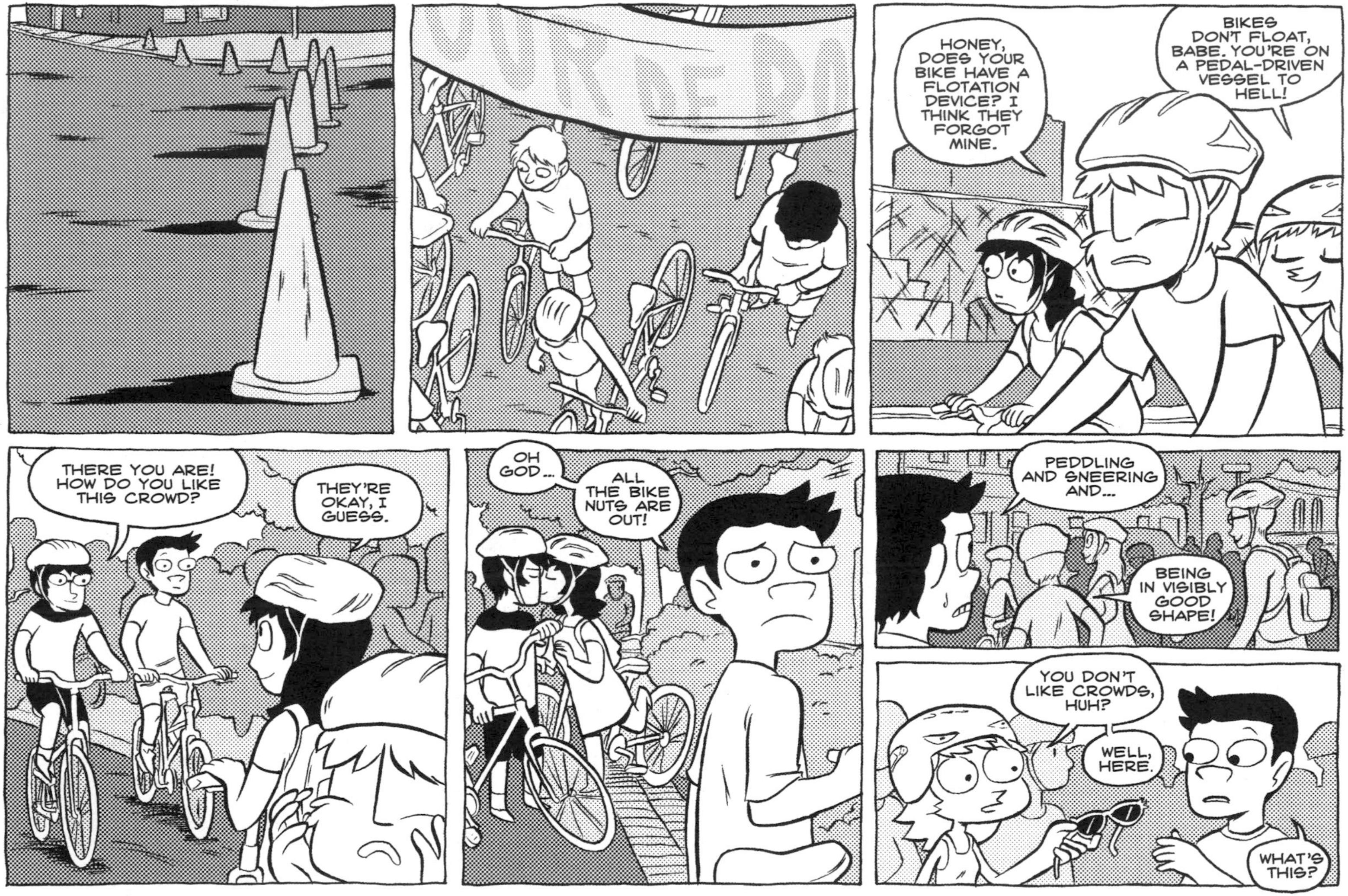
HONEY, DOES YOUR BIKE HAVE A FLOTATION DEVICE? I THINK THEY FORGOT MINE.
BIKES DON'T FLOAT, BABE. YOU'RE ON A PEDAL-DRIVEN VESSEL TO HELL!
THERE YOU ARE! HOW DO YOU LIKE THIS CROWD?
THEY'RE OKAY, I GUESS.
OH GOD...
ALL THE BIKE NUTS ARE OUT!
PEDDLING AND SNEERING AND...
BEING IN VISIBLY GOOD SHAPE!
YOU DON'T LIKE CROWDS, HUH?
WELL, HERE.
WHAT'S THIS?

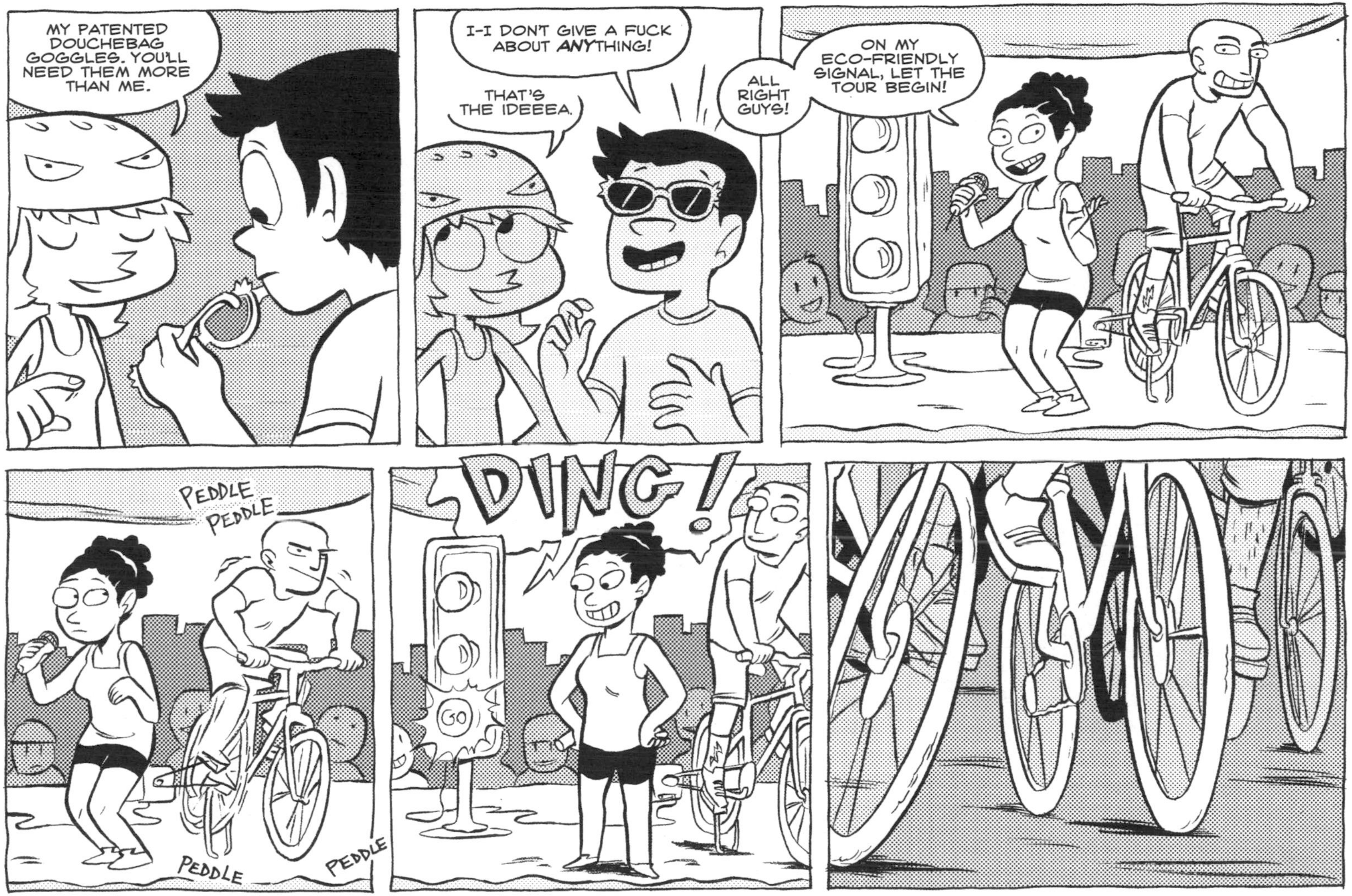
MY PATENTED DOUCHEBAG GOGGLES. YOU'LL NEED THEM MORE THAN ME.
I-I DON'T GIVE A FUCK ABOUT ANYTHING!
THAT'S THE IDEEEA.
ALL RIGHT GUYS!
ON MY ECO-FRIENDLY SIGNAL, LET THE TOUR BEGIN!
PEDDLE PEDDLE
PEDDLE
PEDDLE
DING!
GO

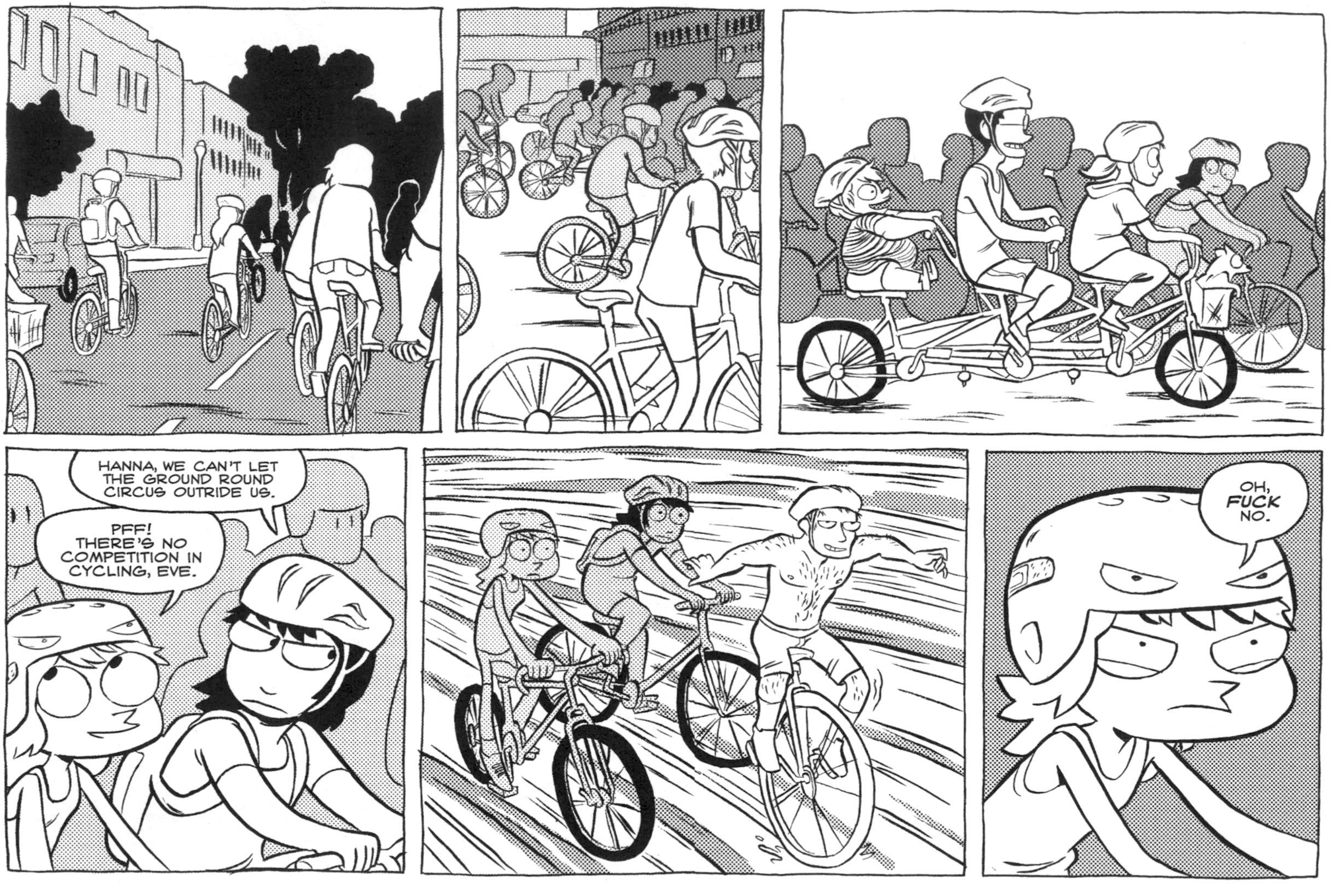
HANNA, WE CAN'T LET THE GROUND ROUND CIRCUS OUTRIDE US.
PFF! THERE'S NO COMPETITION IN CYCLING, EVE.
OH, FUCK NO.

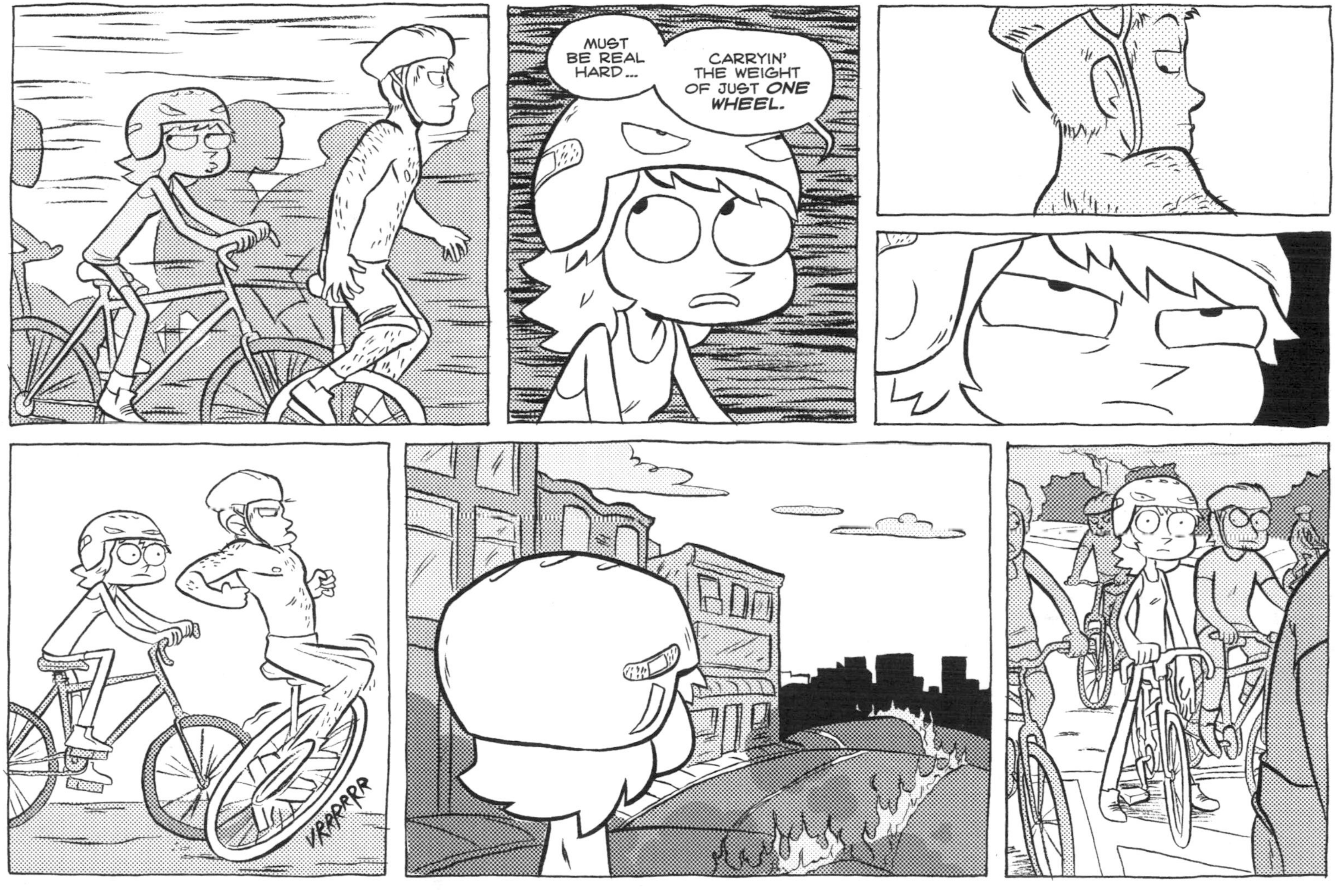
MUST BE REAL HARD...
CARRYIN' THE WEIGHT OF JUST ONE WHEEL.
VRRRRRR

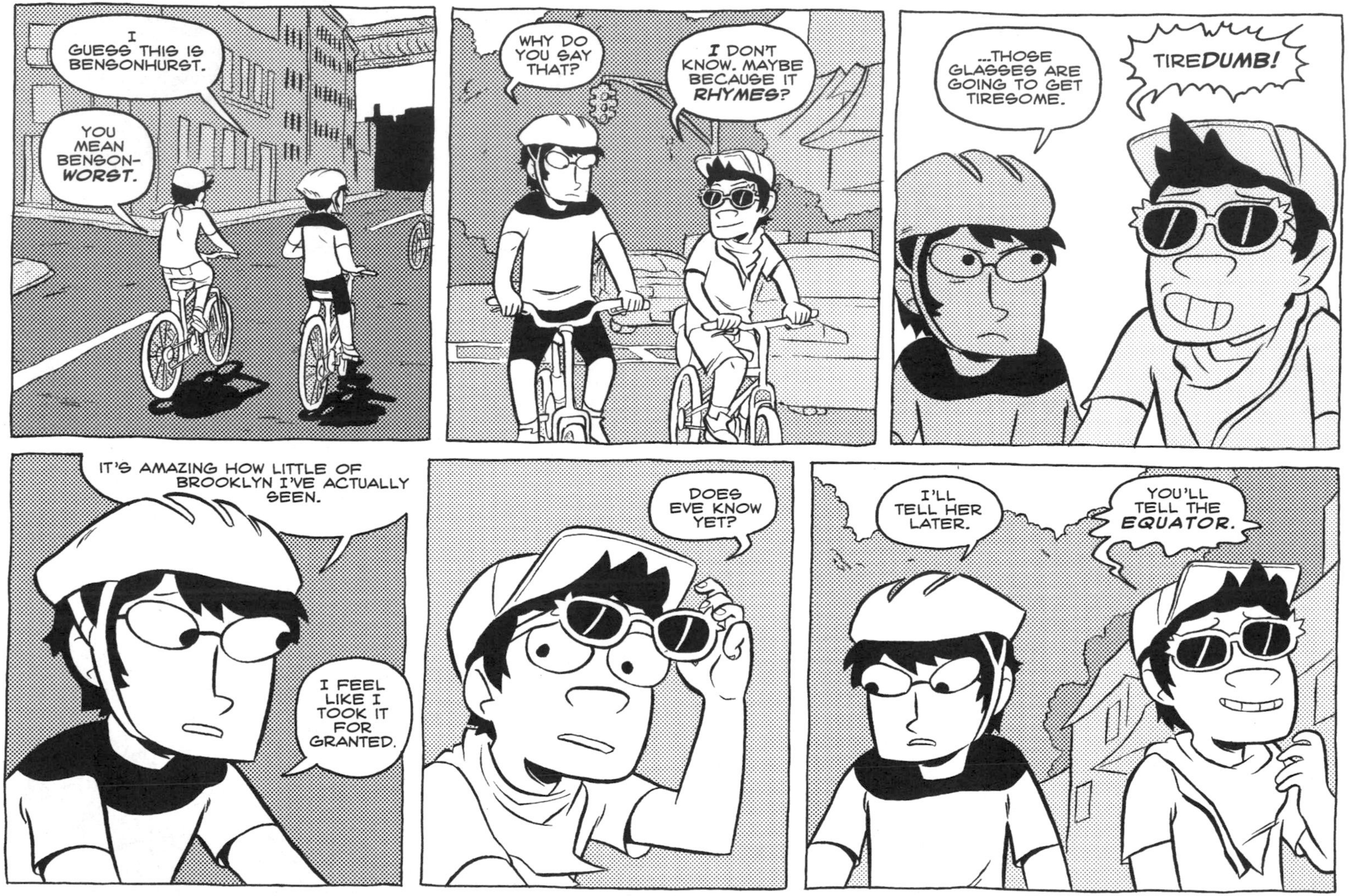
I GUESS THIS IS BENSONHURST.
YOU MEAN BENSON-*WORST*.
WHY DO YOU SAY THAT?
I DON'T KNOW. MAYBE BECAUSE IT *RHYMES*?
...THOSE GLASSES ARE GOING TO GET TIRESOME.
TIRE*DUMB!*
IT'S AMAZING HOW LITTLE OF BROOKLYN I'VE ACTUALLY SEEN.
I FEEL LIKE I TOOK IT FOR GRANTED.
DOES EVE KNOW YET?
I'LL TELL HER LATER.
YOU'LL TELL THE *EQUATOR*.

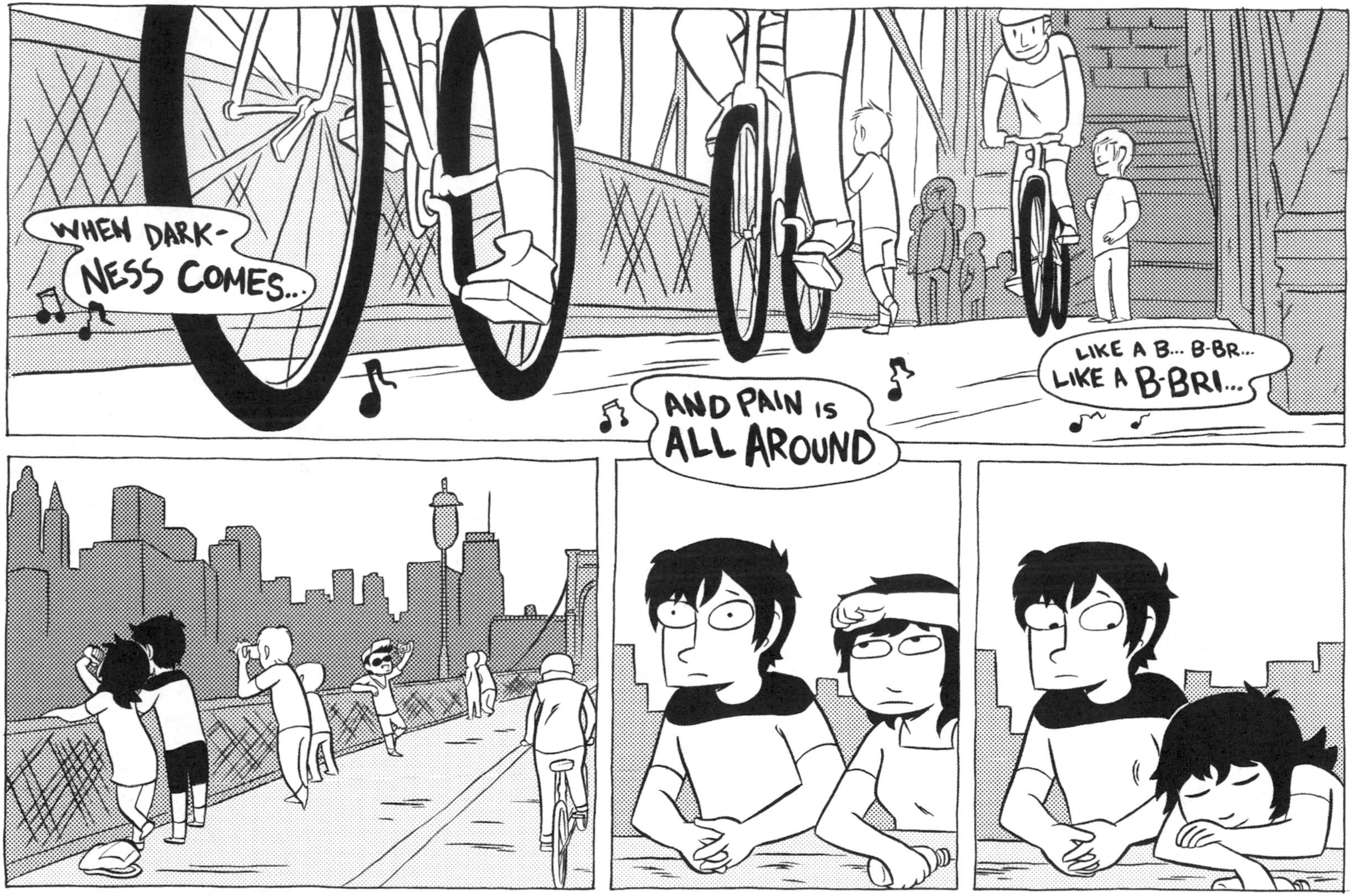
WHEN DARK-NESS COMES...
AND PAIN IS ALL AROUND
LIKE A B... B-BR... LIKE A B-BRI...

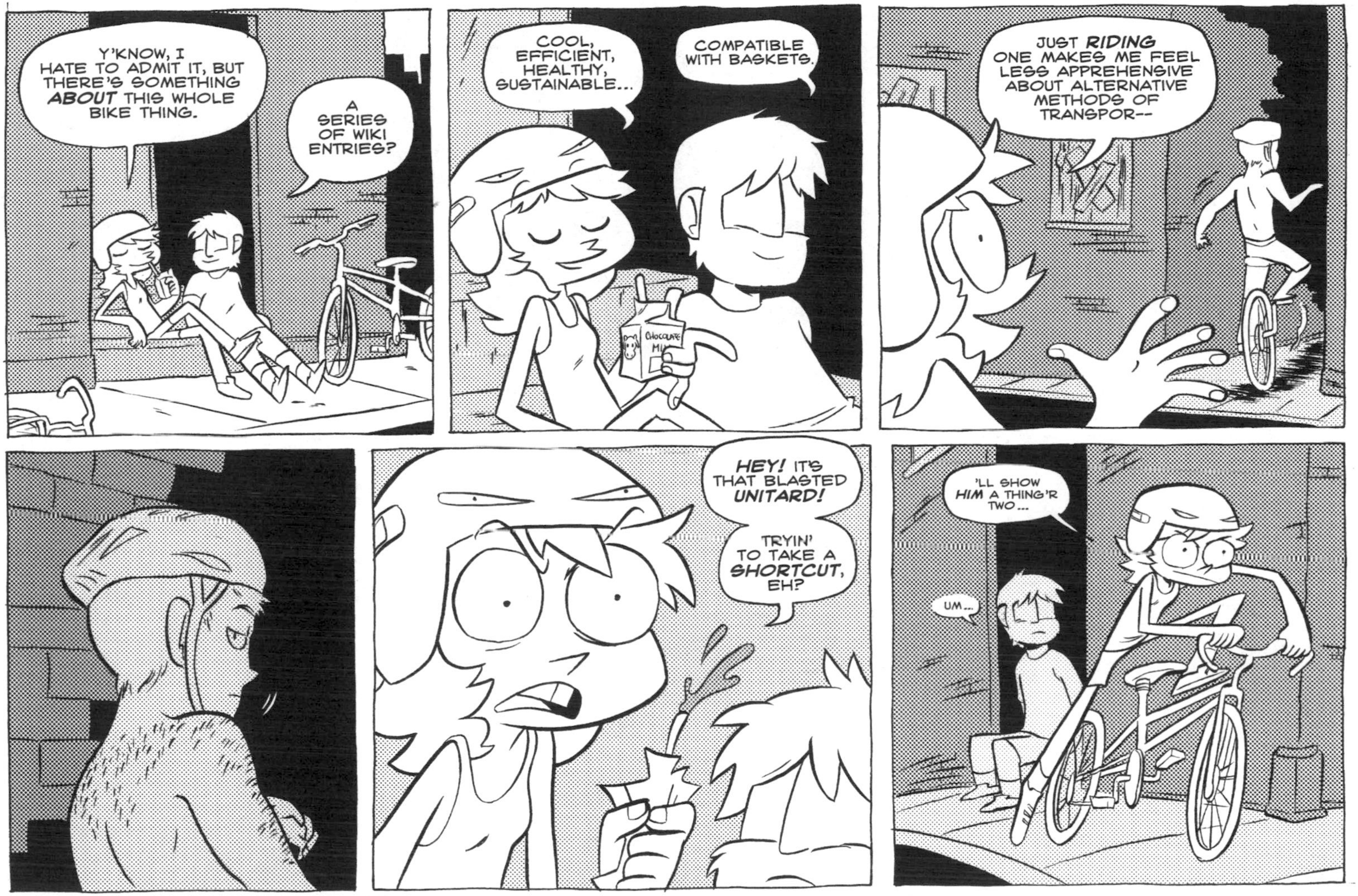

Y'KNOW, I HATE TO ADMIT IT, BUT THERE'S SOMETHING ABOUT THIS WHOLE BIKE THING.
A SERIES OF WIKI ENTRIES?
COOL, EFFICIENT, HEALTHY, SUSTAINABLE...
COMPATIBLE WITH BASKETS.
CHOCOLATE MIL
JUST RIDING ONE MAKES ME FEEL LESS APPREHENSIVE ABOUT ALTERNATIVE METHODS OF TRANSPOR--
HEY! IT'S THAT BLASTED UNITARD!
TRYIN' TO TAKE A SHORTCUT, EH?
'LL SHOW HIM A THING'R TWO...
UM...

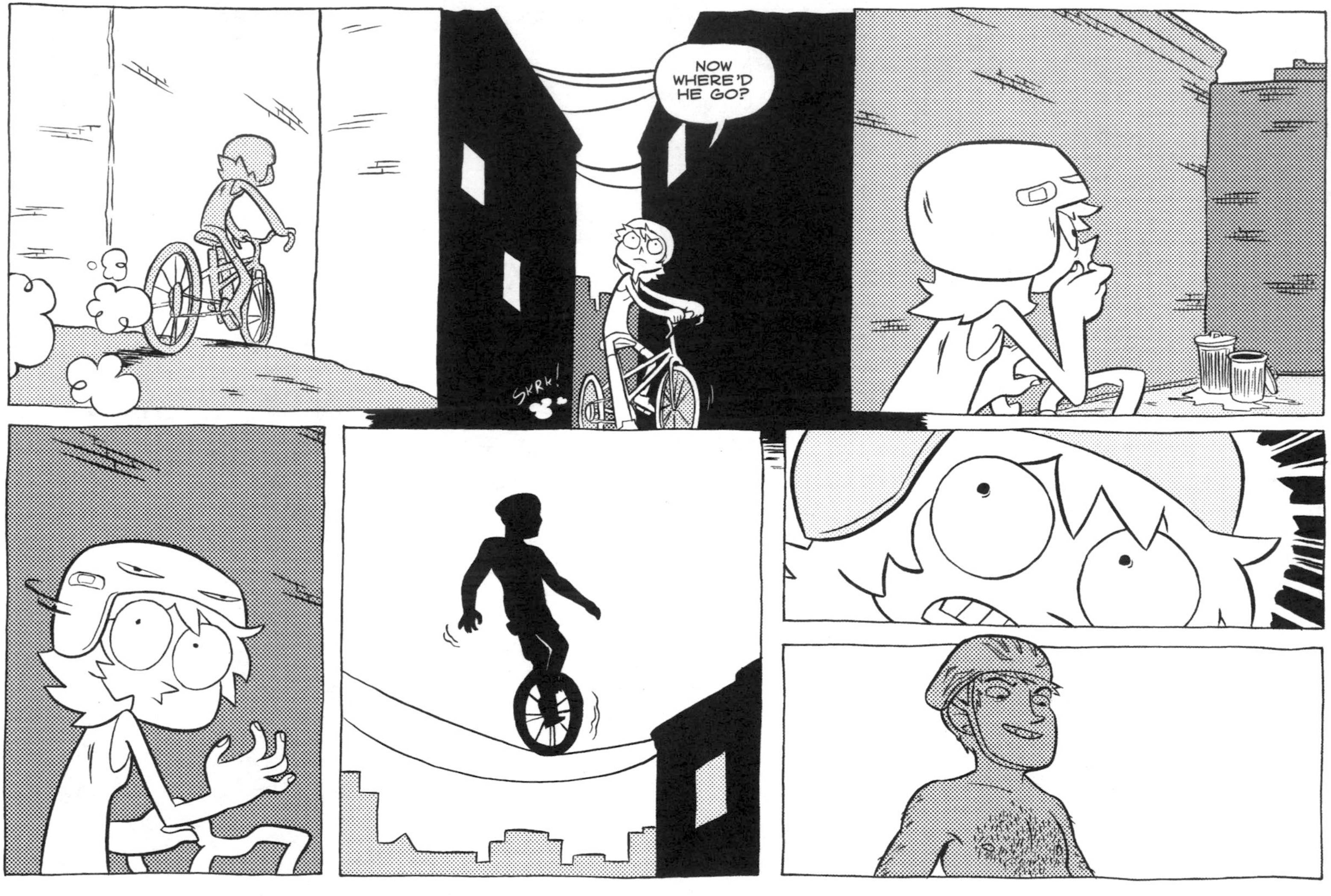
NOW WHERE'D HE GO?
SKRK!

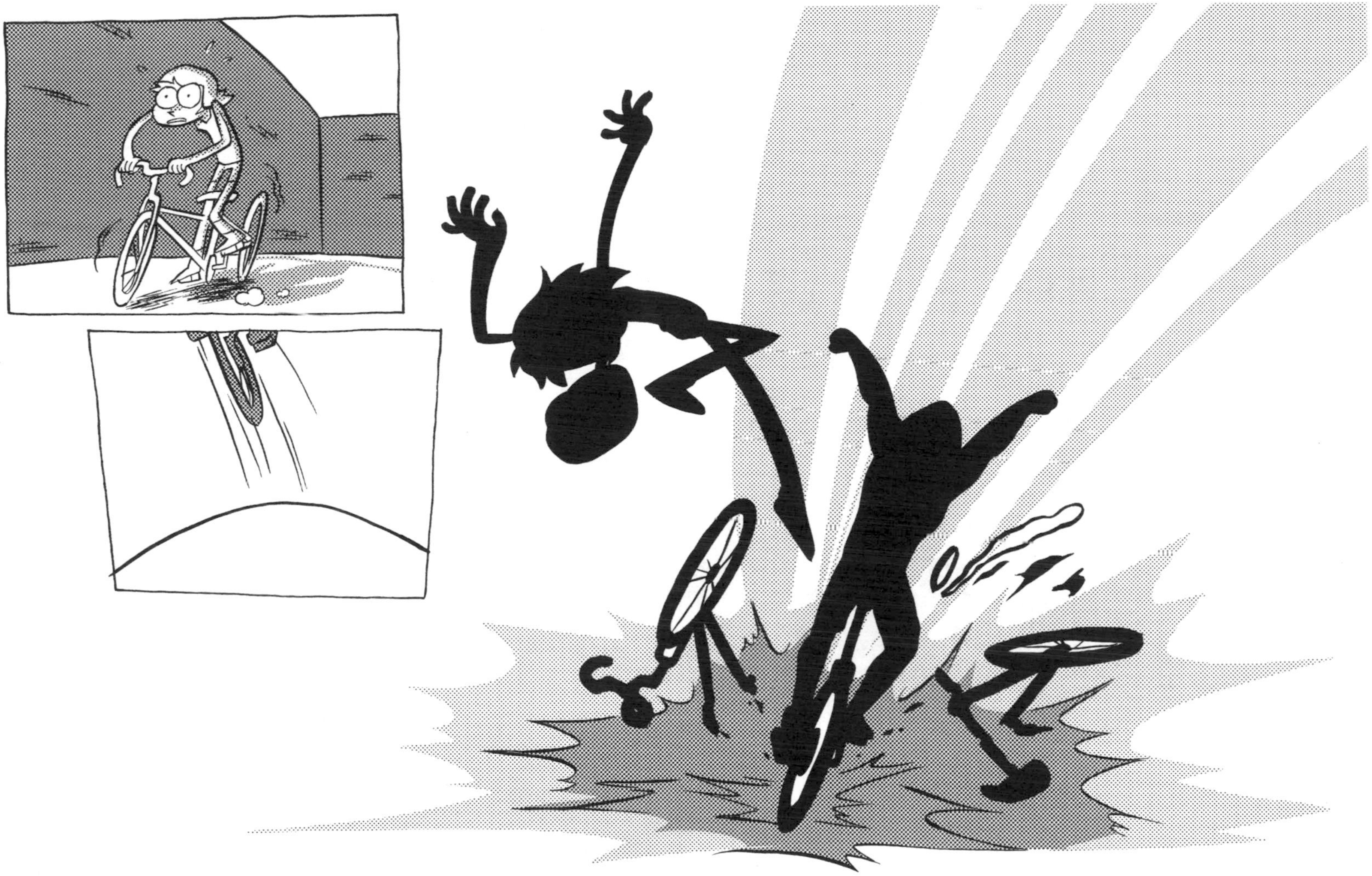

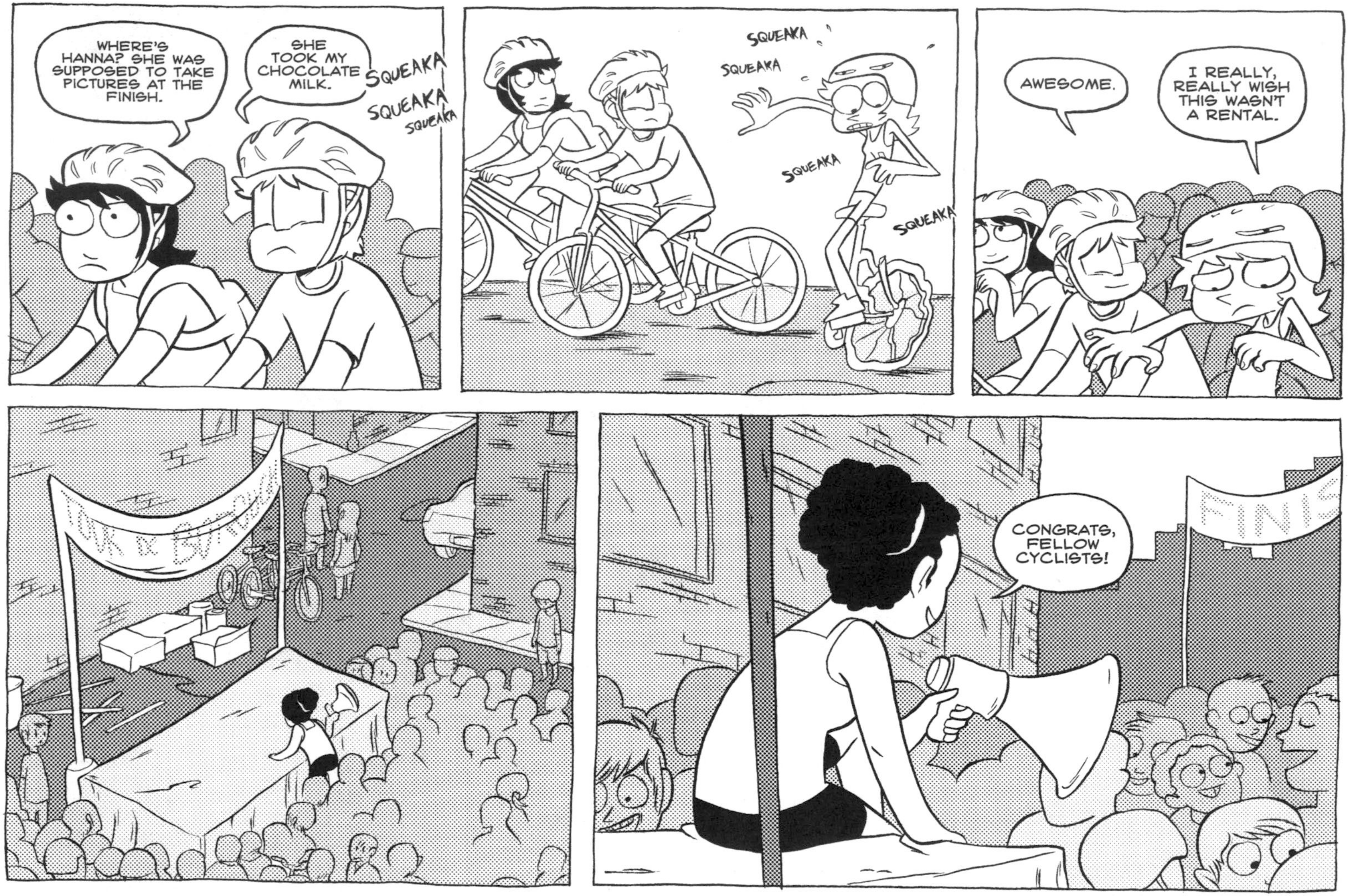
WHERE'S HANNA? SHE WAS SUPPOSED TO TAKE PICTURES AT THE FINISH.
SHE TOOK MY CHOCOLATE MILK.
SQUEAKA
SQUEAKA
SQUEAKA
SQUEAKA
SQUEAKA
SQUEAKA
SQUEAKA
AWESOME.
I REALLY, REALLY WISH THIS WASN'T A RENTAL.
CONGRATS, FELLOW CYCLISTS!

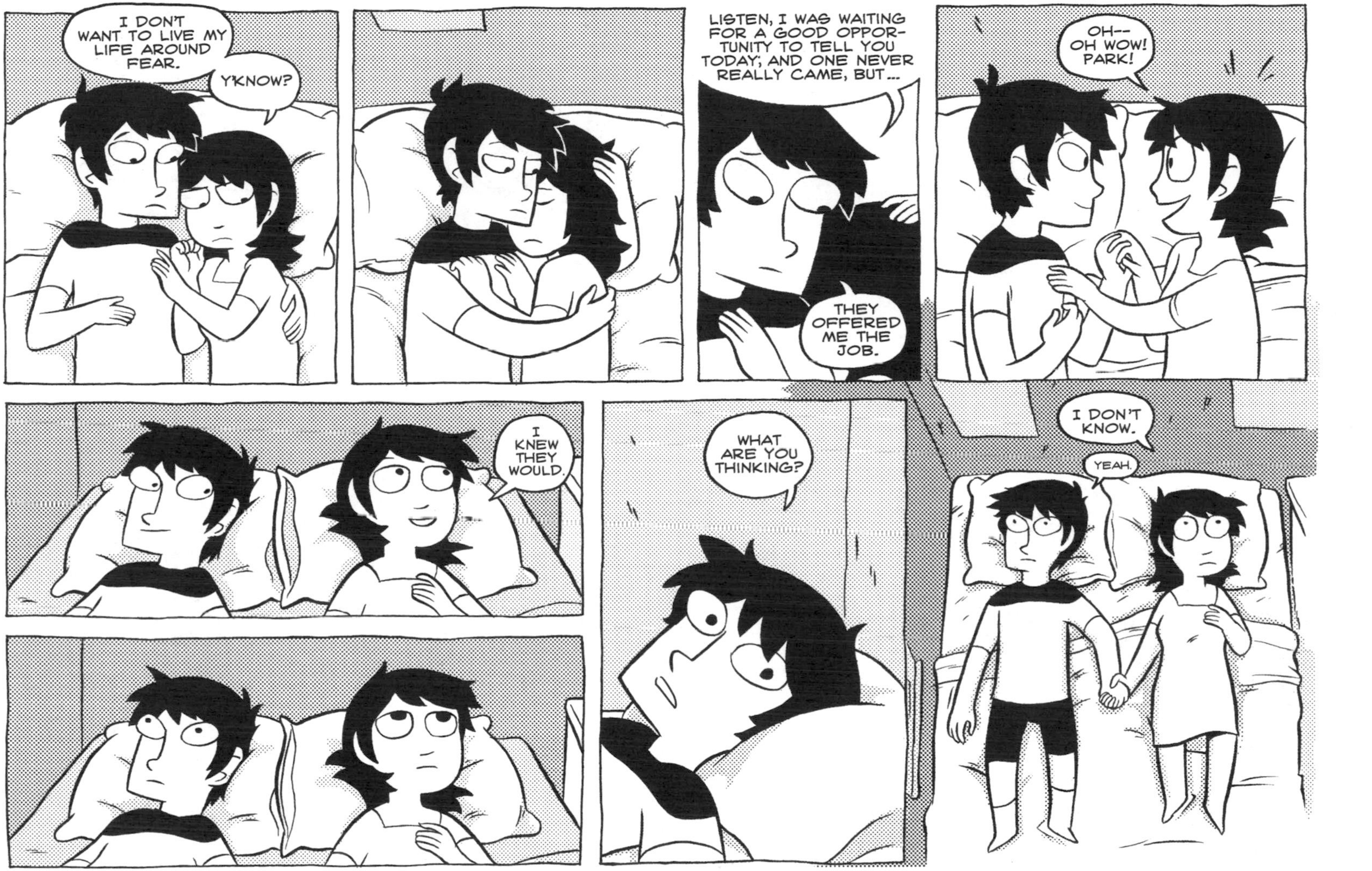
I DON'T WANT TO LIVE MY LIFE AROUND FEAR.
Y'KNOW?
LISTEN, I WAS WAITING FOR A GOOD OPPOR-TUNITY TO TELL YOU TODAY; AND ONE NEVER REALLY CAME, BUT...
THEY OFFERED ME THE JOB.
OH-- OH WOW! PARK!
I KNEW THEY WOULD.
WHAT ARE YOU THINKING?
I DON'T KNOW.
YEAH.

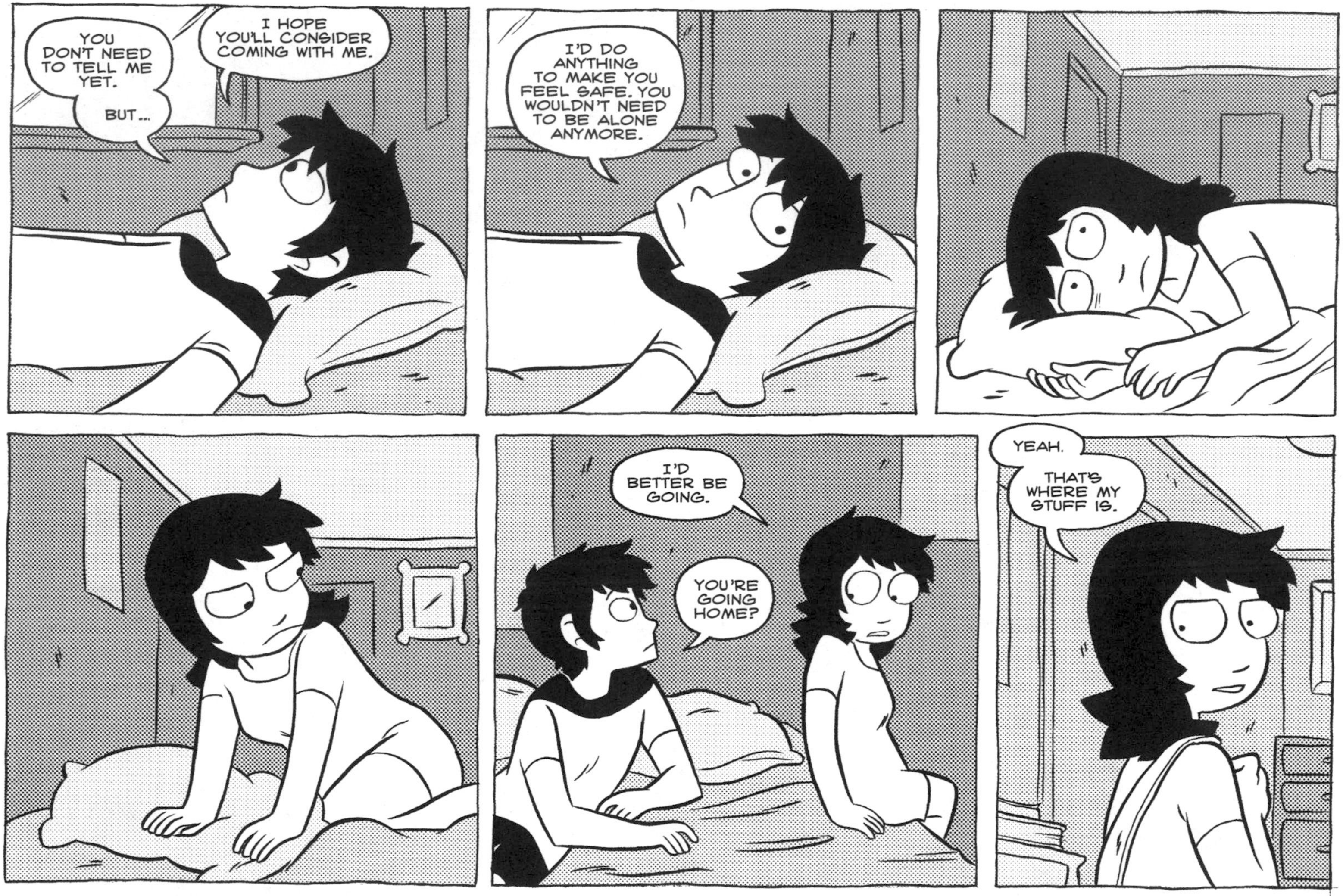
YOU DON'T NEED TO TELL ME YET.
BUT...
I HOPE YOU'LL CONSIDER COMING WITH ME.
I'D DO ANYTHING TO MAKE YOU FEEL SAFE. YOU WOULDN'T NEED TO BE ALONE ANYMORE.
I'D BETTER BE GOING.
YOU'RE GOING HOME?
YEAH.
THAT'S WHERE MY STUFF IS.

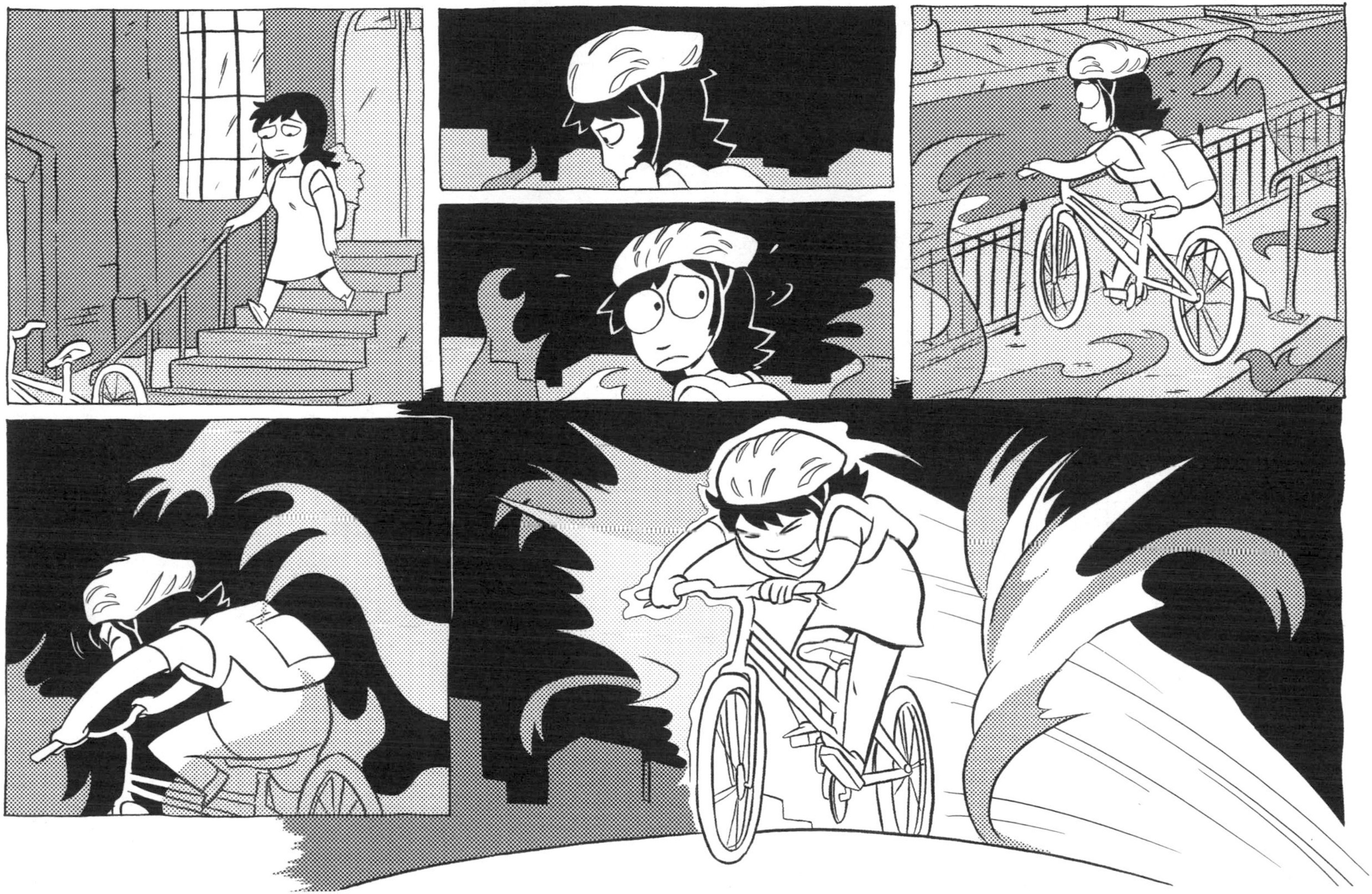

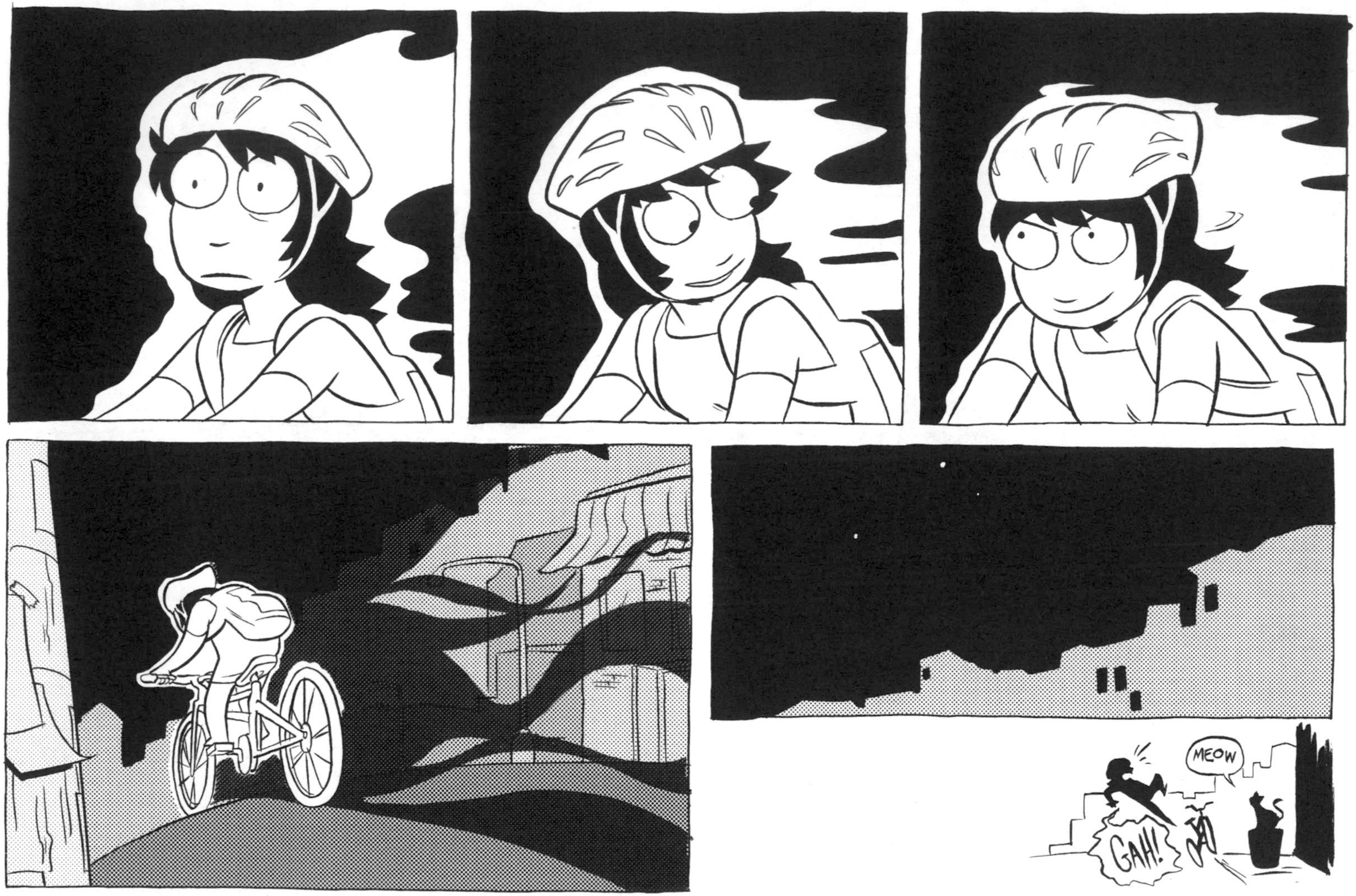
MEOW
GAH!

139

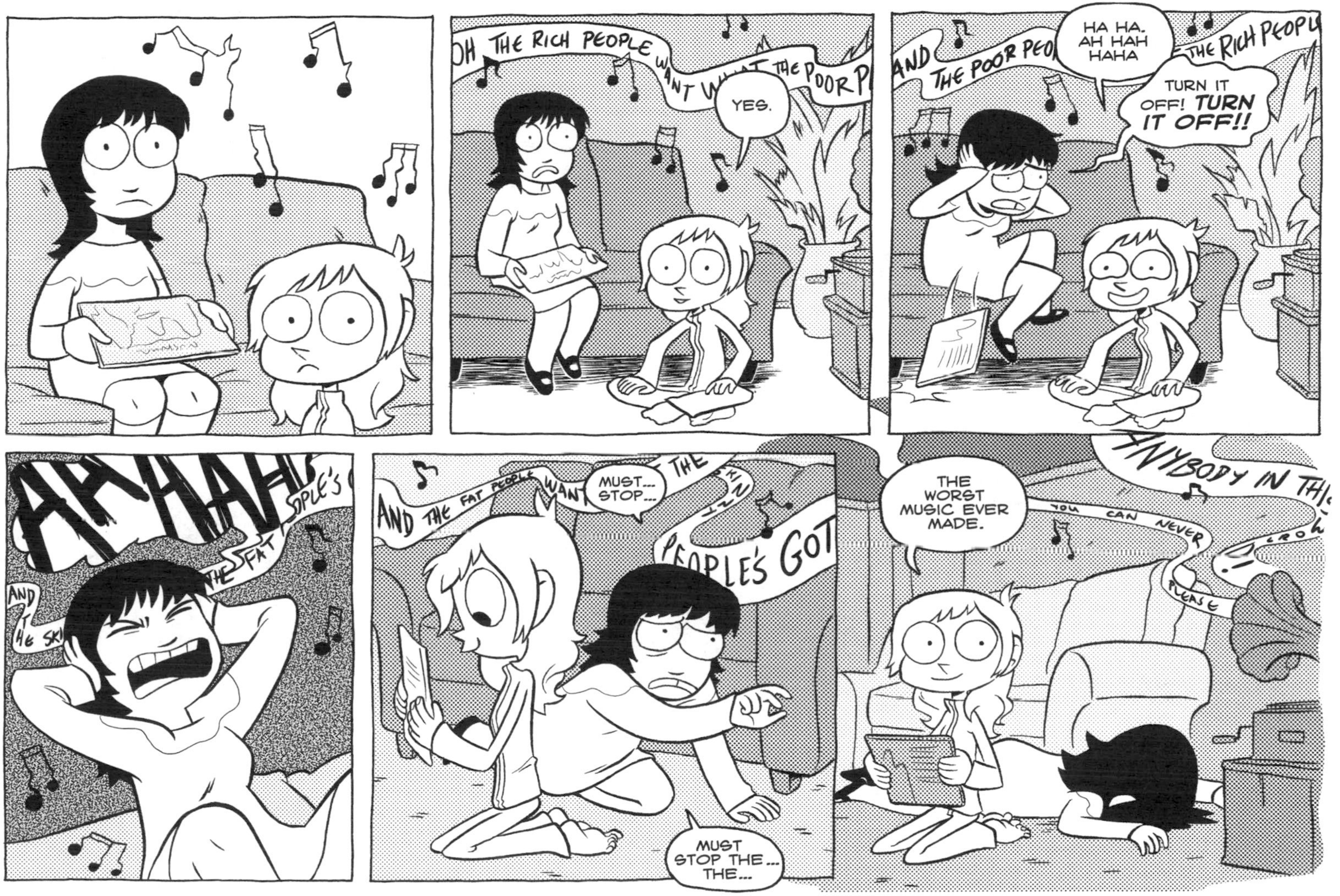
OH THE RICH PEOPLE WANT WHAT THE POOR P
YES.
AND THE POOR PEO
HA HA. AH HAH HAHA
THE RICH PEOPL
TURN IT OFF! TURN IT OFF!!
AHHAHH
AND THE SKI
THE FAT PEOPLE'S
AND THE FAT PEOPLE WANT THE
MUST... STOP...
PEOPLE'S GOT
MUST STOP THE... THE...
THE WORST MUSIC EVER MADE.
ANYBODY IN THI
YOU CAN NEVER PLEASE

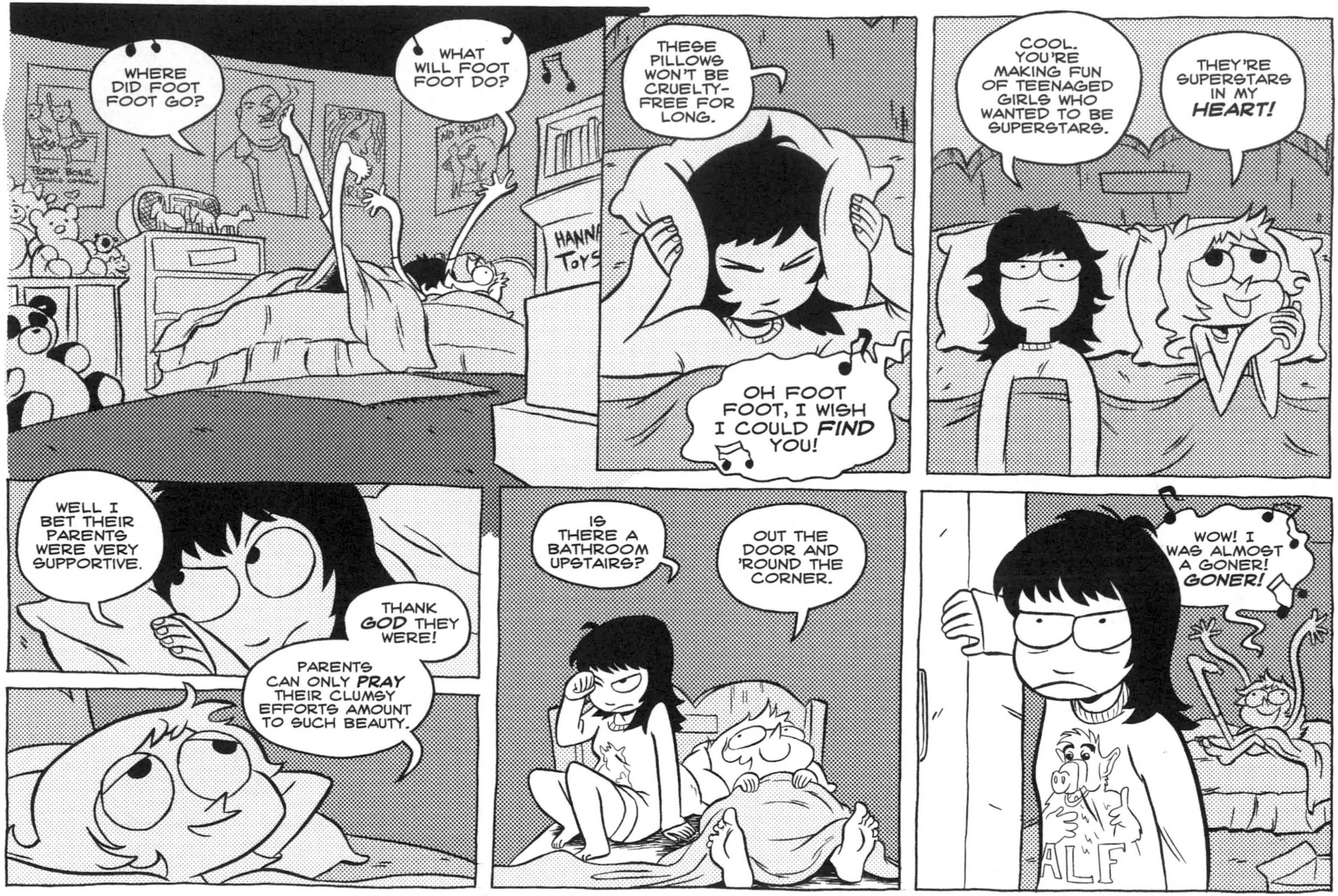
WHERE DID FOOT FOOT GO?
WHAT WILL FOOT FOOT DO?
HANNA TOYS
THESE PILLOWS WON'T BE CRUELTY-FREE FOR LONG.
OH FOOT FOOT, I WISH I COULD FIND YOU!
COOL. YOU'RE MAKING FUN OF TEENAGED GIRLS WHO WANTED TO BE SUPERSTARS.
THEY'RE SUPERSTARS IN MY HEART!
WELL I BET THEIR PARENTS WERE VERY SUPPORTIVE.
THANK GOD THEY WERE!
PARENTS CAN ONLY PRAY THEIR CLUMSY EFFORTS AMOUNT TO SUCH BEAUTY.
IS THERE A BATHROOM UPSTAIRS?
OUT THE DOOR AND 'ROUND THE CORNER.
WOW! I WAS ALMOST A GONER! GONER!
ALF

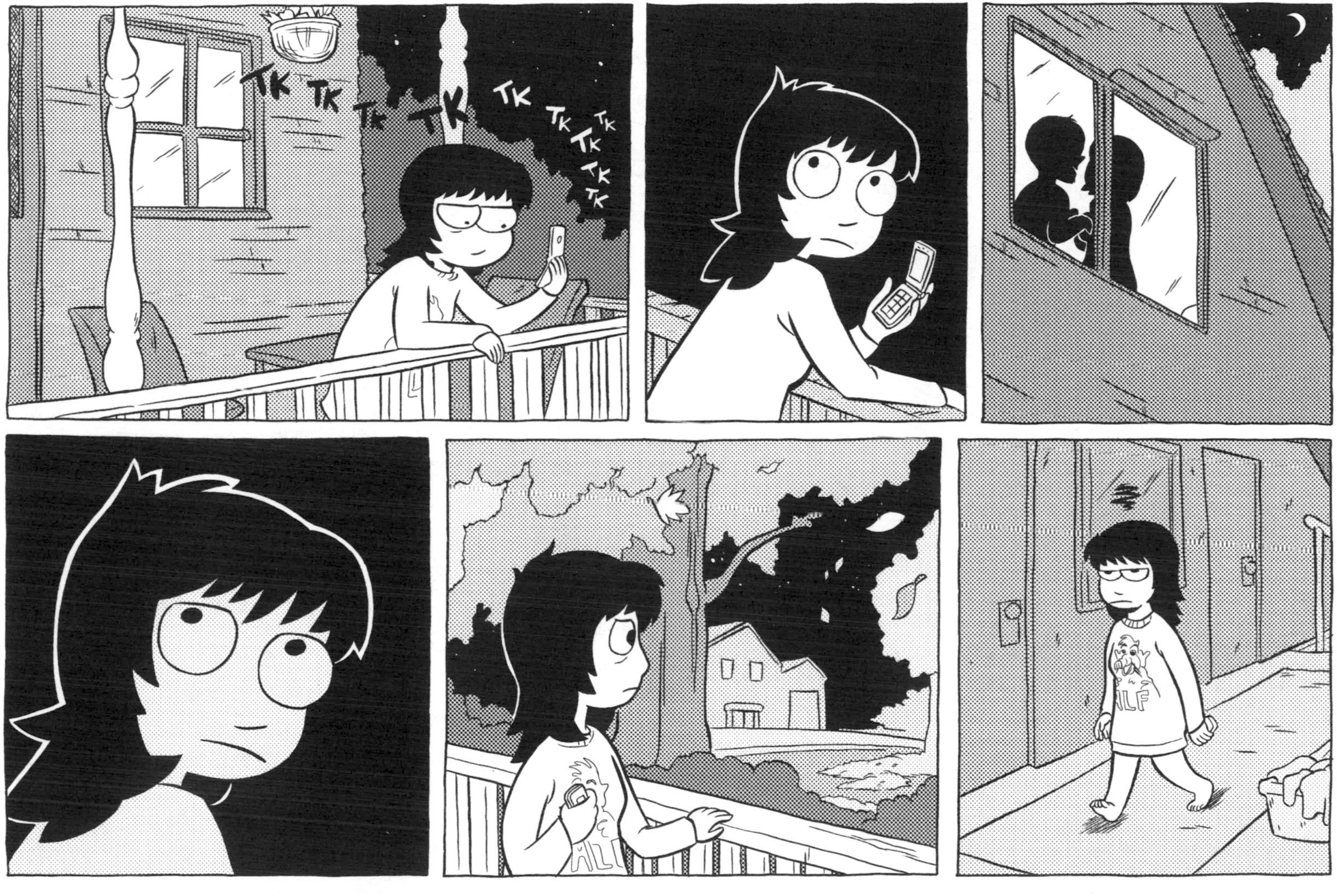
TK TK TK TK TK TK TK TK TK TK TK
ALF
ALF

144

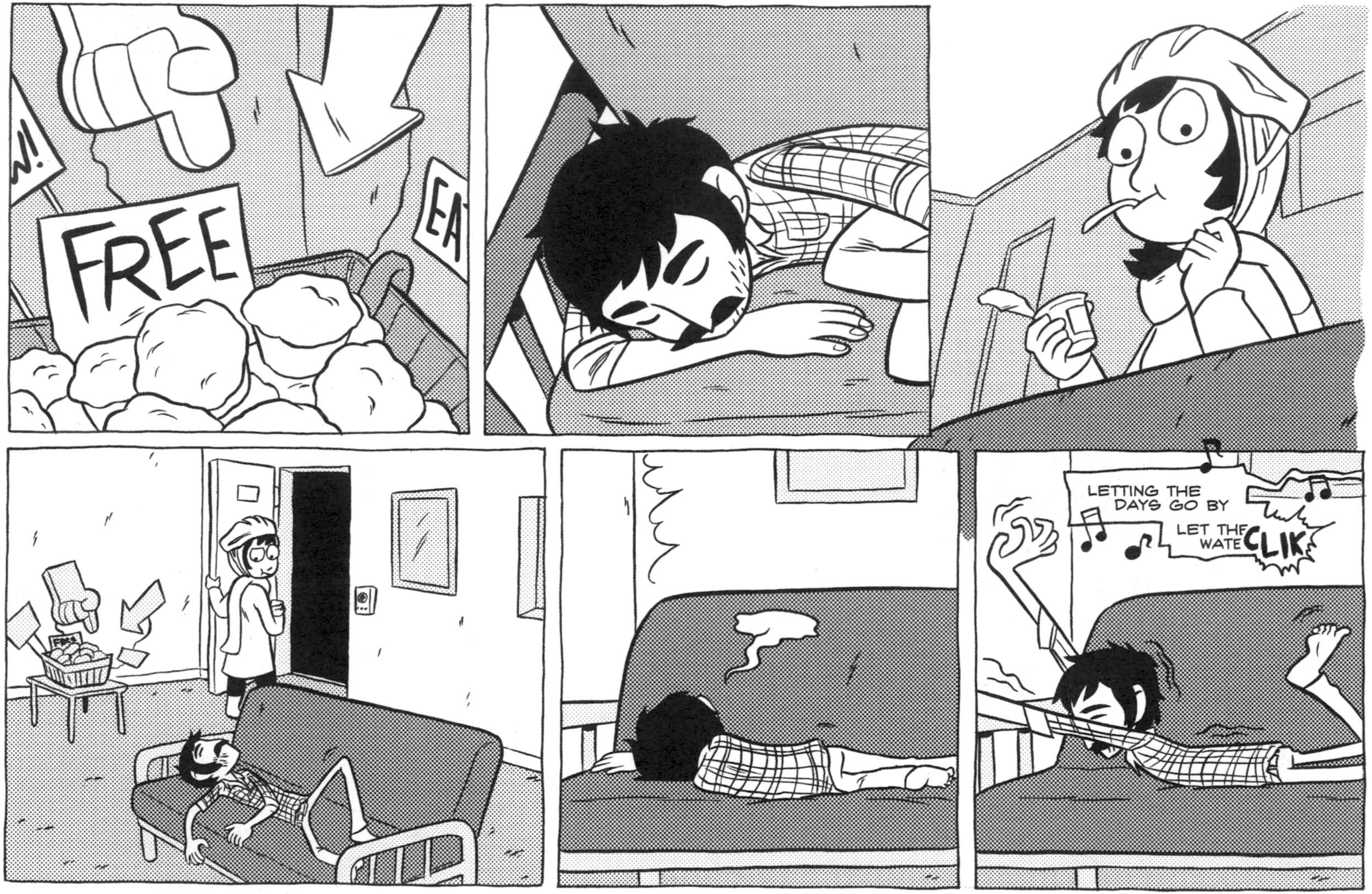
FREE
EAT
W!
LETTING THE DAYS GO BY
LET THE WATE
CLIK

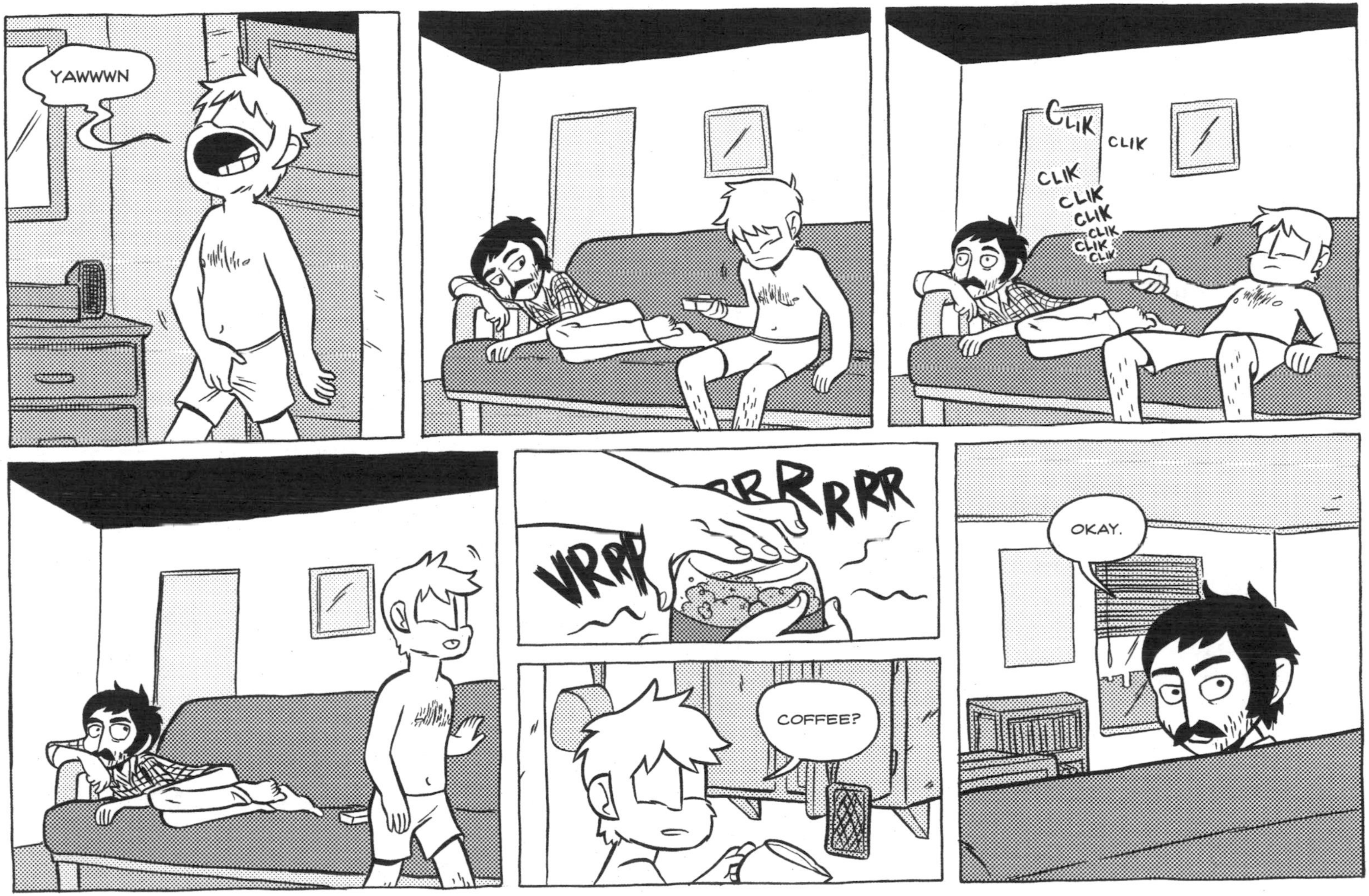
YAWWWN
CLIK CLIK CLIK CLIK CLIK CLIK CLIK CLIK
VRRP RRRRRR
COFFEE?
OKAY.

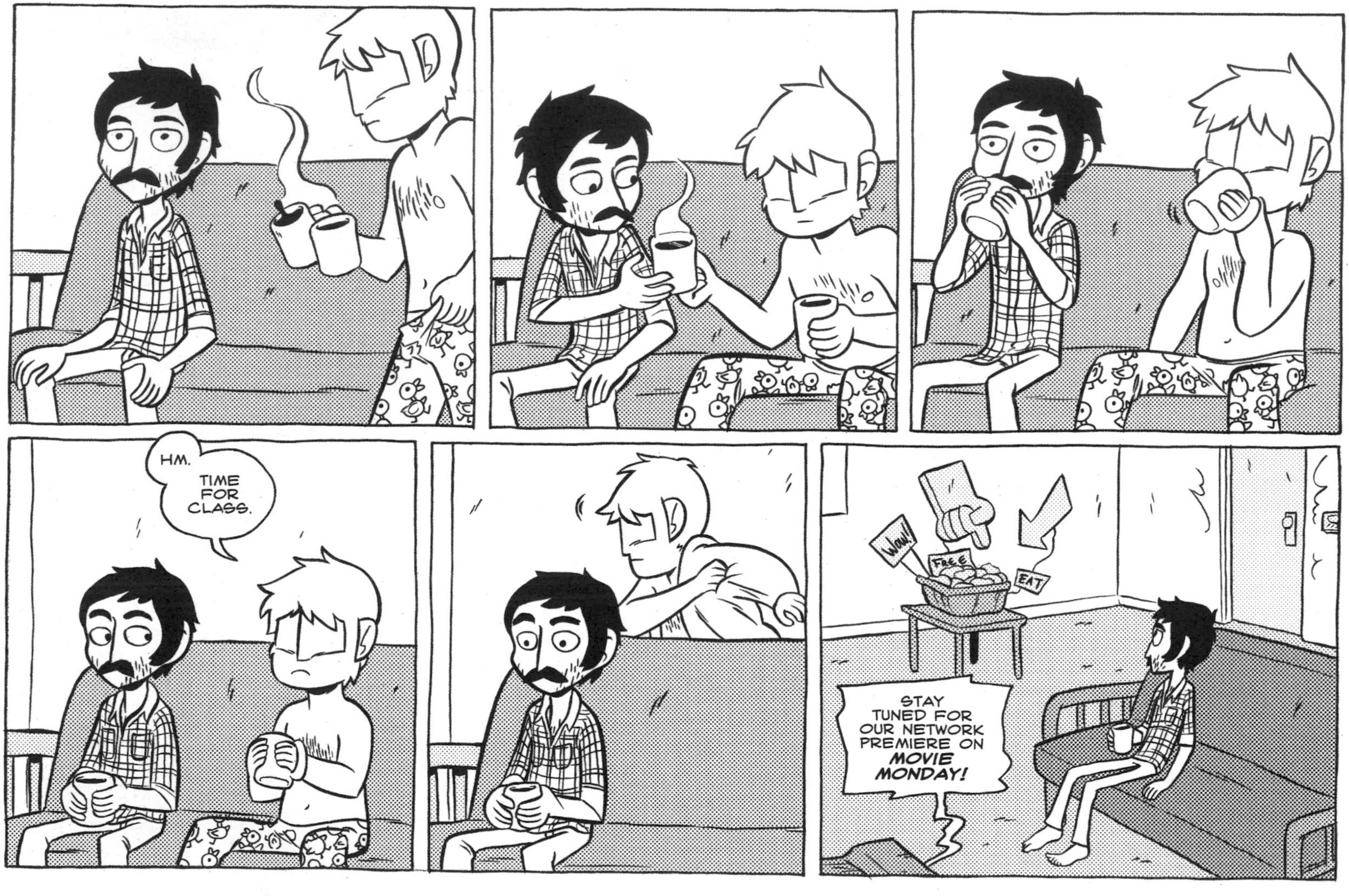
HM.
TIME FOR CLASS.
WOW!
FREE
EAT
STAY TUNED FOR OUR NETWORK PREMIERE ON *MOVIE MONDAY!*

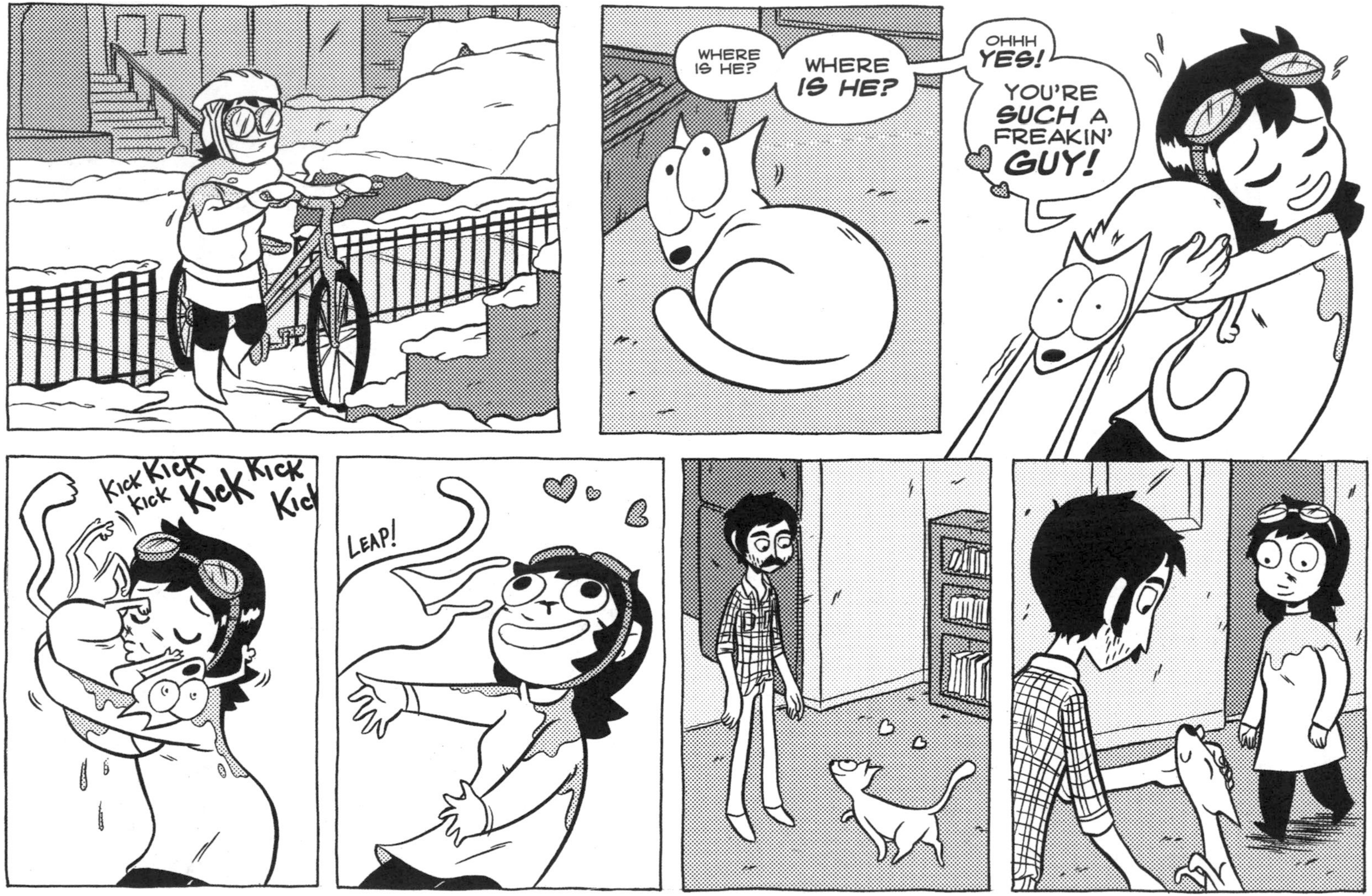
WHERE IS HE?
WHERE IS HE?
OHHH YES!
YOU'RE SUCH A FREAKIN' GUY!
KICK KICK KICK KICK KICK KICK KICK
LEAP!

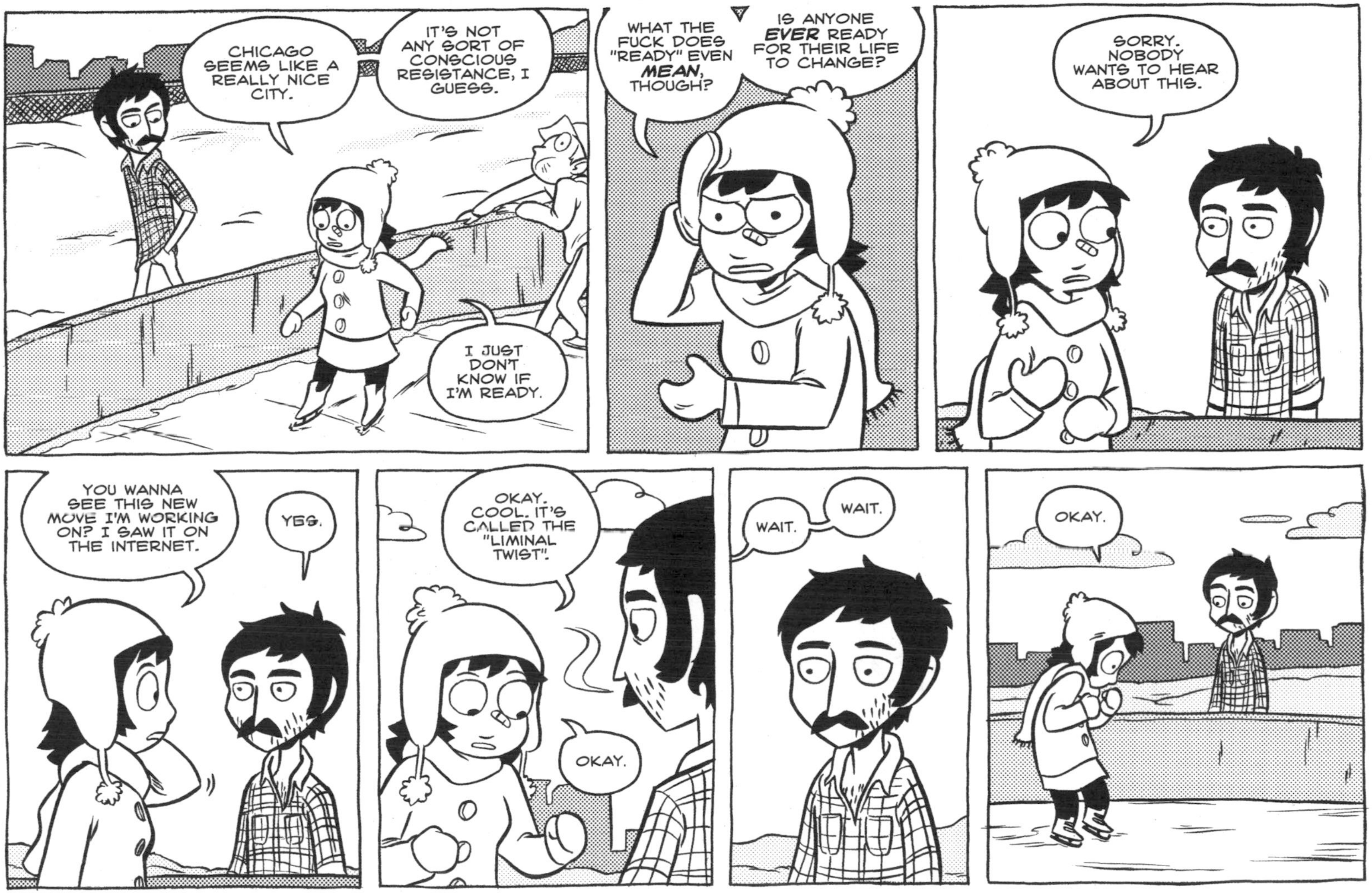
CHICAGO SEEMS LIKE A REALLY NICE CITY.
IT'S NOT ANY SORT OF CONSCIOUS RESISTANCE, I GUESS.
I JUST DON'T KNOW IF I'M READY.
WHAT THE FUCK DOES "READY" EVEN *MEAN*, THOUGH?
IS ANYONE *EVER* READY FOR THEIR LIFE TO CHANGE?
SORRY. NOBODY WANTS TO HEAR ABOUT THIS.
YOU WANNA SEE THIS NEW MOVE I'M WORKING ON? I SAW IT ON THE INTERNET.
YES.
OKAY. COOL. IT'S CALLED THE "LIMINAL TWIST".
OKAY.
WAIT.
WAIT.
OKAY.

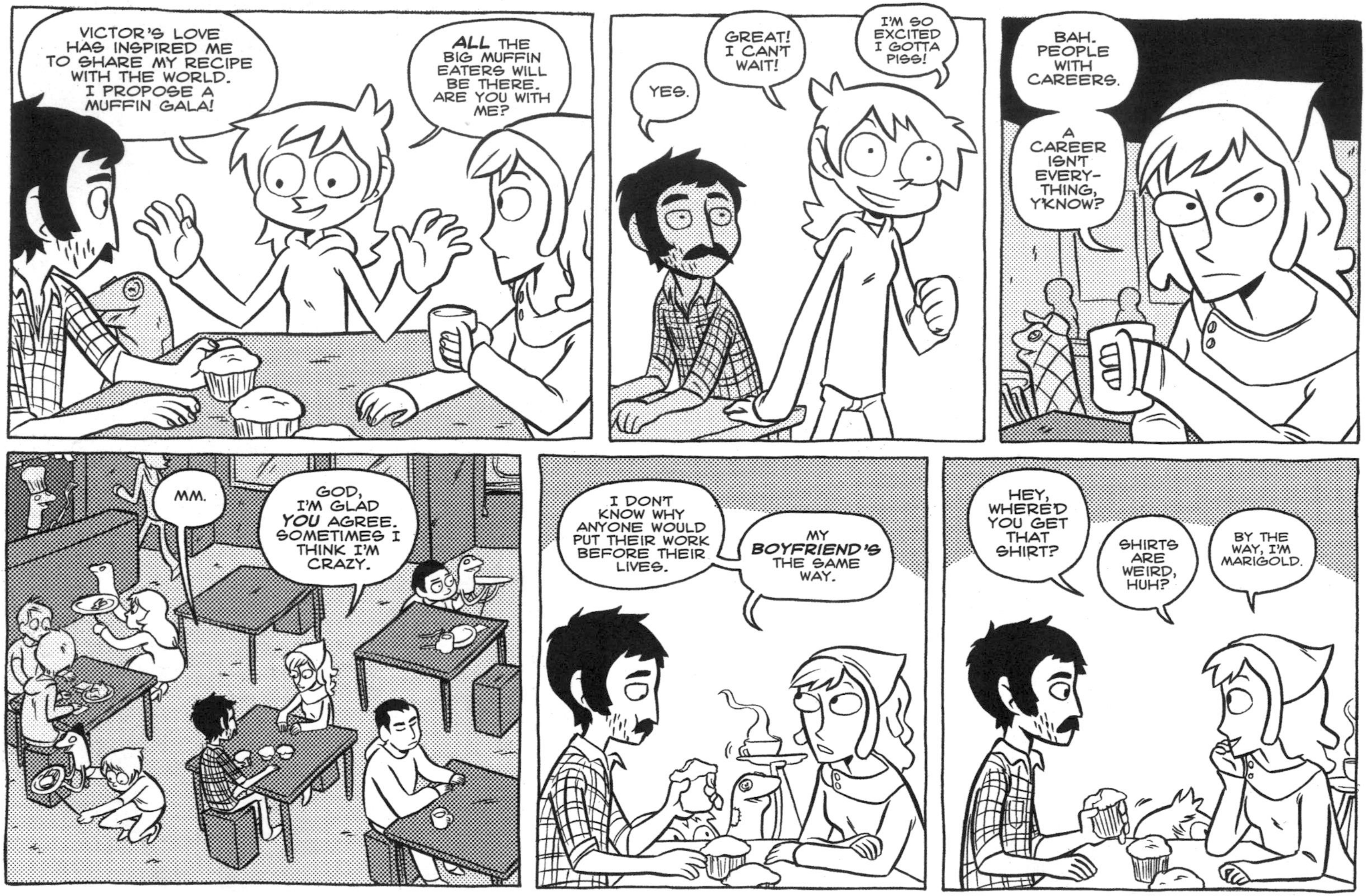
VICTOR'S LOVE HAS INSPIRED ME TO SHARE MY RECIPE WITH THE WORLD. I PROPOSE A MUFFIN GALA!
ALL THE BIG MUFFIN EATERS WILL BE THERE. ARE YOU WITH ME?
YES.
GREAT! I CAN'T WAIT!
I'M SO EXCITED I GOTTA PISS!
BAH. PEOPLE WITH CAREERS.
A CAREER ISN'T EVERY-THING, Y'KNOW?
MM.
GOD, I'M GLAD YOU AGREE. SOMETIMES I THINK I'M CRAZY.
I DON'T KNOW WHY ANYONE WOULD PUT THEIR WORK BEFORE THEIR LIVES.
MY BOYFRIEND'S THE SAME WAY.
HEY, WHERE'D YOU GET THAT SHIRT?
SHIRTS ARE WEIRD, HUH?
BY THE WAY, I'M MARIGOLD.

155

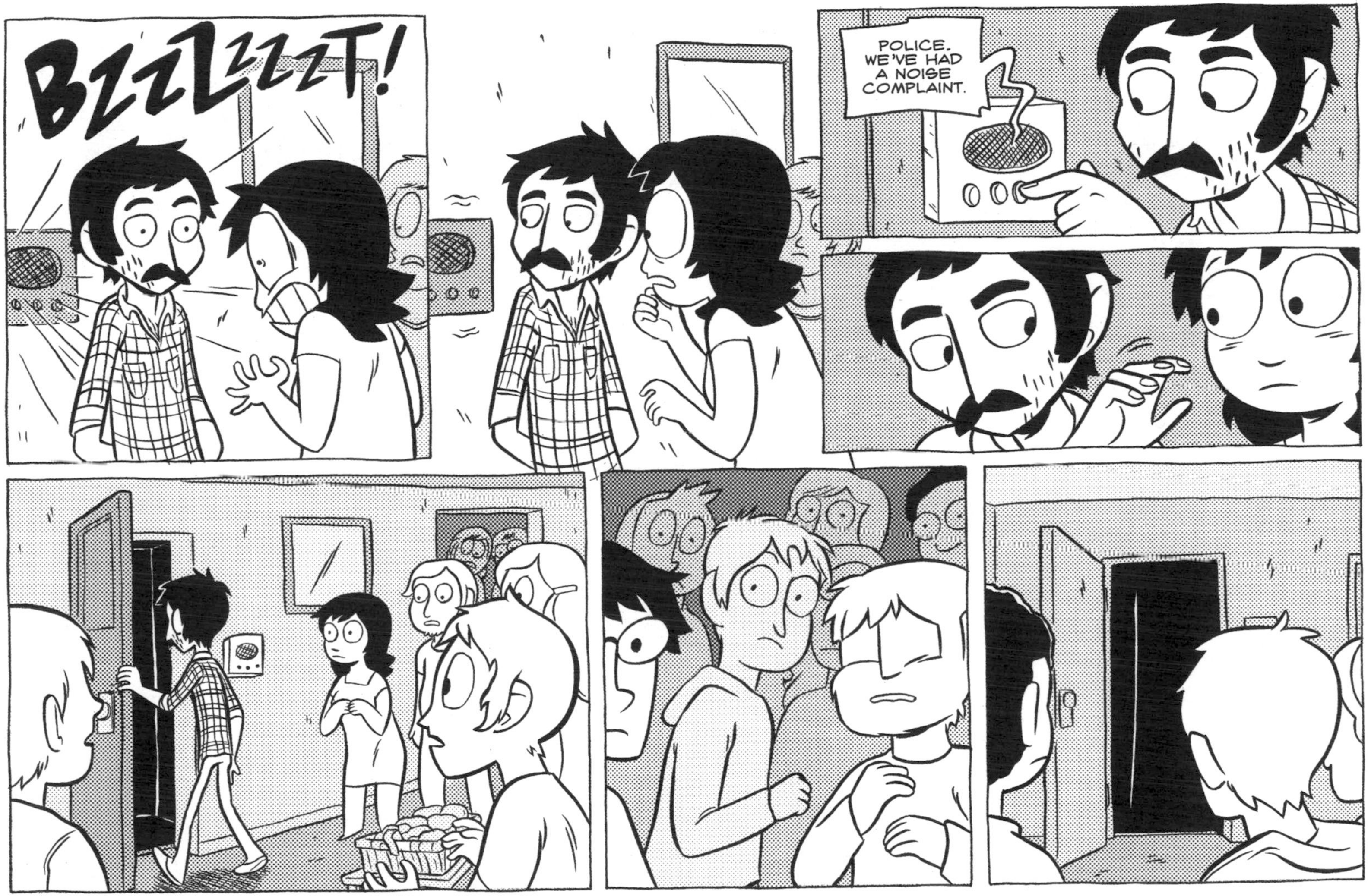
BZZZZZZT!
POLICE. WE'VE HAD A NOISE COMPLAINT.

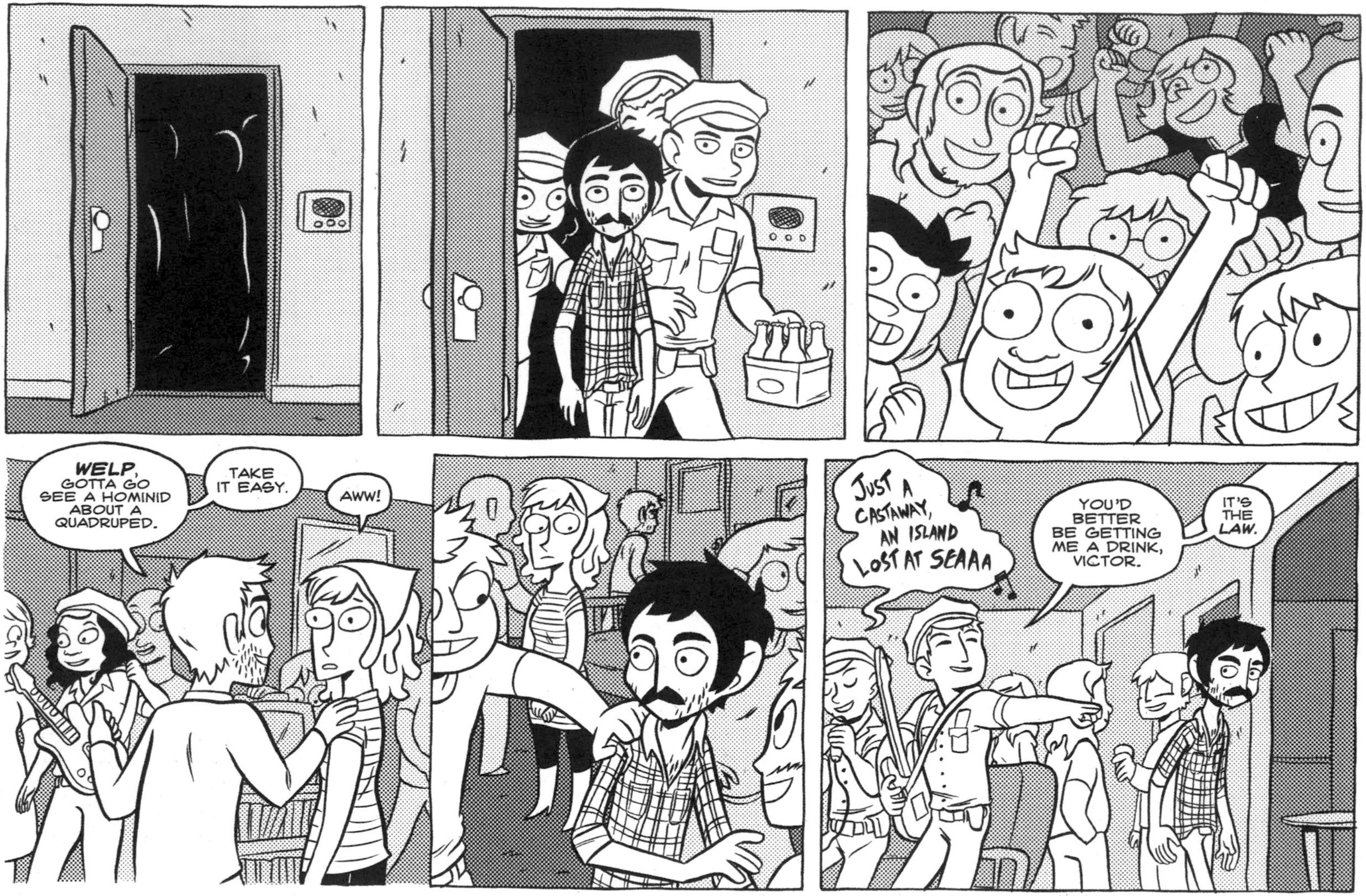
WELP, GOTTA GO SEE A HOMINID ABOUT A QUADRUPED.
TAKE IT EASY.
AWW!
JUST A CASTAWAY, AN ISLAND LOST AT SEAAA
YOU'D BETTER BE GETTING ME A DRINK, VICTOR.
IT'S THE LAW.

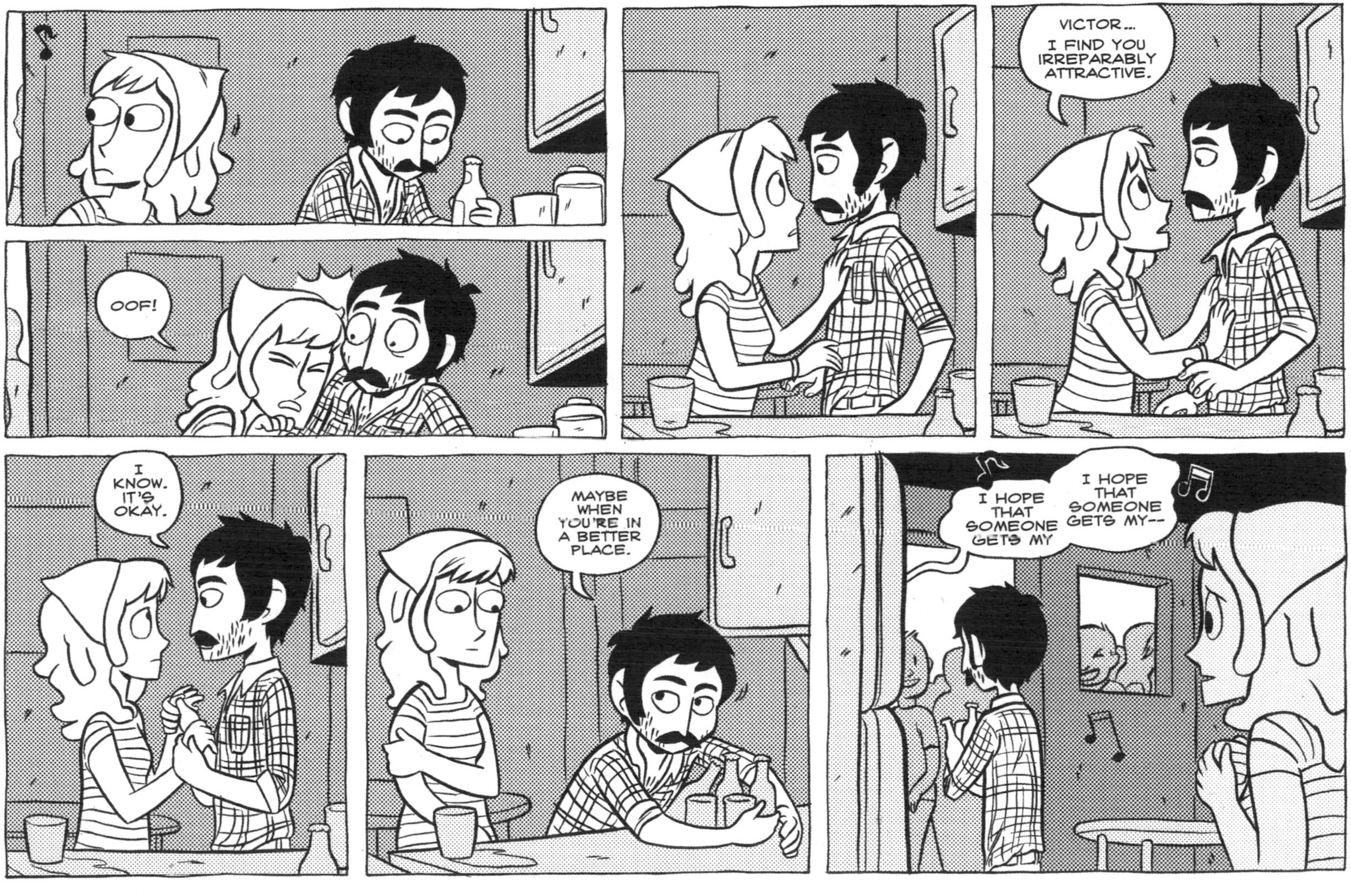
OOF!
VICTOR... I FIND YOU IRREPARABLY ATTRACTIVE.
I KNOW. IT'S OKAY.
MAYBE WHEN YOU'RE IN A BETTER PLACE.
I HOPE THAT SOMEONE GETS MY
I HOPE THAT SOMEONE GETS MY--

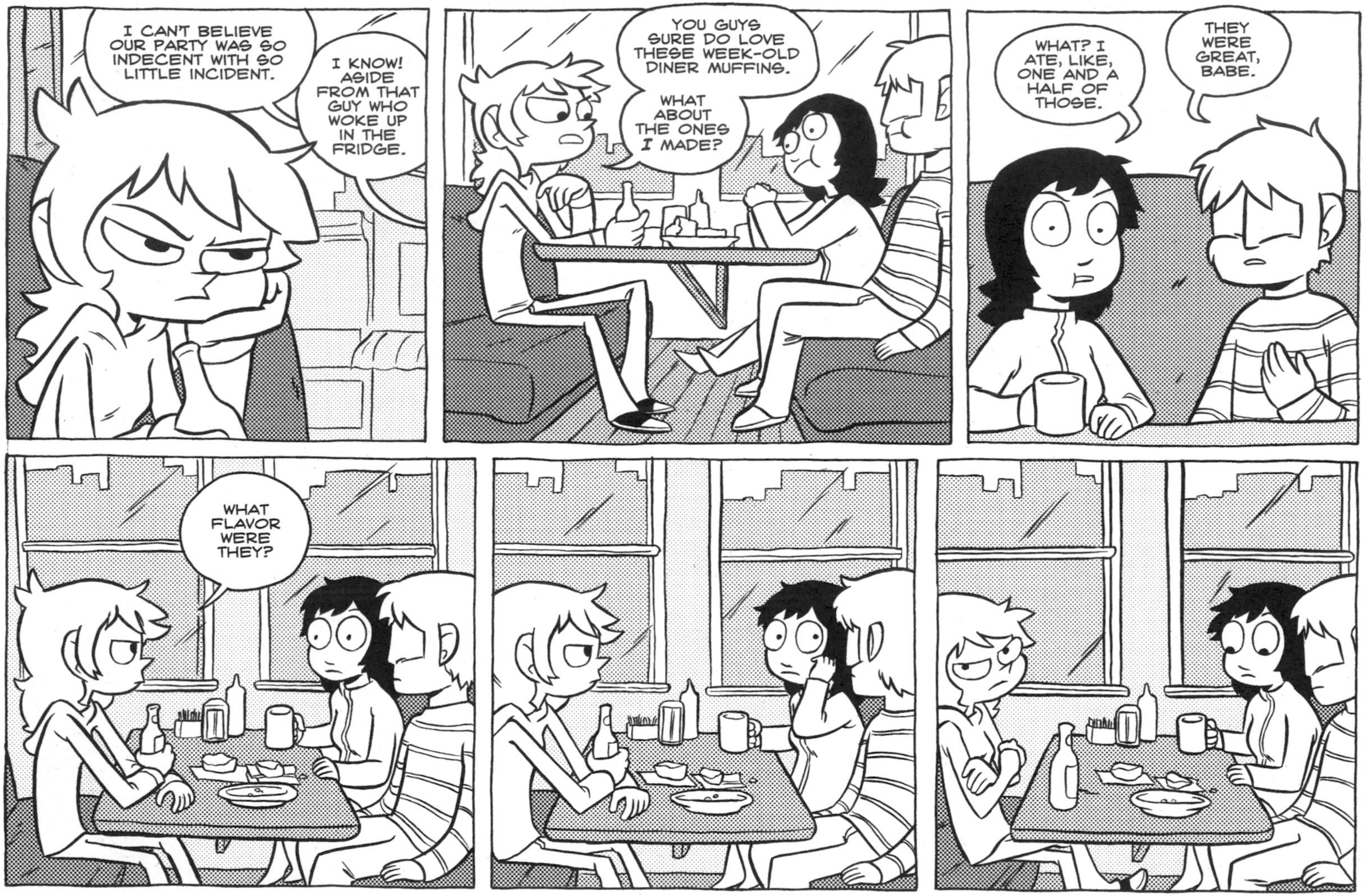
I CAN'T BELIEVE OUR PARTY WAS SO INDECENT WITH SO LITTLE INCIDENT.
I KNOW! ASIDE FROM THAT GUY WHO WOKE UP IN THE FRIDGE.
YOU GUYS SURE DO LOVE THESE WEEK-OLD DINER MUFFINS.
WHAT ABOUT THE ONES *I* MADE?
WHAT? I ATE, LIKE, ONE AND A HALF OF THOSE.
THEY WERE GREAT, BABE.
WHAT FLAVOR WERE THEY?

166

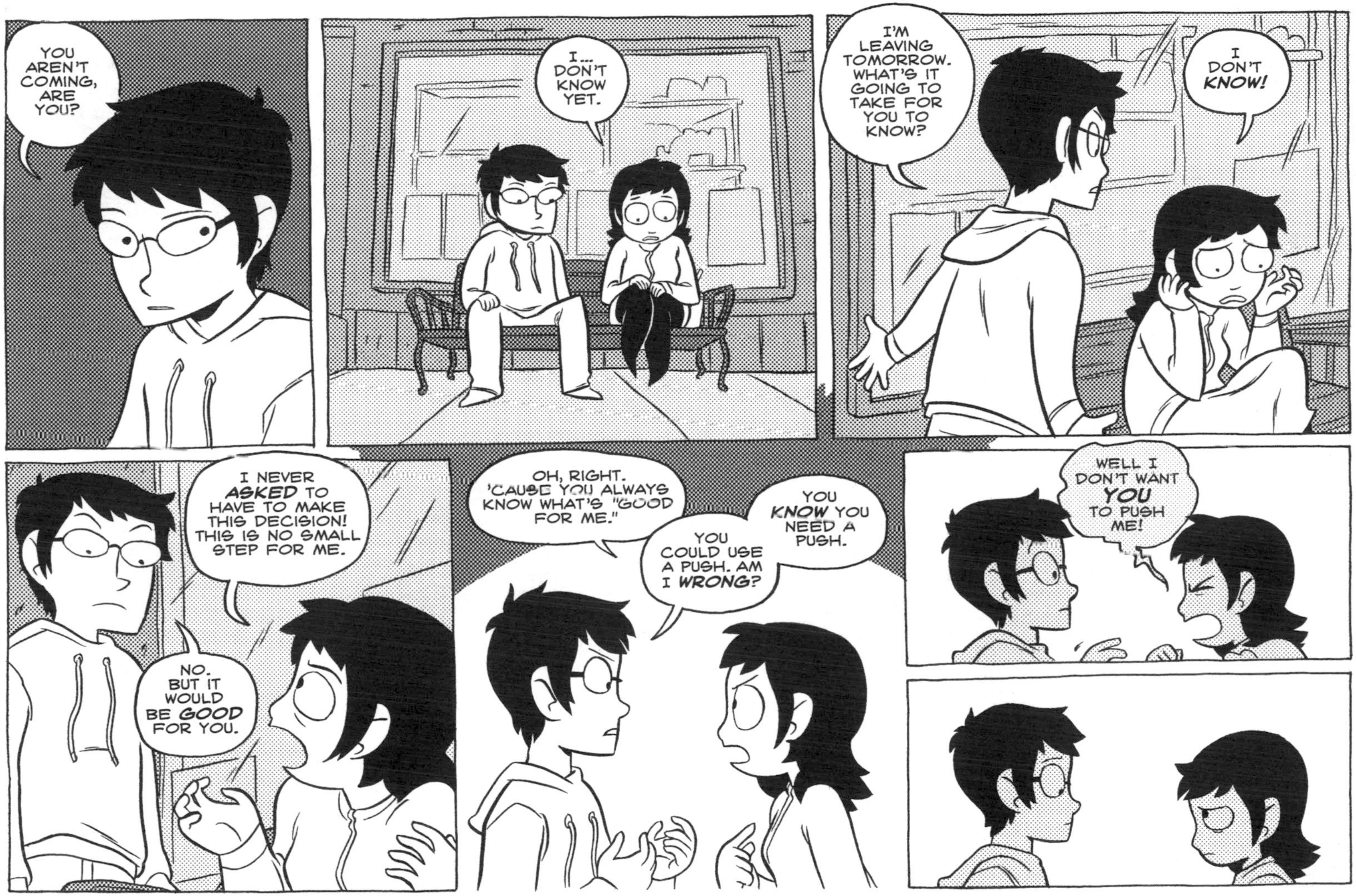
YOU AREN'T COMING, ARE YOU?
I... DON'T KNOW YET.
I'M LEAVING TOMORROW. WHAT'S IT GOING TO TAKE FOR YOU TO KNOW?
I DON'T KNOW!
I NEVER ASKED TO HAVE TO MAKE THIS DECISION! THIS IS NO SMALL STEP FOR ME.
NO. BUT IT WOULD BE GOOD FOR YOU.
OH, RIGHT. 'CAUSE YOU ALWAYS KNOW WHAT'S "GOOD FOR ME."
YOU COULD USE A PUSH. AM I WRONG?
YOU KNOW YOU NEED A PUSH.
WELL I DON'T WANT YOU TO PUSH ME!

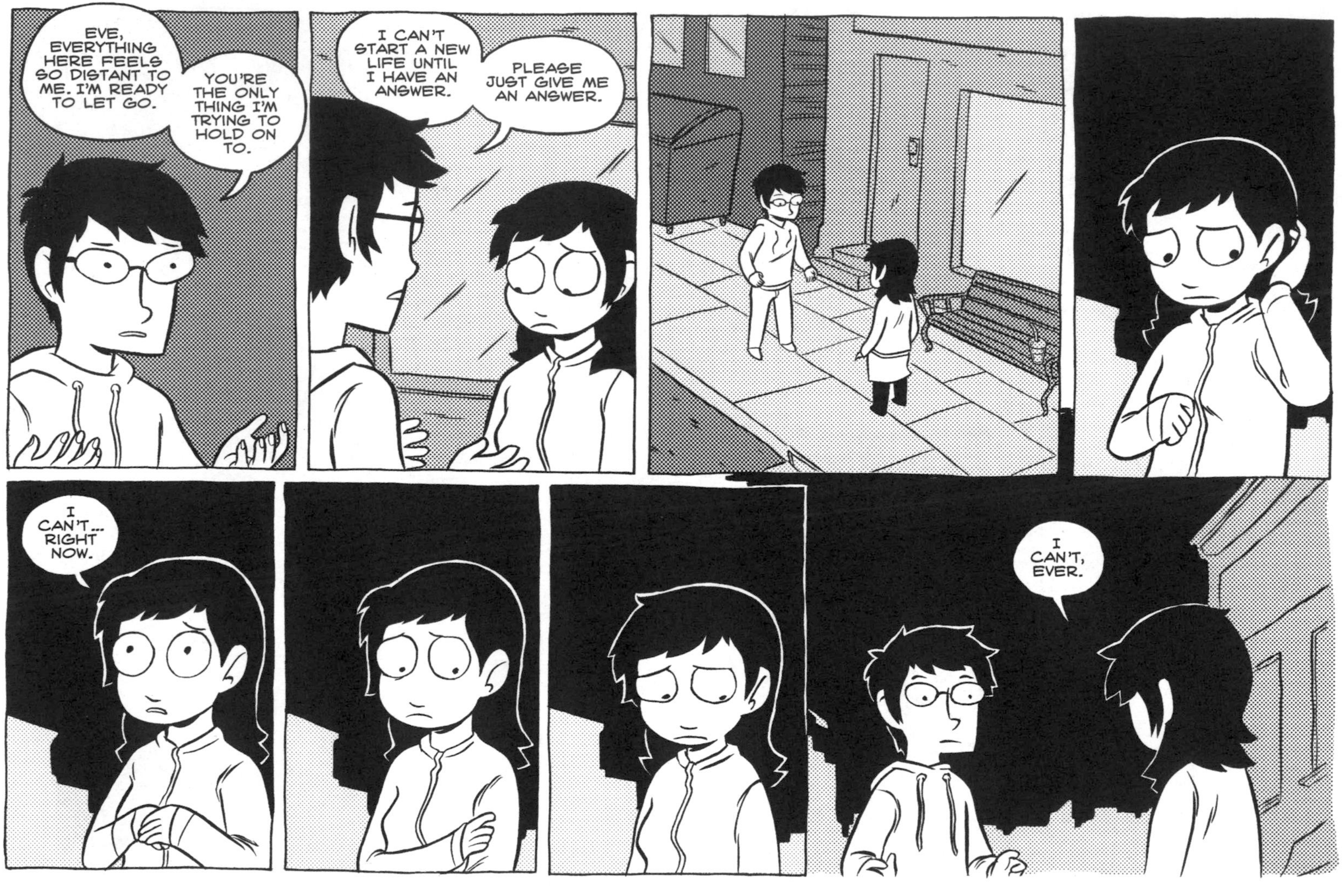
EVE, EVERYTHING HERE FEELS SO DISTANT TO ME. I'M READY TO LET GO.
YOU'RE THE ONLY THING I'M TRYING TO HOLD ON TO.
I CAN'T START A NEW LIFE UNTIL I HAVE AN ANSWER.
PLEASE JUST GIVE ME AN ANSWER.
I CAN'T... RIGHT NOW.
I CAN'T, EVER.

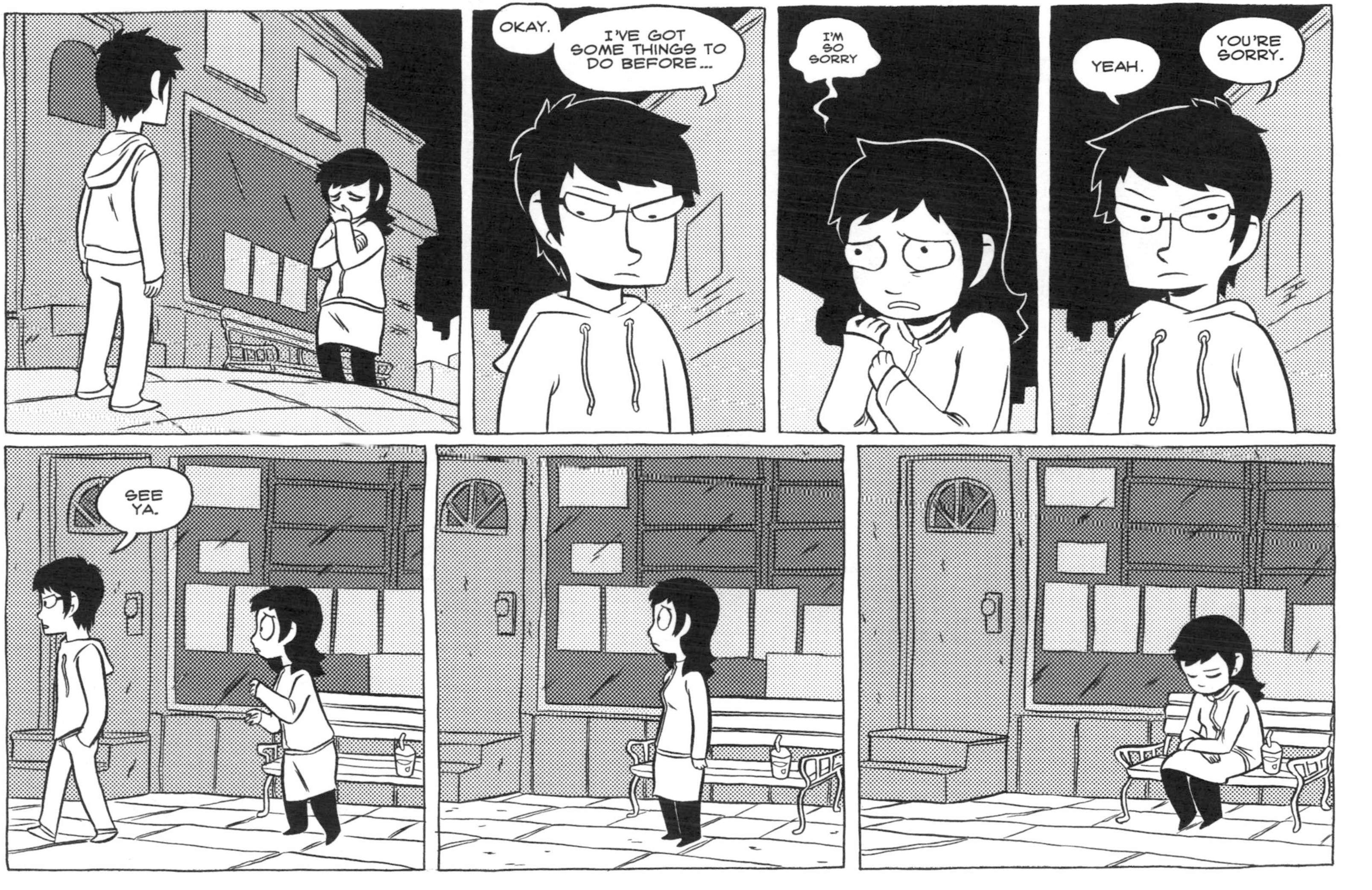
OKAY.
I'VE GOT SOME THINGS TO DO BEFORE...
I'M SO SORRY
YEAH.
YOU'RE SORRY.
SEE YA.

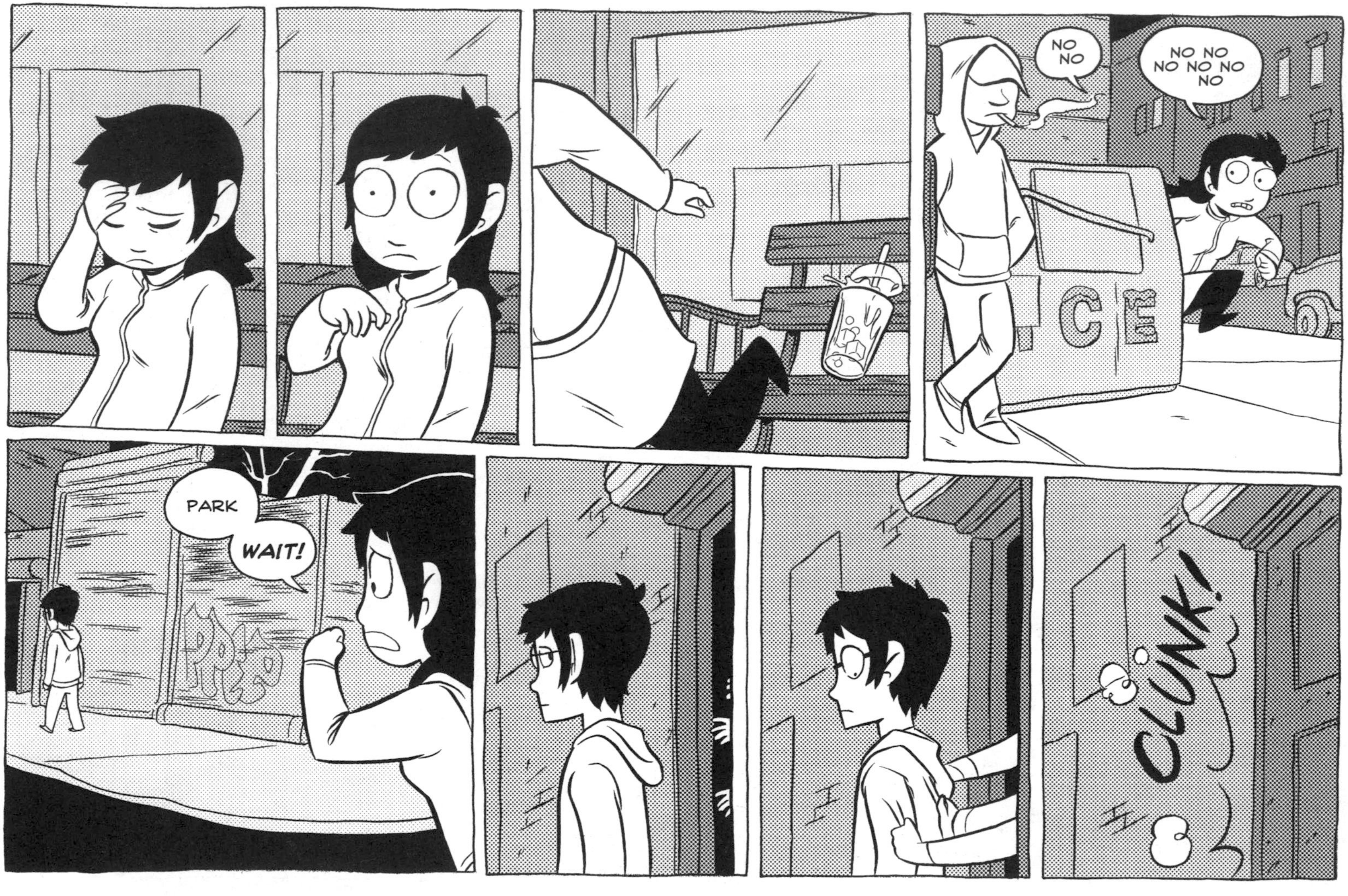
NO NO
NO NO NO NO NO NO
CE
PARK
WAIT!
CLUNK!

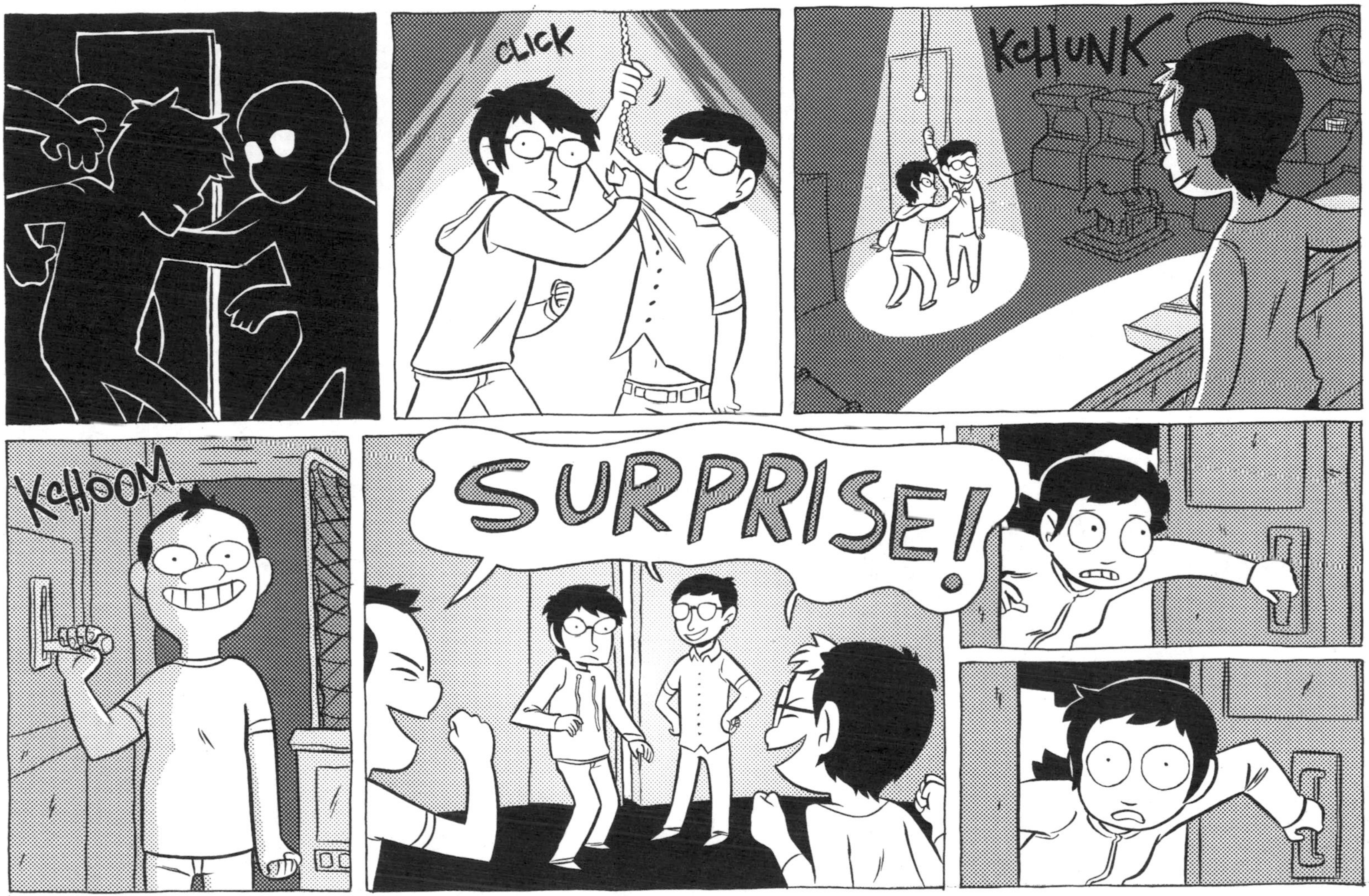
CLICK
KCHUNK
KCHOOM
SURPRISE!

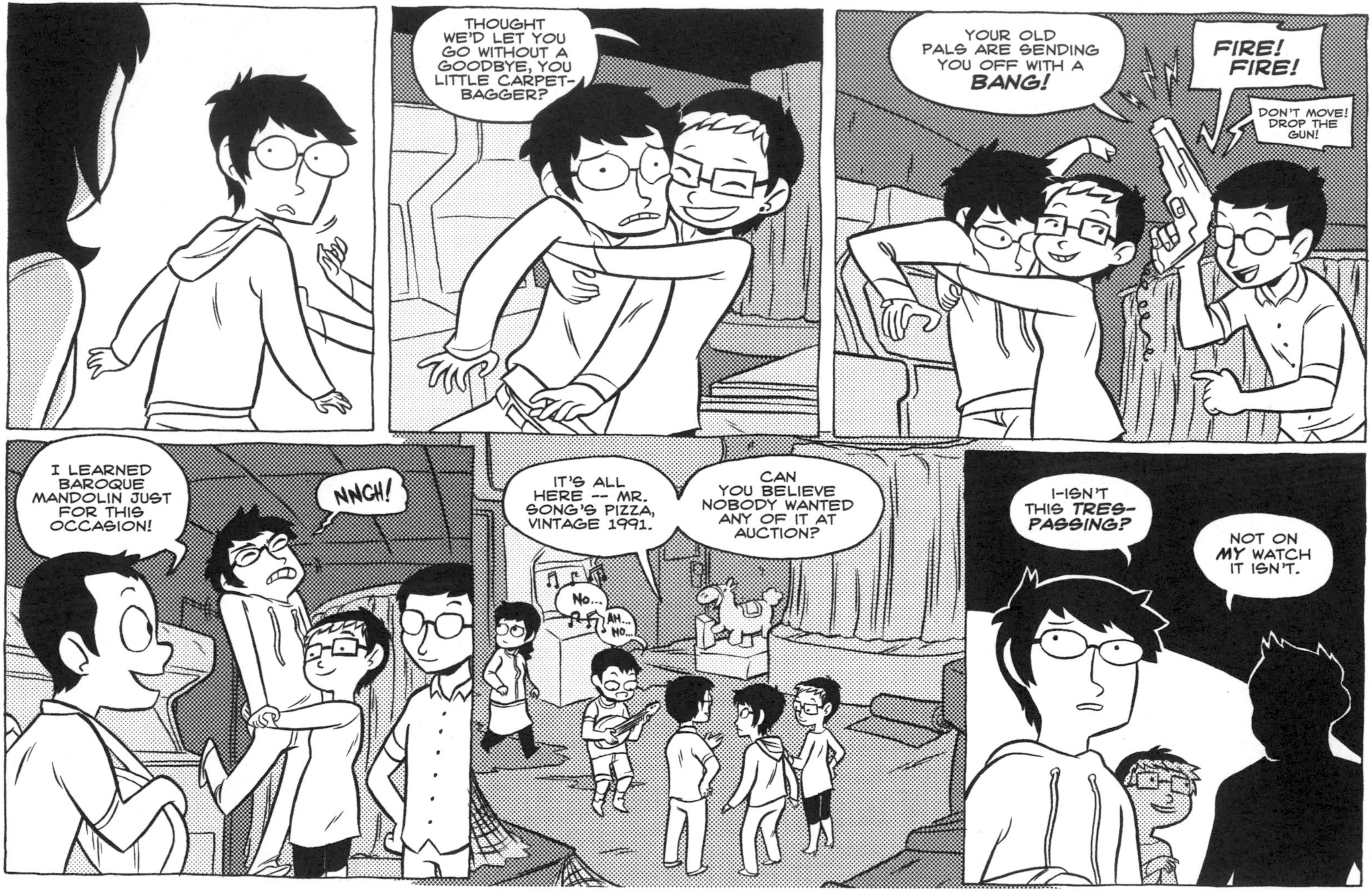
THOUGHT WE'D LET YOU GO WITHOUT A GOODBYE, YOU LITTLE CARPET-BAGGER?
YOUR OLD PALS ARE SENDING YOU OFF WITH A *BANG!*
FIRE! FIRE!
DON'T MOVE! DROP THE GUN!
I LEARNED BAROQUE MANDOLIN JUST FOR THIS OCCASION!
NNGH!
IT'S ALL HERE -- MR. SONG'S PIZZA, VINTAGE 1991.
CAN YOU BELIEVE NOBODY WANTED ANY OF IT AT AUCTION?
NO...
AH... NO...
I-ISN'T THIS *TRES-PASSING?*
NOT ON *MY* WATCH IT ISN'T.

173

174

175

177

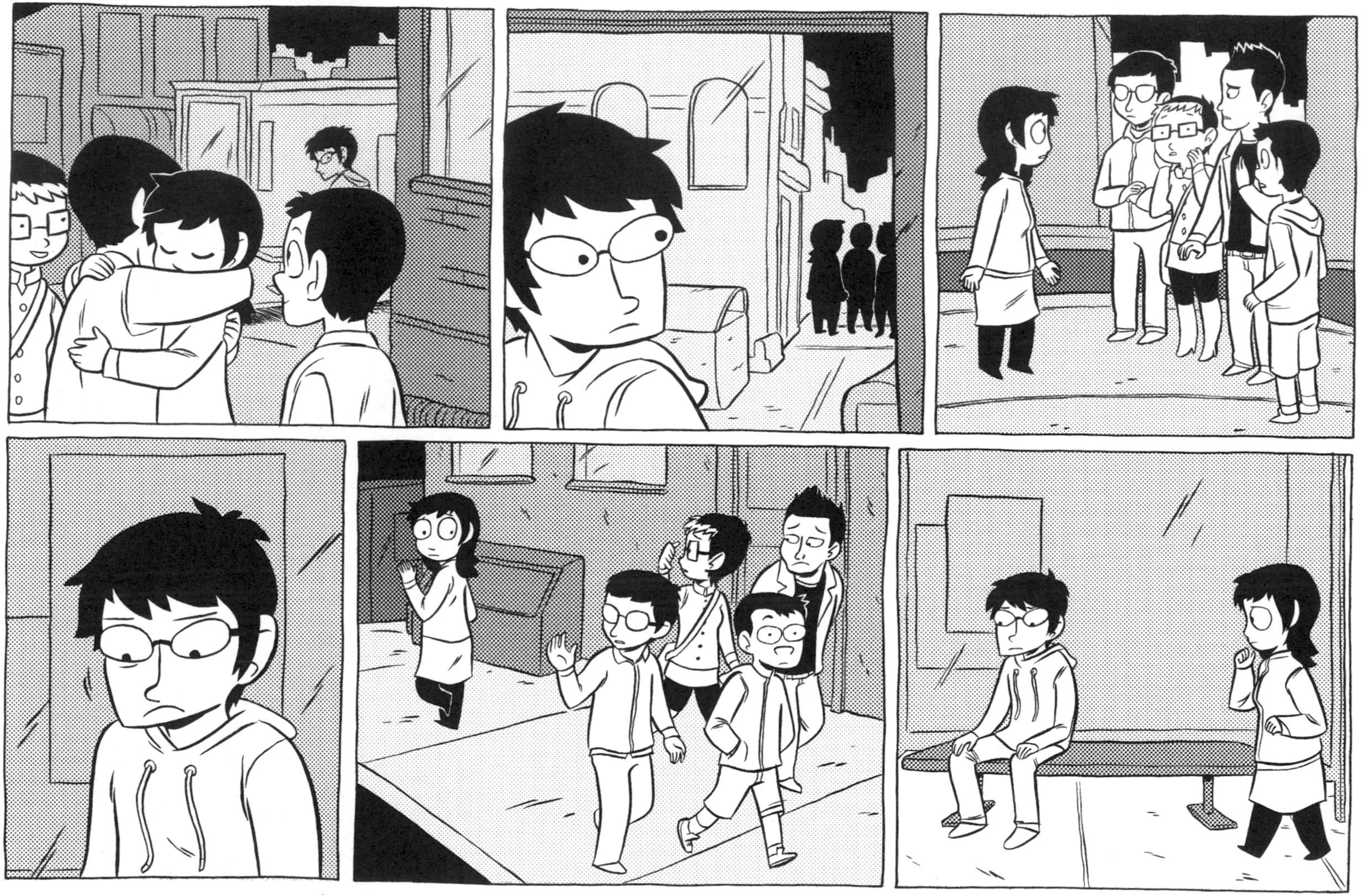

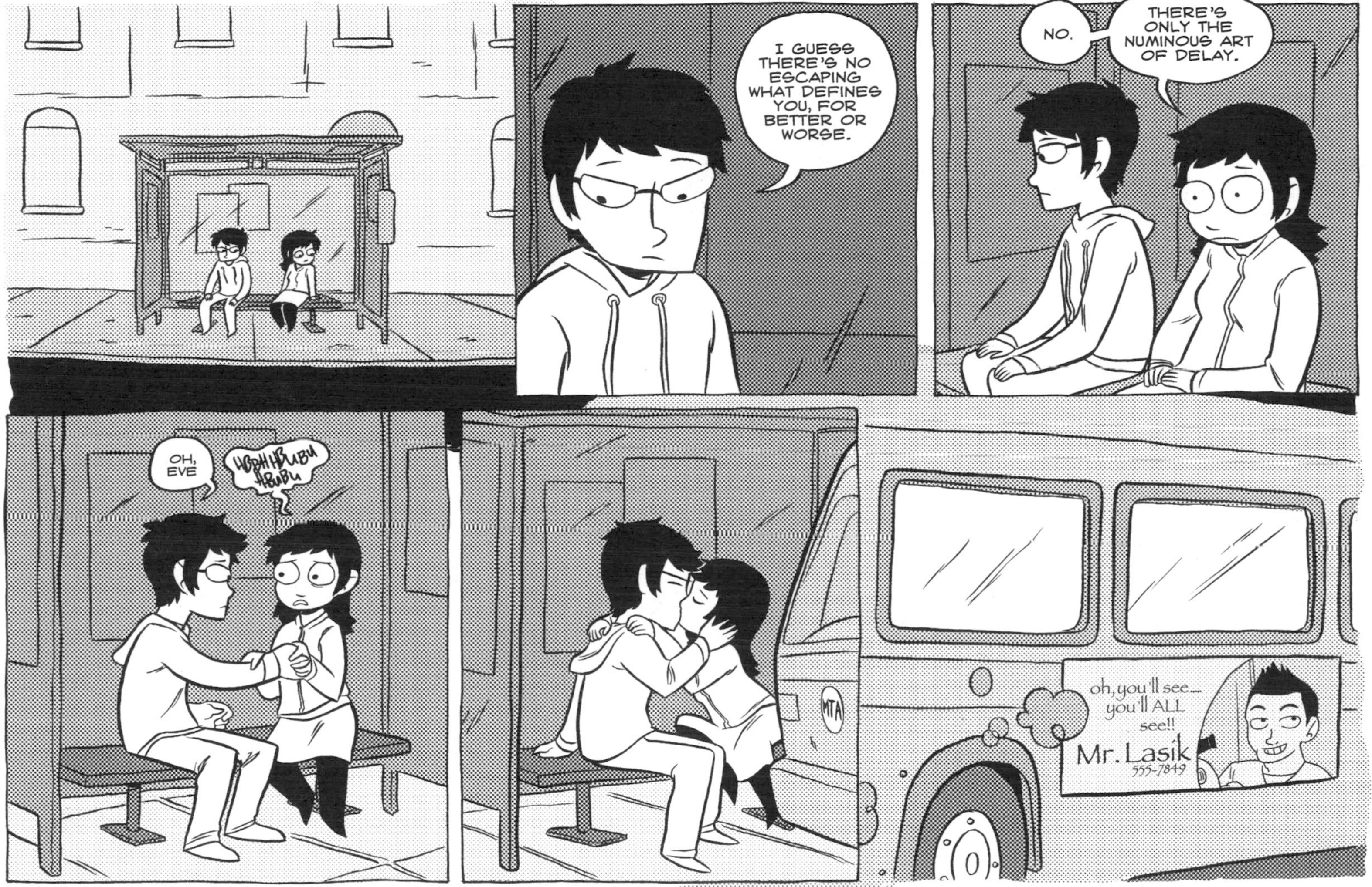
I GUESS THERE'S NO ESCAPING WHAT DEFINES YOU, FOR BETTER OR WORSE.
NO.
THERE'S ONLY THE NUMINOUS ART OF DELAY.
OH, EVE
MTA
oh, you'll see.... you'll ALL see!!
Mr. Lasik
555-7849

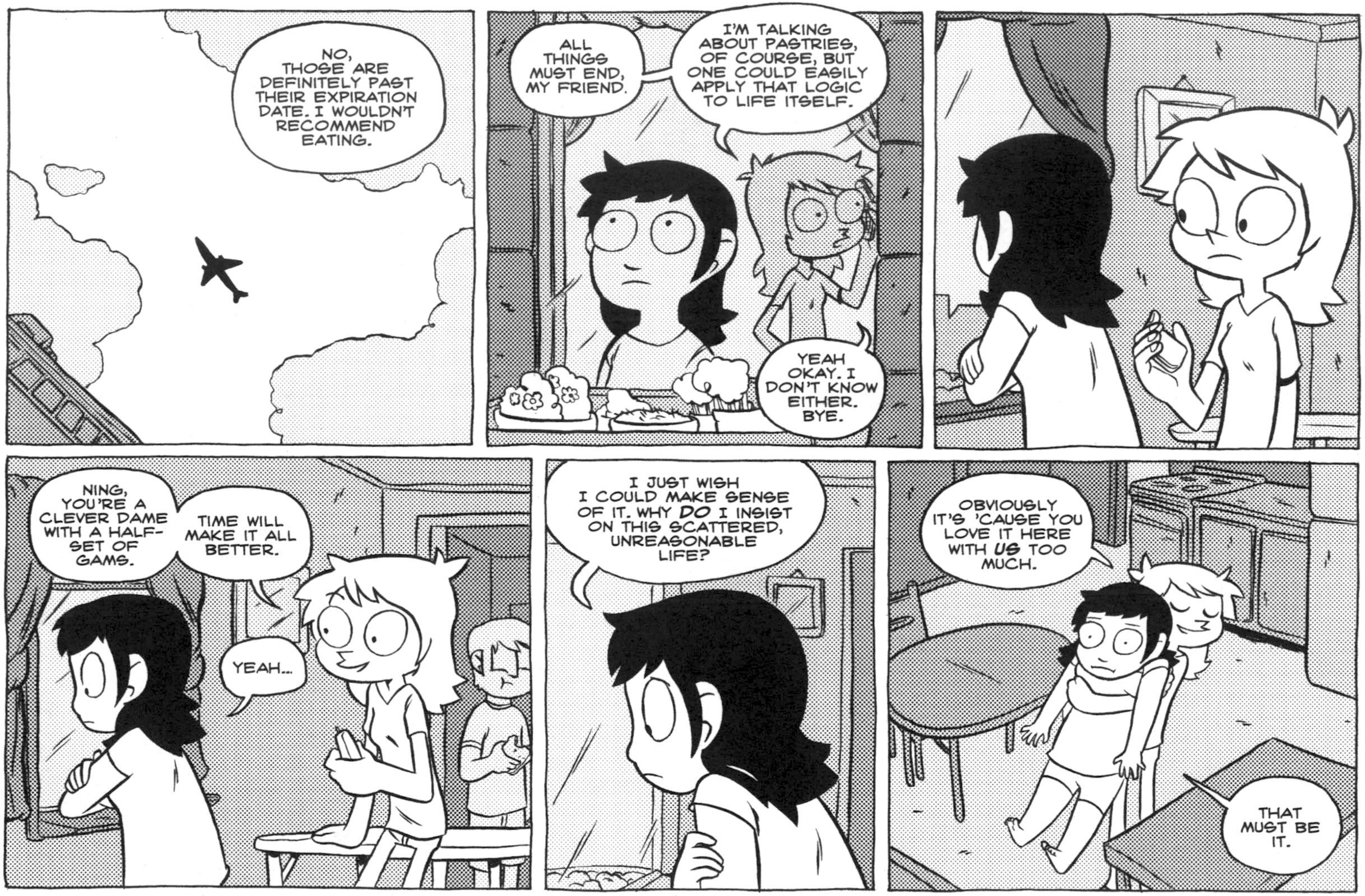
NO, THOSE ARE DEFINITELY PAST THEIR EXPIRATION DATE. I WOULDN'T RECOMMEND EATING.
ALL THINGS MUST END, MY FRIEND.
I'M TALKING ABOUT PASTRIES, OF COURSE, BUT ONE COULD EASILY APPLY THAT LOGIC TO LIFE ITSELF.
YEAH OKAY. I DON'T KNOW EITHER. BYE.
NING, YOU'RE A CLEVER DAME WITH A HALF-SET OF GAMS.
TIME WILL MAKE IT ALL BETTER.
YEAH...
I JUST WISH I COULD MAKE SENSE OF IT. WHY *DO* I INSIST ON THIS SCATTERED, UNREASONABLE LIFE?
OBVIOUSLY IT'S 'CAUSE YOU LOVE IT HERE WITH *US* TOO MUCH.
THAT MUST BE IT.

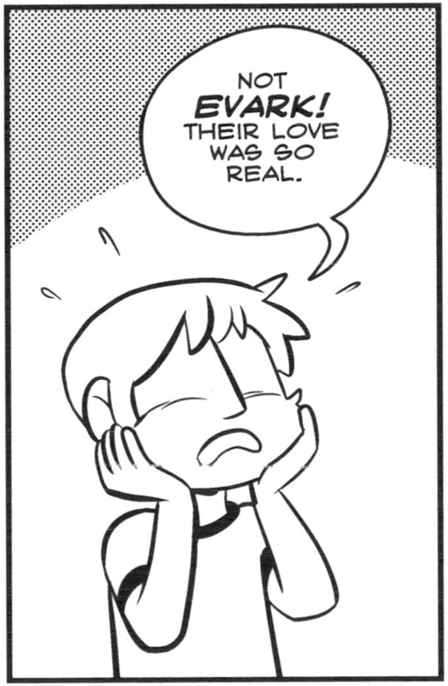
NOT EVARK! THEIR LOVE WAS SO REAL.